The Girl WITH
39 GRAVES

MICHAEL BERES

The Girl with 39 Graves
Michael Beres

Cover photo by Danil Nevsky
Map by Colleen Beres

Thank you to Colleen for accompanying me on research travels as well as doing genealogical research. Thank you to Judi Robinson Laughter for sharing CCC information at the Sweetwater County Historical Museum and pointing out work done by the CCC in the Wyoming high desert and in the Utah mountains and valleys. Thank you to my Father for all the memories he left behind.

"I propose to create a Civilian Conservation Corps to be used in simple work, more important, however, than the material gains will be the moral and spiritual value of such work."

— FRANKLIN DELANO ROOSEVELT, MARCH 1933

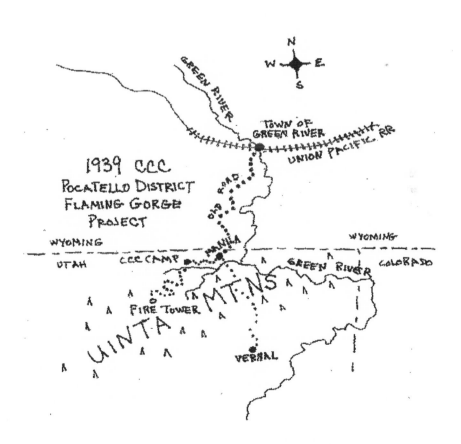

CHAPTER 1—1939

Flaming red hair in Green River was a mystery. Some said Rose Buckles got it from her father's royal Hungarian ancestry. No one could prove it because he Gypsied out of town on the Union Pacific before Rose was born.

During the Depression, Rose learned to make feed sack dresses. Not colorful, but as she got older and winds from northeast Utah plunged through Flaming Gorge Canyon into southwest Wyoming, geologic dust getting into ranchers' mouths and eyes inspired them to offer café meals that kept Rose's hips and breasts in the pink.

Green River is in Wyoming's southwest corner where, like rectangles of fabric, the state overlays Utah's northeast corner. On windy days watching Rose Buckles walk down the street was like watching a monochrome film with red hair penned in by a Disney crew. Town whispers had Rose Buckles so flaming gorgeous, gossip followed like a lost dog. Maybe, rather than the rumored fiddle-playing Gypsy hopping a freight following WWI, a red-headed Irish teamster taking over from Chinese on Union Pacific or Lincoln Highway construction contributed the hair color genes.

Speaking of gossip, how about those FDR shovel soldiers whose begetters could be from anywhere? 1939 gossip had Rose accompanying local boys to the necking rock overlooking the river. So why not one of those Green River

CCC camp boys, or a boy from another camp in the area? Maybe a home-sick city boy from the camp 50 miles south across the state line in Manila, Utah—city boys dynamiting rock adding to all the red dust because Dagget County felt isolated from their county seat and wanted a road over the moun-tain to the "metropolis" of Vernal. City boys stranded in Manila driven north to Green River in government trucks a couple times a month to blow off steam, city boys gawking at local girls, buying beer, and whooping it up at the movie house.

Dammed, the canyon spanning the Wyoming-Utah line eventually became the Flaming Gorge National Recreation Area named, not for Rose Buckles' hair color, as a few elderly locals insisted, but because in 1869 explorer John Wesley Powell christened it the Flaming Gorge Canyon with its reddish walls containing the iron oxide mineral hematite. Before being dammed, the river in the gorge flowed fast like blood in a wild horse, afterwards no so fast.

That summer morning in 1939 Cletus Minch, a local boy fishing the river, was first to find a piece of Rose, a sliced-off hand with a pearl ring. Next day searchers deputized by the sheriff found her head, minus most of her red hair, on the riverbank, and another hand and leg downstream.

Because of limited remains, hair pulled out by the roots, and a mysterious father, legends surrounding Rose's death spread beyond Sweetwater County, following the Union Pacific and Lincoln Highway east and west. Sure, she'd been a sight for men young and old as she sashayed down the street in home-made dresses, but she was also popular with kids and parents, volunteering for the overworked schoolmistress. Rose couldn't afford schooling after high school, but wanted to teach. After death she lived on in ghost stories, a spirit teacher in late night tales at kitchen tables, around campfires, or while waiting to switch on the living room console radio to catch distant stations when sky waves get the ionospheric bounce. One story, in town but also rippling across the globe via WWII troops, had Rose's bits and pieces riding high desert wild horses at night, searching for the rest of her.

Like any good ghost story, Rose bounces to far corners of the Earth the way the black and white newsreel in a darkened movie house—music and narrator loud as hell—jumps from celebrity to celebrity—Lou Gehrig, Albert Einstein, Marion Anderson, Edward Hopper, FDR, Chamberlain, Mussolini, Hitler—and from topic to topic—The 1939 New York World's Fair, Anacin versus Aspirin, Civilian Conservation Corps successes, War in Europe, *Gone With the Wind*, and footage of last year's Miss America beauty pageant.

On this particular night the newsreel's interrupted by a guy in the audience yelling, "Come on! We ain't got all night!" Funny thing, nobody else yells during the newsreel, and nobody tells the loudmouth to pipe down. Like he's the only one in the movie house except the old man peering out the projection booth porthole. Beyond cigarette smoke in the projector's flicker, the old man sees plenty of others down there, heads and shoulders leaning away from the loudmouth, distancing themselves from his yammering until the feature finally begins. Some arrived at the theater with bottles of beer. Now, with the loudmouth yelling, the old man's glad he made the boys swig their bottles and leave them in the Green River Brewery box in the lobby.

A Ford Model T Runabout with Pickup Body rattled down the dark street, lifting dust from the pavement. The Runabout's one working taillight blinked on and off—bad connection. Newspaper pages floated in the wake of smoke and dust. A *Green River Star* 1939 front page landed beneath a streetlight. Top headline: "FDR Serves Hot Dogs to King and Queen at Hyde Park." Sidebar headline: "Cops Still Baffled in Local Girl's Bloody Murder." The Ford model matched what the sidebar victim's girlfriends called her. Runabout.

"What's his name, Rose? A powwow behind the dance hall's nothing but a fishermen flipping his fly."

"Not a fisherman. He's from the Utah camp. Knows my name and soon I'll know his."

"Runabout's the name those city boys'll be calling you at their nightly gabfests. Runabout, Runabout, Runabout Rose."

"You mean hard to get Rose. I've dated a few and there've already been boxing glove rhubarbs over me."

"City boys will be city boys."

"Boys when they join the three Cs, but hammering rock gives them muscles everywhere."

"I remember Miss Watt in history saying Marco Polo discovered fishermen in Arabia drying fish and hammering them with rocks to feed cattle."

"I bet that smelled good."

"You better watch yourself, Runabout Rose."

"The only place I watch myself is in the mirror."

"You're a real pip."

The Ford Runabout's leaky radiator, combined with red dust, mimicked blood spatter on the newspaper lying in the street. As the Runabout disappeared into the darkness, a big band intro to a vocal began, the music loud but raspy, a record's grooves sliced by too many dull needles.

During the late 30s it became routine at the Green River movie house to have a cheerful or romantic phonograph record playing over the PA system after the feature. The PA system/phonograph setup aglow in the ticket booth closet was the work of a local young man named Tom who dabbled in radio and electronics, a young man who would eventually become a radioman on a B-17 bomber that would be shot down over Schweinfurt, Germany. Before that last flight Tom told his buddies about the girl named Rose with red hair, hip-hugging dresses, and a pearl ring supposedly left by her runaway father. Rose Buckles who'd been sliced, diced, and scalped back in Green

River before the war. Speaking of death was common among bomber crews. Like Tom a couple others on the crew were jazz fans and Tom told how the old man running the movie house wouldn't let him play his recording of Billie Holiday's "Summertime." On takeoff of that final flight, the guys in back began singing "Summertime" as the engines droned and the B-17 threatened to shake itself to pieces.

But that's another story. For now it was a June evening in 1939 at the tail end of the Depression as a gang of Civilian Conservation Corps boys shoe-horned their way through the exit doors on either side of the ticket booth. The light-bulbed marquee above the ticket booth read "*Mr. Deeds Goes to Town*, starring Gary Cooper and Jean Arthur." The music from the loud-speakers mounted below the marquee was Hoagy Carmichael's "Stardust" on a 78-rpm record so scratchy you'd think it was being played on a radio in a lightning storm.

Thirty-nine CCC boys fanned across the sidewalk, a few throwing arms around one another's shoulders as they crossed the empty street. Some resembled men, most looked like kids. Green River folks, asleep or listening to their console radios at this hour, preferred to think of them as decent young men, even if many were city boys from that camp south across the state line in Manila, Utah. Decent young men much like the mostly country boys who served at the Green River town camp. The Green River camp boys had become locals, supplying leftover kitchen scrap to feed livestock. CCC young men, no matter where they were stationed, built roads, bridges, fences, and cattle guards. They got 30 dollars a month with 25 sent home. Surely the city boys from Manila must be as wholesome as the ones from the local camp.

The baritone on the movie house loudspeakers continued his scratchy "Stardust." The men from Manila swayed to the melody and looked to the night sky as they headed toward two open-back trucks, one a GMC, the other an older, heavier Dodge. Thin, trousers held high with belts hour-glassing their torsos, the men laughed and hooted, a few lit cigarettes that glowed like vacuum tube filaments. One man joined in singing "Stardust," taking over from the baritone fading behind them.

To an observer in Green River that night, the young men might have seemed cheerful, yet their faces lit by yellowed streetlights revealed tension. Could have been the obvious—city boys far from home and war imminent. But there was something about the way they glanced to one another. One young man jabbed his partner's ribs after they'd climbed into the back end of their truck. He whispered something about a pact levied in Barracks Three. If it hadn't been for the pact, it might have been a perfect Hoagy Carmichael night of nostalgia. If it hadn't been for pinching strands of the girl's hair with sweaty fingers while agreeing to the pact, there might have been more discussion about there being exactly 39 of them on an evening in 1939.

"Stardust" ended at the movie house, but the record kept turning, putting out a 78-rpm cat scratch dirge that weighed down the men climbing aboard the trucks, smokers grinding butts in the dust like they'd been taught at camp. Only after the trucks were loaded—three in each cab, the rest in the open stake-sided flat beds—did the truck engines drown out the 78-rpm cat scratch. Jethro, a Georgia baritone, tried his best to continue "Stardust" using his Hoagy Carmichael imitation, encouraging pals in his truck to join in. But after crossing the Lincoln Highway bridge and turning onto the rutted Flaming Gorge Road, it was too loud and bumpy for singing. The 50-mile drive went from high desert to mountains as they headed south. Jethro sat on floorboards shouting in a mock Charlie McCarthy voice that he needed "ass burn." Jethro was having a girlfriend heartache headache and what he really needed was aspirin.

The stake sides of the big Dodge truck rattled and swayed, dust from the lead GMC coming over the cab and into the bed where the men held on, those in the center lying or sitting on floorboards, those at the perimeter hanging onto the stakes and side rails and peering over the cab. Jethro could have tried "Stardust" again when the truck, still in high desert, stopped halfway to camp, but because of the Barracks Three pact no one felt like singing. When the driver cut the engine, wild horse hoof beats sounded in the distance, but it was too dark to see them. After the hoof beats faded, a non-singing tenor looked heavenward before leaping off the back of the truck.

"Hey, Mr. Deeds, are we back in your hometown yet? It's like the song. I never seen so many stars. No moon, but I can see your faces."

"Night vision," said another young man with a deeper voice. "It'll come in handy when we go to war."

"FDR won't take us to war. He's like Mr. Deeds."

"I'll bet you a carton of Camels he takes us to war."

The lead truck had vanished, but several men who'd been on it appeared on foot, teeth and eyes glistening in starlight against a landscape going from high desert to mountains. One man held a radium dial wristwatch near his shadowed face.

"Hurry up! We need help!"

It was dinosaur bone dry and cool after the heat of the day's sun. Boots on the road raised a dust cloud above a ravine cut when rain was more abundant. Sandstone and quartzite powder got inside the men, ruining the aftertaste of beer, popcorn, and cigarettes, making it seem the workday was still inside noses and mouths. A section of jaggedness south against the horizon of stars resembled cathedral spires; another to the north resembled a castle lookout. Pebbles kicked up by boots tagged along like scuttlebutt threatening to reveal the pact. Whispers turned to grunts and giggles of nervous laughter. The discord of voices cracked the shells of manhood.

"Where is it?" shouted one young man.

"This way."

"Did he heel and toe out of here?"

"He's down there."

The dark ravine at which they stopped was haloed in dust visible in starlight. Silence, followed by a moan.

Eventually the young men slid down into the ravine causing more dust. After a few raised voices, the grating of metal on metal, and a long drawn out scream, they climbed back out and ran. An engine started reluctantly in the distance, one gear ground into another, and the heavy Dodge labored into the night with 38 men onboard. Because of all the legs dangling off the back and sides of the open truck, it could have been a huge bug skittering across the parched earth. It took some time for the dust to settle.

The only sound in the ravine was the ticking of the GMC's engine as it cooled. Below the front corner of the overturned GMC, starlight reflected in a pool of black blood. Nearby, a shadowbox sagebrush lizard skittered beneath the wreck.

CHAPTER 2—2011

Morning. Detroit's Greektown. The revered Gianakos restaurant nestled among older structures. Towering next door the Casino Hotel's upper floor balcony windows reflect a rising sun. Sounds of restaurant ghosts below the apartment as Niki awakens. Her husband pacing. The past. Niki and her husband visiting before the daily opening when her father ran the Gianakos.

Death for Niki's father was swift, a fall from the roof above her head into the alley. Death for Niki's husband was drawn out, cancer oozing from walnut-sized prostate, moving from nodes to bones to brain. After her husband's death, Niki retrieved her maiden name to establish authority over the restaurant and apartments. After her father's death she hired a manager to run the place, supervising various shifts, *déjà vu* sounds coming from below.

The neighborhood was also a ghost. This was most apparent during her morning run. Crazy woman in her 60s imagining she's younger. These days neighborhood bustle consisted of gamblers looking for street parking for their visit to the Greektown Casino to give away their money.

She ran through the alley, saluted the spot where her father was found, and headed out onto the street toward the park. Although Greektown had become an island surrounded by abandonment, smells from childhood remained. It was garbage day, trash at the curbs. She thought of a Greek dance tune she'd recently heard. "Agapi Kai Alithia" which, appropriate to the morning, translated to "Love And Truth."

She thought of the Ukrainian woman named Marta Voronko, with whom she'd shared messages. When she returned from her run she'd check her email. Messages with Marta were part of being a crazy woman, the two of them sharing suspicions about the deaths of fathers and grandfathers simply because Niki's father and Marta's grandfather had been in the Civilian Conservation Corps in 1939. A long story detailing why a Ukrainian grandfather would have been in the CCC in the US. Two longs stories why Niki and Marta were suspicious of what everyone else considered accidental deaths of careless old men.

Niki's mantra, as she ran through her neighborhood, changed from Greek tunes to CCC repeated over and over. CCC, CCC, CCC…

Lunchtime, Chicago's Ukrainian Village. The Bakery Café was peaceful until Demidchik, the neighborhood Russian, pinballed on wobbly legs through morning traffic, nearly being hit by a Lexus, pushed through the rain-spattered door, and spotted his prey. Demidchik wore Lenin look-alike wool coat and cap. He sneered as the door's brass bell jingled merrily, his voice like a Department of Streets and Sanitation dump truck unloading gravel.

"Lazlo Horvath! Gypsy from Ukraine! There are few left from old country! Mexican fence jumpers and Arab women with burkas invade neighborhood!"

Ria, the café proprietress, frowned from behind the pastry display case. When Lazlo ignored Demidchik the tirade continued. "I speak of this godforsaken corner of Chicago, not Ukraine, our bride basket for Arabs…Not so funny?"

Lazlo stared at his newspaper. "Has Demidchik awoken from a vodka nightmare?"

Demidchik grinned. "I slept in Russian cemetery last night. Papa Joe is not buried here, yet he speaks to friends through tunnels dug during the Great War."

"Did Stalin's slave laborers run into Hitler's digging the other way?"

Demidchik shook his head as he marched to the serving counter, eyeing pastry, but settling for coffee. He retrieved coffee pitcher and cup from the counter and plopped down at Lazlo's table, spilling some of Lazlo's luncheon borsht. He removed his cap, sat smugly yet surprisingly silent after his initial outburst, drinking cup after cup of black coffee poured from the insulated pitcher. Lazlo placed his newspaper on the table behind him and bent to his borsht bowl to finish what remained. Demidchik, whose few remaining scalp hairs stood at attention from wool cap static electricity, pounded the table and ranted on a new topic.

"Killer's trademark! Force open victim's mouth until jaw breaks, stuff mouth with contaminated Chernobyl soil. Russians cut Ukraine's energy and sabotage nuclear plants, ignoring borders. Putin is Prime Minister, but will again be President. Russians like Putin are chessmen. When things happen in Ukraine, a Russian has made a move. Therefore, killer is Russian! It will be proven when CSI's study hair found at scene!"

A bull's-eye erupted from Lazlo's borsht bowl as Demidchik pounded his fist. Lazlo looked out the window. Although rain had ended, traffic was still snarled. This morning an easterly from Lake Michigan reminded Lazlo of a spring storm blowing in from the Kiev Reservoir years earlier during a trip to see his brother who worked at the Chernobyl plant, his brother flown to Moscow only to lose his hair and die in Hospital Number Six.

It was April 2011. The Chernobyl disaster's 25th anniversary was at hand, Japan had experienced its earthquake, and Demidchik sat across from Lazlo shouting incoherently. Rather than speaking of earthquakes, nuclear threats, or his usual tirade about "foreigners" invading their Chicago neighborhood, Demidchik squawked about a serial killer.

A younger Demidchik had been "cured" in a Kharkiv asylum, immigrated to the US, and, unable to find a satisfactory Russian neighborhood, moved to Chicago's Ukrainian Village. Demidchik barked broken English from a mottled visage with a salt-and-pepper goatee shaped like a penis. Ria asked Demidchik to lower his voice when she came to the table to refill the coffee pitcher. Construction workers at another table, hard hats beneath their chairs like World War II helmets painted orange, glanced with uncertain smiles toward Lazlo.

"And now," groused Demidchik, "with killer loose, Russian Mafia has eye on me,"

"Mafia with only one eye cannot be very effective," said Lazlo.

"Effective? My phone is bugged! My car is bugged!"

Demidchik turned to the construction workers, their lips squeezing away smiles. Two were African American, one Hispanic, the fourth Caucasian. "Pakistani doctor put something inside when he removed appendix! They work together, these Mafias. Mafias create serial killers! Killing Ukrainians, Americans, even Al-Qaeda if Obama was smart enough to hire them!"

The construction crew, at first amused, now stared at Demidchik.

"You think I am April fool?" asked Demidchik.

"April Fools' Day was last week," said Lazlo.

Demidchik lifted his coffee pitcher as if giving a toast, gulped the remaining hot coffee directly from the pitcher, wiped his mouth with his sleeve, took a few deep breaths, exhaling coffee steam through yellow teeth, put on his worn Lenin cap, and stormed out, slamming the door, the brass bell jingling furiously.

"I should give that man my wife's tamales," said a Hispanic worker as the construction crew paid their bill, all of them laughing. On their way out they tipped their hardhats.

Ria brought tea to the table. Ria's hair was long, the color of bread crust and tied in back. Her homeland was a former Hungarian-speaking village in what was now the Czech Republic, not far from Lazlo's roots in the former Hungarian-speaking portion of Western Ukraine.

"I'm sick of Demidchik's bride basket joke," said Ria. "We should be proud Ukraine was known as the breadbasket, not make jokes about it. You've been here since breakfast, Lazlo. Are you practicing ESP?"

Lazlo motioned toward the stack of newspapers on the table behind him. "I'm keeping up with news about the serial killer."

"Still the Kiev Militia investigator. Tell me what you've discovered."

"The killer has moved from Kiev to Odessa. The first victims were older, broken jaws and contaminated soil stuffed into their mouths."

Ria sipped tea and licked her lips. "And now victims are girls like my cook, who would have been trafficked if not for you. You don't need Internet, Lazlo. Your years in Kiev gave you telepathy. Go to State Street and see if Chicago needs a special investigator."

"They don't believe in ESP, and I'm too old, even for special services."

"Old-schmold. Contact your Kiev associate. The two of you are keenly aware of the past, sharing *déjà vu*. Do you know the opposite of *déjà vu*?"

"No, what's it called?"

"*Jamais vu*, another French term meaning things not yet seen. Call Janos, Lazlo."

"You are a Gypsy fortuneteller, Ria."

"The Bakery Café uses telepathy rather than Internet." Ria smiled and held her glass two-handed. "Lazlo Horvath is thinking of connections

13

between the serial killer, long-term radiation, and the upcoming Chernobyl anniversary. Everything and everyone is connected like in that Six Degrees of Separation movie. Were you aware a Hungarian named Karinthy came up with the theory? Your friend Janos in Ukraine is Hungarian. Call him."

"Last time I called Janos was when I'd barged into the investigation of that old man found beneath a bus on North Avenue. They said the driver started out not knowing a drunk was underneath. Instead of believing them, I go to the family, who insists he's not a drunk, and with their permission I'm allowed into the morgue. The body crushed, the face intact. He was no drunk; his face had a look of determination. The examiner showed me a locket of hair from the man's wallet, red hair. Afterwards I discovered none in the family had red hair. A simple locket of hair and I can't let go. The Chicago detectives said I reminded them of Columbo. The head of detectives told me I could be charged with interfering. Our alderman told me to fuck off."

Ria looked out the window. "And so you called Janos to discuss the tradition of saving hair from loved ones. Kiev detectives with Hungarian creative spirit, partners reading one another's thoughts. Ilonka and I were like that. Life is not for waiting, Lazlo. Life is for contacting friends and creating love."

Lazlo wanted to grasp Ria's hands and ask her to dinner. But last time he asked, Ria reminded him about her lover, Ilonka, who died of breast cancer, saying she'd meet another Ilonka one day. Lazlo stared into Ria's eyes until the café door opened. An old Ukrainian woman from the neighborhood held the hand of her great granddaughter. Ria smiled and there were smiles on both the ancient face and the fresh face of youth as the brass doorbell jingled them in from the now sunny street. The little girl immediately ran to the display case containing jelly and cream-filled pastry. Ria left the table.

A small patch of sky was visible between buildings across the street. A dark northeast horizon, the spring storm heading across Lake Michigan where it would give Detroit a taste of rain and continue into Canada. The man run over by the bus was still on Lazlo's mind. He visualized wide tires doing their work on the torso, blood oozing. Although he could not recall the man's name, he remembered the eldest son. Outside the morgue the son asked if Lazlo was from his father's past? No. The son complained a Greek woman from Detroit had called, asking about the health of his father, about the year 1939, about hair saved. The son told the woman his father was 90 and to mind her own business. A Greek woman from Detroit, the year 1939, hair saved, a dark horizon, and now this Chernobyl killer. Yes, he'd call Janos.

CHAPTER 3

Tea rather than coffee left Guzzo sleepy as he sat on the edge of the bed. The silver tea glass holder's finger loop was too small so he held the hot bottom. On the holder's edge, "Odessa, Ukraine," was engraved in both English and Ukrainian.

The table resembled a half-eaten crime scene—eviscerated cheese-filled strudel, puffs of powdered sugar, blood-red jam oozing from crepes, tea stains on doilies surrounding the samovar. Guzzo recalled the table having squeaked its way into the room on casters needing oil. The wheels were several inches in diameter, caster hubs gray, cracked rubber treads. Guzzo imagined shell-shocked refugees rummaging through post war trash, yanking casters off crushed gurneys, and saving them for future use at hotels yet to be.

Guzzo put down his tea glass, glancing at his tattooed wrist. During a lay-over in Germany others had gotten the usual eagles and weapons. His tattoo was different, the word *STORM* in all caps with an arrow pointing toward his hand. He wondered what the Ukrainian word for storm was and how it would look in Cyrillic. Probably pretty weird like a scream not screamed despite the painful wrist application.

Guzzo's mind time traveled during the night, the blood of strangers searching for his spirit. Leftover dreams from Sicilian ancestors, the violence of family feuds.

Vera was the only person to whom Guzzo confided his morning thoughts. He once told Vera, sleep was like being in the mind of a death camp commandant at dusk, the huge pleading eyes of prisoners glowing in sunset while he selects dinner wine. Vera said she also had disturbing dreams because her parents were, "The last of the red hot dissidents," and because her grandparents had survived to reveal the worst of Stalin's starvation of Ukraine.

Vera was Guzzo's anchor. The irony? He would never have met her if he hadn't accepted assignments passed through the Chicago fishmonger named Pescatore, who received his instructions from another Pescatore in New York. In another lifetime before Nine-Eleven, Guzzo asked his Chicago Pescatore how assignment messages arrived. It had been noisy in the office that day, the fish grinder in the adjoining room so loud Guzzo felt it was safe to ask.

Pescatore paused to wipe guts from his long filleting knife on his apron. "Messages come to market inside special fishes. I can tell by the look in their dead eyes which carry messages, and from what part of the country or world they originate."

Aware of the term, "Sleeping with the fishes," Guzzo apologized for asking and during subsequent visits asked innocuous questions about the fish business, such as what was done with the ground up fish guts from the noisy machine next door?

"Oh the grinder? We put the mix into barrels and sell it to a company where they separate the juices, dry the byproduct, and use a pelletizing machine to make animal feed."

Pescatore obviously had many connections—fish product connections as well as crime families as well as intelligence agencies. How else would information for assignments be gathered if not for connections? And money. No matter his being careful when meeting Pescatore, Guzzo hoped some day, by being attentive, he'd be able to determine the source of non-fish-business funds.

Guzzo cinched up his pajama bottoms, stood from the bed, and walked around the serving table to a full-length closet mirror. He leaned close and examined his eyes, which were neither dead nor bloodshot. He could not lean too close because of his Stetson hat brim. He smiled at himself, adjusted the crease in the hat purchased at a Kiev shop. Beyond the mirror's image of the smiling cowboy in plaid pajama bottoms was the view out the sliding door to the balcony. The morning sun had climbed, the sky blue, the Black Sea Harbor brown, and Vera's kimono blowing between her legs in the sea breeze red and semitransparent in sunlight.

Sounds of the sea had been replaced by Odessa's morning traffic, people scurrying in Ladas, Skodas, and scooters as they snaked between trucks and buses. A bus accelerating reminded Guzzo of the Chicago assignment— the early morning pint of bourbon, the fat rear tires, a push. An especially loud V-twin motorcycle rumbling like a mountain lion reminded him of the Colorado Rockies assignment—a man and his straight-pipe Harley Davidson so badly dismembered, scattered, and burned, DNA tests and Milwaukee factory records were required. Although assignments had begun with old men, younger persons searching the past were added. Not children. A California man had been babysitting a grandson. Not yet two, the boy stared wide-eyed at Guzzo while he performed his task using a kitchen towel to suffocate the man. When the boy laughed, trying to get out of the highchair to join the game, Guzzo carried the highchair out of the kitchen and closed the boy in a bedroom. Strange, he now recalled that before death, the old man pulled a piece of paper from his pocket and held it up, as one would present a crucifix to a vampire. The paper had strands of hair taped to it. Not knowing what else to do, he took the paper from the old man and put it in his pocket. Later, away from the assignment, he saw the hair was red, the tape and paper yellowed with age. Nothing was written and he burned the paper with the hair. The way the old man held the hair up, and a vague story of men saving strands of hair, stayed with him. The story wasn't from Pescatore, but from a conversation recently overheard in a Chicago park at a family reunion, a relative going on and on, saying, "Sure he's old. But what about that hair he saved? Who's that belong to?"

Guzzo's full name was Anthony Ulysses Guzzo, the Ulysses from a great uncle who, in the 1920s, fled Mussolini's war on Sicilian Mafia to become a Chicago produce importer. Guzzo's parents moved to Tucson, Arizona, because of his mother's allergies. Family called him Tony. Everyone else, beginning in grade school, called him Guzzo, or sometimes Smiling Guzzo. The only use of his middle name was on official documents. Even the girl-friend he almost married didn't know his middle name.

Following a tour in Bush Senior's first Iraq war escorting supply convoys, Guzzo got a law enforcement degree at University of Arizona and worked Security on the Arizona-Mexican border where migrants paid to either walk to their deaths, or be sardined into vans leading to shitty jobs. He was intro-duced to the Mexican drug lord who tried to hire him. When Guzzo refused, the drug lord, paying off East Coast favors, put him in contact with the New York fishmonger who sent Guzzo to the Chicago fishmonger. Over time, non-drug-related assignments rolled in. Ulysses was how Guzzo thought of himself—a king battling full circle back to his roots, a fisher of ancient men.

On assignment in Kiev ten years earlier, Guzzo captured Vera with his smile. Both were at the Kiev airport after the Twin Towers fell. Neither could get a flight into the US. They spent several days together. Vera agonized over her pre-green-card past—activist parents executed while she hid in a closet clutching a headless doll during the twilight of the Soviet era. Guzzo put on the smiling face of American business. The aftermath of Nine-Eleven became their bond. With help from Vera's contact in a Ukrainian security agency she was able to get papers, Guzzo brought her back to the US, they married, and had two girls in the span of two years. They lived in Orland Park, Illinois, outside Chicago where Guzzo had easy access to his intermediary.

Several years earlier Vera said she'd never return to her homeland, but here she was. After sightseeing in Lviv and Kiev, Guzzo, Vera, and their pre-school girls were in the middle of a weeklong stay at a five-star Odessa resort hotel. Vera was ten years younger than Guzzo and still awaiting US citizenship. The girls, four and five, were Americans through and through. Vera taught them Ukrainian, but they had no trace of Vera's accent. Arriving in Ukraine, his girls magically transformed themselves into Ukrainians. This morning they enjoyed a giggly room service breakfast in bed watching Ukrainian television cartoons. It wasn't until the hotel nanny picked the girls up for a children's museum outing that Guzzo threw aside the blanket, sat up on the edge of the bed, had more tea from the samovar, and put on his new Stetson.

Vera and both daughters were petite blondes with high cheekbones, very Russian. Guzzo was light-skinned for a Sicilian and had the thin face, large hands, and soccer-ball shoulders of a Ukrainian laborer. As long as he didn't speak, they passed for Kievians escaping the cold. Vera spoke Russian and Ukrainian, completing the window-dressing for his assignment.

Being April, Odessa should have been warmer, but the weather was cool. Even so, April Fools' celebrants cavorted on the beaches. Guzzo's family trips outside the hotel involved shopping and sightseeing well away from the beer and vodka-guzzling students, polluted brown water, and shipyards. Sunbathers gathered across the boulevard on the beach—some walking, some standing and swinging their arms to ward off the chill, and a few nearly naked skinny souls reposing on colorful blankets pasted to the off-white envelope of the beach like postage stamps dedicated to Stalin era famine victims.

When Vera turned back to the room and walked in from the balcony to place her teacup on the samovar table, Guzzo took off his Stetson and bowed flamboyantly.

"You're wearing black market hat," said Vera, flipping her blond hair back and slithering out of the kimono. Now naked, she pointed to Guzzo's feet. "If you bought cowboy boots I would put them on. I see pajama flag is up despite the reason for us coming to Odessa."

"When you mentioned Smirnov on the phone I didn't realize it was the nanny. She turned me on. And please, Vera, no more about reasons."

Vera turned toward the bathroom. "Smirnov is a common Russian name. Nanny is a grandmother, if that is your preference." She paused at the bathroom door, facing away from him. "I agree we consider this vacation rather than what it is for you. If pajama flag is still up, work-related questions will cease."

Guzzo pulled her away from the bathroom doorway, threw aside the Stetson, and pushed her onto the bed. Gulls shrieked, traffic roared, and a musky Black Sea breeze blew in through the open balcony door.

CHAPTER 4

Researching the deaths of Father and Grandfather lured Doctor Marta Adamivna Voronko to an Odessa beach. She'd taken the train from Kiev for an Odessa Children's Rehabilitation Center conference and, while there, text messages came in insisting information about Grandfather's murder on September 11, 2001, was available. With the time difference, Grandfather died after news of planes hitting their targets had traveled the world. The last text message claimed the time of death was chosen; she could obtain further information that night near the beach sanatorium at the Frantsuzky Boulevard tram's last stop.

The messages contained cogent details. Grandfather was a US citizen during the Roosevelt administration, and Father, whose research she continued, died in 2009 in another so-called "single vehicle accident" in the Carpathians. Father was a careful driver, habitually spitting over his shoulder before driving. The mention of spitting for luck convinced her.

Marta had given her e-mail address and phone number to other genealogical researchers. She was aware of researchers wanting secrecy due to ancestral involvement in Ukraine's wartime Jewish pogroms. Because of guilt suffered by past generations and Zionist investigations, a trip to the beach at night did not seem odd. As a precaution she carried a canister of what the woman at her self-defense class called double-strength pepper spray.

Marta sat cross-legged on the sand down the hill from the tram stop near the sanatorium, a slight breeze off the dark sea. Freighter lights moving away from port brought thoughts of other cities on water, especially Detroit in the US because one of her contacts was from Detroit.

At the designated midnight hour, several couples strolled the beach. One woman was topless despite the April chill. As the couple passed close, the man spun around. He was bottomless, the shadow of his penis wagging against Odessa's lit skyline. It appeared the man wore a dark sweatshirt and the woman wore the matching sweatpants. Marta imagined them shivering while making love on the beach. She recalled the hotel brochure saying the beach below the sanatorium was "clothing optional," thought of Sonia's arrival next day, and imagined the two of them topless.

Away from the harbor the sea smelled fresh. Would this meeting provide secrets from Grandfather's past and vindicate Father's compulsive search? Would she learn about strands of hair from Grandfather's past? Would she meet another deranged researcher like the old woman in Kiev's Botanical Gardens who insisted Nazi descendants caused Chernobyl, economic strife, and terrorism? The woman's age could have been anywhere between 60 and 80. She wore a long dress, hiding her feet, and had come close to Marta. The woman smelled like rotten mushrooms. As the woman told her story, Marta felt she was breathing air from beneath the woman's dress. She recalled the woman wore a faded and tattered maroon sweater covered with strands of gray hair.

The old woman's story came to Marta like a whiff of dead fish in the surf. Nazi descendants lived underground not only in Ukraine, but also throughout the world, especially in the US West with its many caverns. The woman said besides wars and economic crises, Nazis recently joined up with anarchist Mormons in Utah.

Nothing was impossible when it came to Internet conspiracies. Perhaps underground Nazi descendents of World War II scientists, having tapped heat from Earth's core, caused climate change. Yes, World War II scientists, bypassed for the Manhattan Project, joining up with anarchist Mormons and right-wing radicals.

Marta would have preferred whoever sent the texts had identified himself or herself. Perhaps it was Niki Gianakos from Detroit with whom she'd shared emails. She recalled recently recounting the meeting with the old woman with Niki after Niki told of her life and research, detailing her husband's death from cancer and the more recent mysterious death of her father. Like Marta's grandfather, Niki's father had been in the CCCs in Manila, Utah, in 1939. Niki spoke of road building through canyons, a rock shaped like a castle, and a fire tower in which one could live. The same details Grandfather had passed on to Father. If she were meeting Niki tonight they'd have much to share.

When a man from behind said, "Good evening," in English, Marta stood, spun around, and grasped the can of pepper spray in her jacket pocket.

He was tall, hatless, and either wore a thick overcoat or lifted weights. He spoke rapidly in a soft voice, a Southwestern American accent evident. "No worries, ma'am. It's about sharing information. It's about grandfathers."

Marta spoke as best she could in English. "You know me, how?"

He stepped closer. "Another American searcher—Hey, don't be frightened."

"What is your name?"

"Jethro. Yours?"

"Mine is Marta. Jethro is familiar, but your accent—"

"No worries. My grandfather was southern. My folks moved west."

"Your grandfather and grandmother are dead?"

"Murder-suicide, according to the Georgia state police."

THE GIRL WITH 39 GRAVES

"Yes, a friend found this in American newspaper archives."

"Well then come on, Marta. We'll walk up the hill to the lights. Should have planned another meeting place. Had no idea it'd be so dark. We'll go to the sanatorium at the top. Have a bottle of mineral water and maybe some vodka. You coming?"

When she paused, he said, "I forgot to mention the reason for meeting. You see, I realize now, all of them saved strands of hair."

"Whose hair?"

No answer. Father spoke of hair Grandfather had saved. Rather than Grandfather being buried with his envelope of hair, Father gave it to her to keep in a safe place. The envelope was tucked away in her jewelry box back in the apartment. Too much information. The man had given her none. Why should she reveal what she knew?

"Very well," she said finally. "We'll go to the sanatorium."

As they walked, Marta tried to keep her distance. He wore dark slacks and a long-sleeved shirt. He spit over his left shoulder as they climbed, reminding her of Father and making her feel less apprehensive. But as the hill steepened he came close, their elbows bumping.

"Excuse my butterflies," he said, touching her arm. "I'm excited to learn what you know."

He was on her before she could react. She tried rolling away downhill but he flattened her face into the sand. The sanatorium lights at the top of the hill shadowed him. When she turned to scream his gloved hand covered her mouth. His other hand had both arms locked behind and his legs intertwined with hers like steel cables.

He spun her around, his face close. "Nothing personal, Doc. I need to support my family."

When she tried screaming again his hand plunged into her mouth. She bit down, but his hand went deeper, beyond the range of jaw muscles, ripping her mouth so wide she thought her jaw would break. And then it did break, pain shooting into her skull with an explosive crack. Her reaction lifted him into the air and she managed to free one hand. She pushed into her pocket, grasped the pepper spray, flipped open the safety cap, and sprayed wildly toward his face.

He flung the canister away and grasped her throat with both hands. She pounded his face, shoulders, and arms. Not able to breathe, she focused on the lights of the sanatorium up the hill. Help would come. A policeman at the tram station near the sanatorium would hear her gasps. But the man squeezed her neck so tightly she was unable to gasp, and finally the lights in the distance dimmed and she was back at the conference earlier that day. The conference at the wonderful Rehabilitation Center founded by a loving father following his daughter's death. Marta had wanted to tell Sonia about the Center, about a loving father, about her own grandfather and father, about the strands of hair.

Sand in her mouth. How would she be able to kiss Sonia with sand in her mouth? And then, suddenly, there was the taste of dirt...

CHAPTER 5

Next morning, while the girls giggled in the bathtub, Guzzo and Vera, wearing the hotel's so-called Black Sea robes, sat in the sun on the balcony.

"I hope they are safe," said Vera.

Guzzo placed his hand on hers. "They're fine, Vera. I tasted the water."

"I was concerned about depth."

"The water's not deep. As long as we can hear them—"

A ship's whistle sounded across the harbor. Vera pulled her hand from beneath his and put her hand on top. "Did you speak with your concierge this morning on your way in, Tony?"

Vera called him Tony when she was angry. Acting matter-of-fact concerning victims annoyed her. He put his hand back on top. The sleeve of the robe slid back, revealing his *STORM* tattoo. "The concierge gave me the newspaper."

Vera's hand on top again. "Was there news of the woman?"

"No."

Vera stared at the horizon. "I wish the return to my homeland had been without the woman. I saw scratches on your face. Did the girls notice?"

Guzzo's hand back on top. "A boy lost his beach ball. I scratched my face chasing it into the bushes. We're on the beach, Vera, staying in a five-star hotel with guaranteed pure water. Last week we visited your city and old neighborhood. What more could a mother ask?"

Vera turned to him. "You're itching your eyes. Does it have to do with the dirt?"

Guzzo did not answer.

"The one you copied has what Americans call *modus operandi*. I heard it on the late news. Suffering is in the trademark." Vera put her hand to her throat. "Stretching the victim's mouth until the lips split and stuffing the mouth with Chernobyl soil. News broadcasts speak of vampires though it has nothing to do with drinking blood."

Guzzo stood, went to the balcony railing, and whispered harshly. "One more word, Vera, and we'll lose the girls because we'll both be locked up after I beat the shit out of you! I needed to follow the M.O. to the letter! I wore gloves and at no time did my skin contact the soil provided!" He turned, aware his usual smile was absent. "We have two more years! You were there when we signed on!"

Vera looked back to the room where the girls giggled in the tub. "I'm sorry. In Kiev I worried intelligence agents might recognize me. Here, with more Russians around, I need to remind myself I'm from America."

Guzzo went behind her chair and held her shoulders. "Okay, babe. It's the black robes talking. Enough said. Agreed?"

"Agreed." Vera stood, lifted Guzzo's right hand from her shoulder and kissed it. "We should check the girls."

Sirens sounded in the distance. The hotel lobby concierge stared out the west entrance at an electronic billboard flashing news in both Ukrainian and

English—a comparison of the current world economy to that of the 1930s, news of oil spills and soaring oil prices because of Russia's games, Orthodox Easter coming on April 19, updates of the nuclear disaster following the Japanese earthquake and tsunami, and finally a mention of the upcoming 25th anniversary of the Chernobyl disaster on April 26. But then the billboard went back to the recently celebrated "Fool Day, The National Day of Laughter" and how important it was for everyone's physical and mental health to take time to smile toward others and laugh at oneself. Many Odessians, hearing distant sirens, assumed revelers, having consumed too much vodka, had moved their extended April Fools' celebration out into the street where it did not belong.

Guzzo stayed on the balcony while Vera checked the girls. Perhaps, like him, Vera was concerned about the change in assignments. With genealogical family researchers, instead of stalking victims at retirement communities in the US, a second and third generation was involved. Why had a bunch of old men, most of them dead, saved strands of reddish brown hair in the first place? If it was money, following money was always dangerous.

Vera was aware of Pescatore's worldwide connections, and was familiar with Ukrainian and Russian intelligence organizations and Mafias. She, of all people, should know the local Russian Mafia was being contacted in case her husband left loose ends on the beach, the same Russian Mafia who had Vera in their clutches before he snatched her away. Perhaps agents covering his tracks would see the Star of David he'd drawn in the sand prior to dragging the body into the surf. Would they leave it to implicate a Zionist zealot? Passover started next day and what better time to kill someone whose family might have been involved in a pogrom? Or would they, or children at play, erase the Star of David?

Guzzo took a deep breath of Black Sea air, coughed, leaned over the balcony, spit, and watched as his spittle sparkled in sunlight before landing on the windshield of a hotel Mercedes shuttle van parked at the curb. When there was no reaction from below, Guzzo turned from the balcony railing and walked to the bathroom to be with his beautiful girls.

CHAPTER 6

Mariya Nemeth and Janos Nagy were a strange Kiev couple. Janos speaking Hungarian while they lay in bed before dawn, "We are a strange Kiev couple."

Mariya speaking Ukrainian, "I prefer the American *sidekick*. Lazlo said we could have been *sidekicks* in strip clubs. Your hair black, mine blond."

Janos switched to Ukrainian. "Like Lazlo's, mine is graying. I considered stripping, had tassels and a pouch prepared."

"You'd get large bills tucked into your pouch. Not like the *hrivnas* tucked into my g-string."

Janos sat up in the dark. "I thought you made a fortune in clubs."

"As you know, my fortune came from what was left of Viktor's savings. Perhaps we should sell the Audi he left me and we'll have more fortune."

Janos lay back on his pillow. "I was joking."

Mariya poked Janos in a lower rib. "Sorry I mentioned Viktor. Speak of something else. Do your butt cheeks still itch from the Mafia bomb outside your office window?"

"The doctor says bits of glass should have worked their way out months ago, yet whenever I sit, especially in my car, it's like ingrown hairs."

"Since Lazlo spoke of the man beneath the Chicago bus with strands of hair in his wallet, hair dominates conversations. My hair, your hair, the feeling like ingrown hairs. You should drive the Audi."

"You don't like my Skoda?"

"Only the color; the bright orange matches your butt. The Audi's seats are comfortable. Give the Skoda to your sister. She can't always borrow Marta's car."

"Too analytical," said Janos. "Instead of discussing cars, and Sonia's lover, we'll make love."

"I thought you had a breakfast meeting with an irate husband."

"An irate husband who suspects a cheating wife takes second place."

"Would an irate same-sex partner be treated to a breakfast meeting?"

"Of course."

"Janos, what color did Lazlo say the hair in the old man's wallet was?"

"Reddish brown."

"I'm glad the strands of hair under the bus weren't blond like mine."

When the apartment telephone rang, Mariya suffered a momentary flashback—She's still married to Viktor; he phones but the call cuts off; she rides her bicycle frantically, zigzagging through Kiev traffic to Viktor's video store; the smoke from the fire resembles an angry python in the sky; the fire so hot policemen and firemen will not let her near.

The flashback's horror was amplified whenever private investigator Janos Nagy—the man she accompanied to the compound for trafficked young people near Chernobyl to solve Viktor's murder, the man who almost died at the hands of Mafia rapists, the man who now shared her life—was not home.

"Mariya, it's Sonia. Is Janos there?"

"No. What's wrong, Sonia? I hear something in your voice."

"I'm here. I'm…cell phone. The connection is…"

"Sonia?"

"I'm back."

"Tell me what's wrong before we lose the connection."

"I'm at the window; this should be better. I called because of Marta. She doesn't answer her phone."

"She's at a conference. She probably turned it off."

"I tried last night on the train from Kiev. She didn't answer when they rang the room. This morning when I arrived at the hotel—I don't think she slept in the room."

"I'm sorry Sonia, I—"

Sonia interrupted. "We were to meet for breakfast before the conference. She registered our room. When I came here—Wait, there's someone at the door."

Garbled voices and a loud clattering before the connection went dead.

Mariya tried calling Sonia back several times. Each time, after the message saying the cell customer was not available, she hung up and waited to see if Sonia would call back. The singsong recording reminded Mariya of her mother's voice when she was a girl in Uzhgorod. Mariya's mother, who insisted she use the city's Hungarian name, Ungvár.

A girl of 16 after a day at school, excited about a field trip to the Carpathian caves and…

"How much will this so-called field trip cost?" asks her mother in her singsong voice.

"I don't know yet."

"Surely the bus alone will cost me a meal."

"I'm not sure, Mother. I'll find out."

"From where does the bus leave?"

"Right here, in Uzh...in Ungvár."

A slap, her mother angry because she almost used the non-Hungarian pronunciation.

Mariya had not spoken to her mother in decades. The last time was a call Janos encouraged. After news of shutting down the "Chernobyl Exclusion Zone Factory for Trafficked Children," she called to tell her mother she was safe. Mariya's mother said it was good she was safe and hung up, the same way the recorded singsong voice comes to an end with a definitive click.

Kiev Private Investigator Janos Nagy was called Gypsy, a name inherited from his mentor, Lazlo Horvath, when both were in the Kiev Soviet Militia Unit prior to Chernobyl. Comrades named him Boy Gypsy and Lazlo Father Gypsy. Lazlo retired to Chicago and wanted Janos and Mariya to move to Chicago. Visas were ready; it was only a matter of time.

For Janos, cases these days were not dangerous as in his past. The vow to stick with Kiev domestic matters and avoid standoffs with Russian Mafia was his promise to Mariya. They'd met two years earlier. She needed a detective to determine if the death of her husband Viktor in the fire at his video store was an accident, as authorities said, or murder, as Mariya suspected. Mariya's analytical mind teamed with Janos' thoroughness led to deep shit, leaving them no choice but to escape various branches of police, the SBU, the Russian Mafia, and traffickers hiding young people inside the Chernobyl Exclusion Zone.

Janos' experience, first in the militia working with Lazlo in Soviet days, then as a private investigator during Ukraine independence, taught him there was always another doorway leading deeper into the human soul's shit. When

Mariya called about his sister Sonia, he knew by the tone of Mariya's voice, one of these doorways had opened.

"I repeatedly tried calling Sonia back. She was in Marta's hotel room in Odessa and someone was at the door. After that the phone went dead."

"Perhaps a quarrel," said Janos. "Their relationship has been difficult, especially with other women *and* men in the mix."

"It's not about their relationship," said Mariya.

"How can you know? You said the phone went dead."

"Sonia took the overnight train from Kiev and was supposed to meet Marta for breakfast. When she went to the room, it appeared Marta had not slept there."

"Aha."

"Janos, your sister was serious. Sonia and I have become close. It's not a quarrel. They agreed to meet at a certain time and Marta's not there."

Later that afternoon, with no word from Sonia, Janos called the central militia office in Odessa. After numerous transfers, he got through to the chief homicide investigator who said Sonia was brought to the militia's morgue to identify the body of Doctor Marta Adamivna Voronko. Marta was found that morning near Chkalovo beach. Although she was in the surf, and the cause of death was suffocation, her jaw was broken and radioactive soil was stuffed down her throat, copycatting other nighttime murders committed during the last year in and around both Kiev and Odessa. The flaw in Janos' conversation with the Odessa militia unit office was not lack of consistency of the phone system, but lack of brains on the other end of the line.

"Perhaps I misunderstand. You take my sister into your basement morgue, show her Doctor Marta Voronko's body complete with broken jaw and Chernobyl soil, she identifies the body, and you allow her to walk out of the building unattended?"

"It's difficult understanding if you shout."

Janos lowered his voice. "Very well. Where the hell is my sister?"

"We told her to wait. She was put in a room and one of our female officers was going to accompany her and—"

"Why didn't someone follow her?"

"I don't know."

"Do you know anything? Did she walk out under her own power, or was she dragged out?"

"As I said, when we left her in the room she was distraught, but physically she was fine."

"Have you cordoned off the area?"

"Of course."

"How many officers and how large a perimeter?"

"Bring your Hungarian ass down here. We can use it to measure the perimeter!"

"Shouting at the brother of a woman you lost? I'm a Hungarian vampire. I'll come there and suck blood. And while I'm on my way, I'll contact Odessa militia officials I can trust!"

CHAPTER 7

When Sonia Nagy walked out of the Odessa militia office interrogation room, down the stairs, and out to the street, she paused in sunlight wondering how much time had passed and why no one had stopped her. The terror on Marta's face in the brightly lit room with officers and a morgue technician standing opposite the body, combined with alcohol scent and walls lined with body drawers, had been unreal. Someone had tried to properly close Marta's mouth to ease the facial expression and done a poor job. The change in bone structure was obvious. When Sonia saw specks of dirt in the corners of Marta's mouth the taste of dirt came into her own mouth.

Sonia had wanted to kiss Marta this morning instead of sitting on a bench across the street from the militia office. Was she practicing the Ukrainian superstition in which one sits before a journey? Was she breathing? Was this really sun on her face? Perhaps a hair dryer in the hotel bathroom. Marta waiting outside for her turn. Sonia will go to the door, open it, and Marta will take her usual morning shower.

A rush of air was followed by a hiss and squeal. When Sonia no longer felt the sun, she realized a bus had stopped. She boarded the bus. It turned several corners and headed away from city center. A breeze from the window blew her hair across her face. Back at militia headquarters the door to the interrogation room had been left slightly open. Sonia recalled overhearing two young male officers in the hallway.

"Where was she found?"

"Chkalovo beach. At first we thought she'd fallen off the yacht club pier. Last year a drunk fell off and drifted there. But dirt in the woman's mouth points to the Chernobyl killer."

"Is this the first time he's left a victim on a beach?"

"They're usually found in alleyways near a bar or dance club."

"Perhaps Chkalovo beach offers a clue, since it's the official nude beach."

"Why haven't they changed the name? Chkalovo was a Russian test pilot. They changed other Soviet names."

"That's the point. It wasn't a nudist beach in Soviet times. Using his name's an insult. Bathers hurriedly disrobing the way a pilot would if his flight suit caught fire."

"If there's any hurrying at Chkalovo beach it's to run from flabby old men with dicks hanging out. Did you hear about the Mir space station cosmonaut's dick?"

"No."

"Our cosmonaut's up there for months. He gets taller, but also sleeps nude and his dick grows. When American astronaut comes on, cosmonaut shows the American who says, "I thought you were all Russians up here. Are you from Texas?"

"What does this have to do with the Chernobyl killer?"

"It's simply a joke. You have one better?"

"A legend about Chkalovo beach and why it's named after the Russian pilot. He's older, wants to be a cosmonaut, but fails the physical. Depressed, he moves to Odessa and wanders this beach searching for youth A flabby yet well-endowed Chkalovo whose dick hangs out one leg of his shorts while balls hang out the other decides, what's the use, removes his shorts, and the nude beach is born. Seeing him naked causes jaws to drop. And when he sees their jaws drop, he becomes angry, gets hold of radioactive dirt, and does something about these dropping jaws."

The laughter of the two militiamen walking down the hallway was inside Sonia's head trying to get out. She hadn't laughed. Instead, she opened the door, saw the sign for the stairway, and left the building. It seemed important to go where Marta was found. Perhaps, in a parallel world, Marta would be there waiting for her.

Sonia sat on the side of the bus facing the beaches. The bus stopped at Arkadia beach with its restaurants and people sitting beneath a rainbow of umbrellas. The parade of people exiting the bus was colorful. Sonia looked down and realized she, too, was dressed colorfully in turquoise slacks, white blouse, and red jacket. Marta would have liked the colors.

The bus whined as it climbed a hill and the sanatorium came into view. Sonia stood in the aisle swaying back and forth in her other world where militiamen joked. A teenaged boy laughed when she almost fell into his lap. The driver stared in his rearview mirror, pulled the door lever, and announced the sanatorium stop in a gruff voice. After Sonia stepped off, the laughing teenaged boy pushed her aside, ran around the front of the bus, and the driver shouted. When the bus and the teenaged boy were gone, Sonia crossed over in a daze, taking the pathway around the sanatorium to the zigzag beach stairway.

Green and red militia tape cordoning off a square appeared up the beach when the stairway turned on the steepest part of the hill. Two uniformed militiamen standing guard eyed her as she walked close. They looked to one another and shrugged as she knelt on pebble stone and wept. When one of the militiamen walked her way, she stood and ran inland past him.

In the dune bordered by grass, several couples sunbathed. A few were nude. They lay on blankets in a hollow protected from wind. After she passed the couples and crossed over the grassy dune, a man wearing a dark blue sweatshirt appeared. He wore no bottoms and had an erection. When she changed direction, he came toward her.

He was muscular, his head bald and egg-shaped. Hair surrounding his penis was bushy and black and she thought, he is a pervert trying to impersonate a younger Khrushchev. The man blocked her path, making her stop. His thick eyebrows rose as he smiled.

He spoke Russian. "I'm here to inform you this is nudist beach. On nudist beach, one must go at least half way, as I have done." He paused a moment before frowning and shaking his head. "No? Then I must become nudist beach security."

Rather than knocking her down and raping her, he held her erect, threw her purse to the ground, took off her jacket, ripped her blouse open, and reached around to undo her brassiere. His strength outweighed the resistance she could offer. His rotten fish breath was hot. In seconds she was topless. He let go of her, nodded approval, and spoke seriously and slowly.

"You will not investigate fathers or grandfathers. Leave Odessa and return to Kiev. Your lover is gone forever and you will be gone forever if you do not walk away. Chernobyl killer will continue if you do not leave and remain silent." After staring at her a moment, he turned and walked briskly toward the sea, his chunky white buttocks disappearing over the dune.

Sonia put her brassiere and torn blouse back on, grabbed her purse, and ran back to the sanatorium stairway. The teenaged boy who'd pushed out of the bus sat on one of the benches using binoculars to spy on the nudist beach. Because her blouse had lost its buttons, she put on her jacket and zipped it up. She took out her cell phone and saw it was turned off. She turned on the phone, shaded its screen with one hand, and selected her brother Janos' number.

CHAPTER 8

C lairvoyant moments are chronic for brooders. The word in Hungarian
folk tales is *telepátia*, carrying wider meaning than the English word.
Two floors below Lazlo Horvath's apartment window, pedestrians of diverse
ethnic origins walk or stand at bus stops. Shoes, some obviously old and
worn, tread carefully on uneven sidewalks screaming from crevices and cracks
for repair. Pothole patches like stray puzzle pieces sag beneath the wheels of
buses flying "heavy" between stops.

A woman in full black burka with a narrow eye slit walks on the uneven
sidewalk. A newspaper headline said French officials were voting to ban face
coverings. Lazlo had nothing against the woman, but the orthodox costume
brought thoughts of death. Perhaps the grim reaper minus his scythe with
two olive-skinned little boys in tow? Might the boys someday become terrorists? He'd been a scythe of death several times, killing in self-defense in the
Kiev Militia, and again afterwards as a private investigator.

Two deaths weighed on Lazlo, two boys he'd never forget. An eight-year-
old from his building crushed by a delivery van as he ran for an orange Frisbee.
After befriending Lazlo, the boy decided he'd be called Gypsy in his neighborhood gang. Lazlo tried convincing Jermaine to quit his gang, but failed.
Lazlo purchased the Frisbee. Therefore, Lazlo was the fly in the ointment of

Jermaine's life. Jermaine would have gone on to become whatever a black man can become in a world where sidewalks are obstacle paths and bombs are buried in streets. The van was a bread truck. Earlier today, Ria's hair in the morning sun at the café was the color of bread crust. Past, present, and future there in the street. *Telepátia.*

After the burka and two boys were gone, a young man appeared, reminding Lazlo of the other boy he'd killed. The young man carried a guitar case, not much different than the violin case of the boy he'd shot dead 50 years earlier near the Hungarian and Romanian borders in what was then the Ukraine Republic of the Soviet Union.

Mandatory Soviet Army tour long before Chernobyl. He and Viktor assigned to arrest deserters in the region simply because they both speak Hungarian. To their officers, nothing but a matter of worthless boys killing worthless boys. Insane officers still angry with Khrushchev and his Cuban missile fiasco. Lazlo gripped the windowsill and closed his eyes

A snowy day in the eastern Carpathian foothills. The driver stays in the truck on the main road as Lazlo and Viktor trudge the back road. A violin playing as they approach the farmhouse. The deserter's file indicates he comes from a family of violinists. Lazlo and Viktor hope he'll hide so he can stay the winter and help with spring planting. Deserters are common, many forgotten. When Viktor knocks, the deserter with violin in hand answers. As noted in his file he has red hair. Mother and sister appear, both with black hair. The sister, perhaps 16, pleads as the deserter gives himself up. The mother says her son's hotheadedness is inherited from a long-lost grandfather, a redhead who ran away to America.

The redheaded son asks to bring his violin. He retrieves the violin case, reaches inside, turns with a pistol, and shoots Viktor in the chest. Viktor falls back through the open doorway. The pistol turns toward Lazlo. The struggle to release the safety and pull the trigger moves Lazlo's rifle too high. The bullet explodes the deserter's forehead. The women scream. Bloody bits of red hair streak the snow as the driver drags the deserter and Lazlo carries Viktor to the truck. Both are alive, but die while the truck speeds to the nearest hospital.

When Lazlo visits the farmhouse again with his captain, the deserter's father is home. He gives them the violin to bury with his son, saying villagers called his son Red Gypsy. Mother and daughter have put strands of their hair into the violin case. The mother weeps in another room. The daughter stares at Lazlo with dark eyes. Except for the visit with his captain to confirm what happened, there is no further investigation. Back at camp Lazlo's comrades baptize him with the name Gypsy, insisting the name migrated from the deserter's soul to his soul when he avenged Viktor's death.

Lazlo opened his eyes. The woman in the burka with two boys reappeared, coming from the other direction. She seemed to look up toward Lazlo's window, reached deep into her garment, pulled out a cell phone, held the phone to her eye slit, and thumbed in a number. Suddenly, across the room, Lazlo's cell phone rang with its Kafkaesque pinball tone. The woman in the burka spoke on her phone and resumed walking.

Lazlo hurried across the room, almost tripping on a rag rug. He flipped the phone open, "Janos Nagy" on the display. They spoke their usual Hungarian.

"Janos, I knew you'd call. Time there?"

"After midnight, Laz."

Lazlo sat at his kitchen table. They discussed the Chernobyl serial killings. Not only had the killings migrated from Kiev to Odessa, but now his friends Janos Nagy and Mariya Nemeth were drawn into the investigation.

"Your sister's lover, dead?"

Janos spoke softly. "I'm with Sonia. Marta was found on Chkalovo beach. But there's more. Sonia goes to the beach after the militia loses track of her. An obvious Mafia thug rips off her blouse and gives her a warning. She's not to investigate Marta's death, or the death of Marta's father and grandfather.

But on the same night of Marta's killing, a waitress in Kiev is killed. Her name was Keresztes and, like my Mariya, she was originally from Uzhgorod."

"Keresztes is Hungarian, common to the area when I was a boy," said Lazlo.

"The Chernobyl killer does not discriminate, Laz. Along with contaminated soil, a Star of David was drawn on her forehead using her blood. No fingerprints."

"Marta did not have the Star of David mark?" asked Lazlo.

"No Star of David," said Janos. "But her jaw was broken and soil was in her throat. Also, some of her hair was pulled and shoved into her mouth. Odessa detectives say she was killed on the beach and dragged into the shallows. But listen to this. I checked the airport; it would have been impossible to fly from Odessa to Kiev that time of night. Therefore, that night there were two so-called Chernobyl killers."

"Copycat or cover up?"

"Cover up," said Janos. "Doctor Marta Adamivna Voronko's research into the death of her father is connected to his research into the death of his father. The grandfather was an American citizen who moved back to Ukraine and married after World War II. There's a US connection with Mafia smell. It goes back to before the war. Sonia said the year 1939 is significant. That, and something about a girl's hair."

"Janos, if you smell Mafia—"

"Yes, next time we'll need to speak carefully."

After hanging up, Lazlo opened his laptop, using the Internet for a trip into the past.

1939—Joe Lewis KOs John Henry and, on a dare, New Jersey bartender Tony Galento; Eleanor Roosevelt resigns the DAR to protest denial of Marion Anderson's appearance; Shirley Temple turns ten; Al Capone released from prison on parole; the New Deal on the wane as war in Europe approaches; in Rome a pope dies and another is elected; after German troops move in, Czechoslovakia ceases to exist and the Carpatho-Ukraine is in conflict, with Czechs, Ruthenians, Ukrainians, and Hungarians at odds, Hitler and Stalin stirring the pot; the "Beer Barrel Polka," originally written by a Czech named Vejovoda, gets rewritten in the US and becomes a hit.

Although Lazlo was not yet born in 1939, Father shared stories with Lazlo and his brother Mihaly when they were boys. Their farm was once in Czechoslovakia, and before that, the Austro-Hungarian Empire. Contention as far back as Father could recall—the famine of the 1930s when Stalin's troops came for their grain, Jews rounded up by Nazis, Nazi-backed Hungarian Army declaring war, formally annexing Carpatho-Ukraine in 1939.

Transcarpathia was the rope in a tug of war. The city of Uzhgorod, originally called Ungvár under Hungarian rule, was at the center. Now, with Janos telling about the Kiev waitress from Uzhgorod murdered and a Star of David on her forehead, Lazlo wondered about the role of Hungarians in the fate of Transcarpathian Jews. Silence on the subject, passed down through the Soviet educational system, was obvious. He recalled hearing epithets of local men against Jews in each language of the region—Hungarian, Slovakian, Ukrainian, and Russian. Older men spoke of troops collecting bodies of those who'd starved to death following Stalin's famine. Younger men made up conspiracies—why were no Jewish bodies collected?

During his Internet search, Lazlo stumbled upon women's hairstyles. Curls, lots of movie star curls. He closed his laptop and closed his eyes. There'd been no movie house in his Ukraine village. Only a record player to entertain themselves. His memory retrieved Father's words, whispering in Hungarian.

"My sons, it was so bad during 1938 and 1939, I wished escape. But there was nowhere to go. Some speculated before the first war, heading to America, working, having children there, and coming back to buy farmland. A mistake because Stalin collectivized the land. However, going to America before the first war gave an advantage to sons born there. They retained US citizenship, returning to take advantage of Roosevelt's programs. If I'd been born there, you'd be Americans and we wouldn't need to whisper about our past, present, and future."

Lazlo opened his eyes to a dark apartment. He stood and went back to his window. The marquee of the Ukrainian restaurant across the street, once a movie theater, was brightly lit and he thought of Janos Nagy, Mariya Nemeth, Janos' sister Sonia, and Doctor Marta Adamivna Voronko. He looked at the time on his cell phone, did a quick calculation. By now it would be dawn in Ukraine. Because he'd been a Kiev Militia investigator for years, Lazlo could see, hear, and smell the Kiev dawn—the bakeries opening, traffic beginning to move, church bells. In spirit Lazlo was still there, still a militia investigator on a case of special interest.

What was the significance of the soil traced to isotopes in contaminated Chernobyl soil? What could the Star of David drawn on a waitress' forehead in her own blood mean? Jewish vengeance against Hungarians? What about Doctor Voronko's hair placed in her mouth after her murder? Could it have anything to do with the old man beneath the bus on North Avenue with strands of hair in his wallet? Perhaps Janos, Mariya, and Janos' sister Sonia had visas prepared and he'd soon see them here in Chicago.

The sound of music came from a passing car. Not Ukrainian music or salsa, not hip-hop or classic rock. A big band blasting from loudspeakers, the bass notes booming. Lazlo opened his window and leaned out. The music faded as a shiny classic '40s coupe with an oval rear window disappeared up the street. Was it Glenn Miller or Benny Goodman?

It must have been Benny Goodman. When he and Mihaly were boys Father had gotten hold of some of Goodman's records. Father compared the rhythms to Gypsy music. He recalled Father dancing in the house, the music turned low so passersby would not hear. As the tom-tom drums beat in the background, he recalled Father whispering in English, "The King of Swing."

Had a '40s coupe playing a Benny Goodman tune really driven past? Perhaps the black coupe, having rolled off a Detroit assembly line decades earlier, was like a crow, an omen. He recalled Mother saying for Gypsies, seeing a single crow was a bad sign. The smell of Mother's hair came to him from the past. A smell like fresh linen she has warmed at the hearth and brought to his boyhood bed. Despite the crow, it was time for sleep.

Hair, something about hair affecting events. Not Mother's hair, not Doctor Voronko's hair, but hair saved. Instead of being buried with the dead, hair from the dead is often saved. Hair in a wallet would definitely be from the past. Hair in a man's wallet might be from a dead wife. But the hair in the wallet of the old man killed beneath the bus on North Avenue was not gray. The hair in the old man's wallet was reddish brown, definitely from a young woman a man does not want to forget.

CHAPTER 9

January 1939. Bela Adamovych Voronko, age 21, arrives New York on Cunard White Star *Aquitania*. At dock, with US passport, he's separated from others, taken to a port authority office, and told to wait. The room has benches, yet he's alone. In past it must have been packed, hands and hair creating horizontal gray areas on otherwise white walls. Two caged windows on one wall remind him of a Gypsy zoo monkey exhibit. A calendar between windows shows the China Clipper flying boat taking off from San Francisco Bay. In 1935 he'd cut the same photograph from the Uzhgorod newspaper and hung it high in the barn safe from chickens. A brief memory—the barn smell, chickens clucking. Here smells are pipes and cigarettes puffed beyond the caged windows. Men's voices tempt Bela to look inside. But the uniformed escort said sit and wait. So he sits, recalling the journey that seemed half his life.

Although the ship was at sea a matter of days, Bela's journey from Uzhgorod, began in 1938 when he was 20, and had taken months. First, the Prague train and the American Consulate General's office to prove he'd been born in the US. Next, back to Budapest for a three-month stay with Cousin Gabor and wife Katica. Perhaps his interlude in Budapest would result in tension easing in his Carpathian homeland. He should have known better when his passport was stamped with the flying eagle over the swastika.

Katica studied English at Budapest University and evenings prepared Bela for a fresh start in his birth country. Daytimes he worked at Cousin Gabor's barbershop, learning the basics. After leaving Budapest, trains through Austria, Germany, and France to the port of Cherbourg were ripe with war rumors. Passing through Germany, swastika flags were waved by increasingly larger groups of young men in brown uniforms. Would it have been better to join the Hungarian Army? But how could he join men becoming angrier as the train neared the French border? Discarded newspapers claimed tension in his homeland was worse than ever.

In Paris, awaiting the train for Cherbourg, he admired the magnificent station and stared at thousands of people scurrying about. In Cherbourg, waiting overnight for *Aquitania's* departure, hundreds slept on floors and benches in a Cunard White Star building. Separate sections for men, women, and families. Wild rumors in semi-darkness. One old man claimed Nazis were on the march following the tracks, would be there by morning, and young men would not be allowed onboard. At daylight the old man mocked younger men with his toothless grin.

On the huge *Aquitania*, with its four funnels, more rumors. A Polish joker insisted the ship, built before the Great War, was taking a northern passage and would be scrapped in Greenland. At a glassed-in world map on deck, the joker traced the new route, using each day being colder as evidence. "It's January, what do you expect?" said a well-dressed man. With this the joker stared ominously at the sky.

While waiting in the port authority room, Bela wondered why the Polish joker, the old man from Cherbourg, and others were not here? Was this a special room? Had America signed a pact with Hitler to have Carpathian Hungarians sent back?

Suddenly, sounds from the caged windows became chaotic. Screeches, whines, and loud voices as if from zoo monkeys. Then the flutter of Benny Goodman's clarinet, more screeching, and Bela realizing someone was tuning a radio. The radio settled on news. He'd learned enough English to understand an earthquake had caused thousands of deaths in Chile in South America.

A man in a white shirt and blue tie brought a file to one of the windows. The man inhaled deeply on a cigarette held in one corner of his mouth and blew smoke from the other corner before motioning to Bela. During the interview the cigarette did not leave the man's mouth, he did not look up from the papers, and he repeatedly blew smoke. When Bela retrieved his copies, the smell of smoke came with them.

With US citizenship intact, Bela followed directions attached to his papers and walked toward Grand Central Station. He stared up at buildings, dodging pedestrians and cars, trying to look American. In his homeland he would have stared at the ground, not because buildings there were not tall, but to watch for horseshit piles. There were fewer horses in New York, all of them down side streets. Main streets and sidewalks were smoothly paved, so it really was possible to walk with one's head in the air, smelling the bakeries, delicatessens, and shops steam cleaning clothing. Engines, horns, and people speaking loudly filled his ears. A newsboy shouting "Earthquake!" while holding up a bundle of papers reminded Bela of a Gypsy singer.

The wool suit given Bela by his parents was thick, loose, and unfaded. It belonged to Uncle Sandor, who enjoyed dumplings and pastry. Bela's original threadbare suit switched with Uncle Sandor's newer funeral suit before the coffin sealing. Bela's mother brushed the suit and packed it carefully in his bag. He wore it during his passport photo in Prague, in Budapest for a farewell dinner, and finally during the train journey to France so he'd look exactly like the photo. The suit remained in the bag for the trip across the Atlantic, safe from sickness and overflowing toilets. While washing older clothing he'd worn on the ship in the washroom for men at the immigration office and steaming it dry on a radiator, he discovered a lock of gray hair tied with a ribbon deep in the suit's vest pocket. His mother had forgotten Uncle Sandor wanted to be buried with a lock of his dead wife's hair. Perhaps the hair would bring him luck, perhaps not.

Having been only four when he left the US, few memories remained—a train ride from Ohio, the rolling and pitching of a ship, another train to Uzhgorod from Trieste. In boyhood, the farm outside Uzhgorod had been a wonderful place. But with Stalin and Hitler one could easily lose track of the name of his country and even his village. Although now a man, Bela sometimes felt like a little boy running away from home.

The dilemma for Bela's family came when he was old enough for recruitment. With American citizenship he could escape recruitment from one side or the other, from east or west, from the chaos infecting his homeland. The last was the Hungarian Brigade in their supposed fight to hang onto their sliver of western Carpathia.

Jews suffered most, even those who made it overland to the *Aquitania*. They traveled third class. One day, passing a chained-off stairway and smelling the steam forced Bela to the outside deck covered with ice so he could vomit. Because of ice accumulating during the trip, he didn't make it to the rail and added his meal to hundreds of others frozen like stalagmites where deck chairs should have been. At port, Bela looked back at the ship and watched as poor souls from third class slipped and slid over the deck ice in New York's sun, climbed wearily down the ramp, and just when he thought he might see a smile or a Jew kneel to kiss the ground, they were whisked away like cattle to a barge headed for Ellis Island. Bela was not alone watching the Jews. Others also watched, many with contempt.

As he walked along the street nearing the train station, Bela saw several huge American automobiles. One he recognized as a 1939 Packard. Father had shown him a photograph in a magazine back home, saying because

Grandfather was born 100 years earlier in 1839, the Packard's year in America would be Bela's lucky year.

At Grand Central Station, Bela purchased his ticket for Youngstown, Ohio, home of Uncle Stephan and Aunt Helen. Uncle Stephan was his father's brother. Aunt Helen was a Polish woman his uncle met in Ohio. Stephan and Helen Voronko would become Bela's new family. Uncle Stephan had written he might get Bela a job at the pig iron plant, but because of unemployment made no promises and said there were other options.

One was the US Army; obviously Hitler and Stalin were determined to take the world to war. Whether the US declared war or not, Bela knew there'd be growth in the Army because America would at least need to protect its shores. He had come from a ship packed with passengers on every deck. With his fresh understanding of English, he overheard British crewmembers with experience from the first war discussing the next war as if it were a ship whose smoke and guns would soon appear on the horizon. They said *Aquitania*, usually called Ship Beautiful, was a sardine can because of the need to escape from the war to end all wars.

The voyage gave Bela time to think of girls with rosy cheeks and multicolored skirts at holiday festivals. Especially Nina Zolotarev, whose photograph was in his luggage. Instead of fingering his aunt's gray hair in his vest pocket, he imagined fingering Nina's golden hair and recalled the time he'd felt her breasts against his chest as they kissed in the barn when he took her inside to show her the photograph of the China Clipper. Their goodbye kiss at the back door to the cottage where she lived with her parents and seven brothers and sisters. He'd kissed other girls goodbye, but none was like the kiss he and Nina Zolotarev shared.

The final goodbye was at the Uzhgorod train station. His mother's tears washed her face. His father joked about a cache of food hidden from Stalin's troops and the huge feast they'd have once he was gone. Bela had been able to hold back his tears. But now, having thought of Nina, and recalling his hurried goodbyes, he was overcome with guilt. Others left behind and he was in America. At the Uzhgorod station his mother said although Nina Zolotarev's mother was Jewish—her maiden name Weizman—villagers agreed to secrecy. On a wooden bench waiting for the train to Youngstown, Bela wished Nina were with him and felt a tear run down his cheek.

Behind him, facing the opposite direction, two women spoke.

"So, tell me, do you really think she's dead?"

"I'll tell you exactly what I think. They'll declare her death official and bury her so they can get on with their war. Men don't want Amelia Earhart messing with their planes, or their plans. Men run the newspapers and radio. They can kill and bury her whenever they want."

"So, you think she's alive?"

"Could be, but what difference would it make to all the so-called leaders? FDR and Chamberlain, but especially those goose eggs Stalin, Hitler, and Mussolini. They get boys jumping up and down and nobody gives a hoot about Amelia."

"I saw Mussolini in the newsreel. They call him *il Duce*. Ladies in the theater were swooning over him."

"You have got to be kidding."

"Of course I am, Kiddo."

Both women laughed.

Bela wondered about the meaning of giving a hoot, then smelled cigarette smoke. He turned and saw both had lit up. It was unusual to see women smoke. He stared until the younger one glanced his way. She had blonde hair and a red hat. When she smiled he knew his face was as red as her hat. He turned about and recalled the heat of a bus that had passed close during his walk to the station. He was alive, in America waiting for a train.

Not far from Grand Central Station, where tracks emerged from tunnels and crossed a switching yard, two men wearing coveralls and carrying suitcases entered a work shack. Each placed his suitcase on a worn workbench. One suitcase black, the other brown. One man short and stocky with an unlit cigar in his mouth, the other tall with a moustache. They took off gloves and put them on the bench. The tall man lit a cigarette while the other relit his cigar. When not blowing smoke, their mouths steamed in the unheated shack.

The tall man glanced out the single frosted window. "How're your boys doing?"

"Not so good," said the stocky man. "Flu got Sammy."

"How's the other boy? What's his name?"

"He's named after me."

"Sally Big Shoes?"

The stocky man pulled a revolver from inside his coveralls and took aim. "Don't get smart, Hebe! His name's Salvatore!"

The tall man raised his hands. "Take it easy."

The stocky man kept the revolver aimed. "You're the one asked. So I'll ask you something. How're your niggers in Detroit?"

The tall man lowered his hands, smoothed his moustache. "All right, let's get on with it."

The stocky man put his revolver away. "Good. We finish and get the hell out of here."

Each took out a key, unlocked clasps on his suitcase, and opened it. They switched positions and inspected the case the other had brought. The tall man prodded newspaper-wrapped bricks inside the black suitcase. He tore off a small corner of newspaper, pushed a finger inside, and tasted off-white powder clinging to his finger. The stocky man flipped through stacks of bills tied with string inside the brown suitcase.

"It's turning into morphine," said the tall man.

"Don't worry," said the stocky man. "It's been stored in a cool dark place."

The tall man smiled. "Did you know prior to 1920 they sold this stuff alongside aspirin?"

The stocky man laughed. "It'll give Detroit niggers a painless death."

"They're customers," said the tall man. "Even Luciano gives them that much."

The stocky man closed the brown suitcase, fastened the clasp, took the key off the table, pocketed it, and put on his gloves. "Are we done? I got appointments."

The tall man closed and fastened the black suitcase and put on his gloves. "I hit a raw nerve?"

"Yeah, a raw nerve. The Lucianos ain't nothin' compared to the Cavallo family. You purple gang guys should know."

The tall man continued smiling as he picked up the black suitcase, opened the shack's flimsy door, and tossed out his lit cigarette. "We don't use that purple gang name."

"Ancient history, huh?"

"Yeah, the same history says Mussolini chased your family from Sicily."

The stocky man paused, shifted the suitcase from right hand to left hand, and turned. The tall man held a revolver and smiled.

"Take it easy, Sal. I hear Little Sal's carrying a stiletto. You and him need temper control. Your family was out of Sicily before Mussolini's purge. It's real easy stepping on your toes. That how you got your name? We got wars coming. Get along and we'll cash in. So what say—?"

"All right," interrupted the stocky man. "I get your point. Let's scram before some yard dick gets nosy. Next time I'm sending a runner. He'll have bigger shoes than me."

"No more dirty work?"

"No more dirty work. My family name's sacred."

The tall man nodded, put his revolver away, and motioned the stocky man through the door. Both looked side to side before leaving the shack, then went in opposite directions, stepping across railroad tracks and snow mounds. A steam locomotive's whistle wailed from low to high pitch as it emerged from a tunnel.

Salvatore Cavallo walked behind a row of snowed-in boxcars to the Packard where Lonzo waited with the engine running. Cavallo imagined steam from the Packard's exhaust piped into the shack with the Jew from Detroit locked inside. But enough with the Jew. Cavallo soaked up the All Weather Town Car's heat. The heater worked better than most in the January cold, the car had a big name, and even sounded big. Once the car was moving away from the yards, Cavallo had to shout to Lonzo in the front seat.

"This thing's like an opera house!"

Lonzo's voice was naturally loud like Lon Chaney Junior. "Yeah, boss. I like it."

Cavallo removed coveralls and boots, put his jacket back on over his shirt and tie. He laced his dress shoes, combed his hair, straightened his hat brim, and put it on. Lonzo drove to three Lower East Side warehouses where Cavallo spread the cash in three separate safes. With the cash put to bed, Lonzo dropped Cavallo at home and took the Packard next door to the apartment house. Cavallo paused to listen to the Packard's engine as it backed in. Lonzo lived on the ground floor, close to the Packard in the attached garage. The other apartments were used for family business, the room above the garage for private meetings.

Inside his own house, Cavallo expected the usual greeting from Francesca. She'd have dinner ready, Little Sal home from his midtown school, and they'd open a bottle of Corvo. Cavallo had tossed his cigar butt and by now he should have smelled garlic, sausage, and pasta. Where the hell was everybody? And why wasn't it hot in here the way Francesca liked?

Cavallo put his hat on the wall hook, walked past the empty kitchen to the living room, expecting Francesca working on an afternoon nap, Little Sal in his room messing with his stiletto rather than homework. Instead, Cavallo's Uncle Rosario greeted him. A bottle of Corvo from the kitchen was on the low rosewood table next to Cavallo's humidor. Uncle Rosario sat in the chair on one side of the table and motioned Cavallo to sit in the chair on the other side.

Even though Salvatore Cavallo ran Brooklyn operations, his uncle, Rosario Vincenzo Cavallo, remained boss in the eyes of other east coast families. Death was the only retirement. Uncle Rosario had come close up against the Lucianos, but was still around after 70 plus years, and still maintained a workable relationship with other families. With Francesca and Little Sal out, Cavallo knew today would be one of his uncle's special visits with some kind of judgment.

After kissing stubbled cheeks, Cavallo sat and stared across the rosewood table. His uncle's eyes were sunken, jaw crooked, wisps of gray hair lit from behind by winter sky visible through the window. What would happen when Uncle Rosario died? Would he establish a similar relationship with other families? Or would war break out like the European war brewing?

Uncle Rosario had already opened the Corvo and, trembling, filled their glasses halfway. They toasted and drank. Cavallo drank most of his; Uncle Rosario took only a sip before wiping his mouth with his sleeve. Several months earlier the doctor said Rosario suffered a minor stroke. Since then he tended to drool. Cavallo and his uncle spoke Italian.

"I cannot drink like before, Salvatore. It's a sign my time is near."

"That sign will have flashing lights, like on Broadway."

A crooked smile. "Better than gunpowder flashes."

"I made the final exchange with the Jew, only he doesn't know it."

"Good. That's the end of it. We've kept the family name unblemished. Because your cousin sits in prison, you and I are the only ones who count."

"You've come here to speak of family legacy?"

Uncle Rosario coughed, took a deep breath, and tapped the rosewood table. "I'm here to speak of legacy in the name of your son."

Cavallo pictured Little Sal sneaking eight-pagers with grainy photographs of naked women into the bathroom and locking the door; Little Sal listening to swing music on the radio; Little Sal learning how to drive with Lonzo, running over the drunk on the sidewalk, and helping Lonzo toss the body into the river. What would Uncle Rosario think if he knew Little Sal had already killed his first man?

"Should we stop calling him Little Sal? asked Cavallo."

"It's not as simple as a name. His first appearance in newspapers cannot be for his arrest. His path must be outside the traditional." Uncle Rosario took another sip of Corvo, followed by a swipe of his sleeve. "You may not agree with Roosevelt, but he has the right idea. Why do you shake your head?"

"What does idiot Roosevelt have to do with my son?" asked Cavallo.

"Idiot Roosevelt is superior to idiot Mussolini in one critical way. He knows how to convince. You knew this was coming. We can't keep doing things the old way. Your namesake, Salvatore Cavallo, will become the family's man of honor, appearing in newspapers and magazines as the Sicilian of reform. Our family funds will push him up the ladder!"

Uncle Rosario stood. Cavallo stood, went to his uncle's chair and they hugged. The order would be carried out. Cavallo only hoped Little Sal would stay in line until his uncle's final stroke. It was January. Uncle Rosario had a hard time with last summer's heat. Although it was several months away, Cavallo thought maybe this summer would finally do his uncle in.

As he escorted his uncle out of the apartment to the car and driver he knew waited in the alley, Cavallo tried to imagine Little Sal, his son, climbing a political ladder. Not a bad idea, as long as Little Sal didn't fall. Yeah, not a bad idea he and his Uncle Rosario came up with.

Over 2,000 miles west, in the dusty town of Green River, Wyoming, a young man named Cletus Minch left the hardware store where he worked. He carried a new fishing rod he'd just purchased and was anxious to try it out. Three girls from his high school class walked along the street. Cletus couldn't help staring at Rose Buckles, the center of attention. Last month a rancher got clipped by a delivery van because both the rancher and the driver were busy staring at Rose.

The setting sun was behind the girls. While the others wore slips beneath their dresses, Rose obviously wore no slip. The sight of Rose's legs tightened Cletus' throat as the girls approached. When they all smiled and said hi, Cletus made what he figured was a grunt.

After passing the girls he dare not turn around. Instead he walked faster, crossing the Green River bridge on his way home. To help forget about his grunt at the sight of Rose Buckles, he flipped his new rod in the air, making it sing and thinking of next morning at the river. Before going inside, he glanced back at Castle Rock standing over town like a statue, and recalled the time he and his buddies climbed it and the kid named Tom almost fell. Cletus' mom sung out his name as the door swung closed.

Fifty miles south down the river, across the state line in the town of Manila, Utah, a young man the same age as Cletus named Decken MaCade had just gotten a ride into town for the first time. Although Decken was a new LEM (Local Experience Man) at the Manila CCC camp, he wasn't local. The Pocatello District transferred him from Salt Lake City earlier in the week because he'd taken a few geology classes and they were blasting a road from Manila through the Uinta Mountains to Vernal. As the camp superintendent put it to Decken that afternoon, "I reckon headquarters thinks we need *expertise* in the geological area." The way the superintendent emphasized *expertise* let Decken know where he stood.

He'd spent the day with the blasting crew from Barracks One, the guys everyone called powder monkeys. No sooner would he get ahead of the blasting to check the age of the rock, someone would be on his behind yelling, "Fire in the hole!" and he'd have to skedaddle.

That evening the powder monkeys invited Decken on a trip to downtown Manila for beer at a few bars and a gay old time at a dance hall. Instead, so-called downtown Manila consisted of rundown houses, post office, gas station, and general store. The powder monkeys bought beer at the general store, drinking it in the back of the truck on the short drive back to camp, and had a good laugh, figuring they'd lured the Mormon into their lair by the promise of Manila's decadence. Decken turned down the beer, not because he was Mormon, but because after a day of blasting he preferred a quiet evening in the library. He found a Uintas Range geology book and cracked it open. The book seemed almost, but not quite, as old as the rock in canyons and thrust faults surrounding the place.

CHAPTER 10

May 2011, Sun City, Arizona. Already 100 outside, but cool in the clubhouse. Scrabble club retirees beyond library bookcases unaware of Guzzo. Amongst Scrabble entry challenges they spoke of air conditioning feeling great after a golf cart ride from condos and argued about health care. The women wanted health care for everyone. The men said Medicare benefits would suffer and universal health care would encourage illegals. One man mumbled mobsters were taking advantage of health care until his wife shushed him.

Another man with a phlegmy voice said, "At least Obama bin Laden's dead." A woman tersely corrected him, "You mean Osama bin Laden." Men chuckled. Women, who outnumbered them, did not.

Guzzo grabbed a thick book from the bookcase and thumbed it in case anyone peered around the corner. *Hitchcock* by Francois Truffaut, plenty of murder photos. Guzzo stared at clips from the *Psycho* shower scene, thumbed forward to scenes of the detective knifed on the stairs, supposedly by old Mrs. Bates.

Guzzo used a knife at a Michigan job after a barroom brawl involving a second-generation researcher conveniently moved outside. Two drunks, one driving off in his pickup, allowing Guzzo to hit his mark. Afterwards Guzzo caught up to the pickup wandering all over the road, then tossed the knife, along with a worn and bloody pair of cotton work gloves, into the bed of the pickup after the guy stumbled into his house.

In Georgia he'd staged a murder-suicide with a 12 gauge double barrel, conveniently loaded with deer slugs and prominently displayed above a fireplace mantle. A white man in his 90s and his African American wife who looked 20 years younger. The house was rural and, because both yelled, Guzzo didn't require a listening device. He recalled the wife's final screech at her husband, whose singing in the shower sounded like a younger man with a deep voice. The guy had just finished a verse of "Stardust." During a pause the wife moved into the bathroom.

"Jethro, I warned you! Your first set of wives left 'cause of that goddamned caterwauling! I mean it, Jethro! I'm younger than you and I can take you on!"

Guzzo went in the unlocked back door, took the shotgun from above the mantle, sat the woman on the toilet seat, shoved the barrels into her mouth, and fired. When the shower curtain flung open, he fired the remaining slug into the chest of the old man. Old Jethro went down without hanging onto the shower curtain and ripping it off the rings. Afterward Guzzo set the scene to appear the wife fired the first shot, then sat and fired the second into her own mouth.

On the beach in Ukraine, he'd told the doctor his name was Jethro to put her off guard. The current job, here in Sun City, would be more relaxed. Fontaine, on the other side of the bookcases, was the one who'd complained about universal health care being used by mobsters. Mrs. Fontaine, who'd shushed him, was aware of the suicide weapon. Guzzo had used a long distance microphone on the golf course facing the condo to listen in when Mrs. Fontaine called her daughter-in-law several days earlier.

"Michelle, he keeps it here on the balcony."

"Does he say what it's for?"

"In case a wild horse runs across the golf course."

"Horses on the golf course?"

"Talk about wild horses is from his CCC days. I tell him to shut up about it."

"Why should he shut up, Mom?"

"Because years ago he said never let him talk about it. But since the stroke, things leak out."

"Do you know what happened in 1939, Mom?"

"A wild horse had to be put down. There's more but that's all I can say about it."

Guzzo continued flipping through Hitchcock, closer to the front of the book, back in time past *Strangers on a Train* and *Spellbound* with its Salvador Dali images of a knife cutting an eyeball, past *Saboteur* with the fall from the Statue of Liberty, and eventually past all the early films to the beginning of the book, where Guzzo began reading.

Eventually Scrabble boards were put away and the players left the clubhouse. Guzzo closed the book, making a mental note to look it up back home. He went out the back exit, retrieved the walking golf cart and bag he'd left there, put on the golf cap hung on the three wood, and walked behind the condos, slowly because of the god-awful heat.

Paul Fontaine's memory was shit. At the dining room table, staring at red flowers, couldn't remember what kind they were. When his wife leaned her cane against his walker and put a plate with a sandwich down, he peeked inside and seconds went by before the words *ham* and *cheese* came to him. Names for things were like Scrabble, trying to get a word to fit.

"Maybe we could take the shuttle into Phoenix tomorrow."

Paul looked up. Lillian's cane now leaned against the table on the far side beyond the nameless red flowers. "I'd rather drive, use my GPS."

"You gave Michelle the GPS with the car."

"I forgot. Anyway, Phoenix is nothing but shopping."

"We have great grandchildren with birthdays. The bus drops us at the door and they have those carts you like."

Paul clamped down, tightening his teeth and chewing his sandwich. He purposely spoke with his mouth full; it bugged the hell out of Lillian. "Okay, fine. Phoenix or bust."

But they never made it to Phoenix. A tall young man in golf outfit came in the door, smiling like hell. Somehow, here was this guy at the side of the table, having come through the door even though Lillian always locked it. A tattoo on the guy's upper wrist—*STORM*. And he had a key. A key! The guy kept smiling and Paul thought maybe he's supposed to know him.

"I'm here to check on things," said the young man.

"What things?" asked Lillian.

Still smiling, the man grabbed the knife Lillian had used to cut bread, and before Paul could put his sandwich down, the man grabbed Lillian around the mouth from behind and cut her throat so that blood the color of roses— Lillian's roses!—spurted across the tablecloth.

It was easy keeping Paul down. Despite his efforts to fight back, the man simply knocked over his chair, sat on him, and grabbed his hands, making him hold the knife. He tried to push the knife at the man, begging back younger years. He felt like a child whining for his mother. Lillian, on the far side of the table, bleeding into the carpet with eyes open, was not his mother. If only someone would help. If only guys from Barracks Three were here. If only he could do something.

The young man opened the balcony door. Paul tried crawling away, was grabbed from behind, thrown atop Lillian, roughed up. Then the rope Paul had tied to the balcony railing as a joke was around Paul's neck and the man carried him. Paul saw the golf course due west with a couple guys looking the other way over the western horizon, the heads of their irons flashing in sunlight as they turned them round and round, contemplating their shots. He saw sky and sun and finally, nothing.

During the condo "sweep," Guzzo noticed a printout on a stack of road-maps in a bookcase. A CCC reunion announcement, October in Colorado. Family members invited to attend for fathers who'd passed. Guzzo recalled seeing the same announcement at another job before Ukraine. The roof job in Detroit's Greektown surrounded by rundown neighborhoods, the old guy spry for his age, clawing the air during his fall.

Guzzo forgot about the Greek, locked the door, went down to his walking cart in the stairwell, and stepped out into the hot sun. He golfed past the pair that had been on the course when he'd hung the old man, tossed his folding cart and clubs over a section of fence hidden behind atrophied bushes, climbed the fence, put clubs and cart into his rental, switched from the golf cap to the Stetson, and drove onto the highway toward Flagstaff. He never flew out of the city where he did a job if he could help it.

On his way to Flagstaff, he took a side trip to Sedona. In an antique shop he came across gifts from the 1930s he knew his girls and Vera would enjoy. He bought bucking bronco mechanical banks for his girls, and a framed newspaper article about Amelia Earhart for Vera. He wanted to teach the girls to save their money and knew Vera was fond of strong, earnest women. For himself, Guzzo bought a framed portion of a front page from a 1938 issue of the *Rocky Mountain News*. A photograph showed Britain's Chamberlain, Germany's Hitler, Italy's Mussolini, and France's Daladier sitting around a table. On the table, an artist had sketched Czechoslovakia carved into pieces. The caption beneath the photograph said, "A Little More of the White Meat, Perhaps, Herr Hitler?"

Guzzo leaned toward the rental car's cool center air vents, and as he stared at his own eyes in the rearview mirror, recalled the eyes of the old man. Although he'd never met the old man, it was as if they knew one another.

He turned on the radio and searched the AM band. He imagined being a talk show conspiracy goon, yelling his lungs out, and because he wasn't one of these, felt better. Then, sure enough, he found a guy crazier than him who compared the current economy to the Great Depression, and compared the President to Adolf Hitler.

A line from a Mel Brooks movie came to mind. *"It's good to be the king."* As the jackass on the radio screamed out of the Camry's speakers, Guzzo said, "It's good to be the killer."

The driver of the red Dodge Charger R/T kept well back, catching only glimpses as they followed the Camry to Flagstaff. His passenger monitored the GPS tracker on his iPhone. They called the unit they'd stuck to the underside of the Camry "bread crumbs on a magnet." They were dressed casually, in shorts and tee shirts. The driver's blue shirt had white lettering saying, "I'd rather be driving a Hemi." The passenger's reddish-brown shirt said "ARIZONA STATE." Both men had shoulders filling their tees.

"You believe in God?" asked the passenger.

"What?"

"God. Do you believe?"

"Of course. I'm Jewish."

"That's what I thought."

"Why the fuck would you ask me that?"

"To get to know who I'm working with, in a friendly sort of way. I was raised Catholic."

"I'm Brooklyn Jewish. I never looked any further back."

"You think they paired a Catholic and a Jew on purpose?"

"How the hell would I know?"

"We didn't get much info. Just watch for those names while we're following. It's nuts when you think about it—following a killer and rather than stopping him, we're told to watch for names." He pushed a button on his iPhone and swiped it to get to his notepad. "Here they are. Cavallo, Polenkaya, Zolotarev, Weizman. That last one's Jewish."

"Were you one of those nerds sitting in line in front of the Apple store?"

"No, the first iPhone came out a few years ago. I got mine last year. Again, about the names. What's it mean trying to dig up names from a hatchet man? The Manhattan briefing was like being with a Wall Street bunch. I know it's not the old days but—"

The driver interrupted. "Old money. The names are the keys. Could be from the war. Treasures, gold teeth, whatever."

"Gold teeth?"

"Shit stolen during the holocaust. The top guys came across something."

"Following a guy who kills old men and women's a treasure hunt?"

"You know what sounds better?"

"What?"

"That Hemi under the hood—5.7 liters, 370 horsepower. I'm going to rent one again."

"Okay," said the passenger, fiddling with his iPhone. "By the way, he's a mile ahead. You can speed up."

The red Charger throbbed as it accelerated through a long curving climb. A road sign said Flagstaff, 25 miles.

CHAPTER 11

Odessa Chief Investigator Voitec was quick to mock Janos' sister Sonia being "an intimate friend" of Doctor Voronko. The discussion went off the rails.

"Your sister's safe, Nagy. Go back to Kiev."

"She's safe because she called me."

"You and I questioned men from the crime scene and guests of the sanatorium. We contacted the lab analyzing soil from the victim's mouth and received preliminary results. Perhaps I should call Odessa's Mayor to see if he knows anything!"

Janos tried to cool Voitec. "I appreciate all you've done. Yet, there's still the question of the half-naked man confronting my sister on the beach."

Voitec sighed. "Hundreds of men on Odessa's beaches fit the description. And please don't criticize our sketch artist. I have budget shortages."

"But the fact your artist is a university student—"

Voitec interrupted. "Stop, Nagy!"

After driving Sonia back to Kiev, Janos and Mariya agreed she stay in their apartment. The apartment Sonia shared with Doctor Voronko was now part of the investigation, including Marta's computer filled with years of professional research, as well as notes of Marta's research into her father's death, and her father's research into her grandfather's death. Fortunately, during an unannounced evening visit, Janos was able to sidetrack a tired investigator while Sonia retrieved not only personal belongings, but also plugged a memory stick into the computer and copied data files. Next day, Janos left Sonia and Mariya to the computer data while he investigated the murder of the Kiev waitress that took place within two hours of Marta's estimated time of death.

The waitress named Keresztes was Hungarian, originally from Uzhgorod. Janos checked other Chernobyl killer victim records, no other Hungarians, and none from Uzhgorod. Next, he visited the laboratory analyzing soil shoved into victims' mouths. The soil must have been gathered from the same spot near Chernobyl. The lab could tell by the unique mix of isotopes. Although the sample from Doctor Marta was small because her body was in the surf, technicians insisted there was enough in her esophagus to make a positive identification. They provided isotope decay analysis graphs proving the match up.

When Janos felt he'd reached a dead end, he contacted his friend Yuri Smirnov of the Ukraine Secret Service (SBU) in Kiev. Janos and Yuri became friends after the Chernobyl Exclusion Zone episode in which Smirnov's old boss was implicated as a human trafficking network co-conspirator. Smirnov, who sustained a severe back injury during the episode, had a new boss who was receptive to communications with private investigators. Wheelchair bound Smirnov offered Vodka. Janos refused and waited while Smirnov downed his glass. Not the day's first; the slur in Smirnov's voice obvious.

"Kiev Militia says Keresztes was a cocktail waitress at a syndicate-run club," said Smirnov. A delay, Smirnov thinking drunk. "Corrupt Kiev Militia reveals snatches, like watching films, a detail here, a detail there. I watch dubbed Hitchcock films. He has *MacGuffin*." Smirnov poured and downed another vodka. "*MacGuffin* in Ukraine and Russia is always money. We have many investigations in progress involving militiamen and syndicates, always looking for the money. If it wasn't for this spinal injury I'd do more."

Smirnov struggled wheeling himself backwards to look out his window. It was a beautiful spring day in Kiev, but when Smirnov turned, his face was ashen like winter sky. Janos considered asking about the pain, but instead turned to his inquiry.

"Tell me about the waitress, Anna Keresztes. Was she a prostitute?"

Smirnov groaned as he turned his chair. "Semi-trafficked."

"Semi-trafficked?"

"Lured to Kiev with a group of girls. The usual job promise from syndicate goons. Cocktail waitress jobs, pay based on selling drinks. As far as we know Keresztes never prostituted. Regarding her murder, we found neither motive nor customer of interest. Other girls at the club said she got along. But there are questions."

"Questions?" asked Janos.

"I dislike the club manager."

Janos stood, walked around the desk, and took his turn admiring the wonderful spring day, blue sky resting atop the spires and greenery of the city. "Does your dislike lead anywhere?"

"He hires many girls and weeds out one or two."

"Can you tell me the club and the manager's name?"

"Janos, I'm office-bound, not the man I was. Investigations for me have become spectator sport, films. When I share information I expect full disclosure in return."

"I understand," said Janos.

"Very well. Keresztes worked at the Chicago Blues Club on Pushkinska Street."

"Near the Czech bar?"

"That's the one, photographs of Chicago teams on walls. Manager is Nikolai Golovko. He insists being called Goalie. In Chicago Blackhawk hockey team photograph Golovko resembles goalie."

"Does the goalie have his mask on?"

Smirnov laughed and winced. "No, but he has scars, and a full head of black hair, obvious hairpiece. Be careful, they named website after him… Yahoo."

Before Janos left, Smirnov again insisted he be fully informed. Asking an old friend to keep him informed was one thing; insisting to the point of giving an order was another. Perhaps pain and vodka had changed Smirnov, or perhaps something else.

Janos parked his Skoda down the street. The Chicago Blues Club was nestled in a long building housing many businesses, its exterior painted a disgusting blue. It looked like a blank computer monitor. He wondered how Mariya and Sonia were doing in their search through Doctor Marta's extensive files. He'd call them after his visit to the club.

Inside the club was also blue, its spilled liquor smelling like ink. A girl, perhaps 18, immediately approached. She wore skintight jeans and a see-through blouse displaying silver nipple rings. The girl's smile, pasted on, reminded Janos of Mariya and her life story. Years earlier she'd also been lured to Kiev. And now here was another girl, one of a dozen or so in the inky darkness near a set of doors to restrooms marked *Babushkas* and *Bubbas*.

The girl held his arm. "I'm Natasha. Would you buy me drink?"

Janos looked toward the bartender, a skinny man of African descent wearing a baseball uniform and cap with Sox stitched on it. Janos allowed Natasha to lead him to the bar. The wall behind the bar was covered with Chicago team photographs.

"What would you like?" asked the African in accented Ukrainian.

"I need to speak with Nikolai Golovko."

The conversation was very short. Golovko came out backed by two who resembled Chicago football linemen. Natasha let go of his arm and stepped back.

"What do you want?" shouted Golovko.

"Shouting is unnecessary," said Janos. "I simply wish to inquire into the death of a former waitress named Keresztes."

"Why should I speak with you? You're not militia!"

Janos held out his hand. "My name is Janos Nagy. I'm interested because—"

Golovko interrupted. "I know this name!" He turned to his linemen. "Get rid of him!"

On the sidewalk, after Janos picked himself up, a militia car pulled up. The driver wore mirrored sunglasses. "Are you Janos Nagy?"

"Yes." He pointed to the club's entrance. "I wished to ask a few questions and—"

"Never mind those ass wipes," said the driver. "Get your car and follow us to headquarters. Chief investigator has critical information."

"We have him!" shouted the passenger, another militiaman in mirrored sunglasses.

"Who?" asked Janos.

"The Chernobyl killer."

Chief Investigator Boris Chudin from Soviet days softened after the Chernobyl trafficking affair. Having given up hair transplants, tanning sessions, and new suits, Chudin was now the official "old man" at central Kiev

Militia office. He'd even given up his pipe, no longer disappearing behind a cloud of smoke.

Chudin stood and they shook hands. "I'd ask you to sit, but we have something to witness. I had my interrogator wait. Especially because of the death of your sister's friend."

Chudin led Janos down the hall to an interrogation room with a huge window on one wall. The room was in shadows, the only light coming from the window to the adjacent room.

Chudin whispered. "We had the one-way mirror installed last year. We found used theater seats for this side. My deputy's bringing the suspect. They've given him lunch and I'm told he's talkative." Chudin nudged Janos after they sat. "The sound's amplified and I'm told they can't hear us unless we shout, but I still whisper. The suspect prefers Russian."

The stocky man in handcuffs and ankle shackles led in by two militia investigators was average height, muscular, perhaps 40. He wore blue work trousers, a blue work shirt, and yellow rubber slippers provided by the militia. His hair was brown, not very long, but naturally curly and thick. His face was round and unblemished, obviously not the bald brute who confronted Sonia on the beach in Odessa.

The man smiled toward the window as he held out his hands to allow a militiaman to attach the handcuffs to the eyebolt buried into the thick table-top. Janos knew the table was bolted to the floor even though he couldn't see the bolts from where he sat. He considered commenting this was the same interrogation room when he was in the militia, except for the improvement of the one-way mirror rather than a darkened corner for witnesses. But not now because he saw in the prisoner's wandering eyes a story was about to unfold.

The head interrogator hung his jacket on the back of his chair before sitting opposite the man. "Vladislav Ivanych Penko, here we are again. It's been years since I've been able to speak the mother tongue. Our stomachs are

THE GIRL WITH 39 GRAVES

full and we have time. Being a bricklayer must stimulate your appetite. You finished everything on your plate. If you'd like water or tea, simply ask. As I said earlier, I'm enjoying our conversation. It's not often I'm in the company of such a well-read person. Please proceed where you left off."

"Where did I leave off?" asked Penko, his voice boyish, despite his size.

"You were speaking of your village during the Chernobyl disaster. You can start there and slowly make your way to the present. As I said, we have time. We're recording and it will make fine reading. Perhaps, as you said earlier, one of the journals with which you're well-acquainted will publish your statement." The interrogator leaned forward in anticipation.

Penko nodded and smiled. He glanced toward the one-way window, then back to the interrogator. "You think my story will interest people?"

"Of course."

Chudin whispered, "A well-educated and well-spoken bricklayer."

Penko licked his lips, folded his cuffed hands, and spoke without hesitation as if giving a recitation.

"Our village was ten kilometers from Chernobyl. But, as a poet would say, the winds of fate were against us. Svetlana and I met in her father's barn. We were in the hayloft when we heard the explosion. At first we thought parents had awakened, found us missing, and searched for us.

"Svetlana and I were separated next day. It was the same all over the region. One family from a village would be moved here, another family there. My family left in minutes, as soon as I ran home. My uncle worked at the plant and knew the danger. We piled into his car and drove south. It wasn't until I was older I discovered Svetlana's family was hospitalized in Kiev because of accumulated radiation due to a departure delay.

"There I was, growing up on a farm away from our village with no idea Svetlana's family had moved to Kiev. They had Russian language books and journals in the farm collective meeting room and I spent my time reading."

Penko looked toward the window, as if to explain. "While other young men smoked and drank vodka, I read. Reading helped me deal with the situation. I lived in the past, before Chernobyl, by reading Soviet history."

Penko looked back to the interrogator. "It wasn't until I was 19, searching for a job after the fall of the Union, that I moved to Kiev. I found Svetlana, but the damage had been done. While working as a waitress, she married a doctor who treated her. I greeted her on the street and we spoke of the accident and the night in the barn. The reason she needed heavy iodine treatments and hospital monitoring was because the bus they took became stuck in mud outside the village, and because everyone got out to push. The contaminated soil splashed in faces as the bus tires spun, especially Svetlana's face. She made the mistake of pushing at the rear of the bus directly behind drive wheels. She had to spit mud from her mouth.

"I told her we should marry because we were together during the explosion. She laughed, saying she already married. I told her I was making a childish joke. She said it was a good joke, and was glad I was able to educate myself and stay away from vodka."

After a pause, during which Penko stared at his hands, the head interrogator spoke. "You said you lost track of Svetlana after this. Tell us about the other young woman."

"The woman at the black market?"

"Yes."

"Very well. It was in the area where automobiles are bought and sold— the open field near Zhulyany Airport where other things are bought and sold as well. The woman had milk tins lined up on a blanket. Each tin was in plastic food wrap. Her sign read 'Magic Soil.' She said it was from a village near Chernobyl that had been plowed under. I was with Sasha, a crazy friend who enjoyed my jokes. I said something to him—I don't remember what—and we started laughing. Others who asked about magic soil turned on us as if we'd pissed on a saint's relic. A man kicked Sasha in the nuts. When Sasha bent forward the man punched him.

"Sasha is dead now. Not from the punch. He suffered an overdose. I came upon him foaming at the mouth in an alley where heroin is sold. The death wagon took him. He was the only person who knew of Svetlana, until now."

Penko glanced at the window, and then back to the interrogator.

"After Sasha's death I returned to the market. The young woman was not always there, but one evening she was there, closing up. I asked about the village from which the soil came. It was twilight when she named my village. A trick in the lighting makes a face familiar. At that moment I knew I must end this selling of magic soil. I told the young woman to stop. She was loading tins into a rusty child's wagon. She said she would not stop. She repeated her claim the soil had medicinal properties. I told her she was a witch. She told me to fuck my mother. I followed her to a shanty made of scrap. Behind the shanty were several rusty buckets full of soil. Inside the shanty were many empty 400 gram condensed milk tins."

"How did you get inside the shanty?"

"Busted through the door."

"And after that?"

"I choked her."

"And then?"

"She lay on the floor but wouldn't stop gurgling. To stop it, I put on my work gloves and pushed my fist into her mouth. The tins of soil were nearby. I dumped one in and sealed her up so she'd know it was time to put an end to it. I used the soil as a kind of mortar."

Penko smiled. "I'm joking. I knew there was no reason to seal her up. Yet, there were all those tins and the buckets full of village dirt out back."

"What made you kill again?"

"As I said, there were all those tins and buckets of dirt. The child's wagon was large. It was dark, the wagon didn't squeak, and I live nearby, so it was a simple decision to take everything because she no longer needed it."

"You also took her money?"

Penko smiled. "You're trying to trick me."

"Forget about money. What about the next time you used a tin full of magic soil?"

"The next time?"

"Yes. There were others."

Penko clenched his fists on the table. "It was soil from my village. These women needed to know the feeling of Chernobyl. It needed to be done!"

The handcuffs attached to the eyebolt kept Penko from slamming his fist on the table.

The interrogator held up his hand. "Please, Vladislav Ivanych Penko. We are here to help. Would you like tea?"

"Later!"

"Very well, later. Now, about the last time you used one of your tins. You said earlier you made a discovery that disturbed you."

"Yes, I go into my closet to retrieve a tin, because of this waitress who's been annoying me, and I find some tins are missing."

"Do you know how long they were missing?"

"It could have been days or weeks. One does not take a daily inventory."

"But you're certain some tins were missing?"

"As I said earlier, I'm certain it was six missing because I stacked them in rows."

"So, when you knew tins were missing, you came into the militia office to report it?"

Penko looked annoyed again. "As I said, I saw news on television about the Odessa killing. Someone killed and used my soil. It was wrong, especially a woman doctor. And then I get this phone call. I never get phone calls. I don't even have a phone. The landlady comes and says I have a call. A man tells me I've done good work. He says it's good these whores and daughters of whores have been silenced and their mouths engorged with the flames of Chernobyl. He's the one you should be after. Can't you see that?"

Penko turned to the observation window. "Can't you all see that? The flames of Chernobyl never go out, even though they buried it. I've read my Soviet history. Jews plot vengeance. A Jew designs a reactor to explode. He comes from 1939."

"1939?"

"Yes. I was told on the streets by others. It's well known, especially among those at the market. The 1939 Jew wants revenge!"

"Revenge for what?"

"The Holocaust!"

"But in 1939?"

Penko laughed. "No, not the Holocaust in 1939. The vengeful Jew was born in 1939. It's well known. He's born somewhere else in 1939. He returns to what was then the Soviet Union to have his vengeance. It's well known on the streets that Jews and Nazis continue to wander our land. They wear disguises. Perhaps, without your knowledge, there are Jews and Nazis seeking vengeance here in your headquarters. Certainly you're aware of the significance of the number 39 equaling to 13 plus 13 plus 13?"

A long pause. The interrogator glanced toward the observation window.

Suddenly Penko struggled violently, knocking over his chair. "You think I'm insane! I have news!" He hung from the eyebolt, his body bent over the edge of the table. He turned to stare at the interrogation window. "Everyone in Ukraine is insane!"

CHAPTER 12

Niki Gianakos had a bad night. The recurring dream of her father falling from the building roof and her not being able to do anything. Up before dawn, some rooms lit in the Greektown Casino Hotel, gamblers preparing to deplete savings. She stood at her window looking down into the alley, waiting for her computer to boot itself awake. This dream had taken a strange turn, instead of modern day cars and trucks in the alley, the vehicles were old, and of course because her father was in the CCCs in 1939, she knew they must have been vehicles from that year. Her Greektown building was old enough. Perhaps her dream was an image from 1939, something she could discuss with Marta in Ukraine.

But the latest email message from Marta was not from Marta. Yes, it was her address, but a man named Victor, who said he was a representative of the Kiev Militia, had sent it. Doctor Marta Adamivna Voronko murdered in Odessa and the militia had retained the computer for evidence. Viktor wrote he'd read saved messages between Niki and Doctor Marta. He attached a translated copy of a report given Ukraine media saying a suspect was in custody and asked if Niki could provide information that might help.

Niki read the report, went to the bathroom, turned on the light, drank a tall glass of water, looked at the ghost of her face in the mirror, wondered why hair along with Chernobyl soil would be stuffed into Marta's mouth, went back to her room, put on her running top, shorts, and shoes, and left the apartment, tucking her key into the back pocket of her shorts with her cell phone and pepper spray as she took the back stairs two at a time down to the exit off the kitchen.

Because downtown Chicago parking was scarce, Lazlo traveled by bus. During weekdays buses ran so close it was often possible to see the next approaching as he climbed aboard his. It was a spring morning with a breeze off Lake Michigan. The lake having retained its winter chill cooled the air.

Two years earlier, on a morning like this, Lazlo had left Chicago, returning to his Ukraine homeland for a short "vacation" during which he almost died helping Janos Nagy and Mariya Nemeth destroy the Chernobyl Exclusion Zone human trafficking compound. Anthony Jacobson, of the Human Smuggling Trafficking Center of Homeland Security, provided critical information to Lazlo, and thus they remained in contact. Jacobson had access to information about all categories of crimes. Lazlo still didn't know the location of Jacobson's office. After Lazlo called, detailing the murders of Doctor Marta Voronko in Odessa, and the waitress named Keresztes in Kiev, they agreed to meet at Chicago FBI headquarters where Jacobson would be given use of a guest office.

As Lazlo stood alone in the bus shelter, staring at an ad for an upcoming Bourne movie, his cell phone vibrated and rang its pinball tone. Janos calling from Ukraine. They spoke Hungarian, trying to make the conversation lighthearted. After general greetings about the time difference and weather, they spoke of the murder.

"How is Sonia?" asked Lazlo.

"She's busy working on medical information."

"Exactly," said Lazlo, knowing Janos referred to Doctor Marta's research. "So, Janos, on the other matter…"

Janos was silent several seconds. Lazlo waited, knowing silence after generalizations would discourage someone listening in. Finally, Janos continued.

"I witnessed the confession. The waitress and other women. It's, as they say in your country, cut and dried. As for the doctor, the same holds true as before."

"Timing's off," said Lazlo.

A pause from Janos, then, "Yes."

The bus pulled up with a loud air brake fart. Lazlo took a seat at the back.

"Cabbage for breakfast?" asked Janos.

"I'll put the phone to my ass," said Lazlo.

"I'll do the same," said Janos.

"Tell me something from deep inside," said Lazlo, trying to keep his voice light-hearted. "The father?"

"A so-called accident. He was on a path toward something, like a violin in the distance, but getting closer. The same with the grandfather, except the violin was practically atop him, close to a resolution of melody. And now for the reason I'm speaking out my ass."

Lazlo laughed. "Go on."

"The grandfather was American."

Lazlo acted surprised to confuse anyone who might be listening. "No shit."

"No shit," repeated Janos, the Hungarian translation doing its job of sounding like a crazy idiom. "Born there, back here at four, then back there when the Hungarian Brigade came calling. First to Ohio to uncle and aunt, then into three Cs."

"I don't understand."

"Pronounce three Cs and think of America's 1930s."

"I understand," said Lazlo. "And I remember the exact year. You have a location?"

"Your state where there's water like the Dead Sea."

"Dead, like I'll be in a few years."

"Find yourself a woman like the one who returned to Ukraine."

"Eva Polenkaya from La Strada?" Lazlo laughed.

"What's so funny?" asked Janos. "The Lake Balaton fishing pole snaps back when properly baited. What about that woman at the café?"

"We're friends. Enough about an old men's love lives. I'm meeting another soon. We'll share two-year-old fishing jokes. I have to get off and switch buses. I'll ask him what he knows about fishing."

"Is he from the homeland travel agency?"

"Yes. He'll point me to the best fishing spots. When we reconnect I'll let you know how aunts, uncles, and cousins are doing. Give my greetings to all."

"You do the same," said Janos. "Best wishes to all on your side, even mischievous family nephews."

This is how Lazlo and Janos always ended their telephone conversations, as if they had dozens of family members, as if this were one of thousands of calls across the globe. But in this conversation, Lazlo knew when Janos referred to "mischievous family nephews," what he really meant was Mafia, most likely the Russian variety.

Anthony Jacobson was a mystery man. For the Chernobyl trafficking case Lazlo met him at the Washington debriefing. Jacobson was African-American but his English had a British accent. Jacobson's contacts provided an overview of world crime. Two years ago Jacobson had gray hair, a beard, and Lazlo guessed him to be in his 50s. Now he was shaved bald with no beard and looked ten years younger. He wore leather boots, jeans, and a flannel shirt as if he'd recently returned from a hiking trip. He sat on the edge of the empty desk in the room with only the desk, two chairs, and a window.

"You look younger," said Lazlo.

Jacobson smiled. "You've got me stereotyped. Or the agency figured how to make time run backwards."

"The agency also altered your accent. You sound like you're from the south, whereas before you had me believing you were British. Perhaps you've had some minor surgery?"

Jacobson glanced at the cell phone he held, thumbed several buttons, and continued. "Let's get to business."

"Of course," said Lazlo, "There've been serial killings in Ukraine."

"The ones involving Chernobyl soil?"

"Janos Nagy contacted me. He was at Kiev Militia headquarters when a man confessed. However, we have a problem. Janos' sister Sonia had a female lover, Doctor Marta Voronko. She was murdered in Odessa at almost the same time as the last victim in Kiev. Someone killed Doctor Voronko and didn't count on the Chernobyl killer coming out of the woodwork."

Jacobson thumbed his phone. "I'm calling my office," he said to Lazlo, turning for a quiet conversation.

Lazlo went to the window. He'd lost his sense of direction in the corridors. All he saw, while Jacobson mumbled on the phone, was an alley being cleared of trash by a blue Chicago garbage truck. He could barely hear the banging as the truck's lift shook out a dumpster's contents, a huge mass of finely shredded paper. Lazlo noticed a double reflection in the window and wondered if the floor he was on was a floor built within a floor, like the one called "the submarine" the KGB installed in the Manhattan embassy.

Shortly after Jacobson's mumbling stopped, Lazlo turned and Jacobson was standing beside him, looking into the alley.

Jacobson placed his hand on Lazlo's shoulder. "Anyone else would have retired after Chernobyl and your run-in with the Russian Mafia. You sure you want this?"

"I'm sure."

They returned to the desk and leaned close as Jacobson spoke.

"The so-called Chernobyl serial killings have been investigated by Ukraine agencies. They agree Mafia groups tried to use the killings to cover their operations. But another connection's emerged. Persons, mostly in the US, but also in Europe, have been investigating what they consider the untimely deaths of elderly relatives."

Jacobson smiled. "I know it seems insane to speak of untimely deaths of the elderly. It's like reading obituaries in which the person of 90 dies unexpectedly. But the information's credible. Some relatives of men who were in the Civilian Conservation Corps in the 1930s are convinced fathers, grandfathers, and uncles died before their time. Because decades have passed, the few remaining are age 90 or more. Relatives now believe the next generation's being targeted because of their investigations. Does this sound familiar?"

"It does. Doctor Voronko was, according to her computer files, researching not only the death of her grandfather, but also the death of her father. The grandfather's name was Bela Adamovych Voronko. His son, Doctor Marta's father, had the same name. According to the files, the grandfather was a US citizen taken back to the Carpathian region when he was four years old. When World War II was about to break out, he escaped back to the US and, unable to find work, joined the Civilian Conservation Corps."

"The good old Fourteenth Amendment. Does the year 1939 come into play?"

"It's the year Doctor Marta's grandfather was in the CCC."

"Do you know where he served?" asked Jacobson.

Lazlo hesitated, wanting to hear Jacobson's theory. "Janos, Sonia, and Mariya are still going through the files."

"There were many camps in Utah and Wyoming at the time," said Jacobson. "Statistically, the supposed untimely deaths are of men from a camp in Manila, Utah, and possibly another in Green River, Wyoming. Both did work in what is today the Flaming Gorge National Recreation Area in northeastern Utah and southwestern Wyoming. At the heart of the statistics, only men who served in the Flaming Gorge region in 1939 have been affected."

"I've heard of the Flaming Gorge," said Lazlo.

"Yes," said Jacobson. "The rocks in the area are red. These days there are jokes that gays descend upon the reservoir in summer. But it's bullshit. I bring it up to disassociate any relation between the region and the fact that Doctor Marta was gay."

"What about uranium deposits?" asked Lazlo.

"Nowhere near enough to have caused a problem; I've looked at classified studies."

"Could the untimely deaths be due to some kind of infectious disease?" asked Lazlo.

"Absolutely not. They all died with their boots on."

"Is there anything else you can tell me?"

"A few were from the south and west, but most of the young men came from eastern and midwestern cities. Specifically, the men from cities were trained for a couple weeks at Army camps in Ohio and Michigan. I've spoken with a woman from Michigan who's investigating the death of her father. She's made her way through several agencies. The FBI, for one, is keeping watch over her. But they can't watch her constantly. I'll find out if she's willing to speak with you. It might take a while. You know how agencies are when it comes to sharing information."

"Of course. But, since I'm here with you in a secure room, may we speculate?"

"Please do."

"After speaking with Janos about Doctor Marta's death, and the deaths of her father and grandfather, a question arose. Have the violent deaths begun in recent years?"

Jacobson stood and walked to the window. "I know what you're aiming at. In one of our agencies, several agents, having gotten older, became more inclined to speak of classified information. Sometimes it's a matter of an old man wanting attention. Other times it's because of stroke or dementia. Anyway, for a while I became involved in taking care of the situations."

"Meaning?"

Jacobson laughed and turned to face Lazlo. "No, we didn't pull their tubes or put pillows over their faces."

"What did you do?"

"The program is called L.L.Bean. Nothing to do with the merchandiser. More like witness protection."

"Why L.L.Bean?"

"Our acronym LLB stands for 'Late Life Bragging.' L.L.Bean naturally came to mind."

"You move old men to secure housing so their secrets remain secret?"

"Old men and old women. It's authorized by FISA on a case-by-case basis."

"You think CCC men knew of things dangerous to national security?" asked Lazlo.

"My thinking is this," said Jacobson. "CCC men in the Flaming Gorge region of Utah and Wyoming knew something extremely valuable, dangerous, or embarrassing to someone or some organization. Whatever they knew, and some theoretically still know, must be very important to this person or organization to have lasted all these years."

After leaving the FBI office, Lazlo walked toward the lakefront. The breeze had diminished and the sun was warm. He sat on a bench at Buckingham Fountain near a plaque commemorating its dedication in 1927. Despite the spring chill, several children ran in and out of the spray laughing and screaming. Lazlo wondered if the fountain had always opened this early. When he saw a city worker come out of a brick pump house imbedded in the sidewalk and walk to a city pickup truck in the distance, he realized the worker might have turned on the pump this morning for its initial test run.

Lazlo tried to imagine what it was like here in the 1930s, especially 1939. Simply swap the modern pickup for a '30s truck, ignore traffic beyond the fountain, and re-outfit the people. Women and girls wear dresses. Boys wear slacks, shirts, and jackets. Men wear suits and hats. Everyone dressed like they might meet someone important. The texture, sounds, and lighting are like an Edward Hopper painting, just enough detail for the mood of 1939.

Lazlo took out his cell phone and called Janos. They spoke Hungarian.

"I hope it's not too late."

"Not at all," said Janos. "We're in computer land."

"Besides the year mentioned, has an American landmark with the word *Flaming* in its title appeared?

"It's where the grandfather served," said Janos. "It bridges two western states."

"We're on the same track. Soon I might be able to meet an American woman who also searches. A question, Janos. The doctor's grandfather was named Bela, correct?

"Yes, why?"

"Perhaps it's simply the name, as in Bela Lugosi movies, but I feel a connection. Here I am in Chicago in 2011 and I keep thinking of the year 1939."

After the call, Lazlo walked across Grant Park and went into the Art Institute. He asked about Edward Hopper's paintings and was told the paintings were on tour. But the gift shop had a Hopper calendar, which he purchased.

On the bus heading north on Michigan Avenue and again on the Chicago Avenue bus heading west, Lazlo flipped through the calendar. Eventually, he stared at the painting *Nighthawks*, in which three people sit in a diner with a single man behind the counter. All three men wear hats. The man behind the counter, in his typical soda-fountain lab coat, wears one resembling a white Army garrison cap. The men in suits at the counter wear felt hats with brims. The woman, sitting with one of the men, wears a red dress, her red hair done up in late '30s, early 40s style. No one smiles. They are, like him, thinking serious thoughts.

The blurb at the back of the calendar said Hopper was spare and strong in his paintings. Hopper admired economy in writing. One of his favorite short stories was Ernest Hemingway's "The Killers."

Lazlo closed the calendar and stared straight ahead as the bus lumbered down Chicago Avenue. Heads bobbed, but the only hats were those worn by a group of boys, their baseball caps various sizes and turned at different angles.

Lazlo imagined it was 1939, the boys in the bus are men wearing hats. He gets off at a stop and walks into a diner. Everyone inside is serious. Two guys in hats tie up some guys and wait. The one they're waiting to kill doesn't show up. He's in bed at a boarding house, having given up. He's going to die, but doesn't seem to give a damn. Even though he's a young man, his circumstances have made him into an old man who doesn't care if he lives or dies.

When the bus arrived at his stop in Ukrainian Village, Lazlo got off through the back door. He must have read "The Killers" by Hemingway long ago as part of an English class. As the bus powered away like a banshee screaming, Lazlo recalled having spoken to the son of the man who'd been run over by a bus on North Avenue. The son was older than Lazlo and the father beneath the bus was 90. Too old for a drunk. What was the man's name? What had been the results on the toxicology report? Certainly there must have been a toxicology report.

George Minkus, torso pancaked on the morgue examining table, dead at 90 with a locket of red hair in his wallet. According to Janos, Doctor Marta's grandfather saved hair. Bela Adamovych Voronko, born in Ukraine. The boy Lazlo shot near the Hungarian and Romanian borders had red hair, the mother saying her son's red hair was inherited from a grandfather who ran away to America. Again, the word from Hungarian folk tales came to mind. *Telepátia.*

CHAPTER 13

Cold March morning, 1939. Columbus-bound bus outside a Youngstown, Ohio, recruiting office, destination Fort Hayes, being used as a Civilian Conservation Corps induction center for men between 18 and 25. "Jeepers Creepers" on a radio as they file out to the bus. A woman volunteer wonders aloud if "Jeepers Creepers" was played at an FDR party. Cheeky city boys sneer at her comment. The volunteer says, "The three Cs will take the starch out of 'em."

Several wore suits and ties beneath overcoats; some wore wool sweaters, no overcoats. A few well-dressed family members, gathered to see their boys off, were aware of worn and tattered fabric. All the young men except one were skinny. A few had sunken eyes, shirts bunched up at their waists, belts too long. One had used a rope to hold up his trousers.

The CCCs did conservation work, giving unemployed young men something to do. If accepted, they enrolled for a six-month renewable period and received 30 dollars a month, 25 of which was sent back to families. Although the Great Depression was supposedly winding down, obviously several getting on the bus hadn't had a decent meal in a while. By the looks of relatives seeing them off, neither had they.

With his parents in disputed western Carpathia, Bela Adamovych Voronko designated Uncle Stephan and Aunt Helen as family. Their name was Voronko; no questions raised when he presented his application. European war rumors heightened the mood of volunteerism; CCC enrollees figured they'd eventually join the armed services. Some FDR critics claimed the CCC was one of many stepping-stones toward war.

FDR critics aside, the CCC was considered one of FDR's most successful programs, especially because of the resuscitation of land ravaged by slash and burn farming, negligent mining, and forest fires. CCC projects included erosion control, building fire roads through national parks, and erecting park buildings. Most importantly, they planted millions of trees, thus giving them the name "FDR's Tree Army."

Morning sun warmed the bus and windows began steaming up. Eventually a recruit opened a window. Others in window seats, including Bela, immediately stood and struggled with their windows. Several were jammed, the driver up front yelling back, "It's an old crate! You're lucky you got those open!"

"How long we gonna sit here?"

"Keep your shirt on. You mugs think I like sitting here? One time in hot weather waiting for the go-ahead we made it a meat wagon and I drove to the morgue."

Bela could see the driver grinning in his rearview mirror.

"I bet they were niggers," mumbled a fat boy up front.

The driver's grin disappeared, he turned, stared at the fat boy. "Don't start out a bad egg in the Cs. They got special camps for Negroes. They work hard as anybody. Talk like that, maybe they'll send you to a Fatty Arbuckle camp. You're not boys, and you're sure not men." He raised his voice. "From now on consider yourselves enrollees!"

Bela's window seat was on the right where the crowd had gathered to see them off. The enrollee beside him leaned forward to peer out the window. Bela leaned back.

"Thanks. Mom came but Pop's got a job in Chicago. Mom and I are living with my aunt and uncle. My uncle's here to make sure I don't make tracks. I hear they give you steak, mashed potatoes, and ice cream every night." He had sand-colored hair sticking out from beneath his cap. The cap was plaid with earflaps tucked inside. Bela decided to practice the English he'd been working on since his arrival in January.

"Do you think it's cold where they're sending us?"

"I'm used to cold. Like I said, I'm from Chicago, but we had to come live with my aunt and uncle."

"For English lessons we read a short story from Chicago. Is it true there are criminals with guns in overcoat pockets?"

"Yeah, during prohibition. But that ended when I was a kid. What story did you read?"

"Something about murders by America's famous Hemingway."

"Probably 'The Killers.' I read it for school. Teacher said it was literature, something people will be reading years from now."

Bela wondered what the world would be like years from now when someone else read "The Killers." Perhaps, like the character in the story, everyone would have a different opinion of death; perhaps they'd view death as a gift. Thinking of death and his family and Nina Zolotarev trapped in his abandoned homeland saddened Bela. He held out his hand. "My name is Bela Voronko."

"Mine's George Minkus."

After they shook, Bela said, "I'm glad to meet you, George."

"Yeah," said George, looking out the window.

Bela smiled toward Uncle Stephan and Aunt Helen, wondering how long they'd stand there. Aunt Helen was chilled, moving her feet up and down. Finally, a man came to the bus, spoke to the driver, the bus started up, the driver ground the transmission into gear, and the people outside stepped back. As the bus roared, Bela smelled exhaust coming out a pipe below his window. Exhaust flattened the paper flower in Aunt Helen's hat as she and Uncle Stephan waved. The driver gunned the engine and finally got the bus moving with a lurch. Bela waved out the window, then leaned back so George could do the same.

The bus hit a bump, lifting everyone from their seats like a dance jump. The driver shouted, "Hope that wasn't a hobo! I ran over one once taking a nap! Something I'll never forget!"

After the driver shifted into second gear he yelled for them to close the windows. When an enrollee with a high-pitched voice at the back shouted, "Hey, there's Myrna Loy and some Hollywood stars come to see us off!" several heads turned and a few on the left jumped up in the aisle to get a look.

"Those ain't Hollywood stars," said another enrollee. "The one looks like Shirley Temple's my sister."

"She sure don't look like you," said the high-pitched voice.

"Don't get wise or I'll—"

"Sit down!" shouted the driver. "I don't need no Mickey Rooney or Clark Gable enrollees! And shut them windows!"

On the highway the smell of exhaust cleared, a fresh breeze coming in a window left open a crack. Houses and buildings spread thin and soon there were farms with fields being plowed for spring. A tractor in one field was red and shiny. When the farmer turned to inspect his plow he sat taller as if to show his pride. Perhaps, after years of depression and the dust bowl, any farmer with a new tractor would be proud. Farther down the highway more fields were being plowed. What fascinated Bela were the perfectly straight rows, like rulers had been used on the black Ohio dirt. Back home, only farmers with the best horses would have straight rows. On the Uzhgorod to Prague train he'd seen dead horses carved up at the side of the tracks. Soldiers had to eat, but without horses to plow fields…

Bela turned to George. "The office woman said we would go out west after Fort Hayes. I wonder if there are horses."

"We'll probably end up in the desert," said George.

Bela looked at George's thick plaid cap. "Your cap will be hot."

"They'll give us hats," said George. "We'll get outfits for all kinds of weather. Maybe we'll be in the mountains. I heard they got lots of work in the mountains."

"I was a boy near the Carpathian Mountains."

"You'll be right at home. That's snazzy."

"Snazzy?"

"Yeah. I mean, that's good."

"Okay," said Bela. "Snazzy."

George stared past Bela out the window with a heartsick look. "Well, Bela, I guess now that we've said so long, we're really in for it."

"Why do you say so long? You can leave in six months if you don't like the CCCs."

"So long means goodbye. What's your accent? What country you from?"

"Accent is a mix of Hungarian, Ukrainian, and Slovakian. As far as country goes, it's a long story."

During the rest of the journey George told stories of being a kid in Chicago—baseball during the day, hide-and-seek at night, and kids he missed after they lost their apartment and had to move to Ohio. Bela told of his girlfriend Nina Zolotarev back home, the China Clipper flying boat photograph hung from a nail in the barn, his aunt's hair found in the pocket of the suit they'd switched before putting his uncle in the grave, and learning how to cut hair from his uncle in Budapest. Judging by somber looks on the brash city boys, most conversations had become melancholy. One young man across the aisle announced that his fortuneteller aunt reminded him 13 plus 13 plus 13 equaled 39 and therefore 1939 was an unlucky year. Whereas someone would normally make a smart-ass remark, no one commented. The driver glanced into his rearview mirror, nodded, and smiled knowingly.

The Packard was tall enough for hats and big enough so four men had plenty of room. Salvatore Cavallo Junior, no longer called Little Sal, sat in front with driver Lonzo. Salvatore Cavallo Senior sat in back with Uncle Rosario, who'd decided to come despite chest pains, insisting mountain air, as they drove through the Appalachians, would do him good.

They drove southwest out of New York, dropping down north of Philly to Route 30. Sal Junior wanted to drive, but Uncle Rosario said it was better Lonzo drive.

"I thought we'd be taking Route 6 west," said Uncle Rosario.

Cavallo, sitting next to his uncle, waited a moment to see if Lonzo would answer, then said, "Recruitment's at Fort Hayes outside Columbus. Route 6 goes too far north."

"So, you up there," said Uncle Rosario. "How does it feel going into the CCCs?"

Silence. Lonzo glanced in the rearview mirror, his eyes narrowed. Outside, trees along the highway were bare skeletons. Silence grew into tension Cavallo felt in his gut. He wished Uncle Rosario wasn't along so he could straighten Little Sal out. Maybe mention Little Sal taking along the stiletto from Grandfather's trunk stored in the attic. Finally, Cavallo broke the silence.

"Your great uncle asked a question. You so swell-headed you can't answer?"

"Just thinking."

Uncle Rosario broke in, his voice strong. "While you are thinking—turn and look at me when I speak!"

Sal Junior turned and smiled.

"This is no ordinary drive. We're heading in a new direction. You'll have time to be headstrong, Salvatore. But now I must say some things. Are you listening closely? If not, there are others who will rise to the top. Would it not be better that you rise to the top?"

Salvatore stared at his great uncle in the back seat, saw the seriousness in his wrinkled face. "Yes, Great Uncle."

"Wipe the smile! Men in power do not trust snitch smile!"

"That's better," said Uncle Rosario when Salvatore looked serious. "Life is a ladder. If you don't climb, others in the family will grab your ankles and pull you down. When I say there are others, I'm serious." Uncle Rosario sat forward and raised his voice. "A bullet through my great nephew's head is not how your journey should end! Do I make myself clear?"

Cavallo turned and looked at Uncle Rosario with surprise. Lonzo stared into the rearview mirror. Salvatore began to look back to the front out the windshield, but turned and stared back at his great uncle.

Uncle Rosario continued, a vocal strength from long ago. "I do not make decisions lightly. Cavallo family members, living and dead, support this effort. Take me seriously, Salvatore, or family from old country will come for you. Even though your father sits beside me, I can say it. If you do not make the effort, expect to be taken for a different ride." Uncle Rosario's voice grew louder. "At the end of the ride someone will piss on your grave! The family name is all-important! It's our legacy!"

Uncle Rosario coughed and took a deep breath. "You *will* succeed in the CCCs. Next will be the US Army. You'll do what you are told. Eventually, you'll realize your potential, go to university, and seek a government career. Your path is like this road, Salvatore. If you veer to the side, you'll die!"

Salvatore, Lonzo, and Cavallo all stared wide-eyed at Uncle Rosario. Lonzo was the first to look away; there was a slow-moving truck he needed to pass.

Uncle Rosario continued. "The future is built on political power. Without power and the establishment of the Cavallo name in Washington, our name will be buried. Your father and I have chosen you, Salvatore, because you are the most intelligent and resourceful of the young men in the family. If you don't wish to follow the path paved for you, tell us now and we'll turn back to New York. If we turn back you'll become another of the boys who stand around waiting for something to start. If you want to be another of the boys, say it now!"

Salvatore stared at Uncle Rosario. His father next to Uncle Rosario had sunken into the shadows. Uncle Rosario moved forward in the huge car, lowering the jump seat behind Salvatore, their faces inches apart. A horn blared and the Packard swerved, but neither the young man nor the old man flinched. From the far corner of the back seat, Cavallo watched as his son placed his hands on both sides of Uncle Rosario's face and kissed him on the mouth. Uncle Rosario smiled, Cavallo in the back seat smiled, Lonzo smiled, and finally Salvatore smiled.

Uncle Rosario remained sitting behind Salvatore in the jump seat with his hands on the young man's shoulders. Salvatore had finally turned and now looked out the windshield. It was as if Uncle Rosario were aiming Salvatore ahead, making certain he knew his destiny.

Cavallo, in his back corner, spoke. "Things were looking up in '37. They were making more Packards. Then in '38, when I get one, FDR's magic turns to horseshit. This 1939 model has a big selling feature."

"What's that?" asked Lonzo.

"They're making only a thousand. Next year they don't even know if they'll make Packards."

"Ain't that the shits," said Lonzo.

After a lunch stop at a diner along the Susquehanna River, Uncle Rosario told Lonzo to get in the back seat and had Salvatore drive while he sat up front with him. As the huge Packard labored up the first long incline of the mountains, Salvatore shifted down to second gear, pressed the accelerator to the floor, and the Packard's V-12 roared.

Uncle Rosario laughed and turned to Cavallo and Lonzo in back. "He knows how to be in control. We have the fuel, now we have the engine."

Salvatore gripped the wheel with one hand and the shift knob with the other. The Packard passed other vehicles as if they stood still. He had to honk the Packard's twin horns to move several out of the way.

Uncle Rosario moved closer on the wide front seat. "Are you angry with drivers who do not make way?"

Salvatore glanced toward his great uncle only briefly, yet in this glance he knew Uncle Rosario needed him to agree with everything, and also to perform exactly as expected. Although he'd pounded the horn ring to move an especially slow truck to the side, Salvatore smiled and said exactly what he knew his Great Uncle wanted to hear. "There's no reason for anger, Great Uncle. It's simply the speed of my hand to reach the horn."

"Try leaving your thumb on the horn ring. This is how I've operated through the years. My thumb always on the pulse of the family organization. Firm knowledgeable patience is the way to properly control a family. Do you understand, Salvatore?"

"I understand."

Uncle Rosario paused as they passed yet another car, then asked, "Will you accept future control of the Cavallo family?"

"I will accept control of the Cavallo family," said Salvatore.

Uncle Rosario moved even closer. Salvatore felt his Great Uncle's moist breathe on his face. "Will you establish the prominence of the family name for all time to come?"

"I'll do it," said Salvatore, staring straight ahead and shifting back to third gear as the Packard topped the incline.

Salvatore glanced down. Uncle Rosario had taken out a pocketknife and opened it. Salvatore glanced back and forth to the road ahead and to what Great Uncle was doing. Uncle Rosario pressed the tip of the blade into his right palm and drew blood. Salvatore glanced at the speedometer—80. He had both hands on the steering wheel, which began to vibrate.

Suddenly, Uncle Rosario grabbed Salvatore's right hand from the wheel. The Packard lurched sideways, but Salvatore quickly straightened it. Uncle Rosario opened Salvatore's palm and made a quick cut with the tip of the blade. Then he folded the knife, put it away, and held Salvatore's right hand tightly with his right hand so their blood mixed.

Salvatore glanced at his Great Uncle, who stared at him with a deadly serious look. When Salvatore glanced into the rearview mirror, he saw his father and Lonzo staring at him wide-eyed. Ahead, the road was wide open, the Packard nearing 100.

Uncle Rosario let go of Salvatore's hand, handed him a handkerchief, kissed his cheek, and moved back to the far side of the seat. "Perhaps you can slow down, Salvatore Cavallo. On this day, especially, you must arrive at your destination without spilling family blood. Mixed in your blood is the family fortune. It will be your responsibility to keep the fortune as well as the family name intact."

As the Packard slowed, Salvatore thought about what his uncle said and stared at his right hand gripping the wheel, the handkerchief hanging out like a white flag. For a while he'd taken it seriously. But thinking about all the damn work he'd have to do in the future as he slowed the Packard made him drowsy. From the time he became aware of his family's business, he'd been impressed for what it got him. Now, driving his uncle, his father, and Lonzo in the Packard felt like a long haul. Maybe a pep pill, when he got a chance to sneak one from his suitcase, would do the trick. Yeah, one of the pep pills he'd gotten from a truck driver at the old man's main warehouse. And later, in FDR's Tree Army, when he needed a boost, all he had to do was find a trucker willing to give up some bennies for a few bucks. He'd stuffed double sawbucks inside the lining of the suitcase that was going with him to camp.

The induction at Fort Hayes took a week. The zigzag train trip to Green River, Wyoming, took four days. It got warmer during the journey, dust sifting into the coaches and onto the leftover WWI uniforms provided. By the first of April, fresh but dusty enrollees were on trucks heading south across the Wyoming-Utah state line on a bumpy, unpaved road. Conversation in the back of one truck was a shouting match.

"This thing ain't got no springs!"

"It's an old one! 1933 Dodge, I think!"

"Close that flap! The dust was bad enough on the train!"

"Why's the dust red?"

"Maybe it's got dried blood in it!"

"The Flaming Gorge carved by the Green River has cliffs of red sandstone!"

"Hey, we got a professor on board!"

"Believe me, Jack, I'm no professor!"

"Back in Wyoming there wasn't much of a river!"

"The guy at the ticket office said they finally got rain down in Texas and Oklahoma!"

"Maybe the dustbowl's over!"

"Yeah, everywhere except in here!"

"I thought we were going to that camp back in Green River!"

"Nah, they got a bunch of country bumpkins there!"

"That's high desert country! We're heading south into the Uinta Mountains!"

"It's the professor again! Is it true they got wild horses on that desert?"

No answer.

Originally organized by men from Kentucky in 1935, and moved about the country the following years, Company 3544 had settled at Camp Manila, Utah, located in Sheep Creek Canyon. The work in the Flaming Gorge region included building roads through hard rock, stringing telephone lines, providing erosion control, repairing cattle guards, and building the Carter Creek Bridge. In 1937 enrollees built the Ute Mountain Fire Lookout Tower near camp.

The men arriving in April 1939 were added to existing re-enlisted enrollees, local experienced men (LEMs), officers, and enrollee leaders and assistant leaders already in place. The new enrollees arrived in time for the evening meal, were given denim work clothing, and assigned to Barracks Three with two veteran enrollees. After a pep talk, the new enrollees promptly fell asleep.

Next morning, a field bugle sounded reveille at 5:45 a.m., they were rushed to the latrine building for morning cleanup and shaves, at 6 a.m. barracks leaders lined enrollees up for exercise, then had them make beds and prepare for barracks inspection by a district inspector. At 6:30 breakfast was served in the mess and they were told they would be allowed a full half-hour to eat this first day but were expected to finish in 15 minutes from then on. On their first day, at 7 a.m., the time they would usually board trucks for work duty, the camp superintendent gave a speech in the center of the compound.

The superintendent pointed out how the buildings at Camp Manila were arranged in the shape of a pine tree and that each barracks building was clearly marked by a sign: Barracks One, Barracks Two, Barracks Three, and Barracks Four. Barracks Five, used only in winter, was currently boarded up. He launched into a speech about sticking with the men in their barracks, the fact they were no longer boys, and they'd be treated as men and not boys as long as they acted like men. "Horseplay on trucks or on the job leads to accidents; I've seen some in my time here. When I finish my speech, you'll go on trucks to your work site for the day. Lunch will be provided at exactly 11:45. There'll be plenty to eat. Normally we'd offer coffee at lunch, but because it's warming up we've switched to ice water and lemonade. You'll get an hour for lunch and rest. Be careful with cigarettes and pipes because we're dry around here. Then it's back on the trucks at 4:30 and back here at 5:00. Evening meal is at 5:15. We expect neatness at all times. If you eat like a pig we have a "pig table" in the corner. Free time begins at 5:45. Evening classes begin at 7:15. If you're good with mechanics, we could use some garage help working on the trucks. They're pretty old, especially the Dodges. We have only two newer GMCs. Enrollees with three chevrons are barracks leaders, those with two are assistants. Follow orders or you'll get on the honey bucket brigade sooner than you'd like. I don't need to tell you what that is. As for fights, take them up with your leader. I don't like to see grudge matches, but if need be, we've got some well-worn gloves and a ring set up behind the mess. A sergeant will be at your first work site. He's a non-commissioned officer."

The superintendent paused, shaded his eyes with his hand, and looked up at the bright morning sun already high in the sky. "We have a fine record of work done by Manila Camp. You'll see some of it the next few days, especially the Ute Mountain Fire Lookout Tower southwest of camp built in 1937. Big enough a man could live in it. Skilled and disciplined men built that tower. I hope you're the same.

"You might have seen wild horses from the train. Mostly they're up in Wyoming in the high desert around Pilot Butte, but once in a while you'll see some here. When you got off the train in Green River I'm sure you noticed Castle Rock north of town. In his free time one of our assistant barracks leaders is chiseling a replica at the foot of the fire tower for posterity. That's the kind of dedication I admire. Have fun out there, men. Dismissed!"

Fifty miles north, in Green River, Wyoming, Decken MaCade and another young LEM from Salt Lake City named Morris were being treated to breakfast at one of the town cafes by the camp superintendent of the Green River CCC camp. The previous evening Decken gave a presentation about geology in the area while Morris gave a presentation about the wild horses. The café was bustling with ranchers in town for an equipment auction being held by the bank on foreclosed ranches. The café had large front windows overlooking the street. Several pickup trucks, mostly Ford Model As, were parked on the street outside, but there were also a couple tractors and even a horse tied at the hitching post.

"I want to thank you men for your presentations," said the superintendent. "Later today there's a car heading down Manila way to take you back."

Decken and Morris both nodded as they chewed their potatoes, bacon, and eggs. Decken swallowed and was about to thank the superintendent when a round of whistles erupted from several ranchers at tables near the front windows. When Decken turned he saw a redhead walking across the street toward the café. As she stepped up onto the boardwalk between two pickups, she held one hand up to hold her hair in place in the dusty wind, which blew her dress between Venus-like legs, causing more whistles and table talk.

"Ain't she the purtiest thing?"

"Sure is. Hope she comes in here."

Frank Grogan, the elderly town sheriff, was at the counter getting a thermos filled with coffee. "That's Rose Buckles, boys. Careful how you talk about our locals."

"All's I said is she's purty."

"Better leave it at that."

"Hey, she's coming in."

The door swung open like magic for the redhead named Rose Buckles. A rancher with hat in one hand flinging it open with his other hand. Once Rose was inside, the café went as silent as church except for a song playing on a radio behind the swinging kitchen door. The few ranchers who still had hats on took them off and put them in their laps. When the boy serving tables pushed through the swinging door from the kitchen with both arms balancing plates, he saw Rose and paused. Just like in the study of geology, time stood still as Rose found a place at a table with a couple locals and smiled at Sheriff Grogan who was on his way out with his thermos of coffee. When time resumed, so did the bustle. Behind the swinging kitchen door, Bing Crosby sang, "You Must Have Been a Beautiful Baby" louder and softer on the radio as the door swung back and forth, back and forth.

Across the street Cletus Minch left the front window of the hardware store after a long pause watching Rose walk down the street. Obviously he'd been told to get back to work.

CHAPTER 14

Zolotovoritska Café, Kiev, had opened only last year in 2010. Today was its first anniversary. It was lunchtime. Mariya, facing a corner-mounted television beyond Janos and Sonia, watched as new arrivals, dodging colorful anniversary string hung from the ceiling, looked confused, not knowing Sonia's tears were for Doctor Marta. Sonia's vacant stare beyond Mariya a flashback to the morgue—skin drained of blood, mouth closed uncomfortably, facial structure altered, dirt specks on dry lips.

Janos reached across the table and touched Mariya's hand. "Anything new on television?"

"No mention of Odessa or Doctor Marta in the captions."

"The Chernobyl killer confessing is like the 2001 American terrorist attack," said Sonia.

"How?" asked Janos.

Mariya recalled scanning data retrieved from Doctor Marta's computer. "Sonia, we haven't told Janos everything."

Sonia wiped her eyes. "Doctor Marta's father and grandfather both killed in single vehicle accidents on remote roads. On Nine-Eleven the grandfather loses control and runs into a tree. Almost ten years later, the father loses control and slams into a ditch. Both thrown through their windshield."

"How does the date matter?" asked Janos.

"The US terror attack was early in the day. News reached Ukraine later." Sonia stared straight ahead, thinking before she answered. "Marta's grandfather was over 80. Supposedly he'd stopped driving, but still had his old car. Marta's father warned him not to drive, especially at night. He went out alone, long after news of the terror attack reached Ukraine."

Janos asked, "You're saying Marta's grandfather was killed when news was focused on terrorists?"

When Sonia remained silent, Mariya spoke. "Marta's father insisted the grandfather taking a late night drive was impossible. Someone took him to the remote location and staged the crash into the tree. Marta said her father's death, though not occurring on the day of a news event, was similar. Both thrown from cars on remote roads."

"Tell Janos about the American connection," said Sonia.

"Marta contacted a Detroit, Michigan, woman whose father knew her grandfather. Both were in the American Civilian Conservation Corps in 1939. Marta's grandfather was in the US in 1939 and immigrated back to Ukraine after the war. There were CCC details in Marta's notes. A fire tower, a rock shaped like a castle, hair Marta's grandfather saved in an envelope…"

According to militia and SBU's Yuri Smirnov, a connection existed between the Chernobyl killer and Russian Mafia, who disliked disruption of trafficking operations.

Janos stayed with Mariya and Sonia until Chief Investigator Boris Chudin assigned a militiaman to guard them. The trafficking connection led Janos to Eva Polenkaya who worked for a committee of parents organized to find lost children. It began drizzling while Janos used his GPS to locate the apartment. He recalled his last visit to Eva Polenkaya had also been accompanied by drizzle. On the previous visit she'd provided information about traffickers using the Chernobyl Exclusion Zone, information that almost got him, Mariya, and Lazlo killed.

Eva Polenkaya lived in old Kiev. When Janos left his car a sudden wind gust released droplets from chestnut trees. He recalled last time he was here rain drops were larger, coming off leaves. Today droplets came from buds ready to burst.

Eva Polenkaya's apartment, on the top floor with a view of the city, was cluttered with books and papers on various tables and chairs. Eva was an energetic, well-endowed 60-year-old with long black hair. She walked quickly but gracefully behind her huge desk piled with stacks of paper. "Besides working for parents of the missing, I hold together remnants of La Strada's anti-trafficking network. The modern world has lost its memory. But now business."

"I've not lost my memory," said Janos. "Thank you for inviting me. Have you thought of anything regarding Doctor Marta Adamivna Voronko?"

"Yes, her grandfather dying during Nine-Eleven turmoil along with his American connection. He's born in the US, brought back here at four and, being able to retain US citizenship, returns to the US in 1939. Then back here during Soviet times after the war he marries and has children. I assume KGB had eyes on him. The Civilian Conservation Corps connection is significant."

Eva stood, came around to the front of the desk, put her hand on his shoulder. "I didn't want to say it on the phone. Did you know Doctor Marta Adamivna Voronko came to see me?"

Janos stood and held both Eva's shoulders. "Really? My God, I had no idea!"

"I know about her grandfather, Bela Adamovych Voronko, and Doctor Marta's father who had the same name. I recently had contact with Anthony

Jacobson in the US. For security we used an outside line. He's been in contact with Lazlo Horvath in Chicago—you look surprised. Good, I like surprises." Eva went to her drizzle-spattered window. "I was going to share something with Doctor Marta, but I worried it might cause problems. You see, Janos, I have a key."

Mariya and Sonia packing for her stay with Mariya and Janos. The handsome plain-clothes militiaman in Sonia's apartment hallway smiled each time she placed a box outside the door. The last box contained underwear and she felt a slight blush. He was a big guy, stood to one side between her apartment and the stairwell. A glimpse of his shoulder holster was reassuring.

Placing boxes outside the open door was fine, but Mariya insisted Sonia stay within sight. Sonia held a box of towels beneath which she'd buried Marta's jewelry box containing the lock of red hair. Mariya said wait but Sonia thought one more box out the door wouldn't hurt. She'd get another smile, the world not entirely insane.

The militiaman was gone. Sonia leaned out and looked the other way. No one. She put the box down and stepped out in time to hear the stairwell door click closed. Perhaps the militiaman sneaking a smoke in the stairwell.

Sonia left the apartment door open, walked two doors down to the stairwell. When the stairwell door opened, another man—taller, darker—smiled at her. Suddenly, she was lifted into the stairwell, a hand over her mouth from behind, yet the man was still in front, smiling. Thick hands shoved her to the edge of the stairs. At the next landing she saw the handsome militiaman lying awkwardly, eyes open, a blood puddle surrounding his head. But he'd just smiled at her! And now the dark smiling man and another had her! She tried to scream but her throat collapsed as though the entire building rested on her. Her last thought was of the jewelry box buried beneath towels.

A brass key, long blade with many serrations, no identifying marks or engravings, the kind used for bank safe deposit boxes. Janos looked back to Eva Polenkaya.

"I don't understand."

Eva went back behind her desk. "My husband—God rest his soul—said it's a copy, given him after the breakup of the Union. It was supposed to unlock a safe deposit box containing kickback money given a Kiev party boss. After the breakup, the boss, on his deathbed, revealed he wanted the money to do the world some good, implying there was more money than anyone could count. My husband joked it was the key to the kingdom. He said there was more to the story, the key actually to a safe deposit box that contained another key, which would lead to the money. He wanted to track down the money, use it to help find missing children. Unfortunately, the key has become useless. The man who provided it was named Alexander Zolotarev. He died after giving the key to my husband, and, as you know, my husband's dead. When Doctor Marta Adamivna Voronko visited, I discovered the Voronko family and the Zolotarev family had dealings in Soviet days and earlier, before World War II. Zolotarev family members left Ukraine during a pogrom before the war. I thought the key might provide information for Doctor Marta's research. I was going to give it to her during an upcoming visit, but now…"

When Eva did not continue, Janos asked the obvious. "You said the key has become useless. I understand the man who gave it to your husband's dead, but how is the key useless?"

"I'm sorry," said Eva. "How could you know? My husband held the key too long. You see, the safe deposit box that was supposed to contain a key to the fortune was located in a bank in one of the Twin Towers destroyed in New York on September 11, 2001."

Janos sat in his car gripping the key, rain hammering the Skoda's roof. He wanted to call Lazlo, but it was early morning in Chicago. The rain had chilled him. He started the Skoda and turned on the heater.

A key given Eva Polenkaya's husband by a man named Zolotarev. The Zolotarev family chased from Ukraine during a Jewish pogrom. Many Jews were forced to leave or ended up in concentration camps. Many hid valuables. Perhaps the deaths of Doctor Marta and others doing family research was rooted in Ukraine's past.

Janos returned the key to his pocket and was about to pull away when he noticed a black Mercedes several cars back. He'd seen the Mercedes pull up when he arrived. Shortly after Janos pulled away from the curb and headed down the street, the Mercedes followed. Rather than go back to Mariya and Sonia at the apartment, Janos drove toward Kiev Militia headquarters to see if the Mercedes followed. But then his cell phone rang, the display showing it was Mariya.

Guilt, Mariya insisting she accompany Janos to the morgue. If only she'd stayed at Sonia's side. If only they'd stacked boxes inside behind a locked door. If only the plain-clothes militiaman had not been overcome.

She's still there, running down the stairs, cradling Sonia's head, rocking her, trying to bring back life. She's still there, yet she's here in the basement morgue, Janos squeezing her hand as Chief Investigator Chudin takes them first to the militiaman's body, then to Sonia's body.

Afterwards Chudin left them alone in his office.

"You've saved my life so many times, Janos."

"They would have found another way. I shouldn't have left. We must both live with it."

"We need to find who did this. What did Lazlo say?"

"He asked if our visas are in order. 1939, something in the US. After the autopsy and cremation and a brief service, we'll fly to New York and begin our search together."

Mariya hugged Janos tightly. "Together."

CHAPTER 15

Several Harleys were backed into the curb, yet Ogden Avenue's Bent Spoke bar was quiet. Lazlo ordered a Sam Adams. The bald bartender with many tattoos smiled with missing teeth. "Things get lively later. After eight hours in an office cubicle, they change to leathers and up Ogden they come. Depending on the weather, of course."

"Of course," said Lazlo.

A back room, pool being played. Although Chicago's smoking ban went into effect a couple years back, Lazlo picked up occasional whiffs. Perhaps a door out the back. On the bar top a Harley tank with legs was labeled "Tip Jar" with a footnote, "This used to be our smoking fund to pay fines when they were affordable, Goddamit!"

The bartender washed glasses, put them on a drying rack, then came back and stood before Lazlo. A stereotypical moment. The bartender, towel in hand, wiping at the bar where nothing's spilled. The bartender's neck creases formed the tattoo line of demarcation, a rainbow of color down beneath his sleeveless tee shirt. Lazlo wondered if Bent Spoke was a gay bar, its name referencing more than roughly handled motorcycles.

"Is asking if you're a cop out of line?"

"Why should it be out of line?"

A coy smile, "You're here for someone other than Sam Adams. You want a pad and pen?"

"I've got a good memory."

"So, get on with it."

"Very well, a patron named Minkus." A pause, the name familiar. "While researching the name I discovered a motorcycle club. I need to know if he's been here."

"What if I say no? Will you slide off and leave?"

"I haven't finished Sam Adams. Saying you've never heard the name is archetypal. Yes, I was a policeman in another life. There are things I could tell you, the way you paused. You've heard the name. An answer will send me back to my apartment to apply what I've learned. Did you hear about the Ukraine case? That's where I'm from. Investigators contact me. Women are killed by suffocation. Radioactive soil from Chernobyl stuffed into their mouths. Their jaws broken because the hand stuffing the soil is large. You have large hands, but many have large hands. The killer wears gloves, remnants of gloves found on women's teeth. I'm a man of detail. All I ask is confirmation of your knowledge of the Minkus name."

The bartender walked from behind the bar to the back room doorway and shouted, "Moss, there's a guy here I think you should see!"

Moss was skinny, in his 70s or 80s, hard to tell. Lazlo was reminded of Willie Nelson. Moss struggled out the doorway, hanging onto the doorjamb, then made his way along the bar holding on with both hands. He wore a knit hat, sideburns and beard sticking out below the hat like hay hanging out a horse's mouth.

"What you want?"

"Important family information. It will harm no one, but may help younger persons down the road. What can you tell me about a motorcycle club member named Minkus?"

Moss turned toward the back room, motioned to the bartender standing in the doorway. The bartender gave a come here head tilt and two bald men joined them. Not as old as Moss, both weighing over 100 kilograms, or at least 250 pounds.

Moss said, "He wants to know if there's someone named Minkus in the club."

When the 250 pounder wearing a leather vest said, "Which one?" Moss lay his head down between his arms on the bar.

"Jesus, Bird, he didn't ask how many there were."

"Well, how the fuck did I know? I thought he was a friend."

"He's no friend," said Moss.

The two heavies moved in, held Lazlo's arms below the shoulders.

"Please do not drop me. I'm old and experienced."

"What do you mean?" asked Moss.

"I'm from the old country. I've been thrown out of many bars. Ukraine bar thugs are especially brutal. You know what happens to police who dare to enter a Ukraine bike bar? Sometimes they live, sometimes they don't. Ukraine bike bars are notorious. The bikes outside contain parts from every brand of motorcycle. Please allow me to stay. If you throw me on street without hearing questions, later your minds will be occupied with thoughts of what I was searching for. What good is that? And who would be hurt if I asked questions?"

Moss nodded toward the two who responded by letting go of Lazlo's arms.

"So, go on," said Moss.

"Gentlemen, were there two men named Minkus?"

Without being asked the bartender brought two glasses of cheap domestic from the bar tap and handed them to the thugs.

"Don't you want anything?" Lazlo asked Moss.

Moss slid from the stool, undid his belt, and dropped his jeans. The jeans stopped at his thigh and he pushed them lower to reveal a half-full urine drainage bag.

"Can't have beer," said Moss. "Doctor's orders."

"I'm sorry," said Lazlo, watching Moss struggle to pull up his jeans. His boxer shorts were red, his legs white table legs.

After dealing with a complicated belt buckle, Moss spoke. "Buddy Minkus' old man was run over by a bus and Buddy couldn't drop it. Kept having theories about who wanted his father dead. Cops give him zilch, so he takes a lone wolf trip searching for clues. Says his father was pushed. While Buddy's on his trip, cops come asking about him. Turns out he's done a horizontal park in the Colorado Rockies, gone over the side, and him and the bike are a mess. They don't ID him for a couple weeks."

"What about the other Minkus?" asked Lazlo.

"Couple weeks back, Buddy's son Cory decides to take his own trip west to, as he said, find himself. Another lone wolf, another Minkus." Moss smiled. "I'm a poet and don't know it."

"I'm familiar with the oldest Minkus run over by the bus. I spoke with a son having the same name, George Minkus."

"George is Buddy's older brother," said Moss. "Came here after Buddy disappeared. He's not a biker. Drove a rice burner hybrid. We told him about Buddy's theory someone pushed the old man. Buddy was a Vietnam Vet like me. Plenty of Rolling Thunder rides."

"I'm on the same journey," said Lazlo.

"Rolling Thunder?"

"Determining whether someone pushed or the old man fell."

"You should talk to older brother George again."

"I called before I drove my rice burner here. He said he knew nothing more. That's when I went online and was led to the Bent Spoke."

"What kind of rice burner you got?" asked one of the thugs.

"Old Honda Civic."

"They are dependable," said Moss. "Want another beer?"

"No, thank you. I must go. Good luck with your health."

Next morning was sunny but cool for spring. At first Guzzo grabbed tan shorts he'd worn in Arizona from the laundry basket, but after stepping outside came back for tan cargo pants. He did his own laundry, careful nothing remained in pockets. After the last trip, Vera asked, in front of the girls, how it went. Guzzo saw himself smiling in the hall mirror as he retrieved from his bag gifts he'd picked up in Sedona.

In the backyard, Guzzo raked the lawn still brown from winter. He told Vera a Chicago suburb yard should be neat. Lately she'd begun questioning his jobs. When confronted, she gave her usual answer. She was interested in everything he did, her curiosity driven by her need to be assured of his safety and her desire to help. Vera knew many things, like the weapons, ammo, and equipment in storage facilities near major airports, but she didn't know everything.

A lawnmower started nearby, its engine running rough, threatening to die. Guzzo wondered if it was the same neighbor he'd helped the previous year by reattaching a throttle spring. He stopped raking and looked toward the noise. It was beyond his house, not visible. Vera stood at the kitchen window, watching him while she spoke on her cell phone. He made a point to ask later about her phone call. If the answer was unsatisfactory, he'd eventually find her phone and check recent calls. Once, after she was on the phone, he saw no recent calls and questioned her. Vera's answer came fast. She'd wanted to call a preschool for the girls but decided against it at the last second. When he asked if she had another phone, she became angry. Guzzo waved to Vera in the kitchen window. Vera waved back, saying something into the phone.

During a barbeque last fall, he'd been able to overhear two wives. He'd gone to his garage to fetch charcoal. Coming back around the corner of the house, he paused after cutting through backyards.

"Vera's from Ukraine."

"Does she work outside the home?"

"Give me a break. She's got two little girls."

"What does Tony do?"

"Shipping or something. Out of town stuff when he's busy."

"He was in that first Iraq war, wasn't he?"

"Yeah, he's got that tattoo."

"Maybe he's in one of the intelligence agencies."

"Could be."

Guzzo smiled at his reflection as he passed his garage window, recalling a Hitchcock film he'd recently seen, the television screen reflection observed by the housemaid at the mountain home near Mount Rushmore as Cary Grant sneaks along the balcony. The housemaid holds Grant at gunpoint as James Mason and Martin Landau escort Eva Marie Saint out to the airplane idling on the runway. *North by Northwest*, that was the movie.

After the job in Sun City, where he came across the *Hitchcock* book by Francois Truffaut, Guzzo ordered it at a bookstore, and also checked Hitchcock videos out of the library. Hitchcock's film names often came to mind. Penny, the well-endowed Greek neighbor bending to examine bulbs surfacing in her garden, reminded Guzzo of *Rear Window*. When Penny stood and turned to explore her yard, she saw Guzzo and waved.

He and Penny chatted at the corner fence post for a while. How the kids were doing, the spring weather, promises to get together more this summer. Penny said she'd just gotten off the phone with Vera and this enhanced Guzzo's neighborly mood.

He fired up his Sears lawn tractor and began pulling the lawn aerator he'd rented the day before. Halfway through the backyard, he felt his phone in his hip pocket. Without shutting off the tractor, he checked the display. The blank text was from P, meaning he'd be expected at the fish market the following Monday. He'd have lunch at his favorite restaurant, and afterward meet Pescatore. He put his phone away, put the tractor in gear, and pushed the throttle.

George Minkus Junior's wife left Lazlo and George alone in the living room. On the coffee table was a framed photograph of George and another man, arms around one another's shoulders. George had short salt-and-pepper hair, round face, and was heavyish. The other man was thinner, had a runaway beard, and wore a red, white, and blue star-spangled do-rag.

Lazlo turned the photo toward him. "I assume this is your brother Buddy."

George nodded.

"You didn't mentioned him after your father's death."

"You didn't ask."

"I'm trying to help."

"Help? After Dad died you weren't any help. Even after the toxicology report."

"Remind me. What were the results?"

"Alcohol level only .05, so he wasn't drunk. A trace of Valium, so they chalked it up to that. He was a nervous man, always looking over his shoulder."

"Did he talk about the past?"

"Not much. He was in the Navy in the Pacific, their carrier was torpedoed, but he seemed more positive about it than his earlier stint in the CCCs."

"Any details about the CCCs?"

"He was in Utah building roads. He got a mailing one time about a reunion. My brother and I found it in the garbage and asked about it. He said it was a long time ago and most of the guys were dead. Buddy thought it meant something. That and the hair."

"The lock of hair that was in his wallet?"

"Yeah. Buddy asked Mom and was shocked she didn't know about it. He said Dad carried it in his wallet as long as he could remember and why didn't Mom know something?"

"What was your brother's theory?"

"Buddy said he asked once after Dad and Mom returned from a party. Dad was drunk and Mom had Buddy help him upstairs. Buddy said he emptied Dad's pockets and, when Mom wasn't listening, asked about the hair. Dad said it came from Wyoming. Buddy asked who in Wyoming, and Dad kept repeating Wyoming over and over until he passed out. After that, no matter how Buddy brought it up, Dad denied he'd ever said it.

"After Dad passed, Buddy researched CCC camp information on the Internet. Supposedly the camp was in Utah, but the closest town of any size was in Wyoming. He found a camp pamphlet listing Dad's name along with the rest of the guys. Buddy copied the pamphlet. I gave a copy to Buddy's son Cory. You want one?"

"Yes. I assume Cory's solo motorcycle trip has to do with this."

George stood to fetch the copy. "Cory's trip will probably end up in Utah. The reason I'm giving you this is because maybe you'll find Cory and send his ass home."

"Before something happens?"

"Yeah. If there's anything to this, you'll not tip Cory's hand."

"I had a brother who died unfairly. And the sister of a good friend was recently murdered because of what she knew. You can trust me."

The Toyota Camry was smooth, quiet, and being a popular car, blended in. Unless anticipating back roads, Guzzo rented a Camry. Although the drive from Chicago to Detroit was not far, he never used his own car on jobs. He rented the Camry under an assumed name from an agency near the airport. His own car was in the airport long-term lot.

With the traffic snarl through Northwest Indiana behind him, he put the Camry in cruise and tuned to a new wave music station. At a construction area along Interstate 94, the pavement was potholed enough to wonder if this could be considered a back road. Perhaps a heavier vehicle with good ground clearance would have been in order. During his visit to the fish market, Pescatore mentioned potholes in infrastructure-starved Detroit.

The mark's name was Angela "Niki" Gianakos, daughter of Nick Gianakos, the tough old bird from last winter. He was surprised how soon he was returning to Detroit. He wondered if he'd left a loose end there or farther north in Michigan when he staged the son's death. Pescatore said no, simply a nosey strong-willed daughter.

Nick Gianakos had "fallen" from the rooftop of the building housing his Greektown restaurant. Before going to the apartment to bring him up to the rooftop, Guzzo arranged tools and spread tar at the base of a roof vent. It was typical of maintenance Guzzo overheard the old man being warned against doing. After retrieving the Greek—a difficult job, the guy wiry and tough—Guzzo threw him off the roof. In the alley he made sure the old guy was dead, put his fingerprints on a putty knife, smeared tar on hands and knees, went up to the roof to leave the tools behind, and paused for a moment to look at the nearby Greektown Casino Hotel to make sure no one had watched. That night, rather than drive out of town, he stayed in the hotel. He'd checked in the day before and, though he wasn't a gambler, took time to lose some money.

Pragmatism instilled by experience gave Guzzo a sense of operating from a carefully-crafted script. The unfolding assignment like a movie being filmed with him the director. He's also the editor, using common sense to cut unwanted segments, leaving nothing to chance. As for other operatives, certainly there were those doing research, filtering it down the line. Eventually the mark would be assigned to Pescatore. Sometimes, alone on his way to an assignment, Guzzo caught himself wondering if having a wife and two girls would go on forever, or if his lone wolf status would someday need enhancement.

Guzzo adjusted the cruise so his speed on the GPS matched the posted limit. In the construction zone he tucked in behind trucks, giving drivers who didn't exercise common sense the fast lane. Guzzo leaned toward the rearview mirror and smiled. He'd rented a nondescript Camry for his last drive to Detroit. A woman this time. Sometimes, in his business, anticipation was common sense.

CHAPTER 16

In 1937, Manila, Utah, CCC crews built the fire lookout tower on Ute Mountain overlooking canyons studded with forested thrust faults and the Flaming Gorge in the distance. In 1939, forest service vehicles had been damaged and the Ute Mountain approach road needed fixing. The final climb was a tan backdrop against blue sky after winding back and forth through wooded mountainside and cathedral-like spires. Weather was perfect, the superintendent said. Sure, always cool in the morning. Easy for him to say.

With limestone dust on faded denim, the young men moving rock blended into the backdrop. Higher on the road around a bend, hidden behind scrubby trees, a tan 1939 Buick Century Sport Coupe also blended in. The two men in the Buick had removed jackets earlier and thrown them into the back seat. The Buick was big enough they could leave hats on, but every so often one of them removed his hat to handkerchief his head. The tall driver had wide shoulders. The passenger, watching the CCC men through binoculars, was stocky and short with sloped shoulders. Both had loosened their ties. The stocky man with the binoculars wore suspenders.

"Back east a tree would give shade."

"Could be worse," said the driver. "This thing isn't black,"

"I don't get it."

"Black absorbs heat. The boss gave us a black coupe last summer. Like an oven." The driver removed his hat, wiped his head before putting it back on. "What's going on down there?"

"That local man. LEMs they call 'em. What's that stand for again?"

"Local Experienced Men. Why you watching him?"

"He's giving Little Sal a hard time."

The driver removed his hat again and fanned air from outside into the open window. "If we don't do something Little Sal'll run to papa."

"Long way to run," said the stocky man.

"He'd figure a way to phone the old man."

"Maybe he'll get himself into one of them grudge matches. District officer the boss paid off says a grudge match with boxing gloves might do him good. I'd say he's on his way." The stocky man handed the binoculars to the driver.

Down at the job site, one young man shoved another, the other shoved back, and soon they were rolling in the dust. The LEM, instead of breaking it up, yelled at other men in the crew. They seemed reluctant but finally a few moved in, pulled the scrappers apart, and stood them up. The yelling was barely audible in the Buick because of the distance.

The driver adjusted the binoculars. "Little Sal's in trouble again."

"He'll give us the shit tonight. Careful you don't let him hear you call him Little Sal."

"Yeah, like never letting the old man hear us call him Sally Big Shoes."

"Or letting the old man know about the pep pills."

"How else we supposed to stay awake?"

"I mean the ones Little Sal takes."

Having given up the binoculars, the stocky man in the passenger held a newspaper.

"Any good news?" asked the driver.

"Mostly war in Europe. Says here the new Pope is concerned."

"He should be. What's his name?"

"Pius, same as the dead guy. Hey, they're using the Yankee Clipper to take mail back and forth over the Atlantic. And another piece about poor old Lou Gehrig. Ain't that the shits?"

The scuffle down at the work site seemed to have calmed. Some men sat in the shade of the two trucks, others sat in the shade of a boulder.

"What's going on now?" asked the passenger with the newspaper.

"Lunch," said the driver.

"What we got?"

"Baloney sandwiches from the café, coffee left in the thermos, water in the jug."

"A beer would hit the spot."

"Later, after we meet with—What do we call him?"

"Sal, until he says different." The stocky man folded his newspaper into a fan and used it. "Hope they cleared those big rocks we straddled coming up. I thought we'd punch a hole in the gas tank. You haven't smelled anything?"

"I was careful. I don't need calling Lonzo about gas leaks. You got the new phone number written down?"

"In my wallet. I hate calling Lonzo. Whoever heard of the driver talking for the boss?"

"Cavallo's Uncle Rosario's calling the shots."

With Brooklyn hot Cavallo enjoyed his back porch. Since sending Little Sal to the CCCs he was alone most evenings. And what the hell kind of companion was Lonzo with nothing but yeah boss this and yeah boss that? Even at the office or a warehouse with the boys he felt alone. Uncle Rosario's grooming of Little Sal putting a curse on him. Sure, it was 1939 and times were changing, but why so fast?

Because the covered porch was on the second floor, Cavallo could see over the backyard wall and bushes. Between houses across the alley he had a view of the baseball diamond next block over. Boys, all arms and legs, playing batter-work-up. Little Sal used to be one of those boys. An argument had broken out and soon fists would be flying. If only kids didn't grow up.

Little Sal had turned into a repeat of so many boys in the family, needing to show how tough he was. Like the time Cavallo saw Little Sal use his baseball bat on a baby rabbit out of its nest behind the backstop. Not to show off; he'd been alone, the other boys gone home for supper. He remembered turning away as Sal slugged the rabbit again and again. Goddamn kids. Probably good he's growing up in FDR's CCC.

Behind him Cavallo heard the maid rattling pots and pans in the kitchen. Cleaning up his mess because Francesca was already in bed. After returning from taking Little Sal to training camp in Ohio, he and Francesca not only ate alone, now they slept in separate bedrooms. And where had she gone today? Shopping, or Canasta with her Daughters of Isabela cronies.

When the doorbell rang inside the house, Cavallo knew Uncle Rosario and his bodyguard would be waiting within the enclosed front porch. After the maid let Uncle Rosario in, the bodyguard would head back to the car and the car would show up in the alley where the driver and bodyguard would wait for the signal to leave. Cavallo stood to look over the back wall. Sure enough, there was the Lincoln, the bodyguard and driver visible through the windshield. The bodyguard had been with his uncle a long time. The driver was a kid Little Sal's age, his cousin Joey's boy, cigarette hanging out his mouth. The timing was perfect, the Lincoln pulling up in the alley just as Cavallo hears his uncle wheezing at the second floor landing.

After a hug, and the request for Corvo, after the maid was gone, Cavallo and Uncle Rosario sat across from one another in their usual places on padded wicker chairs.

Uncle Rosario made a motion like swinging a bat. "I see baseball boys."

"Yeah, made me think of when Little Sal used to play.

"You still calling him that?"

"Hard not to, since we both got the same name."

Uncle Rosario nodded. "I wouldn't know, the Lord chose girls for me and your aunt."

"I've seen girls play baseball in the park a couple times."

"Not my girls." His uncle took a sip of Corvo, returning the glass to the side table. The sign for business. Next would come a statement. Always a statement rather than a question.

"I'm here because of news from Utah. One of our men looking after things called my office. Salvatore picking fights doesn't accomplish goals. The world is changing. We must change with it. I told them to put your son on the phone next time they call. Instead of calling me, they'll call you. Timing is critical because of European turmoil. Italy's signed a so-called Pact of Steel with Germany, boots are marching, and soon Roosevelt will be unable to resist adding ours. If your son doesn't succeed in the CCC and go on to the post prepared for him in the Army, we lose our opportunity."

Uncle Rosario must have seen the reaction on Cavallo's face.

"Why do you shake your head?"

"Forgive me. I was thinking of Sal's boyhood. I'll not simply speak with him. I'll put the fear of God in him. Francesca disagreed with this. Yet I made her understand. I'll not allow him to shame his father!"

Uncle Rosario smiled and nodded. "Good, I needed to hear this."

Camp Manila had five barracks buildings, along with a latrine building, mess hall building, education and recreation hall building, administration building, and motor pool garage. The camp was originally designed for 200 men, 40 per barracks. The buildings were angled; from surrounding cliffs they formed a pine tree shape on the valley floor. Being it was 1939, and it looked like war was coming, the CCC was cutting its ranks and Barracks Five was empty.

After evening meal, during free time, Barracks Building Three on the other side of the latrine was usually quiet, most men at the recreation hall. But this evening the barracks was noisy with excitement because of the upcoming grudge match. The commotion started at the work site. Henry Gustafson, assistant barracks leader, complained about Salvatore Cavallo sitting in the shade instead of working.

"I'll sit anywhere I want, Henrietta."

"Why not climb on top of the rock and get a suntan while you're at it?"

"I'll climb a bigger rock, maybe Castle Rock up in Green River."

"You'd have trouble there," said Henry, trying to walk away.

Sal went after Henry, grabbed his shirt and spun him around. "I'll climb it! Not that glass of milk replica you're carving. The real thing! Why you so interested in rocks anyhow?"

Henry straightened his shirt. "It's educational."

Sal sneered and looked around at the others. "Educational."

"Like that rock shading you. You'll be long gone and it'll still be here."

Sal held up his fists. "You're all wet! I'll never be gone!"

One of the older LEMs at the work site heard the commotion and came over, pulling Sal away. "All right that's enough."

"He started it!" shouted Sal."

"You guys looking for a grudge match, I'm sure the superintendent can oblige."

That's how it started. And now before sunset Henry Gustafson was due to meet Sal Cavallo in the boxing ring behind the recreation building. A couple men sided with Cavallo, but most sided with Gustafson, the assistant barracks leader. Including Jimmy, the Big Apple, Phillips, the barracks leader, and George Minkus, seated on the bunk of their friend, Bela Voronko, who was stooped down arranging the inside of his footlocker.

Bela had a photograph of the China Clipper flying boat taking off from San Francisco Bay taped to the inside lid of his footlocker. It was identical to the photograph he'd clipped from an Uzhgorod newspaper and hung in the barn. News from Carpatho-Ukraine was grim in newspapers and letters from his mother didn't help.

Beyond the open footlocker, Jimmy and George shared a bottle of Coca Cola, alternately pouring some into their tin cups. George held the bottle up. "Bela?"

"No thank you."

Sal Cavallo, in tee shirt and shorts at the far end of the barracks, pounded one boxing glove into another, showing off footwork, bragging he was going to, "Pulverize Henry." Henry wasn't in the barracks and several men with nothing better to do stood watching Sal.

"Glad I'm not fighting him," said George.

"He ain't so tough," said Jimmy. "Henry and I were here before you guys. Henry's quiet, but when someone throws a punch, he's got a little Joe Louis in him."

"He's got colored blood?" asked George, smiling.

"Nah," said Jimmy. "Not that."

"We all contain red blood," said Bela. "No matter where we're from."

At the far end of the barracks, Sal yelled the Brooklyn Dodgers were the best team. Apparently someone mentioned another team and sent Sal into a rage.

Bela asked, "Do you think Sal's anger is real?"

"I don't know," said Jimmy. "I've seen this before, a guy looking for a fight. Like I said, Henry can take care of himself. Except I wouldn't want to be in Henry's shoes." Jimmy took a swig of Coke. "Guys like Sal, the fight's never over. You see him showing off his stiletto the other night? Sal the Stiletto we should call him."

"He's like brown shirts in old country," said Bela. "Something haunts me. I feel I've been here before, or I'll be here in future. Rather than brown shirts, last night I dreamt of a man dressed in black, one who carries knives and guns. As you Americans say, Sal is one who fails to keep his shirt on."

When Jimmy and George laughed, Bela laughed with them.

Jethro, the Georgia baritone, was walking past and heard some of their conversation. He stopped and did one of his Clark Gable impressions. "A normal human being couldn't live under the same roof with him without going nutty."

Jimmy said, "Hey, that's from *It Happened One Night*."

Earlier that day, 50 miles north in front of the Green River post office, a rancher sorting mail couldn't help glancing up the street at two girls leaning against a red Dodge pickup truck. Pretty girls, damn pretty in their home-made flowery dresses. Even as the rancher drove away in his old black Ford pickup, the image of the girls leaning against the Dodge followed along, down the dusty road, up into the hills toward Castle Rock. The image would pester him tonight, that's for sure. The way they laughed, the girls were probably discussing boys, maybe CCC boys from the Manila camp, city CCC boys like wild horses.

Back at the post office another rancher passed by the girls leaning against the Dodge. He caught the front word of the conversation. "Rose…" and was gone.

"Rose, are you saying you've already dated guys from the Manila camp?"

"You bet. Gal from Rock Springs has a car and knows the camp brass. She's dated guys from the Green River camp *and* the Manila camp. Says I'm a pip. We've gone to dances and the Arrowhead Bar a couple times."

"They let you in Arrowhead?"

"No reason not to. My girlfriend with the car is 21."

"But if your girlfriend doesn't pick you up, how are you going on a date with this camp boy? What's his name again?"

"Salvatore."

"What kind of name is that?"

"Italian, very romantic."

"How's he going to get up here to Green River? Someone dumping him off the back end of one of those trucks?"

"He's got a car."

"Come on, Rose. They don't get paid enough for gas, let alone a car."

"He's from New York. Some employees of his father are in the area on business and they're going to let him use one of the business cars."

"This guy's so sweet on you Daddy already sent employees to bring him a car?"

"Maybe. From what I'm told there've already been boxing glove rhubarbs over me."

"Well, Rose, I'll say it again. You don't know what you're getting into."

"I know as much as anybody."

The town boy named Cletus walked past, tipping his cap. The girl with Rose smiled. Rose put her pearl ring to her lips as if kissing it and looked down the street like there might be a parade coming her way.

No rain for days, the grudge match behind the recreation building a dusty one. Not an elevated boxing ring, simply a rope between rusty pipes welded into old truck wheels. The match ended at sunset with a knock down followed by cheering and slaps on backs. Barracks Three men were still celebrating at the work site next day, going over details, especially the final decisive punch.

But the day after, job site talk was subdued. Henry Gustafson not in his bunk that morning. Maybe winning triggered something in Henry. Yeah, wins the match so he can do anything. Must be why he was gone. The loser sure wasn't talking.

Two nights later, many expected Henry to reappear. After walking away from the job site he could have hitched a ride into town to celebrate. But no, he still wasn't there.

After lights out, Jimmy and George crawled off their bunks and sat on the floor on either side of Bela's bunk.

"I heard something," whispered Jimmy. "Paul the mapmaker said he saw Sal talking to someone in a car east of the work site."

"Yeah," whispered George. "Sal complaining he'd had too much coffee and going behind a boulder. We thought he might've been sick, but when he finally comes back he's smarting off as usual."

"Was the car the color of the hills?" asked Bela.

"Yeah," said Jimmy. "Another guy with Paul saw it. Said maybe the superintendent sent someone to check work progress. How could someone like that have a new car? It was a Buick sport model. Where'd you see the car?"

"Up in the hills earlier in the week, parked behind dead trees at a hairpin."

"The car Sal was leaning into must be the same one. When the car drove away, Paul and this other guy saw two men in front. Said the Buick's dust was northeast last time he saw it, maybe up the other side of the gorge toward Rock Springs. Since Sal showed up there's nothing but trouble. First he steals cigarettes at Sunday dinner and sells them back, now this. We never used to have so many meetings in the superintendent's office. Powwows with older staff and LEMs afraid to speak up. Henry would be the last guy to go AWOL. He was at camp before you guys. He liked it here."

"Were the meetings about Sal?" asked George.

"Someone mentioned the tan car, but LEMs I thought would have seen it denied seeing it. Scuttlebutt is the meetings have to do with Sal being Italian, or Sicilian. Like, the guys in the car might be looking out for him."

"And if they're looking out for him—"

"We must look out for one another," said Bela.

"How?" asked Jimmy. "Henry was my assistant. I'm going to request you be made assistant barracks leader, Bela."

"Why me?"

"What you've been through. Leaving home and coming over on a ship to escape being drafted by brown shirt's nothing to sneeze at."

"Or maybe it's because of your snazzy accent," added George.

"My accent?"

"Yeah, Count Dracula ready to suck blood."

All three muffled their laughter as Jimmy and George crawled across the floor and climbed into their own bunks.

At the far end of the barracks the entry door opened from the inside and a young man was shadowed against the light coming from the latrine building. He stood in the doorway for a minute before stepping outside and letting the door close behind him. Outside the sound of a vehicle. It stopped, the engine idling with a rumble. Several minutes later the vehicle drove off and shortly thereafter the door opened again. The young man who'd left earlier returned. In near darkness, Bela watched for movement and saw in the shadows it was Sal. Only after Sal was down in bed, unmoving, did Bela lay back on his pillow.

Near sleep, the man in black returned. Bela forced the dream away with thoughts of Nina Zolotarev. But that afternoon he'd been going through a newspaper practicing English and came across an article saying Carpatho-Ukraine citizens having even one Jewish parent were not safe because of Hungarian anti-Jewish laws and Soviet Union annexation. Were they better off running away? Was he the man in black?

CHAPTER 17

Sonia's service, rather than being in one of Kiev's old cathedrals, was in a small chapel. Janos, Mariya, and a long-lost cousin, wife, and two little girls in the front row. The girls reminded Janos of Sonia when she was their age. His little sister dead. In the pew behind them were neighbors from Janos and Mariya's apartment building along with two Kiev Militia investigators Janos once worked with. In back was an elderly Orthodox priest who also showed up at the cemetery.

An old Volga sedan squeezed between rows of iconic statues and dropped the priest nearby. After the younger non-orthodox priest spoke words familiar from family burials long ago, Janos left Mariya with his cousin's family and approached the Orthodox priest.

"Did you know my sister?"

"No. you and I have met."

"I thought you looked familiar."

"I've lost weight. My name is Vladimir Ivanovich Rogoza. I was once in the Moscow Patriarchate of the Ukrainian Orthodox Church. Perhaps you recall I had an office in Kiev."

"I remember," said Janos. "You were complicit in trafficking children."

Rogoza let out a series of wet coughs into a handkerchief he pulled from his frock. "I served my time, first in prison, now in the abbey where the Patriarchate keeps men like me."

"Why are you here?"

Rogoza looked around and leaned close. "Because of the position I once held, and my acquaintance with others in the abbey, I'm aware of pressures being applied from the north."

Janos whispered. "Moscow?"

Rogoza nodded but said, "Based there, operational everywhere, including here."

"Trafficking?"

"Yes."

"What does this have to do with me and my sister?"

"The investigation," whispered Rogoza.

"The investigation of Sonia's death? Or the investigation she was doing regarding the death of her friend?"

"Both. In their eyes *bizness* takes precedence. Their tentacles cover the world."

"You must know more," said Janos.

No answer. Janos waited, staring into Rogoza's bloodshot eyes.

Again, Rogoza whispered. "That the international arm attached to Moscow observes you and your associates is what I can give, Janos Nagy. What I did to children is more than sin. I go where I can to warn potential victims. They watch wherever I go. And now my warning—all I have to give—is that they are watching you."

"They'll get to you eventually."

"I know," said Rogoza. "It's a sacrifice I make willingly."

Janos moved closer, squeezed Rogoza's bony arm, and whispered harshly. "Don't speak sacrifice! My sister is dead! If this is a trap I'll kill you!"

Rogoza winced but continued staring at Janos. "Janos Nagy, in your position I'd feel the same. I know they're here, Mafias as well as SBU. Do not trust those you trusted in the past. I'm alone in the world. Sacrifice is an improper word because of my past. Perhaps my final words will help." Rogoza's whisper was filled with phlegm. "I've heard mumblings concerning the year 1939. Something in the US in 1939. Also mumblings of a key. To what, I don't know. This is all I can say. Go with God, Janos Nagy. I pray I've helped rather than harmed your cause."

Even when Janos let go, Rogoza continued staring at him until he turned and walked slowly to the old Volga driven by what appeared to be another elderly priest. As he watched the Volga drive away, Janos thought of what Rogoza had said—1939, a key, and warning him to be careful of the Mafias and the SBU. Janos' old friend Yuri Smirnov was SBU.

During their remaining days in Kiev, Janos kept Eva Polenkaya's key close. Although they did not speak of it, he and Mariya packed as if they'd never return, two new suitcases added to accommodate the load. They arranged for storage in the apartment basement and removed all but furniture. A simple phone call would be required to vacate. The night before the flight they ate in their favorite restaurant. A Gypsy woman, managing to sneak in, tried her scam on Janos and Mariya. Although they'd both lived in Kiev for years, the obvious scam attempt made them feel alien. The day of the flight Janos sold his Skoda at the open air market and Mariya put the Audi in storage at a garage where the owner would care for it long term or sell it if need be. The nonstop flight from Kiev to New York took 11 hours. When well away from Ukraine, Mariya finally asked about Father Rogoza.

"Why is he out of prison?"

"A fringe benefit of clergy," said Janos.

"Is it safe to speak?"

"I hope so," said Janos. "Our phones are off, buried in our carry-ons. The plane is loud. There's nothing more we can do."

"I'm tired of riddle speech," said Mariya.

"No more riddles, Mariya. Tell me what you discovered about Eva Polenkaya's key."

"As she said, Doctor Marta questioned her. Her name was in Marta's notes. The key came from Alexander Zolotarev. Doctor Marta's family, the Voronkos, knew the Zolotarevs from before World War II. The Zolotarevs, with relatives in Brooklyn, New York, helped Marta's grandfather, Bela Voronko, when he fled Carpatho-Ukraine to escape the Nazis. Bela, who retained US citizenship because he was born there, ended up in the CCCs in 1939."

Mariya pulled out a small tattered notebook she kept with her passport. "I took notes. While adding her research to the extensive research done by her father, Marta came across information from the father that, rather than the box being in one of the Twin Towers destroyed on September 11, 2001, the key might fit a safe deposit box in an old Brooklyn bank. The name Zolotarev has a connection to a Sicilian family in New York. Apparently a Zolotarev was a go-between for Sicilian and Jewish mobsters during the '30s and during World War II. Women of the family listed as owners. Curiously, the box number is 1939."

"Keep this to yourself for now. You can tell me more after we land."

Mariya smiled. "Not too much at one sitting."

Janos nodded.

"Telepathy," said Mariya. She kissed him.

"I knew you were going to kiss me."

"I know you knew."

Chicago FBI building. Same floor, different office. As before Jacobson wore leather boots, jeans, and flannel shirt. Again he sat on the edge of the empty desk.

"I'm sorry about your friend's sister, Lazlo." Jacobson slid from the desk and walked to the window with a view of the brickwork of another building. "Because I've asked, I'm now briefed on anything having to do with Janos Nagy and Mariya Nemeth. Last time we spoke it concerned the death of Doctor Marta Voronko and the fact she was one of several investigating untimely deaths of men once in the CCC in Manila, Utah. A connection I don't understand involves remnants of a Sicilian-based New York syndicate."

Jacobson turned from the window. "That woman in Michigan—the one I'm going to put you in touch with—I called her this morning."

"She's in danger?" asked Lazlo.

"There's reason for concern. FBI Michigan is watching, but they're short-handed. I warned her to be careful and I'd like you to speak with her."

"Before something happens?"

Jacobson nodded as he pulled a piece of paper from his pocket. "I briefed her on your research without names or other details that could cause problems in case her phone is tapped."

"Was it a cell phone?"

"Yes. I turned on encryption on my end, but one can never be sure."

Jacobson handed over the piece of paper torn from a pocketsize spiral notebook. "Her name, address, and cell number. She might be in the process of relocating."

Niki Gianakos, a Detroit address and a phone number. Lazlo pulled his cell phone from his pocket. "May I call her from here."

Jacobson handed his own phone to Lazlo and walked to the window. "Your phone won't get out of the building."

Niki Gianakos answered on the second ring. "Inspector?"

"I'm using his phone. My name is Lazlo Horvath. Jacobson wanted us to communicate. May I call you Niki?"

"Yes." Her voice was soft, yet determined.

"I think we should meet," said Lazlo. "We're searching for answers to questions dating from 1939."

A pause. "I agree we should meet."

"Should I drive there? I could leave tomorrow."

"Because of my conversation on this phone earlier—Is Jacobson with you?"

Lazlo signaled, Jacobson left the window and took the phone. "Niki, after our conversation earlier I understand your need to hear me. I'm sorry— Good, I'm glad you're packing. The Michigan office will have one agent there until then. Yes, I'll give you back to Lazlo."

Jacobson handed back the phone and left the office.

"It's Lazlo again."

"I'm sorry. Without us meeting face to face—"

"I understand. Jacobson said you're packing?"

"I'm leaving tomorrow."

"To Chicago?"

"Yes."

"Do you have somewhere to stay? I can arrange a local short term rental in my neighborhood."

"Someday we'll look back on this and laugh. But these days it's difficult to laugh."

"Recent loss in my homeland makes laughter difficult."

"Tomorrow afternoon, after I drive across the Indiana-Illinois line, I'll take the tollway and stop at the first oasis. I've driven there before, the Lincoln Oasis. Give me your number. I'll call from there. You can tell me an address then."

The New York plan—Two years earlier, after working on the Chernobyl trafficking case, Janos, Mariya, and Lazlo met with US Customs officials and the Ukraine embassy consulate general. Because of their impact closing a trafficking network, they'd received an open invitation at the embassy. After landing at JFK and passing through customs, Janos and Mariya were picked up by a driver and assigned an embassy apartment. They had an informal dinner with the consulate general that evening and were told the phone line in their room was secure and they'd be able to make international calls in confidence.

Janos called Yuri Smirnov. Although it was morning in Kiev, Smirnov sounded drunk, claiming he had no new information about Sonia's or Doctor Marta's deaths. As Smirnov spoke, Janos noticed the slur lessening. Smirnov was being deceitful, especially when he began questioning Janos, asking about location and plans. The conversation with Smirnov was not that of old friends, but a one-sided interrogation.

After hanging up, Janos decided he needed to speak with someone in Kiev he could trust. Chief Investigator Boris Chudin answered on the first ring.

"Janos, I hoped you would keep in contact. I'm sorry I was not able to attend your sister's funeral. Developments here. I hope you understand."

"Have you heard from Yuri Smirnov of the SBU lately?"

"I know of him. There's talk."

"What kind of talk?"

"Smirnov's head is filled with rusty nails."

"Meaning?"

"Muddled thinking. The rust is caused by vodka, the nails are something else. He questions my investigators about your sister's murder as well as Doctor Marta's murder."

"Perhaps he's trying to help."

"No, Janos. Remember when we watched the confession of the Chernobyl Killer? Yuri Smirnov is looking out, as if through a one-way mirror. My investigators say he eventually gets around to asking about you and Mariya at every turn."

"Boris, could you do me a favor and keep an eye on Smirnov?"

"Of course. Should I call you if anything emerges?"

"No, I'll call you."

"Be well, Janos."

Before bed, Janos told Mariya about his conversation with Chudin. Both agreed Smirnov was acting strangely and it was good he didn't know where they were.

Next morning Janos and Mariya left their baggage at the embassy and ventured out into New York City separately to prepare for their journey to be with Lazlo. Mariya took a cab to HSBC Bank, formerly Republic Bank and before that Bank Leumi. Janos took another cab across Manhattan to New Jersey to search for an appropriate vehicle for their journey.

Mariya's accent was helpful. Although she didn't get into the safe deposit box, she provided the number, saying one-nine-three-nine rather than 1939, as one would give a year. After being asked to sign the form and show the key, she was able to see the signatures of owners who'd accessed the box in the past. The last entry was Endora Zolotarev, signed for entry ten years earlier in August

2001. Before that was another request for entry in 1997 by Endora Zolotarev, and before 1997 a long series of entries by a Mrs. Shulamit Weizman.

Pretending to have misplaced her ID, Mariya left the bank. She'd accomplished her goal, verifying Eva Polenkaya's claim that the Zolotarev family, friends of Doctor Marta Voronko's forebears, held claim to a safe deposit box. She called Janos, keeping it simple. He said he was almost finished, and without naming it, they agreed to meet back at the Ukraine Embassy.

Janos was lying atop a bed on wheels when he took the call, trying the bed out for comfort while the salesman was away taking Janos' bottom line offer to the dealership manager.

Rather than rent or purchase a car, Janos decided, after several stops pricing cars, that a home on wheels would be appropriate. He and Mariya had traveled in a camper van during the initial stages of their investigation into the human trafficking case leading to the Chernobyl Exclusion Zone. The camper van had worked well in Ukraine, allowing them to move about covertly. He felt this would also work well in the US.

Unfortunately, camper vans were expensive in the US, with larger motor homes plentiful and cheaper because of the cost of gasoline. The sizeable motor home Janos lay in when Mariya called was supposedly a Class C as opposed to the even large Class A motor homes. He was at an RV rental dealer in Linden, New Jersey, that was trying to sell off used units.

Janos had dealt with salesmen in Ukraine. It was the same here. After hanging up with Mariya, he walked to the front of the Class C and slid into the driver's seat. When the salesman smiled, waving a sheet of paper, Janos knew the so-called lowball offer had either been accepted, or he'd soon hear a story about how the salesman didn't know where the manager's thoughts were that day, or the manager had countered with an offer so close to Janos' offer, certainly he'd make the deal. As the sign at the entrance to the dealership said, "Ready to deal today."

CHAPTER 18

A Hitchcock moment, *scene of the crime* idiom in mind as Guzzo stood at the balcony sliding door. Same room in Detroit's Greektown Casino Hotel. Looking down at the roof of the building from which he'd thrown Gianakos. Staring down, Guzzo conjured up another fall. The daughter in the stairwell, lighting terrible, especially the second floor landing where the single bulb is burned out. She retrieves a replacement but needs a stepladder. Barely enough room for the stepladder on the landing. Two bulbs and holding onto the ladder a juggling act. One ladder leg slips over the edge. Ladder plummets down the stairs. She's found with her neck broken.

When hotel housekeeping knocked that afternoon, Guzzo tried to tell the young woman to leave. Young, blonde, her accent either Ukrainian or Russian, perhaps lured by traffickers and escaped. He held the do not disturb sign up to get rid of her.

Back at the sliding door, Guzzo focused his spotting scope on the black Ford Fusion parked across the street from the Gianakos building. The male driver still there, looking toward the side entrance leading to a maintenance room and the stairway. Light bulbs and ladder would be in the maintenance room. If it weren't for him, Guzzo could have finished by now. The man watching the entrance meant there could be another, perhaps here in the hotel with his or her own spotting scope.

Last evening Guzzo used the remote listening device trying to hear something in the woman's apartment. He heard pots and pans in the kitchen and Greek background music. He considered visiting the restaurant and installing a transmitter to the ceiling of the men's room. But the apartment was up another floor. After dark he moved the listening device to the balcony. The man in the Fusion had his cell phone speaker on.

"You can leave in the morning."

"Back to Lansing?"

"Yeah, maybe we'll catch a congressman with his pants down."

"Isn't that their default?" No answer. "So, what you doing tonight?"

"That bar north of the capital."

"Have one for me."

"See you tomorrow afternoon."

"Late afternoon. I'll need to stop for a nap on my way back."

Guzzo listened a little longer, heard only a fart, took off the earphones, and packed the parabolic microphone away. Knowing the Fusion man was alone made things easier. In the morning, as soon as the Fusion left, he'd finish. For now, he'd rest.

In another hotel room, two men sat watching a rerun of *The Godfather*. Both were beefy, one wearing a sleeveless tee shirt, the other a Chicago Cubs tee shirt.

"To bad they didn't have a Charger at Midway," said the man in the Cubs tee shirt.

"Short notice," said the man in the sleeveless, fiddling with his iPhone.

"Our mark gets his Camry and we end up with a Lincoln."

"Camry's popular, good resale. This one was like knew underneath when I was down in the garage hanging the GPS."

The man in the Cubs tee shirt continued staring at the television during commercials. "Think our mark's here to do the Greek's daughter?"

"All we're supposed to do is watch for names."

"Yeah, I got the list memorized. Cavallo, Polenkaya, Zolotarev, Weizman. Put your damn phone down. It's the scene with the horse's head."

Outside the window of the Greektown Casino Hotel it was dark and quiet.

Morning. Niki gathering baggage for her journey. A family album had shots of baby Damon in her mother's lap. Her mother gone ten years from breast cancer, her brother murdered two years ago. Damon had gotten curious about Dad's CCC stint, visited the CCC museum at Higgins Lake, and gone out for a few beers only to be stabbed by a local drunk.

Niki's original plan was to limit herself to computer, notes, and a few changes of clothes. But maybe after meeting with Lazlo Horvath she'd take a road trip west, visit the Green River Historical Society to meet the woman she spoke with on the phone. After everything was stacked near the door, after recalling the deaths of her husband, father, mother, and Damon, she decided packing the photo album might be a sign it was time to let go, move away from Greektown.

Armed with several water bottles and her keys, Niki unlocked the apartment door. On her way down the stairs to retrieve her van from the garage she heard pots and pans in the first floor kitchen. The restaurant morning crew. Theo, the buxom day shift supervisor, would be in charge. In the corner of the first floor landing, she saw a light bulb box. She kicked it, thinking it was empty. When it flipped she saw a bulb inside. Theo providing an energy efficient bulb to replace the dull one in the ceiling. It would be brighter, making is safer on the stairs.

As Niki turned to step off for the final flight, a door flew open, banging against the wall. With water bottles under one arm, she grabbed the railing with her free hand.

The black Ford Fusion parked in view of the building's side entrance was running, telltale steam from its exhaust. The man inside on the phone. The new trainee dishwasher, a brash African American young man hired by Theo the morning before, eyed the Fusion coming back from the dumpster. He told his trainer, a Greek boy from the neighborhood, the Fusion driven by the "poe" would look "cramazing" with a good set of wheels.

"What the hell's poe mean?"

"Fuzz, man. Plain clothes."

"You wanna work here? Learn English."

The trainee pushed through the door with garbage bags. "Hell should I learn English?"

A water bottle tumbled down the stairs. The woman up the stairs was whiter than Theo the manager.

"Didn't mean to scare you, lady. New here. Takin' out trash."

He pushed through the side door with the bags and held it open for her. She retrieved the water bottle, thanked him, and hurried toward a garage across the alley. On his way back from the dumpster the dishwasher saw the Fusion pull out and drive away.

The previous night the side entrance was so dark Guzzo knew the Fusion agent hadn't seen him. The dumpster near the door helped. He'd placed the new bulb on the first landing and confirmed the maintenance room was unlocked with the rickety stepladder inside. At dawn he was ready, wearing gray workman coveralls and lightweight tactical boots. When the Fusion pulled away he left his room, taking the guest elevator to the basement, then the service elevator back to the main floor and the Casino Hotel's back exit.

The Caravan was at the side entrance, sliding side door open and seats folded into the floor. As Niki began her second trip down the stairs, she heard a door slam. When she turned the corner she expected to see the African American boy, but he was neither in the stairwell nor outside at the dumpster. She unloaded her things into the van and turned in time to see Theo come out the side entrance. Theo held the door open for her.

"What's the maintenance man for?" asked Theo, adjusting a bra strap.

"What maintenance man?"

"He was in the stairwell. I ask what he wants and he smiles. I ask again and he says you called him. Something about the furnace."

"I didn't call about the furnace. Where'd he go?"

Theo shrugged and adjusted her other bra strap. "I don't know. He was right here a minute ago, smiling like hell."

Niki glanced up the stairwell. "Theo, did you get new light bulbs for the stairwell?"

"The stairwell? We've got enough work in the kitchen. You should come see the mess they left last night." Theo headed for the door to the kitchen.

"Wait, Theo."

"What?"

"Can you wait here a minute? I've got to carry another load down and you could open the door for me."

"You want that new kid to help? I'll send him out."

"Sure, okay. I could use help so I don't have to make more trips."

"Or risk falling down stairs that aren't up to code."

When the African American boy followed her up the stairs she had a momentary thought, him watching her ass in jeans. After they'd retrieved the remaining boxes and got back to the van she felt guilty for having thought the boy was watching her ass because he was so damn polite, commenting on her "cool van" when she hit the automatic sliding door button.

She buckled her seat belt, thought about the light bulb on the stair landing again, and turned the rearview mirror lower so she could see the entire van floor. Nothing except the detritus of her life. She turned into the street and heard the van's automatic door lock click.

Back at the side entrance, the African American boy came out with his final load of garbage bags. Rather than the door slamming as it usually did, another door inside slammed and the tall muscular man in coveralls peeked out. When the man seemed satisfied the boy was hidden from view behind the lifted dumpster lid, he hurried out toward the street and around the corner where the red Dodge Caravan was making a right turn two blocks away.

The morning after the phone call with Niki Gianakos, Janos called. Their flight had arrived and they'd stay where they were at least two days. Janos and Mariya in New York, doing their own investigating before coming his way. New phone numbers. After the call Lazlo programmed both into his phone.

At noon Lazlo went out to his Civic parked down the street. He started it and let it run a while. As he sat there, another old man from the neighborhood pulled alongside and motioned to him, the man searching for a parking spot. Lazlo shook his head to let the man know he wasn't leaving. After the old man a new black SUV passed slowly. The windows darkly tinted, maybe a local young man with money to burn. He expected the window to lower, another inquiry about his parking spot. But the SUV continued down the street, turning the corner at the end of the block. The SUV must not have been running long judging by steam out its tailpipe. After it turned the corner Lazlo could not see the SUV but could see its steam. Perhaps it was something, perhaps not. Lazlo knew he was overly suspicious, especially at times like this when someone else is involved. Niki Gianakos, he liked the name.

At three in the afternoon Lazlo realized he'd skipped lunch and munched on cheese and crackers. At 4:30, a half-hour after Niki said she'd call, he decided he'd go to the Lincoln Oasis. He opened his closet, pulled down his gun case, took his keys out and opened the case. Inside was his .38 revolver. Last time he used it was at the range. He stared at it a moment, checked to see it was loaded, then locked it back in its case and returned it to the shelf. He made sure his cell phone ringer was set on high, and went down to his car.

Rush hour traffic, no black SUV, and no other vehicle following his meandering route. Lincoln Oasis west bound, 6:30, an hour and a half after Niki was to have called. He went in, used the men's room, then sat in the open food court sipping a Starbucks coffee.

Time dragged, large trucks passing beneath the oasis overpass rumbled from below. Caffeine made his heart race. He purchased a large bottle of water and sipped that. He watched people parade in and out of the oasis, almost everyone stopping at restrooms before moving on to the food court. Men, women, and children of all shapes and nationalities. Lazlo thought this is how society finishes, everyone on the move, escaping something, searching for something. He couldn't help thinking of this woman named Niki. The sound of her voice played over and over.

This morning he'd showered and put on a freshly laundered red shirt and blue jeans. Perhaps he should have worn a green tie. Yes, that would be appropriate for a Gypsy. Blue jeans, red shirt, green tie, and his blue jacket. Fool.

Because of all the coffee, he needed the men's room again. The phone rang while he stood at the urinal. He finished up, fumbled for the phone, stood at the row of sinks, the men his age on either side eyeing him.

"Yes, it's Lazlo."

"Sorry I'm late."

"Where are you?"

"I'm at the oasis. It's a long story. I'm not sure what I should do."

"Can we meet this evening?"

"Yes, give me an address. Perhaps a restaurant near you."

"We can meet right now." The men who'd been at the sinks were at the wall-mounted hand dryers that sounded like jets on takeoff. They eyed him in the mirror on their way out. When the dryers stopped, he said, "I'm sorry, the noise. I'm in the men's room."

"Well, I have to draw the line somewhere. I'm not coming into the men's room."

There are moments in life in tune with the universe. Moments when God—if he or she or some sort of essence exists—reaches out to adjust brain synapses exactly so. Such moments can occur any time or place—a quiet hideaway, lights turned low, or pushing through the door of a brightly lit tollway oasis men's room, serenaded by an extremely loud toilet flush.

Because Niki also wore blue jeans, red blouse, a blue jacket, and had white hair—but mostly because of her eyes—this became one of those moments. She reminded Lazlo of Olympia Dukakis in *Moonstruck*. Was the bedazzled look on her face because of their wardrobe match, or something else? A coffee grinder whined at Starbucks, a kid took an order at Sbarros, another flush blasted out as a young woman exited the women's room across from the men's room.

They sat at a small food court table in front of the Sbarro kiosk. Rather than carrying a purse, Niki carried an oblong green wallet stuffed with dog-eared notes. She placed her phone atop her wallet on the table. The top two buttons of her red blouse were unbuttoned, revealing a sliver of smooth skin below her neck, lips, nose, and dark blue eyes. Those eyes, staring at him, took him momentarily away from the Lincoln Oasis with long haul diesels rumbling below. They were on a journey, perhaps a Mediterranean cruise, sitting in a restaurant. Soon they'd dock in Niki's homeland. Although her given name was Angela, she said to call her Niki. Not long ago she was only a voice, now she was here, sitting across from Lazlo, the moonstruck fool.

"I drove here because I was worried when you didn't call."

"There was a new boy at the restaurant," said Niki. "He acted like he needed to protect me even though we'd never met. I kept thinking I was being followed. I exited the interstate several times. When I stopped for lunch I thought a man was watching. He left the restaurant at the same time and got on the interstate behind me. I drove slowly until he passed. I was also nervous about coming here. Roadblocks trying to investigate my father's death and speaking with Jacobson have changed my life. What about you? How did you come to this investigation?"

Lazlo told about Janos and Mariya, what they'd gone through during the Chernobyl trafficking investigation. He told about Doctor Marta Adamivna Voronko and Janos' sister Sonia being Doctor Marta's lover. He summarized Doctor Marta's research concerning the death of her father, Bela Voronko, and her grandfather with the same name.

"Doctor Marta and I shared emails." Niki paused, glanced around the food court. "Dad was happy. He was on the committee responsible for reviving Greektown. He owned a restaurant, hired a wonderful manager, and life was good. He loved doing odd jobs. For him to fall off the roof was simply impossible.

"After the funeral I began investigating. I dragged out everything my mother packed away before she died. Among the boxes was one containing letters and papers from Dad's CCC days. I have a Pictorial Review booklet of Camp Manila. All the men in camp at the time were listed. I tried contacting the ones from Dad's barracks. I remember him bringing up guys in the barracks when he was being feisty. In the early days of the restaurant when a hood wanted payola, he'd mention the guys from Barracks Three.

"Anyway, when I tried contacting the men, a pattern emerged. Doctor Marta Voronko in Ukraine was also searching for information about the deaths of CCC men and relatives. Not simply that men and relatives died, but that the ones who died in recent years had so-called accidents, or suicides, something violent. The last one was a man named Paul Fontaine in Sun City, outside Phoenix. In his nineties and he hangs himself from a balcony after knifing his wife. I spoke with a daughter and son. Both said it made no sense. Their dad would never do such a thing. Just like my dad would never go up on the roof to lay down some tar and accidentally fall."

"Your brother also died?"

"A brawl outside a bar. Yes, he was interested in Dad's CCC days, but they caught the murderer who drove off. The guy's in prison. It could have been my brother ended up in prison."

It had gotten dark outside. Beyond Niki, to one side of the Sbarro kiosk through ceiling to floor windows, oncoming westbound headlights and receding eastbound taillights were visible.

"It's been a long day," said Lazlo. "Perhaps we should eat something."

They ate spinach stromboli from the Sbarro kiosk and drank tea from Starbucks. Lazlo watched as Niki ate, and he saw she watched him, smiling occasionally when she used her napkin to capture a stray string of melted cheese. When they finished eating they sipped tea.

"Do you have an idea where I should stay tonight?" asked Niki.

"My God, I didn't arrange for a room. We can easily find one on the north side. A hotel near me on Milwaukee Avenue. We could go there and—"

Niki interrupted by reaching across the table and placing her hand on his. "Lazlo, we're old enough. Do you have room at your place?"

"I...I have a single bedroom but I often sleep on the sofa."

Niki stood. "We should be going."

Lazlo walked her to a red Dodge Caravan. He pointed out his Civic across the nearly empty parking lot.

"I'll follow you," she said. "But first, may I hug you?"

Lazlo was aware of taking a deep breath. "Oh yes, please."

While packing his gear to check out of the Casino Hotel, Guzzo received a text from Pescatore. The code phrase "born again" along with the phrase "loaves and fishes." The former meant there'd been a change in plans, calling off the job he was on. The latter meant he was to meet with Pescatore the next afternoon at the fish market for a new assignment.

On Interstate 94 heading west, he drove into the sunset. In Indiana he was caught in a massive nighttime traffic jam with construction lane closures. Because the Camry had satellite radio he was able to relax listening to new age music. No sense trying to find an alternate route in the notorious Indiana funnel at the bottom of Lake Michigan. When he finally crossed the state line into Illinois, Guzzo noticed the Camry was low on fuel. He didn't want to exit where he would have to drive blocks off the expressway. It was easier to exit at the first oasis on the Illinois Tollway and fill his tank. The Camry got good mileage; the gauge would still read full when he returned the car at Midway Airport. Although there had been lines of trucks slowing traffic in Indiana, here in Illinois there was no construction.

At the Lincoln Oasis gas station he swiped the credit card he used on assignment and began filling the tank. Brightly colored food court vendor signs lit the place. Because of the time involved dropping off the rental, taking the shuttle to the terminal to get his own car, then the drive home, he should eat something.

At the far end of oasis parking lot, a man and woman walked together across the lot. The sound of gas flowing into the Camry's tank along with the chatter of a nearby idling semi created a strange feeling. Guzzo wondered if the second sight he spoke of to Vera was in play. Vera in the kitchen at this very moment filling a water glass at the sink.

The oasis restaurant parking lot was at least an eighth mile away. Guzzo squinted at the pair. They paused at the rear of a minivan and hugged. Again, he thought of Vera. Perhaps she also thought of him. By the time the Camry was full, the man in the distance had gone to another vehicle in the lot. Soon a small car and the van drove onto the entrance ramp and sped away. Guzzo wondered if he'd witnessed a lovers' rendezvous. He recalled Niki Gianakos had a minivan, a red Dodge Caravan like the one that drove off. Yes, the Dodge Caravan was a common vehicle, but still…

No matter. Guzzo pulled the receipt from the gas pump, tucked it into his pocket, and got into the Camry. Instead of getting back on the tollway, he drove slowly over to the overpass oasis building thinking Chinese food would taste good after the Greek food he'd had in Detroit. He'd order carryout, take something to Vera. At home he'd discover not only was he thinking of her, she was thinking of him. Second sight, everything in life and in death, second sight.

The two in the white Lincoln were still in Indiana, following trucks in the dark.

The driver pounded the steering wheel. "I hate this goddamn traffic."

The passenger stared at his iPhone screen. "He's stopped ahead at the oasis."

"All he's going to do is go back to Midway and pick up his car. Hope he does something interesting next trip out of town. And again, this car is boring."

"You and your Hemis."

CHAPTER 19

Dry hot workday, 1939. Dust plumes as men jump from trucks. Barracks, showers, and mess hall. Rock-calloused hands half-clenched as they stand in chow line. Even powder monkeys usually first in line linger like dumb eggs, brains sun-boiled. Could be another reason for listlessness, especially for Barracks Three. LEMs eyeballing Sal, turning with sour faces when he walks by.

Heat late in the day slow-motioned the camp. At mess, tables normally filled were near empty. Four men sat together at the table farthest from chow line, eating listlessly.

Nick Gianakos: "Bela, you give haircuts. What's Sal say while you're cutting his?"

Bela Voronko: "Warnings not to nip ears."

Jimmy Phillips: "Nothing about Henry?"

George Minkus: "Or what he does outside the barracks at night?"

Bela: "Nothing."

George: "Carl the LEM says he's leaving camp for good because Sal blows his wig."

Nick: "Not only with us, or LEMs. Scuttlebutt's the Superintendent's paid off."

Bela: "Anything from you, Jimmy?"

Jimmy: "I wrote Henry's mom. He never got home. I heard in the administration staff meeting a girl from Rock Springs came home bloodied. A minister drove down to talk to the superintendent."

George: "What the hell should we do, Bela?"

Jimmy: Yeah, Bela. You said you had experience with bad eggs over there."

Bela: "A boy who grew up near Zhitomer. His family, starved by Stalin's famine, moved to our village. He had a little sister who did not come with them. Somewhere along the way the boy discovered that, during the famine, his parents pickled his sister in a jar."

The chewing stopped.

George: "You're grifting us."

Bela: "The boy may have seen the jar. He may have eaten. He could not be trusted, especially with girls. One girl from the village disappeared, then another, no bodies found. One day, when he approached a girl much younger, we—How do you say?— intercepted."

Silence.

Bela: "We were not proud of our actions. Yet we knew it must be done. He was a poor swimmer. We set him afloat in the river."

Jimmy: "You mean you—?"

Bela: "Better you not say it. Something was done and not spoken of in the village. I'm sorry if I shock you. Understand, we all agreed."

George: "You think a guy like Sal the Stiletto would—"

Nick: "Sal thinks he can do anything. A guy in my crew got a pep pill from him."

Jimmy: "What can we do?"

Bela: "We watch him."

Jimmy: "If he does something, will you take over?"

Bela: "If a decision is made, it must be unanimous."

Tables near the four began filling, a few slid in at the other end of theirs. The senior Barracks Two leader came over and whispered to Jimmy, who nodded approval. The Barracks Two leader went to the front near the chow line, whistled for attention, and announced that because of the heat dinner would be extended a half-hour. He also reminded everyone to drink plenty and pointed out an extra jug of lemonade being carried in by the mess crew.

At a table near the chow line, Sal laughed loudly as he grabbed a glass of lemonade from the guy across from him. The young men at Sal's table ate quickly, took their trays to the dump table, got some lemonade and, although they were obviously tired, did not sit back down.

Salvatore Cavallo sat in his living room that night. Francesca had gone to dinner with a crony and was already in the bedroom with the door closed and the radio on. Cavallo could hear the radio through the closed door. Earlier it had been an FDR fireside chat, after that swing music, now longhair stuff.

Uncle Rosario called earlier, asking Cavallo again to talk sense into Little Sal; he'd been trouble according to both the boys and the paid off CCC district officer. The boys were supposed to pick Sal up and put him on a phone. Cavallo told Francesca before she closed the bedroom door he was expecting an important call on the new business line. A while ago he phoned Lonzo next door and asked him to come over for a drink.

Lonzo wore his usual suit and tie, but not his driving hat. Lonzo sat across from Cavallo, the small table containing bourbon, two glasses, and the telephone between them. He and Lonzo toasted to nothing. It was good bourbon. Rather than slug it down, they sipped.

"I don't know what to do," said Cavallo.

"You want I should go there?"

"We got four boys there now. Has he ever done what you told him?"

"Only time was when your uncle was around."

"And now my uncle's on my ass wanting me to do something."

"Maybe he should get on the phone with Little Sal."

"Maybe," said Cavallo. "I don't mind taking over when it comes to business. Dealing with Little Sal's different."

"I understand," said Lonzo.

When the phone rang, Cavallo let it ring.

"You want I should get it?" asked Lonzo.

"Yeah, when you do, let the boys know I ain't happy. Tell 'em to put Sal on and maybe you can warn him I ain't happy before you give it to me."

Lonzo nodded and answered the phone.

"This is Lonzo."

"Look, the boss ain't happy. Put him on with me first."

"Sal? Yeah, it's Lonzo."

"Not so good."

"I mean not so good because you ain't doin' your uncle or your old man any good."

"Look, kid, we been through a lot and I gotta tell you something."

"Don't smart-ass me. I'm trying to do you some good!"

Listening to one side of the conversation was the shits. Cavallo grabbed the phone.

"Sal, you goddamn shit! I want listening on your end."

"All right. I'm listening."

"You been fighting."

"So?"

"I'm not finished! You're supposed listen!"

"Okay, okay."

"I got four boys out there watching your punk ass! Uncle Rosario's pissed! You got that?"

"Yeah."

"So, here it is. One more complaint, I'm gonna have a hell of a time convincing Uncle Rosario not to send some of his boys to replace my boys. You get what I'm talkin' about?...Yeah, don't answer. You know what I'm talkin' about. We got men at camp paid off. We got our boys out there. Quit the goddamn fighting. Sew some normal wild oats. You got free time, especially on weekends. The boys'll let you use a car. Your mom ain't here so I can talk about wild oats, Sal. Be a goddamn normal kid for a change!"

No answer.

"You understand me?"

"Yeah, I understand."

"You remember the blood oath? Plenty of others'd like to be in your shoes. Some still in the old country dealing with Mussolini. This is family. You're our future. Look good out there so you can take over the family business and make it legit. You'll have all the luxuries, and all the women you can handle. You got me?"

"Okay. Yeah, Pop, I got you."

It was two in the morning when the Buick Century Sport Coupe drove out of the CCC camp. After putting Little Sal on the horn with Big Sal the night before, the kid demanded wild oats. The others got the word and brought two Rock Spring whores to Dutch John lodge. While the four played cards outside with the radio turned up, the kid had his way with the whores. One ended up with a split lip, the other had some hair pulled out. Both insisted they be driven back to Rock Springs.

"I'll be glad when this job's over," said the driver.

"We're lucky he didn't kill one of those dames," said the passenger after the overhead light in the CCC camp was well behind them.

"I took his stiletto and cleared the bedroom before he went in. He would have slugged them with a hairbrush if there'd been one."

"We should let the old man know he's a psycho."

"Yeah? Who's going to do that?"

"You see the wad of hair he pulled out of that broad's head?"

"Manny'll give her extra."

"If it wasn't for the rest of us being there and hearing the screams—"

"He's hotsquat material."

"What's that?"

"An ordinary Joe would've been fried in the chair by now."

"Is Manny still gonna let him use their car?"

"It's what the boss says."

On the dark road ahead, a couple horses appeared around a bend. The horses ran off when the driver hit the brakes.

"There's those wild horses again," said the passenger.

"Yeah," said the driver. "Wild horses."

Fifty miles north, all was quiet in Green River except for the Ford Model T Runabout with Pickup Body rattling down the street with its load of morning papers. When the runabout passed beneath a streetlight a headline on the top bundle was visible. "Jewish Refugee Ship Denied Port in Florida." As the runabout headed up the street, its one working taillight blinked on and off.

The marquee of the Green River movie house was dark. The last feature ended hours earlier. Because of the faint glow from the nearby streetlight, the large black letters against white were visible. "Next Week, *Mr. Deeds Goes to Town*, starring Gary Cooper and Jean Arthur."

On a side street in town Rose Buckles was awake, thinking of her upcoming date with the boy named Salvatore from the Manila camp. She met him at the Arrowhead in Rock Springs when she got a ride from her girlfriend. Salvatore Cavallo, a romantic name like in the movies. Maybe he was involved with gangsters like her girlfriend said. So what? The main thing was she'd go out with a guy with a car and money for a change. Maybe the Arrowhead and maybe one of those dance clubs. After that, who knows?

Of course he'd realize it was a first date between the two of them, so she'd have to lay down the law. After all, she wouldn't be 21 for a couple years. But she wasn't a glass of milk either, and it sure would be hotsy-totsy to get into practice for when the right guy came along.

A week later the weather cooled, and so, it seemed, had tempers. Even Sal Cavallo's. Paul Fontaine, the mapmaker from South Carolina, said the situation was like the plantations. "Don't you all know? He's the plantation owner's son and we're his niggers. Boss makes like his boy's working, but really he ain't. He gets trucked anywhere he wants on work days, mostly north to the towns in Wyoming for a cool beer."

Each evening at dinner, the Four Horsemen of the Apocalypse, as Nick had dubbed them, sat at their table in the far corner of the mess. The proclamation was made the previous week when it was still hotter than hell. Nick announced he, being Greek, was War, Jimmy, the Big Apple, was Conquest, George was Famine, and Bela was Death.

The other guys from Barracks Three asked if they could join them. The four said yeah, especially tonight because, instead of sneaking out after lights out, Sal had taken off from the job site and wasn't on the truck back to camp. There were rumors of him going AWOL, and good riddance. As the four spoke with one another, the others from Barracks Three leaned in close.

Nick: "Did the guys in the Buick pick him up?"

Jimmy: "It was a Buick. But this time two different guys in the black Buick four-door."

George: "He's a mob kid with protection."

Jimmy: "It figures. I got a closer look this time. New York plates. And when Sal got into the back seat, I seen him holding up a suit on a hanger."

Nick: "What should we do?"

Bela: "Nothing. Perhaps he's gone."

Nick: "I hope so."

George: "What about Henry? Anything more about him?"

Jimmy: "I called his mom again. Hasn't shown up and she's plenty worried."

Bela: "Do you recall the weekend after Henry was gone?"

Jimmy: "What about it?"

Bela: "The work crew from Barracks Two said they found a dead horse in the canyon."

Nick: "What's that got to do with Henry?"

Bela: "Do you remember what the work crew said about horse's remains?"

George: "Too much blood and guts for one horse. They found a boot and laughed it up saying the horse wore boots."

Jimmy: "This is nuts."

It was late, Rose Buckles still in Rock Springs. Sure, she liked having a highball at the Arrowhead. Maybe two. She liked Billie Holiday singing "Summertime" on the jukebox lit up in the dark corner. But Salvatore didn't seem to hear the song and kept jabbering through it. Saying things about country gals searching for guys with money and wondering if that was her plan. Not that she was surprised. Going out with him was a way to show friends and family in Green River she could do what she wanted.

When "Summertime" ended she tried small talk, telling Salvatore the story about Marco Polo discovering fishermen in Arabia drying fish and hammering them with rocks to feed their cattle. He didn't flinch or smile. Instead of commenting he turned to her and pointed out the new moustache he was growing. Even in the darkened bar she could see it was still peach fuzz.

After a quick bar hamburg, which tasted like horse meat compared to the day-old bread slugburgers at the Green River Café, a cop came in. Instead of eyeballing her and the second highball, the cop looked over the two guys watching Salvatore. The guys were beneath one of the few ceiling lights and the cop went over to them. After a gab the cop left the place while putting something into his pocket. Rose wondered if she should have said something. *Hey, mister. I accepted a date with this guy and I don't think I like him. Could you give me a ride home?*

She wished they were at one of the lit tables, especially when Salvatore started talking about New York, saying there were a lot of niggers and kikes who wished he'd never been born because he "Beat the livin' shit out of 'em." Maybe it was the straight bourbons talking, maybe not. His voice went up in volume, more people looking sideways at him in the dark. Rose held her purse on her lap, ready to either leave, or, if necessary, slug him with it. She carried a canyon rock in the bottom for exactly this reason.

A little before midnight, when she could no longer take being part of Salvatore's barroom sideshow, she told him she was expected home. He finished his last bourbon, had some water, took a pill from his pocket, downed it, and escorted her out the door. In the parking lot there was some hubbub about one car blocking another, the hoods who'd given the cop a payoff involved. Salvatore laughed like a hyena, told her to hurry into the Buick, and sped out.

During the drive back toward Green River, he slowed down and said how beautiful she was and how he liked her dress and her shoes and especially her hair. He went on and on, saying he never saw anyone so beautiful, not even in New York. He popped another pill. When she asked what kind of pill, he said aspirin for his headache.

He was quiet a while, then reached over and put his hand on her thigh, bunching the skirt up in his hand like it's in the way and her thigh's his wedge of pie. Rose had been here before and knew how to smile as she pushed his hand away.

When they passed the Firehole Canyon sign and continued heading toward Green River she felt better. But then, as Green River lights appeared, he slammed the brakes and turned south onto a dusty side road toward the river, the top of the canyon, the necking rock. He pulled off the road at the canyon edge. When he stopped but left the engine running she figured to convince him to turn around and go back to the highway. If not, maybe she'd get out and make tracks. It wasn't that far to the highway. She'd been here before and knew her way around.

The dash lights glowed on his face, making him into a comic book shadow. She pointed out the windshield. "The moon sets in the afternoon now. My mom keeps track of it. With no moon the stars are sure bright, aren't they?"

Silence. She rolled down her window and felt a slight breeze off the canyon. She recalled this was the spot she and her girlfriends skinny-dipped down in the river the summer before. He put his hand on her thigh again, same place, moving her dress hem higher.

"I really should be getting home, Salvatore."

The air was fresh compared to the bar. She wished they were still there with other people. What about the men she thought were keeping an eye on Salvatore? She looked back for another car but saw nothing but rocks, scrub, and high desert plateau against the stars.

"It's got to be after midnight, Salvatore. My mom will be looking for me. She might even get my uncle to give her a ride and—"

"And what?" His voice was loud like back in the bar.

"They'll be driving around looking for me. My uncle comes down this road a lot because he knows it's a favorite spot for guys with cars to take their girlfriends."

He let go of her leg. She pulled down her dress hem. "Can we go now? It's our first date and maybe if we go out again—"

"I got me a brand new suit." His voice was low, serious. "And how about this car? I don't go through this much trouble for other girls. They mostly come to me. Here I am, putting myself out for a gal like you and—"

"Please. Take me home now."

He reached out and shut off the lights and engine. His voice changed, the hint of a phony southwestern cowboy accent. "Well maybe I'll do just that. But first we should get out and take a gander at the canyon in starlight."

He got out on his side, came around to her side, reached into the open window and opened the door. "Just in case you all locked me out."

She got out. They'd look at the stars a while, maybe hug and kiss a little, and she'd insist he take her home. He held her hand tightly as they stared at the stars. "I sure am grateful, ma'am, for us being able to share this moment."

The way he spoke made her nervous. "You don't even know me."

He stepped around and faced her, grasping her arms, his face a shadow against the stars. "Don't be a jelly bean. Come on, we'll walk down in the canyon a little."

When she paused, he pulled her forward, "I forgot to mention the reason for us meeting tonight. You see, I realize now, I really love your hair."

"My hair?"

"Yes ma'am. I love your hair so much it gives me butterflies. Here, let me hold it."

"Okay, one kiss. Then I really have to—"

He was on her before she could react. They fell to the ground. She tried to roll away but he flattened her onto rock and dust. The light from the stars made him into a shadow. He pulled something from his pocket and suddenly a blade reflected starlight. When she sat up to scream his hand covered her mouth and she felt it, an intense burning at the side of her belly that took her wind out. His other hand had both her arms locked behind.

He spun her around and threw her back down. Something metal clattered on rock. "Nothing personal, Rose. I need to satisfy my desires."

One hand up her dress, his other hand grasping her hair. The burning at the side of her belly weakened her and she felt the warmth of blood. She screamed and the canyon echoed it back. Somehow he got his trousers down and ripped off her underwear. He entered her. His moves in and out were mechanical. She didn't want it to be like this. Not the first time like this! He lifted her hips from the ground, one hand clenching her buttocks, the other pulling her hair.

She tried hitting him, harder and harder, but he held on. If only she'd brought her purse with the canyon rock from the car. The purse that was between them when he first reached over. Thinking about hitting him with her purse gave strength to her arms and she swung hard, like when she was a kid playing baseball with the boys. Harder and harder until he let go.

She crawled away, stumbled up to the car, reached into the open window, turned in time to see him coming for her, and swung the purse in a wide arc. It smashed him in the head and put him to the ground.

He struggled to get up and went down on hands and knees. She staggered back to the car, holding her hot belly. When it seemed he'd given up, a growl emerged from deep inside and he launched himself at her. He pulled her hair and kept pulling. She fell away but he pulled her so hard by her hair she was lifted from the ground. Pulling and pulling at her hair. Him growling and screaming. The words "I just love your hair!" screamed out. The taste of grit and rock, her face driven into the ground, pounded into the ground as he pulled her hair again and again. Finally, the stars were gone as if they'd followed the moon below the horizon. The pain in her belly was gone, leaving nothing but her head feeling it was being blown to pieces.

Cletus Minch fell in love with fishing gear while working at the hardware store and managed to buy himself a fly rod and reel and the gear to make artificial flies. His prize possession was the leather-trimmed creel basket he got from an old timer named Jake who said he was too old to fish and wanted the creel to go to someone who'd appreciate it.

On fishing mornings Cletus would find a lunch packed by his mom in the icebox. Sometimes sandwiches were made with trout from his last fishing trip, sometimes jam. That morning he could tell by the absence of fish odor his mom had used jam. He packed the lunch in his creel and headed off. The half moon wouldn't rise until after sunrise, but once away from the few lights in town, starlight was good enough.

He passed his old fishing spots from when he was younger and lacked proper boots. At first, shale along the east side of the gorge was loose, making his trek along the river noisy. Eventually the ground stabilized where he knew it would. Near a familiar boulder he saw the gray light of dawn. Some locals called it the necking rock. It was only a mile south of the highway, a favorite pull-off for the handful of boys his age who had access to a car or truck. No such luck for him. With his father out of work, and his mother doing laundry for neighbors, and especially because they lacked ranch land, Cletus knew they chose to have only one son, and no way would they ever be able to afford a car.

Cletus tried a few spots where there were stepping-stones into the river, at first using a junk fly to get his rhythm. At daylight he'd get serious, fill his creel with wet moss, and catch some fish. Getting home by noon with enough cool fish for the week would help feed his family. Plus this summer a few of the neighbors had begun purchasing fish from his mother.

When it was light enough he sat on a boulder, opened his fly box, and selected one of his favorites constructed on the proper hook size. It was reddish-brown except for the purple hackle and yellow wings. He took his time, listening to the river while he fiddled with his gear. The sun would rise behind him in the east and he looked out at boulders he could see lodged in the river bottom. He never went out so deep his high-tops would get soaked. Someday he'd be able to afford the waders he'd been eyeing at the store. Yep, one of these days he'd be standing out there in the middle of the river like the old timer who gave him the creel. He'd have bought the old man's waders but, according to the old man, "Not worth patching anymore."

When the sun finally peeked over the east edge of the gorge and lit up the west side, Cletus saw the shadow of the necking rock above the far shore. The red rock reflected in the undulation of the river, mixing reds into greens and blues. As it got brighter he spotted a patch of moss behind a boulder cluster to the south. Among the boulders was one on which he'd chiseled his initials, *CM*, at the beginning of summer to mark one of his favorite spots. He got up and walked to the moss patch. It looked like green moss had died, turning reddish brown. But as he got closer he realized it wasn't moss. Maybe some other vegetation, maybe something fibrous he could use to make a fly. It wasn't until he bent to pick it up that he realized it was hair. He pulled some hair from the moss, holding the strands up to the light of the rising sun. More red than brown, maybe a red he'd seen somewhere. Maybe the color of yarn they had at the hardware store. When he pulled more hair from the moss, something came with it. At first he thought it might be a slug or part of a lizard or fish that had gotten tangled.

Then he saw something else. Near the hair, near what looked like fish or lizard guts, down beneath the lapping water line—He dropped the hair, jumped back. He dropped his pole. He heard himself gasp. "No!" He stumbled back to the boulder on which he'd been sitting earlier. "No!"

Frank Grogan, the elderly Green River sheriff, had an office at the back of the town hall the size of a closet. The cell in one corner was a flat-barred cube that could hold four men if they all stood. Frank's desk was held up by an ancient treadle sewing machine stand. When he was a young sheriff decades earlier after he left the Army following the Spanish-American war, he built a box where the sewing machine had been. He put on a larger top with a lift-up pad-locked door in order to have a safe place to store ammunition. On the wall was a map of the town, a map of the gorge down to the Utah line, and a photograph of him looking like a schoolboy.

Frank always got into the office early. Nothing else to do since his wife passed. First stop was the café for coffee and eggs, then to the office for a nap, then maybe another trip back to the café to fill his thermos. He sat on a pillow on his wooden chair, propped his feet on his desk and was about to take his morning nap, staring at the grainy photograph of himself as a schoolboy, when the door flung open and the boy himself stumbled inside, breathless.

The schoolboy held a whip. Frank stood, grasping the pain in his chest, closed his eyes, held himself up with both hands on his desk, listening to his gasps for breath and to the boy's gasps for breath. He wanted to tell the boy to go ahead and whip him like a wild horse because he figured the ghost of his past whoring and drinking before coming out west had returned to take him back east to the war. But then the pain in his chest subsided, and the boy spoke.

"Sheriff Grogan!"

"What the hell, boy? Is that you, Cletus? I thought I'd died!"

"Sheriff!"

"Calm down! Calm down. Catch your breath."

The whip was actually the boy's fly rod. His creel had swung around to his back, the strap pressing on the boy's neck. He was wet from head to toe and it looked like he threw up on his shirt.

"What the hell, Cletus? You go swimmin' this morning instead of fishin'?"

"I...I can't understand...I hope I did right!"

"What, boy?"

Cletus shifted his creel from behind his back. "There were vultures. I figured there'd be more, especially later." Cletus came closer and turned his creel to his front, resting it on the desk.

"It's dripping wet, Cletus. I didn't ask for no fish."

"It ain't fish. I didn't know what else to do. There was at least one vulture circling downriver and I didn't know what else to do."

Cletus unbuckled the creel and slowly opened it, looking out the only window in the office. "I didn't want the vultures to get it."

Inside the creel, packed in moss, was a hand cut off above the wrist. A small, delicate, white hand with a pearl ring on one of the swollen fingers.

Frank fell back in his chair, held his chest.

"I hope I did the right thing. There were vultures."

"Yeah, Cletus. You sure did the right thing."

CHAPTER 20

Kiev stakeout dream, militia partners taking turns sleeping, Janos at the wheel, Lazlo in back, dead-end into a red canyon ahead. Janos! The brakes! Lazlo opens his eyes. The sky above buildings across the street tinted red. *Red skies in morning, sailors take warning.*

Wait, he's on the sofa, Niki Gianakos in the bedroom. They arrived last night, driving side streets hunting for parking. When he found a spot he pulled ahead so Niki could take it. After throwing a suitcase and briefcase into the back of his Civic, he found another tighter spot. Niki was surprised having to walk two blocks to his building.

"There are plenty of spots on your street."

"Short-term. A ticket, then the rip-off towing service."

Lazlo recalled a rush of adrenaline when she finished using the bathroom and, wearing plaid pajamas, said goodnight before going into the bedroom and gently closing the door.

They ate breakfast down the street at the Bakery Café. Both wore the same clothes as the night before—red blouse and shirt, blue jeans. Lazlo introduced Niki to Ria telling her they were working a case. Ria smiled knowingly and, on the way back to the window to the kitchen, mumbled, "*Jamais vu*, things to come." The cook, Stella, leaned out and winked. Luckily, Demidchik, the insane Russian, did not show up.

The sun was bright, reflecting off car windows as they walked back to Lazlo's building. A black SUV parked across the street, windows tinted so darkly he could not tell if anyone was inside. Perhaps Homeland Security, FBI, or another agency assigned to keep Jacobson informed.

Back in the apartment they sat at the table outside the kitchen alcove. Niki's cheeks aglow, hair brushed into a bouffant, blue eyes sparkling in the light from the window. She suggested they compare notes and he watched as she went to the bedroom. A few minutes ago he motioned her up the stairs ahead of him. She'd climbed quickly. He'd done the same, subtracting years. When she returned to the table with her briefcase, he said, "You look good in jeans."

She smiled. "So do you. Let's discuss appearances later. We have work to do."

"I'm sorry."

"Don't be sorry."

Niki pulled a dog-eared faded green booklet from the briefcase. "Pictorial Review, Civilian Conservation Corps, Pocatello District, Company 3544, Manila, Utah." The first page had a drawing of a uniformed young man shouldering a pick as if it were a rifle. The second page had a printed message about the booklet being given someone, "Hermione" written in. Following an introduction was another line filled in, "*Erotas*, Nick."

"Hermione was my mother," said Niki. "They met before he went into the CCCs. The way my father signed is frisky of him being that it was 1939." Niki touched the word on the page. "*Erotas* is the modern form of the Greek word *Eros*. There are several ways to express love in ancient Greek. This is the sexy one." Niki glanced to Lazlo and smiled. "You're blushing."

The following page contained certification of the CCC member, the company, camp, date, and commanding officer signature. Next was the district commander's message, photo, and US Army rank. After that several pages with photos of the company commander, inspectors, instructors, surgeons, officers, and local experienced men (LEMs).

"Finally, down to the nitty-gritty," said Niki.

The next group of photos showed young men boarding stake-sided trucks to work sites, moving rock, putting up fences and cattle guards, the interior and exterior of barracks, and, finally, group photos with enrollee name lists.

Niki selected a photo, moved her finger along a row, and stopped. "This is my father. No close-ups, simply part of the group. First time I looked at the photograph years ago I was able to pick him out. He had a great smile."

"I see you in his face, the twinkle in his eyes."

"You obviously want me to blush."

They stared at one another a moment before Niki stood from the table and went to the window. "I need to go to the place my father served, especially after speaking with other survivors. There are things I haven't told you."

After waiting a moment, Lazlo asked, "What things?"

"The research," said Niki. "Others related to Manila CCC men saved strands of hair. The hair obviously came from their time together at camp."

Niki returned to the table, reached into a side pocket, and pulled out a Ziploc bag. Strands of red hair held together by yellowed tape. Lazlo recalled the redhead in the Hopper painting *Nighthawks* and the violinist with red hair he'd killed near the Hungarian and Romanian borders. They were silent a moment, each trying to make connections to the past. *Telepátia* or *déjà vu*?

They went over what they knew, focusing on George Minkus, who died under the bus on North Avenue; his son Buddy, who died in a motorcycle accident; Paul Fontaine, who killed his wife and hung himself in Sun City,

Arizona; Bela Voronko and his son, who both died in single vehicle accidents in Ukraine; Doctor Marta Voronko, recently murdered on an Odessa beach; Sonia Nagy, recently murdered in Kiev; and of course Nick Gianakos, who fell from the roof of his Greektown building.

Eventually they agreed Lazlo should phone George Minkus Junior to see if he knew of his nephew Cory's motorcycle trip, and Niki should phone Jacobson and find out if he has further information.

Lazlo reminded Minkus his brother Buddy died in a motorcycle accident and his nephew was on a similar trip. The phone went dead. When he called back, Minkus said, "Yeah, I hung up. You're a persistent bastard." Minkus gave Lazlo his nephew's cell phone number. "Someone should be able to get hold of him. I don't know why. He's a loner like his old man."

When Niki called Jacobson, he said he was still in Chicago and would meet with them the next afternoon. They sat thinking in silence for a time before Lazlo went to the refrigerator and suggested he make sandwiches for lunch.

"Were you ever married, Lazlo?"

"I had a companion. She became ill. What about you?"

"My husband and I married young. I managed my father's restaurant while my husband worked for Ford. We waited to have children because of strikes. When we tried, we discovered he had prostate cancer. So began years of different therapies. Rather than taking him quickly, cancer made its slow journey to lymph nodes, bones, blood, brain. He was gone mentally before it took him physically."

Niki encouraged Lazlo to speak more of his past. Eventually the story of the violin-playing deserter in the Hungarian-speaking village came out. The redheaded boy pulling a pistol from the violin case and shooting his partner Viktor. Then the rifle, as if on its own, raises and shoots into the boy's head. The wailing women, the father wanting the violin buried with the boy, finding out the grandfather who escaped to America in the early 1900s had red hair, Lazlo being willed the name Gypsy, and finally the phrase, "Boys killing boys."

Lazlo and Niki sat on the sofa. Slowly they both reached out and held hands.

In Rock Springs, Wyoming, off Route 30, a man sat at the wheel of a black SUV outside a truck service shop gate. He was big, wearing a blue windbreaker and Chicago Cubs baseball cap. After a while his partner, wearing a red windbreaker, got into the passenger seat.

"What's up?" asked the driver.

"GPS didn't lie. His Camry's in back."

"You find out where he is?"

"I got a mechanic off to the side. Says our mark's driving a big tow rig down to Vernal, Utah. Something about a cold snap and maybe snow in the mountains overnight."

"Why a tow truck?"

"I can only dance around so much."

"Nothing about Cavallo, Polenkaya, Zolotarev, or Weizman."

"I gave each name a mention. Nothing."

"Guess we drive to Vernal." The driver grimaced as he put the SUV in gear. "Piece of shit Chevy Suburban, 5.3 liter V-8, not enough torque for its weight."

Motoring into Utah from Colorado on US 40 south of Dinosaur National Monument. Elevation 6000 feet, landscape studded with buttes, ridges, and the deep Green River Canyon downriver from the Flaming Gorge Dam.

During the trip on his Harley Davidson Road Glide, Cory Minkus developed a penchant for valleys, mountains, plateaus, and canyons. The ride took him into the setting sun and Vernal, Utah. He filled his tank, bought a sub sandwich and a six-pack of bottles, and pulled into the Best Western Dinosaur Inn. After a hot shower he had a couple beers and his sandwich, then went outside with two more beers to smoke a cigar. Too early in the season for the outdoor pool, so he pulled up a chair at one of the tables, his leather jacket on to ward off the evening chill.

His Road Glide was visible through the fence surrounding the pool, its fenders and tank reflecting pink sky. Halfway through the cigar a tall muscular man in black cargo pants and hooded sweatshirt began eyeballing Cory's bike. His cell phone played "Born to be Wild," the display showing an unfamiliar number. He canceled it, put the phone on the table and took a couple puffs on his cigar. The guy in black still eyeballing his bike. "Born to be Wild" played again and he answered.

"Yeah."

"Cory Minkus? My name is Lazlo Horvath."

"I don't know you."

"I'm an investigator in Chicago looking into the deaths of your grandfather and father. Your uncle gave me your number. I've spoken to men at the Bent Spoke bar and relatives of men originally in the CCC in Manila, Utah. People whose relatives have met with so-called accidents. I hope I'm not being too blunt."

"Uh…yeah…this is quite a coincidence. Manila is up the road. I'll be there tomorrow after I visit a guy in a nursing home."

"A nursing home?"

"It's a long story."

"Can we discuss it?"

Cory stood because the man in black was checking his Road Glide too closely.

"I've been on the road, had a couple beers, and I'm tired. How about tomorrow?"

"I understand. I'll call you tomorrow, say around noon?"

"It's hard answering while I'm riding. I'll call you."

"Around noon?"

"Yeah, noon here is one your time."

"Good. I'll be waiting."

When the man in black straddled Cory's Road Glide, he pocketed his phone and took an empty beer bottle with him.

"Hey!"

The man held his hands palms up like he meant no harm, putting on a broad smile within the sweatshirt hood. "Hey, man. No worries, man."

With his hands held up his sweatshirt sleeves slid down. On his right wrist was a tattoo with the single word, *STORM*.

Cory woke early. He had a headache from last evening's five beers—one long neck going to the smiling guy in black who'd admired his Road Glide—but headache or no, once on the road with the wind in his face, he knew he'd be fine.

He anticipated this morning's ride, not only because he'd end up where his grandfather served in the CCCs, but also because of the scenic loop recommended by the guy in black with the *STORM* tattoo. The guy said he'd been on the Red Cloud Loop hundreds of times, towing cars that went off in hairpins. The guy pointed out his rig across the parking lot, said he was from Wyoming, the last tow leaving him in Vernal where he often stayed over.

"Your tow outfit pays for your room?"

"Hell yes. Better than driving back through the High Uintas Range at night. There's a car off the road on the loop at about 9000 feet I've got to hitch up and take back to Green River. Can't do that at night."

"I was going to take 191 north. Hotel manager says there might be snow at high elevations."

"She doesn't know shit. 191's okay for motor homes. On a bike, I'd take the Red Cloud Loop. West of town you turn north at Dry Fork Canyon. There are signs. I've got a bike myself and the Loop is the way to go, even this time of year."

"What's your bike?"

"An older Sportster 1200."

"Is Red Cloud Loop paved?"

"Mostly, a few gravel sections, but this time of year there's some gravel on 191."

"Okay, guess I'll take the loop."

"You won't be sorry. Maybe we'll run into one another since I'm going that way for my hitch up."

When Cory left the Best Western he saw the tow truck was gone. He rode into downtown Vernal to visit the nursing home where there was supposed to be an old guy who once worked at the Manila CCC camp. He found Decken MaCade by way of phone calls to a local historical society. An old woman gave him the name, said he was at a place called the Mountain View Care Center, but not much else.

The smell was a mix of coffee, baking meatloaf, cleaning fluids, and urine. Mountain View Care Center buzzing with activity. Breakfast was over, lunch, the main meal, already cooking. In an activity room a group of old women and two men seated in a circle of chairs were alternately being tossed a beach ball and returning the toss to a young woman who kept up a constant chatter. In the hall aides took residents for walks, most using walkers, some being held up by an aide on either side, safety belts secured around skinny and plump waists. Most aides were female. They wore light blue slacks and flowery tops. Two male aides wore blues top and bottom. Cory left his helmet on the Road Glide, but noticed residents and aides eyeing his leathers. Should have known nursing homes were hotter than hell. He unzipped all the zippers as he walked down the hall.

Decken MaCade shared a room with another man who was asleep. MaCade had the window bed. The room-dividing curtain was pulled out to give the sleeping guy some privacy. MaCade sat in a wheelchair between the bed and curtain. A label below the armrest of the wheelchair had a printed label with MaCade's name. Hand-lettered below were the words, "damn chair." MaCade faced the window, the windowsill lined with fist-sized rocks of varying colors and shapes. Beyond the rocks, through dingy glass, mountains topped the haze above the trees and buildings of Vernal.

MaCade was skinny and wore bib overalls over a flannel shirt. His ears, both with hearing aides, stuck out a mile. His face was sun-scared. Tubes in his nose led to a green oxygen bottle mounted to the back of the wheelchair.

"Mr. MaCade?"

The weathered face turned toward Cory. "What?"

Cory held out his hand. "I'm Cory Minkus."

"Decken MaCade," said the old man. "Everyone calls me Decken. Sit on my bed. I didn't piss in it. Not lately anyhow."

Cory sat on the edge of the bed facing Decken. "I like your rock collection."

"They're from the Uintas Range, millions of years separating them. "I've been collecting rock all my life. I like your outfit. Leathers?"

"Yes, leathers."

Decken stared at Cory a moment, turning his head at various angles as if he could read his mind. "So, you're visiting. I guess somebody in one of them historical society's sent you."

"Yes, I phoned a woman named Etta Pratt. She works at the Sweetwater County Historical Museum."

"She's a volunteer," said Decken. "Old like me so all she can do is volunteer until she ends up dead or in this place. I'm surprised they let her on the phone. Last time I saw her she said they told her not to answer calls. Things aren't the same around the gorge since me and Etta were younger. Used to be more natural. That all changed when they built the dam in the 50s. I forget the exact year. Everything submerged, even roads and a bridge over the river built by CCC boys. I remember how the electric and telephone lines went right down into the water like there might be fish down there with hookups. Crazy, the whole place turned into fishing resorts and those damn jet skis. Ranchers took the buildings apart and used the wood like they owned it. In the 60s a storm washed away all traces of the CCC camp. Only things left from what the boys did are roads, especially the road from Manila to Vernal, and of course the old fire tower. I guess that's what happens to everything and everyone, including old coots living here. We get washed away."

"Can I ask you about my grandfather who was at the Manila CCC camp?"

"What was his name?"

"George Minkus."

Decken looked down to his lap, closed his eyes. Cory thought he'd dozed off, but he looked up suddenly. "Give me some other names, his buddies when he was at Manila. You should know some of their names if you've been searching."

"Okay, besides George Minkus, there was Nick Gianakos and Bela Voronko."

Decken stared at Cory a while, then said. "Others have come here, you know. They think the 1939 Manila boys from Barracks Three—all of them were in Barracks Three—died in funny ways, and I don't mean out-loud-laughing funny."

"That's why I'm here. My grandfather supposedly fell under a bus. And my father, Buddy Minkus, went searching for answers and crashed his bike in a way none of his fellow bikers back in Chicago would have figured."

Decken started a coughing fit that blew the nose tubes out and had Decken reaching for the call button next to Cory on the bed. Instead of handing the button to Decken, Cory pushed it and stood next to Decken, patting him on the shoulder trying to calm him.

After visiting Mountain View Care Center, and witnessing Decken MaCade maybe having a stroke, Cory took US 40 west. He'd come back later and see if Decken's state of mind was different after the stroke, or what-ever happened following the coughing fit. Yeah, definitely come back and see Decken again, probably tomorrow after visiting Manila and the woman named Clancy at the Lucerne Valley Marina.

Cory would return because following the coughing fit, MaCade had been in a panic, saying crazy things like maybe the CCC boys came back from the dead to kill one another, or time-traveled from 1939 and were killing one another. Decken said they were all jealous, something about a girl named Rose and a guy named Sal the Stiletto. He said ghost boys meet up at the fire tower at night and probably have their way with Rose. He mentioned a place called Castle Rock, but said there was another one, another Castle Rock at the fire tower. It seemed half gibberish, half making sense. During the episode, the two male aides he'd seen in the hallway held Decken down, yelling his name and saying they didn't want him to hurt himself. Decken calmed down after a female nurse came in and gave him a shot.

Cory had stood back from the action, touching the various rocks lined up on the windowsill. The nurse, surprised to see Cory still standing there, told him he should come back later. Cory had agreed and been on his way out, following the nurse, when Decken reached out, grabbed his arm, and said, in a harsh whisper, "See Clancy at the Lucerne Valley Marina north of Manila. See Clancy. She knows all about it."

As Cory rode out of Vernal he could still hear the words, could still smell and feel Decken's breath on his face. Sour coffee breath blurting out, "See Clancy. She knows all about it," as the nurse escorted Cory past the dead-to-the-world guy in the next bed.

Mountain air was good after the visit to Decken MaCade. The slight hangover from last night's beer blown away. At noon he'd stop to call Lazlo Horvath who phoned last night. Later he'd visit the Lucerne Valley Marina, and tomorrow he'd definitely come back to Vernal.

Before getting on the Road Glide in the parking lot, he checked out the Flaming Gorge map he picked up at the visitor's center. The marina and even a fire tower were listed. Also on the map was the Red Cloud Loop recommended by the hooded sweatshirt tow truck driver. Maybe some cobwebs from 1939 were clearing away.

Cory found the sign for the Red Cloud Loop and turned north. Vernal was busy with traffic, but when he made his way through a neighborhood, mountains came up fast. At first there was evidence of strip mining, and a sign telling how phosphates were used for fertilizers to help feed the world. Soon road signs were limited to warnings for tight curves.

The mountains, a mix of rock and trees, were greener than he expected. As the road climbed, it became all gravel rather than sections of gravel like the guy in the hooded sweatshirt said. Riding the Road Glide was slow going in tight hairpins. At higher elevations, despite the bright sun and temperature in the 50s, there were a couple patches of unplowed mushy snow, making it a slow ride following other tracks that had gone through. A slow ride with no way over to 191 unless he rode all the way back down to Vernal. No way he'd turn around now because he was more than halfway through the loop. The road would probably clear soon, the hooded sweatshirt guy saying there were a few rough spots both ways. One good thing about the cutoff, at least there were no other vehicles…until he came around a really tight hairpin and saw the tow truck parked on the wrong side of the road, facing him.

After *Nurse Ratched* injected Decken, the two male aides put him in bed, saying he'd have a nice nap and they'd return at lunchtime. Maybe they turned up his oxygen, he wasn't sure. He opened his eyes and looked toward the window, wishing the young man was still there instead of nothing but his lineup of rocks and blue sky and the hazy view of Marsh Peak at 12,240 feet on the Sheep Creek Loop some 40 miles to the northwest.

After being an LEM in the CCCs, he'd gone back to Salt Lake for a while, until he joined the Navy. Eventually he returned to the Uinta Mountains. He settled in Green River, first working for the mines, then the forest service. For a while he worked at a marina up near Green River. He almost married Etta Pratt some years back, but it was too late, all because of his emphysema. Shouldn't have taken up smoking in the Navy. Doc says good thing he quit when he was younger, otherwise he'd be gone by now. Of course, at 94, it wouldn't be long.

So, what to leave behind? At least something. But if he died before Clancy had a chance to visit…Sure, he told her there'd be something, but what if died tonight? Could happen. And what with Cory Minkus and others visiting, no telling who might get hold of his map. He'd put it in an envelope and marked it, "For Clancy," but if someone else came looking…Bela, George, and Nick in Barracks Three convinced him to forget what they called, the cache. Better off they all went to war, and after that better off if they were all gone from life before anyone found it. Nothing there but the truth, except with all the relatives visiting and the guys from Barracks Three dying the way they say they did…But the guys said to forget the cache.

"Crap," said Decken out loud.

During a weaker moment, after the war, when he'd gotten juiced up and gone up to the fire tower that night…Sure, how could he forget the cache when he nearly lost his arm getting it stuck beneath the Castle Rock replica at the fire tower? Only thing he ever reached that night was the revolver. Crazy old man with a gun hidden in a sock inside an old shave kit bag with a rusty zipper. The bag hidden in the back of the bedside table drawer.

"Crap," he said again as he inched himself higher on his pillows. "Crap."

When he got himself pushed back so his head touched the headboard, Decken eased himself onto his side and stared at the bedside table. He got himself up on his elbow and opened the drawer. The envelope to Clancy and the old shave kit were behind two tissue boxes he'd jammed in to fake the back of the drawer.

He made sure no one was in the room, turning up his aides and listening carefully before he pulled out the two tissue boxes. He listened again, stopped breathing a moment because of his crackling chest, then quickly pulled out the envelope and shave kit, tucked them beneath his cover sheet, pulled a pen and notebook from the table and rolled onto his back. Elevated bed and thick pillows had him sitting almost upright and he went to work, creating a new note for Clancy and rolling the old note with the map on it into a cigarette shape that would fit into one of the six chambers in the revolver.

After renting the tow truck Guzzo had purchased gas containers and filled them. Although the truck was still up above at the gravel hairpin, he'd parked it to the side after pushing the Harley and its passenger off the cliff.

The Road Glide was mangled, but not so badly many of its parts could have been salvaged. Farther down the slope, the rider was not salvageable. The rider left Guzzo with no feeling at all except satisfaction Pescatore was unaware of his failure in Detroit. Pescatore apparently assumed he'd called Guzzo back to Chicago before the assignment was complete.

The body was disjointed, like pulling a heavy rag doll with every-which-way limbs. He put the body at the base of the boulder beneath the bike wreckage. Pouring gasoline was difficult because of the idiotic safety nozzles, using one hand to hold the nozzle safety open while lifting each gas container and pouring with the other hand. The glove holding the so-called safety valves got soaked and he was careful lighting the match. Halfway up to the road the Harley's tank exploded. At the top he tossed the empty gas containers into the back of the truck, threw his gloves onto the floor, and turned the truck around for the drive back to Wyoming. Somewhere along the way he'd get rid of the gas containers and the gloves.

As Guzzo drove north the morning sun was warm on his right side. He recalled his anger with Vera on the back patio of his house early the previous morning before leaving for his flight to Cheyenne and the hopper to Rock Springs.

"There'll be other dance recitals. And there won't be many more assignments."

"Is that according to your fish monger?"

"Yes, goddammit! According to my fucking fish monger!"

When Guzzo came to the end of the Red Cloud Loop, he paused at the stop sign. This was not the time to think about arguing with Vera. Facing east, the dirty windshield of the tow truck was lit by the sun. To his right, 100 yards south down 191, a black Chevy Suburban was parked at the side of the road. As he turned left onto 191 a horn blasted. A motor home coming down the highway from the north swerved, nearly hitting him. He floored the tow truck, pulled the air horn chain, and gave the motor home driver the finger. In the tow truck's huge side mirror a trail of diesel exhaust from the twin stacks hovered above the road. In the distance the motor home had pulled to the side and stopped, probably everything having fallen out of cupboards. Soon the motor home and the Suburban disappeared in the distance. But after a couple miles, when he saw the Suburban topping a hill a quarter mile back, he decided to take another route to Rock Springs. At the junction of 191 and 44 he took 44 toward Manila, heading for the northern route on the west side of the canyon where there'd be more pull offs and opportunities to lose the Suburban that might or might not be following him.

There was no answer when Lazlo tried calling Cory Minkus. He tried again while Niki drove downtown to the FBI office where they'd meet Jacobson. Still no answer.

Two chairs faced the desk, angled toward one another as though whoever prepared the office knew Lazlo and Niki would be there.

"It's good to see you in person," said Niki. "Why are we here? On the phone I had the feeling you were going to tell us to back off."

"Have I ever told you to back off?"

"After I hounded the Michigan FBI, you certainly weren't enthusiastic."

Jacobson smiled. "I like to weed out conspiracy theorists."

"We're not conspiracy theorists," said Lazlo.

"I know," said Jacobson. "I'll get to the point. Before you ask what exactly is the game, we're not sure. It seems CCC men from the 1939 roster of the Manila, Utah, camp, along with relatives, have died statistically outside the norms. More so-called accidents, acts of God, or however else you'd like to put it, than usual. Organized crime and agency interests from the US and overseas have complicated things."

"Exactly what organized crime and agency interests?" asked Niki. "I thought here we'd be blunt."

"All right," said Jacobson. "We're talking a spattering of New York mob groups, including old Italian and Sicilian families. We're talking the Russian mob, the CIA, the Russian Foreign Intelligence Service, the Ukraine Secret Service, and our own FBI, who kindly provided this office."

"What about Homeland Security?" asked Lazlo.

"We take more of an inactive fact gathering role. What few facts we have suggest there was and still is money involved."

"A great deal of money I'm sure," said Niki."

"You're going to Wyoming and Utah?" asked Jacobson.

"Yes." She glanced to Lazlo. "Neither of us has and we think it's about time."

Jacobson turned to Lazlo. "Will your Ukraine friends be meeting you here or out there?"

"I'm not sure. As you know, they're on their way."

"I suggest you start with the town of Green River in Wyoming. The historical society might help, especially since the Manila camp is gone and the gorge was damned. These days there are marinas, fishing, and jet skis. I'll try to have our people keep an eye on things out there, but they can't be everywhere."

"They'll watch for us at the Green River Historical Society?" asked Lazlo.

Jacobson nodded.

During the drive back to the apartment in Niki's van, Lazlo took a call from Janos. When he switched to Hungarian, Niki smiled.

Using their roundabout way of speaking, Lazlo filled Janos in about the Jacobson meeting and getting in touch with Cory Minkus. Janos filled Lazlo in about the Brooklyn safe deposit box and the fact he and Mariya would be heading to Chicago to meet them by way of a box on wheels, giving the length of it in meters, which Lazlo knew was a medium size motor home.

"You won't be able to park in my neighborhood," said Lazlo

"I'll call when we get close."

Lazlo closed his phone. "I'll switch back to English."

"That would be good," said Niki. "Although I like the sound of Hungarian, less choppy than Greek. How soon should I start searching for a parking spot?"

"Turn left at the next street. If there's a spot we can walk to the apartment on Damen and maybe stop in somewhere for a drink."

The Vernal, Utah, medical examiner was a large woman. After the fire crew put out the flames, officers at the scene suggested they go down the embankment and gather the charred remains. The medical examiner pointed out she was wearing hiking boots and slacks and insisted she climb down. The two officers, a man and a woman, helped her.

Although it had been a while since a tourist called it in, the area around the wreckage was still smoldering where underbrush had burned and fallen trees had caught fire.

"What a mess," said the female police officer.

"Yes," said the medical examiner. "Too much of a mess if you ask me."

Both officers watched as the medical examiner pulled a knife from a sheath on her belt, stooped down, and began gingerly poking at the remains."

Next day Guzzo was back in Chicago. During the flight he'd gotten a message to meet Pescatore and went to the fish market directly from the airport. It was noisy in the building; a young man he didn't recognize dumping buckets of fish guts into the fish grinder. Inside Pescatore's private office, as was often the case during their meetings, Pescatore stood behind his stainless steel fish table wiping his filleting knife in his apron. This, even though the fish table and apron were clean.

"Do you bring your knife out especially for me?"

"I bring it out during meetings in the event someone walks in."

"Why am I here so soon?"

"Things have accelerated. The woman you were to meet in Detroit is here in Chicago staying with a man who's become problematic." Pescatore placed his knife on the fish table, went to the cluttered desk behind him, and came back with a notebook and pencil. "I'll write the name and address of the man. Memorize it, then give the note back."

Pescatore wrote on the notepad, tore out the sheet, and handed it over the fish table. Guzzo took the note, but before memorizing, asked, "Both?"

"Both," said Pescatore.

As Guzzo studied the note, the fish grinder in the next room vibrated the walls.

CHAPTER 21

"**S**ummertime" recorded in 1936 by Billie Holiday was played nightly on the Rock Springs Arrowhead Bar jukebox. But 1939 summer livin' really wasn't so easy, especially at Camp Manila down across the state line.

Because of news on the recreation hall radio, first rumor to fly was war in Europe having to do with the girl's murder. A Jewish kid in Barracks One said maybe the girl was Jewish and brown shirts had made their way to the American West.

The fireworks—bigger than the firecracker bundle set off in camp July 4th—began when local sheriffs and state police showed up Sunday morning, everyone in camp dressed for Sunday service and inspection. They interviewed officers and LEMs. Some from Green River knew the girl's parents. Word from senior leaders, with access to the administration building, was the Green River LEMs were helping police question staff and enrollees would be next. Later in the day the camp superintendent said since the murderer had a car, and because no CCC enrollees had access to cars, they were off the hook.

The company commander for the northeastern Utah and southwestern Wyoming Pocatello District showed up at Sunday dinner. Last time he visited was the previous year, so most enrollees had never seen him. Instead of calling for attention, like everyone expected, he got into chow line and sat with his tray at a table. The mess was quiet, not the usual chitchat and clatter. Enrollees at the table with the commander kept their mugs down. The commander was a tough-looking cookie with a center part in his hair and a James Cagney sneer. He tried starting conversations with the enrollees at the table. Most simply nodded yes or shook their heads no. A few glanced to Jethro, the Georgia baritone, who was good at doing a Cagney impression, but Jethro stared down at his plate.

The commander eyed another table where a young man with dark peach fuzz moustache squeezed in. The young man had salt and pepper passed and became the center of attention. He had a bruised cheek and forehead, most likely a grudge match. The commander had been worried the local murder would affect morale. They could use more take-charge young men like this.

When he finished eating, the commander took his tray to the KP table and greeted the camp superintendent who'd just arrived. During their brief conversation the company commander pointed to the table where the smiling peach fuzz moustache not fearful of taking charge sat. Having seen *Public Enemy* when they were younger, many thought of James Cagney pointing out a guy he'd like to do business with. After the James Cagney look-alike commander left, the camp superintendent stood with a puzzled look, then called for attention.

"We've had excitement in camp, but it's over. Authorities agree there's no information here about the unfortunate murder of the young woman. I've sent the LEMs home and starting tomorrow things will be back to normal. As I said when you men arrived, I've seen my share of troublemakers. For a change I'm glad ours are the more juvenile variety. Some of you may think things will change around here, but they won't. Tomorrow you'll be on the trucks to your work sites as usual. Everything on schedule. I'll speak to you again at our evening meal. Oh, and to boost morale the commander gave the go-ahead for scheduled visits to the Green River movie house next week. Because we're short on trucks, we'll go by barracks. Barracks One Monday,

Barracks Two Tuesday, and so forth. We're also short on LEMs, so I'm giving permission for enrollees who've passed their driving tests to take the trucks."

The only enrollee smiling was Sal, the fuzzy-mustached kid. Maybe Sal's bruises were from the grudge match with Henry who went AWOL, but in the overhead lights of the mess the bruises looked redder and more recent. Sal raised his hand. The superintendent felt sweat on his back. "Yes?"

"What movie's playin'?"

The superintendent hesitated, the question not fitting the mood. Finally he said, "*Mr. Deeds Goes to Town.*"

The Four Horsemen at their usual table. George to Bela's right, Jimmy and Nick across from them.

Bela: "Jimmy, you heard anything more?"

George: "Yeah, you were at the administration building."

Jimmy shook his head.

Nick: "Come on, someone must have squawked."

Jimmy: "It's all talk if you ask me."

Bela: "We are asking."

Jimmy: "You're not the one who saw the license plate on the Buick Sal got a ride in."

George: "What's that got to do with anything?"

Jimmy: "Probably nothing. Anyone might stop at a roadhouse."

Bela: "What about this roadhouse?"

Jimmy: "A cop waiting outside the superintendent's office said folks saw a car with a New York plate at a roadhouse on the main highway."

Nick: "Did you say anything about the Buick picked Sal up?"

Jimmy: "No one asked. Before I knew it interviews were over and they said I wasn't needed. They'd already questioned everyone at the Green River camp before coming here and were satisfied nobody in the three Cs did anything."

Nick: "Maybe you should say something."

George: "Yeah, Jimmy. How about it?"

Jimmy: "I don't know. I heard Matt, that LEM from Vernal, talking to the camp surgeon. He said a couple locals swore they saw goons with New York plates and maybe they had something to do with it. He said it could've took a couple guys to...to pull out the her hair."

Nick: "The killer pulled out her hair?"

Jimmy: "Someone right away mentioned Indians...the hair and the way she was slugged with something and cut into pieces."

George: "Cut into pieces?"

The Four Horsemen put down their forks and seemed to shrink into their chairs. Toward the front of the mess, guys at Sal's table sat higher in their chairs, laughing at a joke Sal had apparently told about Hitler because of the way he held his finger beneath his nose.

That evening, before lights out, Sal sat on his footlocker surrounded by the half dozen Barracks Three guys who'd been at his table during dinner. Sal's voice loud enough to be heard the length of the barracks. Earlier, a rumor spread that Sal lathered up and used the stiletto he kept on him to shave off his moustache. Sal got the guys' attention by taking the stiletto out of his pocket, flicking it open, and letting them pass it around before stowing it in his footlocker. He sat on the footlocker, folded his arms, looked around the barracks, and made a speech, a smart-ass look on his face like the company commander.

"Maybe Hitler ain't such a bad guy. Charlie Lindbergh and Henry Ford and America First like him. Says what he means and does it. I say to hell with anyone who doesn't let us do what we want. What you guys think? And how about the way I got myself a clean shave? Better than paying some *Bohunk* a nickel to cut your hair, or your throat."

A couple guys glanced toward Bela. Jimmy shouted, "Lights out!" from the front of the barracks and everyone wandered back to their bunks, unbuckling belts, peeling down to shorts, and climbing beneath blankets. Everyone except Sal who sat on his footlocker, arms folded, staring across the barracks at Jimmy with a strange smile. Finally, after staring back at Sal for a moment, Jimmy reached up to the switch near the door and cut the lights.

To pacify Sal's use of *Bohunk*, obviously referring to him, Bela lay back in his bunk, closed the corners of his pillow to his ears, and buried himself in music. Someone had put on a Benny Goodman record in the recreation hall the other night, and Bela lay there, turning up the volume in his head, the tom-tom drums of Goodman's drummer matching his heartbeat, the drums echoing into a future without Salvatore Cavallo.

When the *Green River Star* reporter interviewed Cletus Minch, he avoided giving details. Sure, he told the reporter he found a hand, but that was it. Last evening, when the paper showed up on the porch, he refused to look at it. His mother said he should at least look at his photograph, but he couldn't. He'd see his photograph today in town all over the place, including the hardware store, but didn't want to talk about it. That's why he left for work before sunrise. Bad enough he'd have to talk to the old man.

Cletus was rounding the corner onto the main street when the car pulled up alongside. There were no curbs in town and the car, a big black Buick, came halfway onto the sidewalk. The window was down and a man wearing a city hat and suit coat said, "Hey, Cletus Minch. I'd like a word."

"Are you a reporter?"

The man glanced toward the driver. "Me and my partner are investigating."

"What do you want?"

"We got word Irish who work on the railroad were down at the river at night. Some might have been there in the morning, before sunrise like now. A bunch of those damn Micks wandered back to their work camp after sunrise. Maybe you saw one of them that morning, either before sunrise or after."

"I didn't see anybody."

"Maybe you did and maybe you didn't. Thing is, we know for sure the Micks who wandered into camp next day were saying things, if you know what I mean."

"What were they saying?"

"Things, kid. You sure you didn't see a couple Micks at the river, or maybe while you were walking? It'd help if you could say you saw somebody, even at a distance. One of the Micks who got back late had red hair like the girl. Not that you'd have to identify him or anything. But red hair on a guy ain't that common except on Micks."

The guy took off his hat and leaned out the window, staring at Cletus, his eyes visible in the dawn light. The guy had black hair slicked back. He smiled as if he expected Cletus to agree with him. The driver spoke.

"Let's go, Manny. He don't want to help."

The guy put his hat back on and straightened it. "Okay, chump. We're going. But don't forget, we're looking into this Mick with red hair and we'll be around."

When the Buick drove off, Cletus saw a New York plate. During the remainder of his walk to the hardware store, Cletus thought hard about the morning he found Rose Buckles' hand. He recalled the quiet, the sound of the river, the sunrise. No matter how much he thought about it, he couldn't recall seeing anyone along the Green River except his own mottled reflection in the current. When he arrived at the hardware store the sun was coming up.

Summer heat had Uncle Rosario laid up at home, a night nurse ordered in by the doctor, and an extra young man from the family keeping electric fans running. The young man tending the fans was named Felice. Long ago he insisted he be called Felix. Unfortunately, his given name Felice was pinned on him, pronounced in a feminine way throughout adolescence and high school. Maybe the taunting made Felice into an odd job runner, maybe not. One thing Felice could be trusted for was to keep anything he heard to himself.

Uncle Rosario was in bed, a lunch tray off to the side with a half-eaten salami and cheese sandwich sticking out its tongue. A bottle of bourbon on the nightstand along with an ashtray with a smashed-out cigar butt. When Cavallo asked if he'd started smoking and drinking again, Uncle Rosario smiled.

"The butt and bottle remind me how things were. Felice and the nurse try to take them away, but a man needs memories. Like being with a woman, nothing but memory."

Felice sat in a chair in the corner. He said nothing.

When Cavallo moved closer to the bed, his uncle said, "Don't worry. I trust Felice with my life. Tell me, Nephew, what the hell's going on with your son in Utah?"

"He's a wild horse champing at the bit. I can't blame him. He's anxious about our plans."

"Tell him to be patient," said Uncle Rosario. "The time for action will come."

"I have told him."

"Apparently not successfully. Our men said he grows a moustache like he's some kind of Clark Gable, or even worse, Adolph Hitler."

"I told him to shave it off," said Cavallo.

"What about that fight?" asked Uncle Rosario. "Don't look at Felice, I'm talking to you."

"The kid isn't at camp anymore."

"Where'd he go?"

"The boys scared him off."

"You sure they didn't do more than scare him off?"

"If they did, they're not telling me."

"They're your boys. You should know. As far as family is concerned, he messed with Sal, so he messed with all of us. Your boys are there to make sure Sal moves up, not out. And to make sure nothing happens to him. Tell him he can swing his weight around later."

Cavallo stared at Uncle Rosario. "Are you finished?"

"I'll goddamn let you know when I'm finished!" After a series of coughs, his uncle continued. "You know I got other contacts out there. What about that murder and the cops seeing New York plates at a roadhouse?"

"The boys called Al in Kansas City. He's driving to Utah right now with Kansas and Missouri replacement plates. He'll hang around to help if there's trouble."

Uncle Rosario picked up the cigar butt from the ashtray on the night-stand, looked at it a moment, then put it back down. "The kind of news I like. Sal knowing there are more men keeping an eye on him should keep him in line."

Cavallo nodded. "I agree. It also helps we got the commander paid off."

"Did it take much?" asked Uncle Rosario.

"We got war coming and anything a guy like him can get is plenty in his book."

Because Barracks Three was working cattle guards in the flatlands all week, the two from the tan Buick and the two from the black Buick stayed in their rooms in Rock Springs. Instead of needing to watch Little Sal during the day, they rested up and one or the other pair met up with him at night.

Tonight it was the tan Buick with the big-shouldered driver and the stocky passenger who waited outside camp where a small side road from the canyon opened onto the main road.

"I'm glad we got new plates," said the driver.

"Who's gonna come along this god-forsaken road in the middle of the night?"

"The cops, maybe. Especially after that girl."

"You think it was a road crew Mick like the guy in the bar said?"

"How the hell do I know?"

"The other boys let Sal use their car," said the stocky passenger.

"We didn't give him our car," said the big-shouldered driver. "That's all that counts."

"We're the ones on the new phone number to the boss every day. The other guys never talk to the boss."

"They talk to the uncle. He's old but keeps his nose wet. We get that note shoved under our door. Says call a number and next thing I know I'm on the phone with the uncle. We got one phone number in your wallet that goes through Lonzo, and now I got this number in my wallet that goes to Rosario. Big Sal hasn't got a clue what's going on. Rosario says shake up the barracks leader and I got no choice."

"What did you tell the kid by the way?"

"I said be careful how he treats Sal because accidents happen."

"I don't see how what you said gives the kid—What's his name?"

"Jimmy Phillips."

"I don't see how what you said gives Jimmy ammo against us or Sal."

"I hope not," said the driver. "Gives me the creeps not knowing what Little Sal'll do next. Like for instance, here we are waiting for a kid who takes pep pills so he can stay up, and we're not even sure if he might have been the one who—"

"Shit."

"Yeah, shit's the only word for it." The driver started the Buick and flipped on the radio to warm up.

"Are we leaving?"

The driver turned the lit radio dial back and forth. "No, I'd rather listen to music on the Motorola than think and I don't want to kill the battery."

"Guy at the bar says the only station's in Rock Springs and it goes off at midnight."

"Remember when the New York Auto Club had that thing about the car radio being dangerous because it distracts the driver?"

"Yeah, so what?"

"Not as dangerous as a kid on the loose, that's for sure."

A distant station buried in static played what sounded like Hawaiian music and driver shut off the Buick's ignition."

Inside the Motorola, the glow of vacuum tubes slowly went from orange to black as the static faded.

Snoring in Barracks Three, along with the ticking of the potbelly stove, had a rhythm. Perhaps a tune he'd heard on the recreation hall record player. Glenn Miller—"Moonlight Serenade" or "In The Mood." Benny

Goodman—"Stompin' At The Savoy" or "Sing, Sing, Sing." Definitely not Kate Smith's "God Bless America." Too much like marching. A guy trying to sleep in a barracks didn't care to think of marching.

With "God Bless America" in his brain, Bela closed his eyes, recalling, during his journey to the US, young men in brown shirts marching up and down the Pilsen station platform. By giving Sudetenland to Germany, Hitler was supposed to have been happy singing his "Deutschland, Deutschland, Uber Alles."

Bela recalled sitting in a window seat of the stopped train, opening his passport and staring at himself. He wore the same clothes he'd worn when his passport photo was taken at the American Consulate in Prague—shirt, tie, sweater and Uncle Sandor's wool funeral suit. Two brown shirts came aboard, staring angrily at each passenger for a moment before moving on. Bela wondered if they would have moved on had he been wearing his original threadbare suit, the one switched with Uncle Sandor's newer funeral suit before the coffin was sealed.

As the snoring and ticking of the potbelly continued, Bela lifted himself onto his elbows and looked toward the far end of the barracks. From his point of view, the placement of the window was directly above Sal Cavallo's bunk. The window faced the latrine building where a single bulb over the door gave off a glow bright enough for Bela to see what Sal was up to. Previous nights, he'd seen Sal get dressed and sneak out. Later, after the low rumble of a motor and wheels on gravel, Sal would return, get undressed and get back into his bunk.

Bela lay back and closed his eyes, recalling a folk tune from home and trying to make it fit the rhythm of the snoring and the potbelly's ticking. He recalled the smell of Nina's hair and tried to block out the smell of socks and trousers drying above bunks in the rising heat of the stove. He tried to recall the feel of Nina's breasts and hips against him, but it was no use. He let go of himself, lifted himself on his elbows again, and wondered what time it was.

Thinking of Nina's hair had made Bela recall the strands of his aunt's gray hair still in the vest pocket of Uncle Sandor's suit packed in the bottom of his footlocker, hair that was supposed to be buried with his uncle.

With most guys being homesick, stories of home made the rounds. Even Sal had one. Throwing a baseball bat after a bad pitch and accidentally killing a rabbit. Bela remembered Sal burying his head in his hands, the rest of the guys looking sad until, suddenly, Sal uncovered his face and laughed like a hyena, saying they were chumps. No one was supposed to make fun of Sal the way Henry had that night. Next day Sal hit Henry in the head with a shovel, claiming it was accidental even though he'd been swinging it like a baseball bat. And of course after the grudge match, Henry disappeared.

Something moved on the other side of the barracks. Bela sat up. Low in the light from the window, both Sal's hands were upraised. Sal held something in one hand. After an audible click, the stiletto blade reflected light from the latrine building.

The driver of the Buick started the engine.

"We leaving?" asked the passenger.

"Ain't it obvious he's not coming out tonight?"

"Suppose he does after we're gone?"

"The hell with him. Least he could do is tell us which nights he wants to jaw."

"I'm glad we weren't the ones he asked about using the car."

"Yeah, but we're the one's picked up Manny when he dropped theirs off."

As they drove into the night, the Motorola's vacuum tubes oranged up and static came from the loudspeaker.

Again, Cavallo was summoned to Uncle Rosario's bedside, Felice in the room with them.

"You know what Al discovered after delivering the license plates?"

"Al called you?"

"I told him to call me. What he said is the important thing. A boy was taken care of as a favor to your son. Everything is being done for your son. He's the family legacy's male heir. It's a commitment he must keep, regardless of his tendency to be headstrong. Do you agree?"

Cavallo was silent.

Uncle Rosario sat taller in bed, his face beet red, hands trembling. "I need an answer! Do you agree making a way to the top of the ladder must be done at all costs?"

"I agree."

"Then you must speak to him!"

When Uncle Rosario collapsed back on his pile of pillows and grasped his chest, Felice ran to his bedside.

But Cavallo's uncle wasn't finished. He motioned Felice away with one hand and motioned Cavallo closer with the other.

"Listen to me," he whispered. "Your grandfather and I worked many years to create the legacy. We put it in the Cavallo name. Perhaps it will help matters—"

His uncle spent some time coughing up phlegm before continuing.

"Perhaps it will help matters with your son if you reveal details of the legacy."

"Details?"

Uncle Rosario spoke more loudly. "Yes, the aspirin company! The heroin your grandfather bought didn't come from the Orient. The heroin came from the stockpile! Without the aspirin company's knowledge your grandfather—"

Another round of coughing.

"You know all this. I repeat it for Felice's benefit. Your grandfather created so much wealth, the family didn't know what to do with it. Perhaps if your son knows the extent of it—"

"You want me to tell my son?"

"His desire for power could be the key."

Uncle Rosario turned to Felice. "Bring me the silver box on the desk… Yes, that one."

Felice brought a small silver box. Uncle Rosario opened it and held up a key. "It opens a deposit box in a London bank."

"What's in the deposit box?"

Uncle Rosario smiled. "Directions to the fortune."

"Directions?" asked Cavallo.

Uncle Rosario pulled Cavallo by his sleeve and whispered wetly into his ear. "Directions to a place safe from even this madman Hitler. Swiss banks."

"The box in London, what's the name of the bank?"

"Bank Leumi."

"Can you tell me the a name on the box?"

Uncle Rosario smiled, one side of his mouth drooling. "Mrs. Shulamit Weizman."

"A Jew?"

"In a Jewish bank! Clever, yes?" And with that Uncle Rosario launched himself into such a coughing fit, Felice retrieved a bowl from beneath the bed and placed it before the old man who continued coughing, spitting, and laughing.

Next day, the two who'd waited for Little Sal the night before spent the afternoon in their room trying to catch up on sleep. They'd finished their morning business with the camp superintendent, delivering the packet of cash and getting him to agree that no matter what Sal did or how he acted, the superintendent would "take care of it." They told him not to worry. War was coming and guys like him were needed. If he wanted to do his part for his country and not be buried either in the ground or in a penitentiary, he'd "take care of things" when it came to Sal.

After the morning putting the superintendent in the pressure cooker, both tried to relax. Although they were dressed in slacks and shirts, they'd removed jackets and shoulder holsters and loosened their ties. The taller man, who usually drove, lay on one of the room beds. The stocky guy, who'd come back from picking up sandwiches at the inn's café, sat on the sofa.

"What kind of sandwiches you get?"

"Ham on rye and salami on rye. Both cut in half."

"Cheese and mustard?"

"Yeah, on both."

The tall guy joined his partner on the sofa. "Ain't you gonna open the bag?"

"Something I should tell you first," said the stocky guy.

"Tell me which sandwich is ham. I'm tired of salami."

"It's important."

"Okay, shoot."

"The other boys who were told to pick up Sal this morning are back. They took Sal to a phone. After the kid gets off the phone he goes nuts."

"More nuts than he is?"

"During the drive back to camp, the kid says things about Jews and a bank somewhere and starts laughing."

"Did the boys say anything about change in plans?"

"Nothing. Even worse was what Big Sal told them after the kid got off the phone. Says we do what the kid says or we might as well dig our graves out here."

"Where's Sal now?"

"In the barracks by himself. What worries me is, if he gets in trouble, we're in trouble."

"Maybe he'll kill himself."

"He can't. When the boss is gone he's next in line."

Late that afternoon at dinner, the superintendent confronted the Four Horsemen. He pulled a chair to the end of their long table.

"I said when you arrived at camp you'd be treated as men if you acted like men."

All four waited.

"Just because Salvatore Cavallo is more often in the mood for a fight than not is no reason for the rest of the barracks to single him out. If I could I'd put him in empty Barracks Five by himself. But I can't do that."

When the four glanced to one another with puzzled looks, the superintendent blew up.

"Listen, boys!" Then more quietly. "I've heard rotten rumors around camp. Believe me, that girl's murder had nothing to do with us. I should know. Not that we're perfect. What I'm talking about is a prime example. If I get wind of any more rumors, like the Cavallo young man somehow related to a crime simply because of his ethnic background, your discharge sheet will make it hard to get into the branch of service you may have wanted. You're not in Boys Town here. I'm US Army and I've got the authority! Do I make myself clear?"

They all nodded.

"If you want rumors, some folks in the towns say an Irish worker from one of the road crews up north was seen hanging around the river the night the girl was killed. That's the rumor I hear, so don't go spreading any of your own."

The superintendent tried on a smile that didn't look like a smile. "By the way, we got this new LEM from Salt Lake City who's working with the powder monkeys. Name's Decken. He knows something about geology. Maybe you've seen him in the recreation building. And maybe you'll learn some local geology from him because next week you'll be working with him helping clear the road to Vernal."

After the superintendent left the table, Bela saw enrollees from other tables looking their way, especially other Barracks Three enrollees. Near the front of the mess, Sal sat facing the other way, obviously ignoring what just happened.

Jimmy pushed his tray to the center of the table. "That was nothing. This afternoon taking a leak in the woods I met up with the hoods from the black Buick who gave Sal a ride."

Silence, all three staring at Jimmy.

"They said leave Sal alone or they'd take care of me like they took care of Henry."

Before classes that evening, Bela, Nick, George, Jimmy and other Barracks Three enrollees gathered camp scuttlebutt. It was confirmed; Sal's goons had gotten to staff *and* the superintendent. During classes even the instructors were spooked.

The plan, doing something was better than nothing. After lights out, they'd put sheets over the windows and turn the lights back on. The two big barge loaders from St. Louis agreed to guard the door and switch out the lights should an officer or LEM show up. Jethro, the Georgia baritone, would have his guitar out so he and Paul Fontaine could do a duet to cover the commotion of them getting back to their bunks.

Maybe after confronting Sal they'd discover he had nothing to do with the Green River girl. Maybe they'd have a sit down with Sal, he'd see none of them was out to get him, and in the end his goons would start looking after the entire barracks.

"It can't hurt to try," said the brain from New Jersey who'd been reading a book his dad sent him called *How To Win Friends And Influence People.* "Everybody's got to have some good in them."

"I say we give it a try," said the kid from Dallas. "Corral him into seeing things our way."

"What if Sal doesn't show up?" asked the New Jersey brain.

"He's always in the barracks after class."

But at nine, Sal wasn't there. And at half past nine everyone was talking at once.

"You want covers on the windows anyway?"

"Leave it."

"How about the lights?"

"I don't know."

"Hey, who's been in my footlocker?"

"Mine, too."

"Anything missing?"

"It's messed up."

"That's why I got a lock."

"What the hell is this? There's some of that new Scotch tape in my work pants pocket."

"It ain't that new."

"It's got hair on it."

"You keep hair in your pocket?"

"Hell no."

"Hey, I got the same thing in my work pants. Tape with hair on it."

"Me, too."

Suddenly the barracks door swung open and Sal walked in, eyeing the St. Louis boys on either side. He looked around at everyone and walked slowly to his bunk. He lay down on his back with his hands behind his head.

The only sound was the rustling of a mouse beneath floorboards. With all the windows closed and draped, it was hot, the smell of the day's work clothes in the air.

Bela approached Sal's bunk. Sal began speaking, all the while keeping his eye on Bela.

"So, I go for a beer and you guys make plans. You got a girl to gang-shag?" Sal stood, his face redder than usual. "Mess with me and my old man'll take care of you *and* your families! You think camp staff's on your side? Brother, that day's long gone. What's the scuttlebutt? One of you go bananas on a local gal? Damn foreigners! You, Bela Lugosi. Or you, Boris Karloff. You come to my country thinking you can do anything. I'm the only one can do anything!"

Sal walked into the aisle and faced Bela.

"What say, Bela Lugosi? Ain't it true some guys do anything they want? Like your man Hitler over there?"

"He's not my man," said Bela.

"I hear your so-called countrymen joined him!"

"Not necessarily by choice."

Sal took a step closer. "Your next gal gonna be from somewhere else? That's how *Bohunks* work. First up in Green River, then down in Vernal!"

Bela waited to make certain Sal was finished. The rest of the men hadn't moved. Finally, Bela asked his question.

"Tell me, Salvatore Cavallo. Are you saying you plan to kill again?"

Sal held his fists up, one leg in front of the other. "What I'm saying, Bela Lugosi, is being the victim's hair was pulled out, and being guys in this barracks are saving hair, we're in this together! A guy might or might not catch himself a ride down to Vernal! Either way I've got torpedoes guaranteeing one thing!"

"And that one thing is?"

"I go down we all go down! I get fingered, there'll be another gal while I got witnesses as to my complete innocence! You guys and your straight razors get me?"

After Sal lowered his fists, Bela took down window coverings and opened windows as others went to their bunks. The only sounds were floorboards creaking, springs squeaking, then silence. For the first time since they'd been at camp, Jimmy didn't say, "Lights out."

After the lights were out, Sal whispered, "Hush little babies, don't you cry."

Outside, mountains on both sides of the valley listened. There was no snoring in Barracks Three that night.

CHAPTER 22

Separate cabs and switching halfway. Janos hauling luggage across Manhattan, eventually getting to the neighborhood of the New Jersey RV dealership. Mariya starting her cab rides later. Together they waited in the entryway of an abandoned furniture store to be certain neither was followed. A homeless woman walking past eyed the two sitting on suitcases.

"Like her we should wear sweaters and coats," said Mariya.

"I agree," said Janos.

Mariya retrieved a pair of rusty shopping carts from a vacant lot. The wobbly wheels were noisy beneath their luggage. Janos let his shirttails hang out. Mariya wore a scarf babushka style. The homeless couple transported their belongings several blocks. Near their destination a Linden, New Jersey, patrol car slowed alongside. When Mariya saw a policewoman staring, she gave the policewoman a mournful smile and kept pushing her rickety cart. The patrol car gone, they backtracked into the alley behind the dealership. After stowing their luggage in the motor home and dumping the carts, the sun was down.

"This will be like driving a building down the road," said Mariya.

"No one expects ducks in the duck blind."

"Where do we go now?" asked Mariya, sliding into the booth behind the driver's seat.

"Tonight we stay here," said Janos. "We have registration and plates. At my request the salesman left the back gate unlocked. I only wish Sonia were with us."

"You and Lazlo will be militiamen again. Knowing one another's mood and intentions will help us solve it."

Janos found utensils, plates, a candle, and matches.

Mariya opened the refrigerator. The light went on revealing empty and warm shelves.

"Come with me," said Janos.

He led her to the side door. Between rows of motor homes, a taco stand across the street from the dealership was so brightly-lit, reflections of motor home glass, aluminum, and fiberglass made the lot into a carnival.

"*Voilà.*"

Together three days and four nights. Clichés sneaking into intimate conversations: "Life is short," and "A rolling stone gathers no moss." Giggling like children in Lazlo's bed. Nervous laughter better than none.

They began their clandestine journey at four in the morning scattering stray cats in Ukrainian Village alleyways, carrying rather than rolling suitcases on gravel. The oven exhaust fan behind the Bakery Café gushed sweet warmth. Luggage stowed in Niki's Dodge Caravan, they retraced the route.

Back in the apartment, Lazlo whispered into Niki's ear. "Just now, in the bathroom, I heard a noise from next door. As of yesterday that apartment was vacant."

"Could someone have seen us in the alley?" whispered Niki.

"The windows face the wall of another building."

"What should we do?"

"Would you feel safe going back to your van alone?"

"Of course."

"I'll watch the alley from my fire escape to make sure you're not followed. Then I'll lug a huge empty suitcase I didn't use down the stairs and to my car. With the van on the other side of Damen on a bus route, you should be safe. Send a simple text message when you arrive. I've got an overcoat in my car. I'll prop it up as though you're with me. After I leave in my car with the empty suitcase, I'll lose anyone who follows, park somewhere else, and walk back to the van. Lock yourself inside until I arrive."

"I have pepper spray. Do you, Lazlo?"

"Yes. Both our phones are on vibrate." Lazlo threaded a key off his key ring. "Take this."

"What's it for?"

"In my small suitcase already in the van there's a metal gun case with a loaded revolver."

"What if—?"

Lazlo interrupted by turning Niki's head to whisper into her ear. "If I don't arrive at the van within an hour, drive to the front of the FBI building downtown. You won't be able to park without being chased away. Keep coming around the block. After that, go to lunch."

"I won't be able to eat."

"But you will eat. The thought of being with my fellow rolling stone will keep me safe."

As soon as he suction cupped the microphone to the bathroom wall he picked up an early CNN broadcast in another apartment, but could tell the two next door whispered. A door opened and closed. He left the bathroom and ran across the empty apartment he just broke into. No one in the hallway.

Back in the lighted bathroom he adjusted earphones. Still movement next door. He looked into the mirror above the sink. His eyes bloodshot. Yesterday he was in the tow truck heading back to Rock Springs. He'd lost the Suburban and Pescatore had texted. A private jet at Rock Springs, the meeting at the Chicago fish market. The Greek woman, Niki Gianakos, back on the agenda, along with Lazlo Horvath, an ex-detective from Ukraine.

Commotion next door. During a lull in the racket, a door banged open. When he ran and peered out, he saw Lazlo Horvath for the first time. A man with wild gray hair pulling a large wheeled suitcase down the hall to the stairwell.

Guzzo went back to listen. Hearing nothing, he pulled the suction cup away, wiped the wall with his sleeve, turned off the light, and hurried after Horvath. When he passed the apartment he checked the knob, found it locked. The Greek woman must have gone ahead.

Horvath's suitcase bumped on sidewalk expansion joints. He went past Guzzo's latest Camry rental. Guzzo paused and watched. A half-block away, Horvath opened the trunk of a Honda Civic and shoved the large suitcase in, pushing it about to make it fit. The Greek woman must have slipped out. It appeared someone was in the car's passenger seat.

Guzzo started the Camry and was about to follow the Civic when a dark SUV with heavily-tinted windows drove slowly past with its lights out.

After Janos drove the motor home through the alley gate, Mariya got out and ran back to close it. Back inside, door locks clicked when Janos pushed the button. "Most large Class A homes had only one door, like our door back there. This Class C is based on a van and therefore has normal driver and passenger doors."

"You are savvy American shopper," said Mariya.

"I also purchased a GPS."

"I'll watch from the back. When we're sure of not being followed I'll make coffee. Both the sink and stove work and I found instant in the cupboard."

After their back road route the eastern sky behind them reddened with dawn. Once on Interstate 80, Mariya sat up front, coffee cups in the holders. The engine throbbing beneath the center console created ripples in the cups like bull's-eyes.

"This beast is noisier than our Ukraine camper van," said Mariya.

"A large V-8 in the doghouse."

"Doghouse?"

"While shopping I learned the terminology. The engine compartment we are forced to squeeze around is called the doghouse."

"Doghouse in America also refers to a place a person in trouble resides," said Mariya.

"Really?"

"Yes, Janos. Bowwow."

Having met Lazlo only recently, Niki trusted him, but mostly worried about him. Perhaps they'd met in another lifetime and, going through ordeals, prepared to arrive at this time, in this place, together.

A few windows lit in apartments where weary Chicagoans made their way to kitchens, and especially to bathrooms. Too much coffee while she and Lazlo whispered their plan. She'd flipped the switch to cancel the interior lights. When Lazlo arrived, the light would not go on. Okay, now she had to pee so badly, she could almost hear Lazlo saying, do what you must. Luckily she hadn't parked beneath a streetlight and no one had come out of an apartment. A bus went by and was a block away. She checked forward and back, unlocked the door with the mechanical button so the automatic headlights wouldn't flash, opened up, got out, pulled down her jeans and underwear, and squatted in the street.

Headlights a half-block back after Lazlo pulled the Civic out of the tight spot. Perhaps he rolled his empty suitcase right past the vehicle. When he turned the corner onto Damen Avenue south, he saw it was an SUV, two in front lit up beneath a streetlight. As expected, the SUV paused before pulling out behind him. This time of morning, remaining unnoticed was difficult.

Instead of continuing to the Chicago Avenue stoplight ahead, Lazlo tapped his brakes for a quick right on Rice Street, a narrow one way, then the next left, then another left, and back onto Damen. The SUV had to hurry to keep track. Back on Damen heading south, Lazlo knew they were following, and now they knew Lazlo knew. The overcoat in his passenger seat had leaned onto the console during the turns and he propped it back up.

He drove down Damen to Grand Avenue. Grand angled northwest. The SUV powered through a stoplight's yellow, its higher headlights glaring. He needed to get back to Niki, but in the process lose the SUV. Therefore he did what any savvy Chicago driver would do. He drove like the bat out of hell, watching for cops.

Northwest on Grand, a sudden screeching turn onto Humboldt Drive, barreling through the park and onto the parkway. He braked hard and cranked the Civic into a narrow street with cars parked on both sides. The SUV kept up, but the narrow street with the SUV wagging back and forth to avoid parked cars provided the solution. He sped back to Damen, north of where Niki waited. Then a quick right down an alley behind businesses. As expected, morning delivery trucks, some almost, but not quite, blocking the alley. He squeezed in front of the cab of a backed-in beer truck.

"Damn!" The SUV made it through, sparks where it touched the truck's bumper.

After the alley he purposely turned the wrong way onto a one-way street. The SUV followed. A car head-on flashed its lights. He nosed into a no-parking zone and the car flew past, a woman flashing her finger then gaping at the SUV's headlights. The SUV backed into an alley as Lazlo pulled out of the no-parking zone to continue the wrong way. But suddenly his driver's door was pulled open and a hand grabbed his jacket at the shoulder.

"Don't make it hard!" shouted a man.

Lazlo eased off on the gas. "Why not?"

"I don't like running!"

"Then you must practice!"

As Lazlo sped up his shoulder belt locked, jacket trying to tear its way beneath the belt. The jacket zipper gouged his neck. The man's feet slapped the pavement. Lazlo's left hand tore from the wheel. The slapping of feet ended but the man hung on, the Civic dragging him, the driver's door smashing him, the man's breathing stronger as if he could stop the Civic by sheer force. Then, suddenly, the grip ended, the door slammed, and Lazlo was able to put his left hand back on the steering wheel. In the mirror he saw the man he'd dragged in the headlights of the SUV. The man jumped up, ran around to the passenger side and got in.

Another alley, another one-way street, but going the right direction. More quick turns, the Civic's engine and tires screaming. A bystander slammed his door shut and pasted himself against his car as the Civic flew past. One side of an insane dialog entered his mind.

"I clocked you going 70. How could you possibly get up to 70 on this street?"

He kept turning, flooring the Civic, braking hard, turning, and flooring it again until the only sign of the SUV was not the headlights themselves, but the beam of headlights before they turned after him.

A parking spot appeared. Unbelievable, a parking spot on the street. Someone leaving for the morning shift, taillights up the street. Lazlo turned off his lights and whipped in, nudging the car ahead. He pulled the overcoat from the passenger seat over him and lay across the console. He heard the SUV round the corner and roar past, going after the taillights of the morning shift worker.

Starbucks on West Division opened early. Changing from his torn jacket into the overcoat from the passenger seat, Lazlo ran through several yards, alleys, and an empty lot in which he fell. He climbed a fence and finally arrived for his red-eye. Inside, he went directly to the men's room, locked the door, and looked at himself in the mirror. His eyes were red, but not as red as the blood on his neck. He opened his phone but it would not go on. He'd also lost the pepper spray from his pocket.

Lazlo materialized at dawn, standing at the passenger side with two paper coffee cups. He told her to start driving as soon as he got in. He put the cups in the holders. When he put on his belt she saw he was wearing an overcoat and saw him dab blood from his neck where he held the shoulder strap away.

"Coffee?" he asked.

"No, I already peed in the street. What happened?"

"A not very nice fellow tried to drag me out of the car; jacket zipper got me."

"Should I stop at an emergency room?"

"It's can't be bad. I held napkins on it and Starbuck's served me. I hung out in the men's room to make sure I wasn't followed. I washed there and would have called but my phone's busted and I lost my pepper spray. You were supposed to leave. But I knew you'd still be here."

CHAPTER 23

Daylight brought headwinds, the Class C like a sailboat wrangling its way forward. Janos and Mariya took turns driving. Even if they uncovered the conspiracy that killed Doctor Marta, could Janos ever hope to confront men a half-world away who broke Sonia's neck and threw her down the stairs?

Janos and Lazlo planned their rendezvous in Hungarian while Mariya drove. Lazlo on Niki's phone, explaining he busted his. As usual Hungarian and shared knowledge would confuse anyone listening. They agreed on an Illinois location where boxes on wheels overnighted. The location had two words. First, a past tense verb for the fate of Ukrainians due to Stalin. Next, second part of a compound adjective for a music genre played at a specific Kiev club. To anyone listening, even a fluent Hungarian, it would have been confusing. To Janos and Lazlo it was obvious. They'd meet at Starved Rock State Park in Illinois.

At the last stop, while the Class C drank its share of Earth's fossil fuel, Mariya purchased sandwiches and a Coke six-pack. When Mariya placed two Cokes in the cup holders while climbing into the passenger seat, she showed a tight-lipped smile. Coke was Sonia's favorite.

Janos looked ahead out the windshield. "I hope we can trace men saving hair to something, or someone. Men saving each other's hair seems unlikely. Something tragic happened."

"Saving locks of hair is universal."

"I agree," said Janos. "Young men at a camp, hair saved…Vengeance?"

"A woman," said Mariya. "It must be the reason, a woman murdered."

According to legend, around 1770 a Native American tribe pursued by two other tribes sought refuge on the sandstone butte along the Illinois River and eventually starved to death. After coming down from the well-worn rock, Niki and Lazlo went to the lodge bar. A wall of black and white photographs gave the lodge's history. In the 1930s CCC men built the place, with its great hall and huge fireplace.

"I wonder where these young men were from," said Niki, staring at the photographs. "Living near water was Dad's heritage. Detroit's Greek community and Henry Ford's five-dollar day wage lures his family and he ends up in Utah. Even though the Green River was nearby, it was surrounded by rock and dust.

"When I was a girl he said most, like him, were from cities and not accustomed to the remote location. One time he said there were occurrences he'd never forget. Not the work or the heat…occurrences. A couple times he brought out the camp pictorial along with a photo album. Inside the album was an envelope with strands of hair. Reddish-brown hair held together with yellowed cellophane tape. He said it belonged to someone special, someone who should have been taken care of the way he took care of Mom and promised to take care of me."

"Do you recall him speaking of threats?"

"I remember news in the local Greek paper. Not an article, a letter some-one sent in. I was learning Greek at the time. The letter said something about a purple gang. I remember, being a little girl, thinking that was cute. Thing is, when I asked Dad, he didn't think it was cute. Later, in high school, I learned about Jewish Mafia working in Detroit back in the 1920s and 30s named the Purple Gang. I asked Dad again. It was one of the few times I'd seen him angry. He said Mafias were devils put on Earth to make things miserable for people in Detroit, especially coloreds. Most people his age used the term *coloreds*. Anyway, being a teenager, I mentioned the color purple again. When I did, something else snuck out. He became morose and told me non-purple Mafias made life miserable in the CCCs…

"That's the last time I remember seeing the hair in the envelope. He'd had enough ouzo, dragged out the album, and what he said while fingering the hair was a simple phrase I'll never forget. 'Poor little Rose.' When I asked what he meant he tried to make light of it. He said, 'You know, like the flower. Like flowers folks put between book pages.' Then he went quiet."

It was dark in the bedroom, not because it was night, but because the thick curtains were closed. He'd lost Horvath and Gianakos. He'd lost his edge.

"Vera, I need sleep?"

"We all need sleep, Tony. The girls sleep poorly when you're on the road. To make things somewhat normal I've signed them up for preschool."

"Jesus Christ, Vera! I've been up 36 hours! Give it a rest!"

Guzzo held his phone beneath the blanket. He'd recently texted Pescatore. He was on call, as requested. He could sleep holding the phone, but not with Vera at him.

The evening went better. The girls were glad to see him, they ordered pizza, he and Vera sat through *The Lion King*, several trips to the espresso machine keeping him awake. They played a kid's version of Scrabble, during which he and Vera smiled conspiratorially, allowing the girls to win. With the girls finally in bed, he and Vera had sex and he felt at peace. Not once after his outburst had Vera called him Tony.

But it didn't last. At the edge of sleep his phone hummed. Pescatore's text said he'd get new instructions in the morning, most likely involving another flight, perhaps back to Rock Springs.

When Guzzo checked Vera, he could tell by her breathing she was asleep. He wondered how Pescatore received information sending him back to the Wyoming-Utah border so soon. Who the hell else was watching? Would he ever get a chance to follow the money? When he finally slept, it was fitful with strange nightmares taking him back to patrols along the Arizona-Mexico border. An old man, not with a Mexican accent, but with an Eastern European accent. He awoke in a sweat. After *The Lion King*, drinking espresso, and playing Scrabble, he'd watched the evening news. There'd been politicians complaining about the border. Politicians speaking of building a wall. A lesson learned. Do not watch news before bed.

It was three in the morning. He washed his face, took a Valium, and returned to bed. For a few hours he'd forget the outside world. Repeating this mantra to himself, he slept.

Outside Cleveland, Janos took over driving.

"No one following," said Mariya from the back bed.

"Get some sleep," said Janos. "I did while you drove."

Janos had gotten a text from Lazlo, new phone, same number. He called, but it immediately went to voicemail. He left a message in Hungarian—he'd text at 100 miles out.

Because of the time difference, Janos decided it would be a good time to contact Kiev. When Boris Chudin's phone went to voice mail, Janos asked, "Anything new about our friend named after cheap vodka? If so, call this number. My phone is off and on, be sure to leave a message."

The Class C pounded down the highway, amplifying expansion joints. It was like driving on the chest of someone in panic. Like listening to Sonia's heartbeat before she's thrown down the stairs.

Niki parked at a campground restroom/shower building, backed in with a view of the reserved campsite. Lazlo checked his new phone for messages.

"They'll be here in two or three hours."

Niki touched his leg. "The van seats are folded away. We could move the luggage aside and nap."

"You are very unruly."

"Thank you."

After their "nap" they took turns using the restroom. A park ranger drove past while Niki was gone. Seeing the insignia on the side of the state park pickup triggered a flashback.

Lazlo inside the Kiev Militia building, which smells like a public restroom. The Chernobyl disaster is in the not-so-distant past and fear of latent radioactivity lodged in scum and dirt looms. Rather than the floor being shiny and clean, it's coated with years of scuffmarks from prisoners being dragged to interrogation rooms.

Niki opened the door and got in. "Are you okay?"

"A flashback to former life. I'm fine now." He glanced at Niki and smiled, having caught sight of a motor home in the distance. "That could be them."

The Class C with New Jersey plates paused at the reserved site. He and Niki waited to make certain the motor home was not followed. When Janos and Mariya emerged after parking the beast, Lazlo and Niki joined them. There were hugs, and more hugs.

"I'm so sorry about your sister," Niki told Janos.

"And I'm sorry about your father," said Janos.

"There are very few in the campground," said Lazlo. "But still, we should go inside."

"Our box on wheels is your box on wheels," said Mariya. "We can cook onboard. I had Janos stop at a food market."

Niki diced an onion and watched as Mariya boiled buckwheat. "What are we making?"

"*Hrechanyky*, fried wheat and meat patties. I'm using ground chicken. I bought mild sauce and a prepared salad."

"In honor of our guests, we have Retsina," said Janos.

"The wine of the gods," said Niki.

Janos rubbed his rear end. "I also bought vodka to ease the pain of sitting in this thing as it tried to shake itself apart."

During and after dinner the four compared notes. Janos and Mariya detailed research Sonia found on Doctor Marta's computer regarding the deaths of her grandfather Bela Voronko, and her father, Bela Voronko Junior. Niki told about the death of her father Nick Gianakos and things he'd revealed while alive. Lazlo went into detail about the Minkus father, George Minkus, the two sons, one of whom was killed on his motorcycle, and the grandson traveling in Utah. Lazlo had tried calling numerous times but was unable to get through. The common threads? Bela Voronko, Nick Gianakos, and George Minkus served at the Manila, Utah, CCC camp in 1939; saved strands of hair; and died in so-called accidents. All went quiet after Mariya pulled an envelope from the pocket of her jeans. Strands of red hair Dr. Marta had in her jewelry box, the hair saved from 1939 by her grandfather, Bela Voronko.

Janos and Mariya insisted they sleep in the low-ceiling bed above the Class C cab. Lazlo and Niki slept in the back bedroom. During the night all four, at one time or another, in his or her unique style, snored. In the morning they sat in the booth behind the driver's seat drinking coffee after having eaten sliced ham fried with a dozen eggs.

"That empties the refrigerator," said Mariya.

Lazlo muttered something in Hungarian, making Janos laugh.

"I think I've heard that one before," said Mariya. But what exactly does that mean?"

Lazlo smiled. "Literally it translates as 'Bring on the Gypsies.' It's an idiom. It actually means, start the music, or start the celebration or party."

"With you and Janos from Ukraine, why did your families speak Hungarian?" asked Niki.

"We're from western Ukraine," said Janos. "Before World War I it was part of the Austro-Hungarian Empire, then part of Czechoslovakia, then in celebration of Hitler and Stalin becoming big hits, they carved off the part called the Carpatho-Ukraine. After World War II Stalin got it and it's now Ukraine. Anyway, Lazlo and I, at different times, went to Kiev to make our fortunes in the Kiev Militia."

"Doctor Marta's grandfather grew up in the same region," said Mariya. "He was born here and able to return with citizenship. Unfortunately, he was on the list of doomed CCC men."

"As was my father," said Niki.

Lazlo touched Niki's hand. "We should be leaving."

"I agree," said Janos. "It's a long drive."

"Bring on the Gypsies," said Niki.

Two men waiting at a Denver airport gate. One wore a short sleeve shirt with parrots, the other a Chicago Cubs tee shirt. Their bags were on the seat between them. The man in the Cubs tee shirt turned to his partner who was fiddling with his iPhone.

"I hate layovers."

The iPhone man slipped it into his parrot shirt pocket. "At least you'll get your Charger at the other end."

"That's what they said last time and I got a Suburban."

"We'll have time to complain. Our mark isn't due for a while."

"How do they know when he'll land?"

The man in the parrot shirt shrugged. "Internet."

"They're following our mark on the web?"

"They discover things that lead to other things." He pulled the iPhone back out of his pocket. "It's called research."

"While you're on that thing, look up the specs for the new Charger on Edmunds."

Etta Pratt turned 90, no longer drove, but still volunteered at the Sweetwater County Historical Museum. Depending who was working, she'd get a ride in from her home south of the river for the 10 a.m. opening, and in the mid-afternoon get a ride back from her daughter, Patti, who taught at the Green River High School. Sometimes Etta helped out in the gift shop, but gave up operating the cash register. These days she straightened shelves or helped out if the curator needed assistance with a visitor or a researcher, which meant watching like a hawk to make certain nothing in the permanent archive was disturbed.

Etta's personal donation to the museum decades earlier had been her extensive collection of Green River newspapers. Although the curator tried to convince her to digitize them, Etta always found room somewhere in the building for the boxes.

"It's not the same online," said Etta. "Part of history is the feel and smell of the paper. It's like a book in your hands rather than one of those Kindle things. I like the color of old newspapers. Some turn yellow, and some turn pink. I wonder how that happens. Don't worry. I'll find a place for my newspapers in the basement if I have to."

That afternoon, as her daughter drove her home, Etta thought back to the 1930s when they drove past the building that used to be the movie house, but was now a tavern.

"I remember so many movies that played there, Patti. It seems whenever I watch a Paul Muni or Jimmy Cagney or Jimmy Stewart movie on TCM I take a trip back in time. Why in the world they made the movie house into a tavern is beyond me. We didn't have a tavern in Green River when I was a girl. Over in Rock Springs they had the Arrowhead Bar. I've got bad memories of that place."

"You're right about taverns and bars, Mom. Maybe the country should have stayed dry like towns down in Utah. But if so, the movie house would probably have become one of those adult theaters, then a video store."

"Some legacy that would have been," said Etta. "The world's turning into casinos and bars. Young people with their breweries and wine tasting and now whiskey tasting in those hillbilly states. And the dancing. Instead of holding hands they're holding onto themselves."

"So, Mom, are you sure you're sticking with TCM? Seems you might be watching other things?"

"Maybe a little. Anyway, I'm sure glad to have TCM and my newspaper collection. You'll make sure they don't burn it when I pass."

"I said I would, Mom. Don't worry."

"A lot of memories in those papers, some good, some bad."

Driving all day and into the evening put the Class C and the Caravan in a KOA in Laramie, Wyoming. They'd stopped at a food store. Dinner that night: pan-fried tilapia with lemon and capers, tomato fritters, and salad.

"If we keep eating like this we'll need two motor homes," said Lazlo.

In bed, he whispered to Niki, "You make me happy to be alive."

"Stay that way," said Niki, kissing him.

Janos bumped his head on the low Class C bunk ceiling. "Enough. Gypsies are asleep."

Outside, at the campsite next door, a man and woman at their campfire smiled to one another listening to the laughter inside the motor home.

"Ain't this the life?" said the man, the flames of the fire flickering in his glasses.

"It sure is," said the woman. "Look at all those stars."

Next morning, as the Learjet 45XR climbed through thin clouds over Chicago's south side, Guzzo made strong samovar-like tea using the microwave and several bags at the refreshment center. Explaining to Pescatore details of pursuing Lazlo Horvath from his apartment and being intercepted by men in an SUV had been pointless.

Back in his seat, teacup on the fold-down table, Guzzo stared at the bull's-eye turbulence in the cup. He looked to the seat across from him. If he weren't the only passenger, he might have commented, the bull's-eye a scene from a disaster flick, a defect in one of the engines. He sipped the tea and decided perhaps he'd make another. He looked out the port window, trying in vain to spot his Orland Park neighborhood and his house through thickening clouds.

So, thought Guzzo, what the hell's going on? How big a stash was there to afford a private jet? When he initially signed on, he assumed he was a lone wolf. This time at the fish market Pescatore admitted there were others. When he asked who, Pescatore mentioned Russians and feds while wiping the filleting knife in an apron smeared with fish guts.

"You'll keep me informed?"

Pescatore put down his knife, wiped his hands in his apron, turned to a cabinet behind him. He retrieved a cell from several and studied it a moment before handing it to Guzzo. "The latest encryption technology. I may need to call you on this one."

"My pockets are full of phones."

Pescatore turned, picked up his knife, and began filleting a fish. "I suppose that's why you wear cargo pants. By the way, there's something I need to tell you from my gut."

"What's that?" asked Guzzo.

"An operation wrapping up requires speedy communication. Swiss banks have become inquisitive. You'll run into others you'll need to eliminate. It's almost over. Time to take care of yourself. The encrypted phone has a duel purpose—urgency toward completion and protection of you and your family."

As Guzzo recounted the conversation, he stared out the Learjet's window. Cloud cover had cleared, giving him a view of farmland, irrigation circles, and other shapes. Like a puzzle, he thought. During the completion of the assignment, would he and his family be able to cash in?

He closed his eyes and allowed the Learjet's engines to lull him to sleep.

Mrs. Hansen, the Green River Historical Society curator, was a tall slender woman in a circa 1950s housedress. She reminded Niki of a schoolteacher, Mrs. Stick-Up-Her-Ass.

"Before retiring to this post, I taught high school history. Covering FDR there was brief mention of the CCC, along with all the other so-called New Deal programs. The local camps are long gone."

"What about structures in state and national parks. Weren't there any here?"

"Not that I'm aware of."

"The roads. My father was at Camp Manila; he spoke of roads, cattle guards, and erosion control work."

"They were building Flaming Gorge dam when my family moved here. Those projects are underwater. We have a thriving community catering to sportsmen and sportswomen. We left city slums behind. Here we have family values. We moved away from Detroit." Mrs. Hansen busied herself with paperwork on the counter.

Niki couldn't recall if, during her phone calls, she mentioned being from Detroit. "It would be nice to speak to someone who was here during the 1930s. I realize it's a long time ago—"

Mrs. Hansen interrupted. "I suppose Etta Pratt."

"Does she work here?"

"She manages a ride in from some of the others. I live on the north side, so there's no way I'm giving her a ride even though she's asked."

Niki could stand it no longer. "Is there something wrong, Mrs. Hansen?"

Mrs. Hansen looked up from her paperwork. "What do you mean?"

"A historical society should be a place for research."

"I do genealogical research myself. It seems to me it might be better if, rather than traipsing around looking for old work sites, some of you CCC researchers would use the Internet. The university in Salt Lake City, for example, has an extensive library of information and photographs online."

"I've been on their website, Mrs. Hansen. I've got every photograph from their archives on my computer. It's in my van. Would you like me to get it?"

Mrs. Hansen stared out the window long enough for Niki to glance there. Lazlo, Janos, and Mariya stood between the van and the motor home. "Mrs. Hansen?"

Mrs. Hansen seemed near tears. "It's just, during the past few years there've been so many of you. I've got work to do, and the museum's collection is so large…"

"I understand. You mentioned Etta Pratt."

"I'll take you to the back room."

Castle Rock loomed above the interstate behind the historical society building. Parked beneath a lone tree in the parking lot, a white Lincoln Navigator had its windows down. The Navigator had Colorado plates. The man and woman onboard wore colorful clothing typical of vacationers. Jennifer, an African American originally named Guinevere (smooth and white) at birth, sat in the driver's seat. Finley (Gaelic for white champion) sat in the passenger seat. Both had short hair and were bare shouldered. They'd finished Subway sandwiches, the crumpled wrappers resting on the console, drink cups sweating in cup holders. Although the Navigator faced Castle Rock, Finley used binoculars to look back toward the historical society building.

"What's going on?" asked Jennifer.

"The Gianakos woman's inside and the others are standing around."

"Any other vehicles?"

"None," said Finley. "The SUV from this morning could be out of our line of sight."

"Maybe one of the crime families Jacobson said to watch for."

"Them, or Russians," said Finley.

Jennifer lifted her iced tea from the cup holder, took a sip, and put it back. "You think there's anything to this?"

Finley shrugged. "With budget cuts, would Jacobson put us on something spurious?"

Jennifer smiled. "Fancy word."

"I'm expanding my vocabulary."

Finley continued watching the three standing outside the historical society building. A mild breeze blew dry air through the open windows. He glanced up at the sky, which was cloudless and clear. In the distance, 20 miles to the east, sun glinted off a jet circling to land at the Rock Springs airport and Finley went back to watching the three people.

CHAPTER 24

Work on the road between Manila and Vernal, Utah, 1939. A plan emerges from dust and heat. The Green River movie excursion looming like an ancient creature from rock shattered by powder monkeys. Seeds planted the previous night when Salvatore Cavallo claimed Barracks Three shared blame for murder. Sal didn't belong in the CCCs; his was a different kind of family. Knowing they'd drive two work trucks on their own because not even one staff driver was available conjured up scenarios as men pickaxed blown-apart boulders.

In retrospect, as old men, they'd think of the plan in terms of a tribe forced to defend itself rather than cowering in a cave. The busted up rocks they banged into truck beds that day were huge. Together they concluded a truck capable of carrying the rock could become a weapon.

Quiet Paul Fontaine cut his arm on a sharp rock. After blood dried over the cut, Paul helped set the mood. "Look, it's a map. My dried up cut's the gorge, Green River in the bottom. Bloodstains are mountains. Town of Green River's up here, Manila's down here. Where blood ran onto my wrist is Vernal. Our camp's here between Manila and the Ute Mountain Fire Lookout Tower."

A few nervous chuckles, but Paul was serious. "Could be a map of where the girl is, pieces spread all over. Imagine her blood drying in the sun for a day before remains were found. Imagine vultures spreading her all over the place."

Only Sal, laughing like a hyena at all the guys looking so serious, hadn't heard what was said. He sat in the shade of a boulder they wished would dislodge. Later he'd meet up with the men in the tan Buick or the black Buick. Out of earshot they spoke of gangster goons and replayed details of the murder. A recent Green River newspaper in the recreation building said her name was Rose Buckles.

Barracks One men, on their second tour at Manila, said Rose was a great gal. At dances there'd been more than a few scuffles over who'd dance with her. Maybe that's why the Green River ladies auxiliary stopped having dances. Too many fights over Rose Buckles.

The 39 minus one Barracks Three men lugging rock into trucks recalled the James Cagney look-alike district commander singling Sal out as a go-getter, and the camp superintendent giving hell to the Four Horsemen. Like the staff owed Sal and his family a goddamn favor!

Sal called the Ukrainian-Hungarian Bela Lugosi, and the Scandinavian kid named Borg, Boris Karloff. Like calling Henry, Henrietta, after hitting him with a shovel. Repeating *Henrietta* over and over until the grudge match. Finally, Henry disappearing, his body probably buried at a work site, maybe that rock pile down in the gully, or a rockslide in the gorge.

The previous night pulled their lives inside out. Many found strands of red hair in work slacks. Others found strands hidden in corners of footlockers, some of the hair with pieces of scalp. The way Sal raved about Rose's hair had those who didn't find strands figuring they would eventually. Who the hell'd believe CCCers? "*Hey, you gotta do somethin' about this guy in our barracks...Please, Superintendent!*"

At lunch break, several huddled behind the GMC. Eventually all 38 swung by because the water jug was there. When it was obvious Sal grabbed lunch and was off by himself, the kid from Chicago nicknamed Silent Joe Palooka, who'd had some college classes, spoke up.

"If we say something, we're in trouble with staff and the goons. If we keep quiet, he kills another girl or someone else. Therefore, we've got to do something."

Quiet Paul Fontaine with dried blood on his arm looked off into the distance. "He enjoyed it. Everyone'll be busy with FDR's war and he'll be out there. We got no choice. He's worse than a wild horse."

The Buick had been a furnace. After putting on fresh clothes, both washed their shirts, slacks, underwear, and socks in the motel bathroom sink and hung them to dry on the hitching post railing out front. It was a bone-dry breezy night. They sat on folding chairs outside, sipping bourbon and watching their clothes dry.

The stocky man looked to the room next door and the empty parking spot in front. "Where'd Manny and Al go?"

"Arrowhead."

"Probably hotter than hell. I'm glad Sal got talked into the movies."

"Maybe he'll get in a rhubarb with whoever hit him up side the head."

"You sure it was a guy slugged him?"

"We gotta think of ourselves. I'm glad we got new plates on the car."

"It'll be eggs and coffee back in Brooklyn. This place gives me the creeps, especially after that thing with the girl."

"Did the boss say anything on the phone about knowing the kid was out that night?"

"Nothing."

"Manny and Al talk to Rosario and we talk to Big Sal."

"Big Sal's got no clue. His Uncle says shake up the barracks leader and we got no choice."

"Maybe we should mention the pills to Big Sal."

"I sure ain't gonna be the one."

"Shit."

"Yeah, shit's the only word for this mess."

Late afternoon, the town quiet. Hardware store, Nan's Drug and Sundry, and the IGA already closed. The setting sun reflecting pink off the canyon. Because the Green River movie house lobby lights were already on, the old man knew Tom had let himself in early. Tom's rear end in work pants stuck out of the closet beside the inside door to the ticket booth.

"Working on your amplifiers?" asked the old man.

"I think a twin power triode tube blew."

"Okey-dokey," said the old man.

Tom spoke from the closet as the old man walked by. "It's okay, got some spares."

"Fine and dandy," said the old man. He went behind the concession counter, turned on the light for the popcorn machine and, glancing at the closet, grabbed a Power House bar. He opened a drawer beneath the cash register and pulled out the candy inventory sheet.

Tom spoke from the closet. "It'd be nice to have a relative die and leave me fortune like that Longfellow Deeds character."

"Only ones dying around here are kids."

"Yeah, Rose was swell."

"But if someone did leave you a fortune, FDR'd figure out a way to grab it." The old man waited. He liked saying things about FDR and getting reactions. "So, Tom, what song you playing on that thing tonight? No alligator swing racket and no Negro jazz."

"I thought 'Stardust' would be nice 'cause the sky's clear enough to see Utah. Tell me again why we're open on a Wednesday night."

"District CCC commander talked to the mayor. Guess it's a special treat."

"You think CCCers had anything to do with Rose?"

"Doubt it. The mayor says have a movie tonight to show the town isn't paranoiac."

"Para- what?"

The old man loved showing off his vocabulary. "It's when folks are frightened of things that shouldn't frighten them."

Tom backed out of the closet, stood wiping one hand on his trousers and holding a sleeved record in his other hand. He turned and walked to the counter. "I thought the mayor was suspicious of those boys."

"Maybe. Amplifier fixed?"

"I'm gonna try it."

"Not too loud."

"Can I make it loud tonight?"

"Sure, no one will be in town but them boys. Might as well give them a nice sendoff. Who's singing the "Stardust" song?"

"Hoagy Carmichael."

"Good, his voice is assuaging."

"Assuaging?"

"It means to bring comfort, what this town needs after what happened to Rose Buckles."

Tom pulled the record from the sleeve and held it up to the light. "They had another church service for Rose this afternoon?"

"Those things are more for people left behind than victims. In a couple weeks the local pastors will call it quits. It's nothing like all the services we had for the big war."

"I wonder when the next war's gonna be."

The old man smiled. "FDR won't take us to war. He wouldn't dare jeopardize our peace."

"Jeopardize or not, my dad says we'll go to war eventually. I figure I'll be a radio operator in a bomber."

"Well, good luck. I still say FDR won't go to war. You going to try that out now?"

Tom held the record sleeve in one hand and the record in the other. "Oh yeah, Hoagy Carmichael with his deep, soothing, crooning, and *assuaging* voice. Too bad Billie Holiday doesn't have a version."

When Tom went to the record player in the ticket booth, the old man reached for the Power House candy bar he'd hidden at the side of the cash register and took a big bite.

Windless, waning moon already set, starlight shadows in rock and shale. Shine of the Green River at the bottom of its gorge spindly and black, awaiting smaller gorges cut over time to feed it. Occasionally, when a sudden storm pours over rock, small gorges come alive like blood veins feeding a heart downstream. One dry mini gorge is alongside the road from Green River to Manila. Some local maps call it a gully, others a ravine. A two-foot culvert, put in during washout road repair, is down ten feet in the ravine. A section north of the culvert is so steep someone placed several half-foot warning rocks at the edge. A sagebrush lizard rests motionless atop the largest warning rock, a black shadowbox image in starlight. A flash of light in the distance startles the lizard into a slither down to the bottom.

From deep in the ravine, the blinding light that frightened the lizard came closer, rays descending the down slope like a parent in a lighted hallway opening a door to check a child. Theoretically, lizards have no such thoughts. But humans do. Young men far from home to earn 30 dollars a month with 25 sent to family might think of parents checking on them.

An engine being gunned followed the light, then the squeal of brake shoes on pitted metal drums echoed into the ravine and far away into the distant gorge. Dust, plowed by skidding tires, advanced into the headlight beams. The engine stopped, the headlights stayed lit. Young men's voices, some testing lines between puberty and maturity, cried out.

"Shit! We'll all be dead!"

"Not yet!"

"Come on! He's a live wire back here!"

"You saps are good as dead!"

"So's your old man!"

"Did you spoon before you used the shiv?"

"Fuck you! She was a flat tire! I didn't do nothin'!"

"That ain't what you said last night!"

"My dicks'll get you!"

"How many did daddy send?"

"Fuck you!"

Young men shadowboxed in headlights. Several grabbed one man and threw him into the ravine. Arms, legs, shoulders, and dust.

"Attaboy! Break a leg!"

A scream, followed by, "Hey! My shoulder! You guys leave me here you're dead!"

Shadowed figures slid down the slope then climbed back up. Rocks bordering the edge of the ravine were kicked down. There was so much dust the twin headlights of the truck resembled movie projectors with busted films. Voices became quieter.

"Now what? I'm not drivin' it in there."

"Everyone here will push."

"Can't we wait for the other guys?"

"No."

From down in the ravine, "Hey! Get me outta here!"

From the edge, "For the girl! Now, push!"

The truck, headlights lit, rolled forward, then fell onto its side, plummeting into the ravine like a train derailing.

A scream. The truck's headlights flashed orange, one after the other, and went out as it overturned to a stop in the black pit.

The slow raspy turning of a pair of rear wheels, then silence until the young man trapped beneath the truck moaned. The sound of another engine came from the north, lights in the distance, dust in the air, young men with arms at their sides standing at the edge like rocks marking the dropoff.

"He ain't dead. Now what?"

"We all agreed! Get the others!"

Running feet, followed by a voice in the distance. "Hurry up! We need help!"

"Where is it?"

"This way."

The voices came closer to the ravine at which some young men stood as sentinels while others slid down on backsides.

"Did he heel and toe out of here?"

"He's down there."

"Is he—?"

"No, but he won't be doin' the Lindy hop no more."

"Oh, Jesus. What'll we do? There were 39 at the movies and only 38 will be back."

"We all agreed on this, pardners. So come along down."

"You ain't FDR."

"Yeah, but I'd have no trouble hog-tying you."

The moaning in the ravine continued. Those on the edge hesitated as if awaiting a boxing gloves grudge match. Two falsetto voices duked it out.

"It's on him but he's not hamburger?"

"I told you we should've used the Dodge."

"What's that got to do with anything?"

"Everybody knows Dodges are heavier than GMCs. We found that out when we had to push it up the hill at the fire tower."

Bela spoke with authority from deep in the ravine. "All of you will come down here! Move over to this corner! Must I wait?"

"But there's blood!"

"I see it! In the dark it's black like—!"

"Like what? Her blood?"

"To hell with blood!" shouted Bela. "We made our vow! When I say lift, we all lift. When I say drop, we drop."

Everyone slid down the embankment. There was a strange smell in the ravine. Sweat, hot metal, and gasoline. One of the guys spun two of the

GMC's upturned wheels. The wobbly wheels silhouetted against the starry sky were reminiscent of the elevated knees of a woman on her back from the deck of flip cards one of the guys had hidden in the bottom of his footlocker back at camp. Yeah, back at camp down in the canyon where everything must be peaceful compared to this.

Finally, when they were gathered, Bela gave his orders. "We will all lift." And a moment later, "Good, on three. One, two, three—"

Metal squeaking and twisting, along with moans becoming screams, pierced the night as the truck was lifted and dropped. A final scream echoed through a nearby canyon. The men in the ravine remained silent until the echo quit.

It took several minutes. But finally the screams became whimpers and harsh wet inhales and exhales changed to…silence.

"That's some crooner. He won't sing no more."

"That's the idea, his mouth's shut for good."

"I wish I was back riding rails. Those were the good old days. Oh, God— Did he have hair on him?"

Bela again. "I felt inside pockets. No hair. We carry her hair. It was part of our agreement. Each received strands and promised. After tonight we never speak of it. If someone asks, he put down money saying he wished to race back from Green River. During accident those of us with him in the GMC became scratched and bruised. Say it back to me."

"Yeah, we know. Scratches and bruises. I got one and so does Joe."

"When camp superintendent asks, Sal waved his sawbuck. The argument over whether the GMC could beat the Dodge was his wager. The sawbuck went back into his pocket. He left without waiting for anyone to cover bet and few were able to get into the GMC with him. Those of you in back jumped out before truck rolled."

"Don't worry. We'll be Charlie McCarthy dummies."

"It's not funny! Do we agree?"

"Yeah, yeah—"

"All of you, say it!"

A chorus of muted voices. "Agreed."

"Does anyone not agree?"

No response except the shadows of fidgeting young men against the twinkling backdrop of stars. One man lifted a cap to scratch his head, another hugged himself and shivered, a third stood at a distance pissing against a rock. Instead of lighting cigarettes like they usually would, they gathered in small groups, their youthful brashness extinguished.

Bela climbed out of the ravine. "Come. We must all squeeze into Dodge."

The upturned wheels of the GMC were motionless as they trotted away. An engine started reluctantly in the distance, one gear ground into another, and the Dodge labored into the night with its load of 38 men. Because of all the legs dangling off the back and sides of the open truck, it could have been a huge bug skittering across the parched earth. It took some time for the dust to settle.

The only sound in the ravine was the ticking of the GMC's engine as it cooled. Below the front corner of the overturned GMC, starlight reflected in a pool of black blood. Nearby, a shadowbox sagebrush lizard skittered beneath the wreck.

There were 38 now. With four jammed in the cab of the Dodge, that made 34 in the back. Bela, wedged in the middle with two hips banging his, couldn't help thinking 13 plus 13 plus 13 equaled 39, and here there were only 38 in the Dodge as it struggled in lower and lower gears up the grades, Joe beside him banging the shift stick against Bela's knee as they neared camp.

Morning on the road between Green River, Wyoming, and Manila, Utah. Cool, sunny, windless, and dry despite distant thunder to the south. Dust had settled back on arriving vehicles, all black except the Green River hospital ambulance closest to the ravine. Behind it, two Wyoming state police cars and the Sweetwater county sheriff's car. Facing north, a Dagget county sheriff's car and two unmarked cars. Down in the ravine the Sweetwater county coroner was in suit and tie, the ambulance driver in jacket and slacks. The cops in blue uniforms with officer's hats and the Army officers in olive drab and tan uniforms with garrison caps looking down from the ravine edge waited for a nod from the coroner. When they got it, several looked toward the sky. The sun was behind them to the east.

"Wrecker's on the way," said a Green River cop.

"Guess we'll need it to get him out of there," said the Pocatello District CCC commander who resembled James Cagney.

"You'll notify next of kin?"

"My camp superintendent'll do it. He knows the young man."

"Too bad when the young get killed."

"You mean like the Green River girl?" asked the James Cagney look-alike.

"You think this has anything to do with Rose's murder?"

"No, my camp superintendent says they were racing trucks last night."

"Don't you have regular drivers?"

"Someone messed up and told the men they could drive them."

"How many were out here?"

"Thirty-eight. Thirty-nine including that one. They're saying he's the bad nickel, arranged the truck race that got himself killed."

"Too bad."

"Yeah, we could've used a man like that in the upcoming war."

"You really think we'll have this war?"

"I've seen this before. It's inevitable."

"Young men like the ones at your camps will be the ones who'll suffer."

"That's the way war goes."

The cops and the CCC Army officers helped the coroner and ambulance driver up the last steep part of the climb from the ravine. The sound of an engine came from the north, the wrecker like a herd of horses chased by a cloud of reddish brown high desert dust.

The tan Buick's tall driver waited while the stocky passenger went to the Manila post office phone booth. After previous hot days, the cool was welcome. They'd been south of camp waiting for CCC crews on the Vernal road but nobody showed. They'd considered driving into camp to find out what was going on, but didn't want to be seen. As the driver stared at his partner jabbering in the phone booth, he looked forward to being back in Brooklyn where everything was closer, not miles away to a damn telephone.

An old man came from the post office and limped the other way without looking toward the phone booth. The stocky guy finished and walked slowly back, stopping halfway to remove his hat, wiping his head with his handkerchief while looking back toward the phone booth, then hurrying to the car without putting his hat back on. He slid in and slammed the door. He stared out at the phone booth.

"The sun made the phone booth a furnace. I'm trying to forget—"

"What the hell is it?" asked the driver.

The passenger suddenly resembled a fat sweaty kid. "Called the camp a couple times. Got a secretary. I can tell something's up when I say I'm a relative. Wants me to leave a message but doesn't ask my name. So I call again and say I need to talk to the superintendent. I make off I'm Big Sal. Next thing I know I'm on the horn with the superintendent and he's telling me he's sorry but has some really bad news and is there anyone with me. I says my old lady's with me. He asks if there's anyone with the two of us. Now I'm in really deep, so I says one of our company workers is here. And that's when he tells me."

"What?"

"Little Sal's dead."

"Holy mother of God. How?"

"A truck accident coming back from Green River last night. Because of where Little Sal was sitting, he got crushed."

"Shit. Maybe we should see the body and make sure."

"He says they took the body up to the morgue in Green River."

When the driver started the Buick, the stocky guy asked, "Where we going?"

"Where do you think? We got to make sure."

An hour later, by insisting they were long lost uncles traveling west, the pale-faced mortician gave them a quick look, patted them both on the shoulders, and next thing they knew they were back in the Buick that felt hot despite the cool day.

"Now what?"

"You heard pale face. He wants us, being we're relatives, to call the parents."

"The boss and his uncle put us out here to take care of the kid and now—"

"Let's head west."

"They'd find us."

"Let's tell Al to call? He's got the inside skinny with Rosario. He's from Kansas City so maybe he won't get burned so bad. Yeah, Al calls the uncle and has him tell Big Sal. Depending how it goes, we figure whether it'd be a good idea to go back to Brooklyn."

Camp Manila, Sheep Creek Canyon. Thunder in the mountains before dawn, but no rain. At breakfast, after announcing the "accident," the camp superintendent gave the day off and left with a couple assistants. Decken considered showing a geology film he'd gotten from Salt Lake, but knew better than to approach the superintendent. Everything was canceled. The only thing planned was an evening service by the district chaplain driving in from Pocatello headquarters.

Decken walked the camp to see what was up. Barracks One, Two, and Four men gathered in the recreation building, several saying they always thought Barracks Three was wacky, not only because of Sal Cavallo, but because Barracks Three "city boys" got too much slack. Whoever heard of trucks out at night without at least one LEM driver? Then there was that European guy with the accent, the hair cutter, and Henry disappearing, and the Buicks with two on board always around Barracks Three's job site.

At lunchtime, someone put cigarettes on the tables. Free cigarettes were usually reserved for Sundays or special occasions, a couple guys always managing to come early, swipe them, and sell them back later. Especially Sal Cavallo, stealing cigarettes one of his specialties. Today at lunch the cigarettes stayed put and Decken noticed men who didn't smoke offering cigarettes to men who did.

Another wacky thing was a full meal of meatloaf, mashed potatoes, and beans at lunch instead of job site sack lunches. The smell of meatloaf baking wafted through camp all morning. Decken heard a couple guys say if they closed their eyes they could be home because it smelled like moms' cooking. After an afternoon with guys speaking quietly and smoking, or playing ping-pong in the recreation building, everyone somehow agreed to put on dress uniforms early because the bulletin board showed a repeat of lunch but with apple pie thrown in.

At both meals, Barracks Three men sat at two of the long tables side-by-side separate from the others. After the short service given by the district chaplain and dinner, Decken, who'd been sitting with other LEMs, walked to the Barracks Three tables and said, "Sorry about what happened, men."

On his way out the door, Decken turned back and saw the Barracks Three men staring at him with strange looks on their faces. They hadn't taken a bite of pie, whereas men from other barracks were finished and either filing out the door or up at the coffee pots.

The sun was low in the west, getting ready to set behind Windy Ridge. Beyond Windy Ridge was Ute Peak and the fire tower, but Decken couldn't see it from here. He had a funny feeling about the fire tower, like it was an eye of God watching. Decken felt there was bound to be trouble in camp, but wasn't sure why he felt that way and walked slowly back to his quarters. The rumble of thunder from miles south rolled across the mountains.

Warm Brooklyn evening, 1939. Salvatore Cavallo on his second story back porch. A baseball game ended in the park a block over and he watched as boys made their way into the neighborhood. It'd been a semi-official game complete with coaches and umpire dads. He wished Little Sal were still a boy, out there on the diamond instead of in Utah swallowing dust. That's what Sal said was his main job, swallowing dust.

Cavallo picked up his wine glass and took a sip. Back in the house the radio console boomed in the living room, Francesca listening to big bands because what else was there to do on a warm summer evening? Music in the house was better than arguing. When he and Francesca argued he didn't mention Uncle Rosario still playing the goddamn godfather. Cavallo took a gulp of wine to finish the glass and poured more from the half-empty bottle.

Things would be better when his uncle died. Cavallo could call his son back from Utah. He'd be Little Sal again, getting in trouble here where he could keep an eye on him. Maybe assign Lonzo to keep him in line. Yeah, good idea. If his uncle died he'd bring Sal back to Brooklyn, make one of the other boys his driver, and give Lonzo a babysitting job with muscle. His uncle, having only girls, had no idea what it took to raise a Brooklyn boy.

As Cavallo was about to take another gulp of wine, he heard a car in the alley and saw Uncle Rosario's Lincoln behind the back wall. The driver jumped out and opened the back door, but instead of his uncle, Felice the fawning odd job runner, got out. Felice wore no hat and, to Cavallo, his hair was too long in back. Maybe his uncle liked Felice because he was like a daughter. Maybe he and his uncle would have a few laughs tonight talking about Little Sal out west sowing wild oats. But when Felice ran around the Lincoln and opened the opposite back door and Cavallo saw the look on his uncle's face, even at this distance, whatever laughter he thought was there vanished.

The back door banged against the wall. The big band music from the living room radio console cut off in the middle of a tune. Uncle Rosario's voice and Francesca's voice and Felice's voice went at it for a while. The only thing Cavallo could make out was his uncle insisting, "I must speak with Salvatore." Then shouting, "No! Only Salvatore! Now!"

Cavallo stood in the hall at the top of the stairs. At the bottom his uncle struggled, trying to climb. Finally, gasping, his uncle motioned to Felice who picked up his uncle and carried him like a baby, the cane pointing the way, Uncle Rosario coughing. Felice put Uncle Rosario in the wicker sofa, propping cushions around him. Tears streamed from his uncle's eyes, coughs erupted like phlegmy thunder. Maybe his uncle would die before his eyes.

Before Uncle Rosario could say anything, the phone rang downstairs inside the house. A moment later Francesca's screams filled the house and echoed out into the neighborhood.

Francesca leaped into the casket. It took three of the boys to haul her out and carry her away. The doctor's pills did no good. She didn't make it to church. At the cemetery she sat in the limousine while Lonzo accompanied Cavallo to the grave. Uncle Rosario was in a wheelchair, Felice pushing. Francesca's ulcer had begun bleeding when they met the train bringing Salvatore's body home. During the funeral luncheon Francesca vomited blood into her plate and was hospitalized. Blood on pasta like spaghetti sauce.

Cavallo and Uncle Rosario did not speak until Little Sal had been in the ground a full week. Eventually they met in the office at the main warehouse. He asked that Felice not be in the meeting. His uncle motioned Felice out. They sat across from one another at the table, the conversation short and to the point.

"I want to find those responsible."

"I agree," said his uncle.

"You said we have funds. Can we use them?"

"Of course."

"Write down instructions. When you pass I'll take this to its conclusion."

"It will be difficult."

"Difficult, but not impossible."

"Do you want me to contact our men in Utah?"

"No, I'll do it!"

Frank Grogan, the elderly Green River sheriff, knocked on the Minch house front door. Not much of a house, not much of a door from the way it rattled. Mrs. Minch was younger than Frank, but weathered from washing and hanging out laundry for townsfolk.

"Cletus is over to his job in the hardware store."

"I told him I'd bring back his fishing creel. I washed it good after the coroner finished."

Instead of grasping it by the strap, Mrs. Minch reluctantly took the creel in both hands as if it were a small animal. "I don't know if Cletus'll be down to the river to fish anymore."

"Aw, he should go fishing," said the sheriff. "I would if I was young. Tell him to come see me. He did his duty and...Well, I'd like to encourage him."

Mrs. Minch stared over the sheriff's shoulder as if there might be an answer in the clear blue sky. "Cletus says fishing won't feel the same. Says the freedom of it's lost."

As he walked back to his office, Sheriff Grogan was glad he'd had his say and hoped Cletus would visit. A buzzard soared above, heading south toward the river. He stood in the center of the street and watched the buzzard for a long time. The buzzard catching the updraft from the gorge, not having to flap its wings, heading south like the mountains there had a morsel on the end of a line and were reeling the buzzard in.

CHAPTER 25

After the Learjet landed, Guzzo drove his rental Camry to the same junkyard truck shop from which he'd rented the tow truck. The alcoholic manager sat on an old car seat in front of the office shack. Guzzo said he needed to do some back road driving. When the manager hesitated, Guzzo lifted his jacket showing his Glock in its shoulder holster.

The yard had several suspicious-looking windowless chop-shop garages. The manager gave no indication he'd dealt with Guzzo before, struggled to his feet, and limped to a three-year-old Ford 350 crew cab, mumbling it was rough looking but powerful.

"I don't need a back seat," said Guzzo.

The manager tried a smile in reaction to Guzzo's smile. "It's what I got. Super Duty Lariat 4 x 4. Geology crew hauled a horse trailer. Got them where they wanted. Raised suspension, dually rears, oversized tires, skid pad, front bull guard. Tough as shit."

Filling out paperwork with bogus California ID, Guzzo noticed a stack of fire extinguishers and emergency medical boxes, most likely lifted from "junked" vehicles.

The pickup smelled of booze and cigarettes until Guzzo was well down the road with windows wide open and air conditioning blasting. Eventually he closed the driver's side window but left the passenger window and two rears down. The 350 sounded good, especially with the passenger window down because the huge exhaust pipe was on that side.

At the airport, cell towers had come into range, pushing through Pescatore's texts. Three more actors to watch for: unnamed New York competition, government agency people who might be watching the New Yorkers, and Russians. With no change of plan indicated, he'd follow through on the original mark and anyone associated with her. If others got in the way, the big pickup would help. During their last face-to-face, Pescatore insisted federal sources were dead on, meaning there was at least one mole.

At Interstate 80 Guzzo upped the back windows and floored the 350. Because shitty smells inundated the truck's fabric, passenger window down would be his routine. He smiled at himself in the rearview mirror. Gas V8, not a diesel like last time. He adjusted the mirror; no one coming on the ramp with him.

Crazy world, everything interconnected like a Hitchcock plot, complete with *MacGuffin*, the thing everyone's after. Could be old money from the 1930s because guys who served in the CCC in Manila, Utah, in 1939 had been marked. A shitload of money hidden away. Russian hounds picking up the scent in Ukraine.

Lazlo joined Niki in the Green River Historical Society's back room. They agreed Janos and Mariya take the Class C to a nearby campground south along the gorge and they'd meet there.

Etta Pratt was a spry old bird wearing a housedress with daises. Reading glasses hung on a silver chain, her eyes blue and clear.

"At my age I say what's on my mind. You two married?"

"We met a few days ago," said Niki.

"How nice. I like it when people just meet." She lowered her voice. "Don't mind the curator. We're supposed to be the historical society. She says, *forget about it.*"

"You mean the '30s when the CCC was here?"

"Folks today have no idea how difficult things were. FDR pulled us out of it. Today it's ranching, oil, mining, casinos and anything else that sends cash to Wall Street. I watch TV." She lowered her voice again. "When I went into the hospital for blood work, they had Fox News on. Can you believe it?"

"I know what you mean," said Niki, glancing back at Lazlo. Instead of smiling, Lazlo stared off toward bookshelves, a strange look on his face. Niki returned her attention to Etta Pratt. "About the Manila CCC camp in 1939—"

"Oh yes, you say your father was there?"

"Yes, we'd like to get a feel for how things were in town. My father said he was taken to the hospital here for an injury and sometimes they came to a movie."

"Let's see. If your father was here in 1939, it was near the end of the CCCs. By then the ladies auxiliary stopped throwing dances. I used to go, though I wasn't old enough. Some of us younger girls snuck in and the auxiliary was afraid we'd hook up with older boys. Anyway, no more dances after the head of the auxiliary got interviewed by the newspaper."

"*The Green River Star?*" asked Niki.

"Yes, my daughter and I still get it delivered. Back then it was a newsboy on a bicycle, now it's that creature in his pickup truck who drives on the wrong side of the street."

"Do you recall stories that might have been in the paper in 1939?"

"Recall?" Etta stood and walked slowly to a closet behind her. "Lazlo—what an interesting name—Lazlo, perhaps you could help." Both Etta and Niki waited a moment. Lazlo stared at the bookshelves as if he were in another world.

"Lazlo?" said Niki.

"Oh, I can help."

Newspapers, boxes of yellowed newspapers from the 1930s. Etta slid one onto a table. "Here it is, 1939."

Niki carefully removed the stack from the box labeled 1939 and began reading headlines. "Amelia Earhart Officially Deceased, Thousands Killed in Chilean Earthquake, Hitler's Demands Never-Ending, Slovak-Hungarian War Begins, Spanish Civil War Ends, Lou Gehrig Gives Moving Speech, FDR Serves Hot Dogs to King and Queen At Hyde Park."

Etta put on her reading glasses and watched as Niki went through the newspapers. She stopped Niki at the paper with the FDR headline. "That was sad. Poor Rose."

"What?"

Etta pointed to a sidebar headline. "Cops Still Baffled in Local Girl's Bloody Murder."

Niki sat down with the paper, put it between her and Lazlo so they could both read the article. After a minute they stared at one another. "Hair," said Lazlo, clearing his throat as if he hadn't spoken for a long time. "Her hair was pulled out."

"Yes," said Etta. "Rose had the prettiest red hair. There are legends in town about the gorge being named after her. Flaming Gorge because Rose Buckles was flaming gorgeous. Of course that's impossible; the gorge was named in 1869 by John Wesley Powell."

Lazlo had once again turned to stare at bookshelves. He was silent a moment, turned back to the newspapers, then to Etta. "Did you know Rose Buckles?"

"She was older than me and my classmates. One thing for certain, we all wanted to be like Rose."

"In what way?" asked Lazlo.

"All the young men made eyes at her. She didn't live long enough. Lazlo is it?"

Lazlo nodded.

"You know something about Rose being murdered?"

"I'm not sure what you mean."

"The way you study my eyes." Etta turned to Niki. "The way he studies my eyes, like a fortuneteller. Rumor was Rose's father was a fortuneteller. Played a fiddle. Some said he was a Gypsy. Supposedly hightailed it before Rose was born."

"Lazlo's a retired detective," said Niki.

"Oh, that's the reason," said Etta.

After a pause, Niki asked, "Did Rose Buckles date CCC boys?"

"She was a little girl when the CCC camps opened. It wasn't until '38 or '39 she dated."

"Did authorities question anyone in the CCC?" asked Lazlo.

"They insisted CCC boys had nothing to do with it. Everyone assumed it was a teamster passing through. Teamsters stopped at bars in Rock Springs. Rose and some of her friends snuck over there. Other rumors besides teamsters, of course. One was a Salt Lake Mormon devil came up and did it as a lesson for their girls. In those days we lived for rumors. One thing keeps the story alive around here is the way she was killed. Her hair tore out and her body cut to pieces. A boy named Cletus Minch, who died in the war, found a hand and took it to the sheriff. If Cletus hadn't been fishing that morning, vultures and wolves would have…"

Etta seemed to be thinking. Neither Niki nor Lazlo interrupted.

"After they found what was left of Rose, we heard they had a ruckus down at the Manila camp, Utah state police called in. Supposedly hoodlums and nothing to do with the CCCs. You've got to understand, the war in Europe was on everyone's mind."

"Are there articles in the paper about this ruckus at the Manila camp?"

"Nothing," said Etta, taking off her glasses. "Some townsfolk thought maybe hoodlums killed Rose. But that rumor died when everything in the news turned to war. I've wondered over the years if the so-called CCC camp ruckus had *something* to do with Rose."

Lazlo looked off toward the bookshelves again. "Do any of Rose Buckles' relatives still live in the area?"

"One," said Etta. "Rose had a younger sister who married after the war and had a daughter. The sister and her husband died from lung cancer. Their daughter moved from Green River down to Manila."

"Rose's niece?" asked Niki.

"She's middle aged, but damn if she doesn't look like Rose Buckles grown up, red hair and all. Maybe, since she's been here with her partner and looked at my papers, she could help."

"Is she researching the CCC camp?" asked Niki.

"She wants to know how her aunt died. I'll write down her phone number and such."

While Etta rummaged inside a huge purse on a table behind her, Lazlo touched Niki's hand. He had a faraway look in his eyes.

"Lazlo, is something wrong?"

"When I was a boy in Ukraine there was an old woman in the village who told fortunes. Funny thing…Etta reminds me of her."

"I've got it," said Etta, turning back toward them with a small address book in her hand.

Mariya drove the Class C while Janos used the GPS to lead them to the campground at which they agreed to meet Niki and Lazlo. Janos leaned forward looking into the oversized outside mirror. "How long has that black SUV been behind us?"

"Since we left Green River. Should I stop and see if it passes?"

"There's a picnic area before the campground. Just ahead, on your left."

Mariya pulled in and watched the side mirror. "I think it passed. Wait. It slowed. I can't see it now."

"Park so the side door faces east. I'll get a message to Lazlo."

"You have a signal?"

"I think so. Marinas are down the road."

After sending a text to Lazlo in Hungarian, Janos saw a rocky outcropping at the back of the picnic area, large boulders that might provide an overview. He turned on the Elvis CD someone left in the dash radio and had Mariya lock the side door behind him. He walked straight away from the Class C, watching the spot where the SUV was last seen. In a minute he was climbing a tall boulder. Near the top the road to Manila looping south along the gorge was visible. In amongst another group of boulders not far past the picnic area entrance the sun shone on the black SUV.

Only a few minutes had passed. Rather than returning to the Class C, Janos slid off the boulder and made his way through high desert scrub. The SUV was backed in, obviously ready to follow when they left the picnic area.

Janos reached beneath his jacket out of habit. No shoulder holster, no pistol. Those were back in the apartment storage in Kiev.

Because of the way the SUV was backed in, he was able to stay out of sight of the side mirrors and the rearview mirror by keeping a boulder between him and the passenger compartment. Eventually, after battling an angry sticker bush, he crawled directly behind the SUV. The engine was off, the darkly tinted side windows open. He smelled cigarette smoke and heard a cough. He expected to hear FBI or Homeland Security men speaking. When the two spoke Russian, he had to stifle and audible grunt.

"Perhaps we should have followed the others."

"Sergi said stay with Nagy and Nemeth. They have the key."

"Does Sergi know what the key opens?"

"Nagy got it from Eva Polenkaya."

"It must be the key to a fortune if Sergi's interested."

"A fortune in US dollars would be good for the economy."

"We'd get Putin medals."

Both men chuckled. Janos crawled away. It was hot in the Class C; Mariya opened windows and shut off Elvis. Janos typed another text in Hungarian to Lazlo.

"You think Russians have been responsible for these killings?" whispered Mariya.

"They're fishing."

"What will we do?"

"Wait for Lazlo and Niki, then decide. Is your international phone charged?"

Mariya pulled the phone from her backpack. "Who are you going to call?"

"It's evening in Kiev. Yuri Smirnov from the SBU home with his vodka. A good time to call a man with connections."

Interstate 80, halfway between Rock Springs and Green River, Guzzo saw them parked near the Firehole Canyon 191 exit ramp. The spot they'd parked, the car's make and model—Dodge Charger, Wyoming rental tags—and the fact there were two men in front made it obvious. Feds or hoods, watching him. He exited at 191 south, the same route he'd taken down to Vernal for the motorcycle job. The Charger followed, a roadmap flipping around in front of the passenger a little too obvious, especially with what looked like a smart phone mounted in a holder on the dash.

Guzzo recalled the hit men from *Bullit* chasing Steve McQueen. All they needed was overcoats and hats. A beautiful day, the afternoon sun bright on the Aspen Range. Guzzo took them on a cruise down 191, turning west on the Firehole Canyon road to the gorge. The Charger took the bait. Pescatore had said things were coming to a head. Guzzo repositioned his Glock further forward beneath his jacket. Although there were other vehicles on 191, the canyon road was deserted. He pulled to the side after a blind curve. The Charger passed. He waited until the Charger was out of sight, then another minute.

He did a U-turn, spinning the dually wheels on embankments. The sound of the engine and stones being thrown came into the open passenger window. Soon they were behind him, heading back to 191. Guzzo glanced at his GPS. No way they had time to get a look at the canyon; they'd U-turned somewhere and were following. He recalled seeing two-tracks heading east into the Aspen Range last time he was here. He turned south on 191 and looked for an appropriate turnoff. The Charger dutifully followed. The first two-track looked like a dead-end. The next had worn ruts and continued far to the east zigzagging up the foothills.

After turning, the 350 created a fog of dust for them to choke on. Around a rock outcropping to the left there was a steep drop-off to the right. He skidded to a stop. By the time the Charger stopped in his dust plume, he was out on the driver's side of the Charger with his Glock in both hands, safety off. The driver lowered his window. The passenger held onto a phone. Both kept their hands in sight. The driver wore a Cubs jacket.

"You've been pulled over before," said Guzzo.

The driver did the talking. "What makes you say that?"

"You know what to do with your hands."

"We're lost."

"Does your friend have a GPS tracking app on his phone?"

"All right, we're not lost. We just do what we're told."

"Who do you report to?"

"It's a phone number; I don't know. Can you quit two-handing that thing?"

"Passenger, I saw your hand move."

"What do you want us to do?" asked the driver. "We'll go back and say we lost you. That good enough?"

"Let's say you turn around here and head back to the highway. Go back to Rock Springs, drop off your rental, and fly away. Can you do that?"

"Sure, if you give us room to turn around."

"You can turn around here."

"How?"

"Back and forth. If you get stuck I'll pull you out with the truck."

Guzzo got back in the truck, belted in, and leaned out the window with his Glock aimed at the passenger who stared at him wide-eyed. He watched as the Charger went forward and back on the narrow two track trying to turn around. When it was broadside and backing up close to the steep drop-off, Guzzo put the truck in reverse and floored it.

The 350 slammed its oversized rear bumper into the Charger's passenger side and shoved it sideways down the two-track until it went over the drop-off and turned onto its roof. He had a road flare from the 350's door pocket out and lit before the Charger stopped rolling. He butt-slid down the shale embankment, Glock in one hand, lit flare in the other. He opened the non-locking gas cap and shoved the flare through the filler flap.

"Nothing personal!" he yelled, pulling the flare back out.

Guzzo knew the Charger wouldn't become an instant movie set fireball, but it had been driven hot, plenty of vapor to keep things going. As Guzzo climbed the embankment, still holding the lit flare, he saw flame at the gas filler door increasing steadily like an idling blowtorch. At the top of the embankment, he turned and stood on the two-track to watch. The driver's door pushed open, but hit shale. The smashed passenger door didn't budge and he could see a piece of a side airbag sticking out a half-open window like a pale tongue. There were shouts and screams. Although he was out of the line of fire, he ducked when one of the men fired a gun several times. More screaming followed this.

It took a while, but eventually the flames at the neck of the tank heated enough to ignite a rear tire and the underbelly. Finally, the gas tank melted through, gas spilled into the air and flared up. Like in *Bullit*, where they'd run into a filling station, the two hoods burned to a crisp. Guzzo doused the flare in shale, threw it into the back of the 350, found a place ahead to turn around, glanced down at the flaming Charger, and drove back to the highway.

After speaking with Etta Pratt, Lazlo left Niki inside with the curator. Traffic groaned on the nearby interstate, almost like city traffic. A sudden feeling of *déjà vu* hit him. On a day like this in Kiev he'd go for a lunchtime walk. Perhaps he should take a closer look at Castle Rock resembling a Kiev cathedral on the far side of the highway. Perhaps he should take a closer look at the white Lincoln Navigator he'd seen parked since their arrival.

As he walked, Lazlo searched the horizon between buildings. He went around back past garbage dumpsters, then into the parking lot where the Navigator was still parked beneath the single tree. Beyond the Navigator Castle Rock was larger than he'd expected, overlooking the town. When he emerged from behind the building it was obvious the male passenger was watching the entrance with binoculars. When the man saw Lazlo, binoculars disappeared and a bare elbow hung out the window.

Lazlo kept walking and soon saw that an African American woman was in the driver's seat. Both had short hair and were dressed in bright athletic clothing. Having been an investigator all his life he doubted they were tourists. He walked the outer edge of the parking lot, staring at Castle Rock, then turned abruptly, as if to walk back to the building, and approached the Navigator's passenger side.

The passenger was perhaps 30, his right arm obviously sunburned. The African American woman was somewhat older. Both stared at him. The binoculars were in the man's lap. Although the engine was off, the woman's hands were on the steering wheel in driving position.

"Good afternoon," he said.

"Nice day," said the woman.

"Are you from around here?"

"We're tourists," said the woman, taking charge.

Body language, a slight movement of her head. She was boss, the young man the recruit.

"I'm curious what government agency employs you."

The young man pulled his sunburned arm inside and looked to the woman. She hesitated a moment. "Excuse me?"

Lazlo leaned on the passenger door. "You've been watching since we arrived. Why didn't you follow the motor home?"

The woman smiled, looked into the rearview mirror pretending to check her lip-gloss.

"I'm alone," said Lazlo. "Obviously I'm not a threat."

"All right," said the woman. "What do you want?"

"Would it be all right if I made a phone call?"

"Who you going to call?"

"Anthony Jacobson."

Both stared with looks of realization they tried to hide.

Lazlo continued. "Jacobson said there'd be people out here. Other parties would be watched. Who are you watching? Yes, you can say you're watching us. But I don't think you followed us here. Someone led you. May I call Jacobson?"

"A man full of questions," said the woman. "Sure, call him. But I've got one for you. When you walked around the building did you see a black SUV back there?"

"I did not."

"Shit," muttered the man.

Lazlo got out his phone, spoke to the answering service. "This is Lazlo Horvath for Anthony Jacobson."

He hung up and the phone rang seconds later.

"What is it, Lazlo?"

"Two of your people are here."

Lazlo handed the phone into the Navigator. The young man simply stared. The woman reached across and grabbed it.

"Yes?...Yes, Sir...I understand...We lost the other vehicle and we're in the parking lot with him" She looked to Lazlo. "He wants to know what you want us to do."

"I suppose, rather than following us, it would be best to look for your original mark."

After getting his phone back and exchanging numbers, Lazlo walked back to the building as Niki came out. They got into the Caravan.

"We should eat something," said Lazlo. "The two in the Navigator had Subways."

"Did you speak with them?"

"Yes, I'll tell you about it. There's the Subway."

As Niki turned into the Subway, Lazlo glanced back and saw the Navigator leave the parking lot and head the other way.

A phone conversation in Hungarian, sandwiches and drinks for four, Niki driving while Lazlo spoke to Janos and watched for the rest area, careful they wouldn't pass it because of the black SUV. After turning in Lazlo retrieved his .38 that had been locked in the gun case inside his suitcase. They joined Janos and Mariya by going through the motor home's side door.

"Except for pepper spray, our only weapon," said Lazlo, checking the cylinder as Niki, Mariya, and Janos watched.

Janos reached out to Lazlo's arm. "You remember Yuri Smirnov?"

"Is he still in Kiev?"

"Yes, I called moments ago. He was playing drunk. Instead of answering questions, he questions me. Asking about location from several angles.

Because of the international phone, I was able to convince him Mariya and I are still in Kiev. It didn't end there. He asked about you, wanting to know if you were still in Chicago. He feigns reminiscing old times, then suddenly asks about Eva Polenkaya. I never told him about Eva or the key."

"You think he's turned over?" asked Lazlo.

"He spoke Ukrainian, saying everyone is searching for something. He might know about the Brooklyn safe deposit box. After speaking with Smirnov, I called our old chief investigator."

"Boris Chudin?"

"His men keep tabs on Smirnov. Their information digs the Smirnov hole deeper. He's been in contact with a woman in the US who speaks Russian. The woman met Smirnov in Kiev during Fool Day celebrations, coincidentally a few days before Doctor Marta's murder."

Lazlo shoved the .38 into his jacket pocket. "They're following the money."

Janos turned to Mariya and Niki. "Lazlo and I need to confront the Russians."

"Only if you are both careful," said Niki.

"We were partners in Kiev," said Janos. "Notorious Boy Gypsy and Father Gypsy."

"The windows are open," whispered Janos as they crawled low behind the SUV.

A moment later Lazlo held the .38 beneath the chin of the driver and Janos held a stubby twig within his sleeve poking beneath the neck of the passenger. More than the sight of Lazlo's .38, their abrupt and demanding Russian/Ukrainian curses typical of militiamen disarmed the two. Soon all four were back at the Class C. They deposited the contents of the SUV's glove box on the table at which Mariya and Niki sat. They'd tied the Russians' hands behind their backs with their own shoelaces and their shoes flopped on their feet. Lazlo pointed his .38; Janos pointed the two automatics taken from them.

"Their spare magazines and cartridges fill my pockets," said Janos in Russian.

"Your pockets must be heavy," replied Lazlo in Russian. "I have their cell phones."

"If I use their pistols on them, one advantage will be a reduction in weight," said Janos.

The younger Russian who'd been the driver looked terrified. The older faked a yawn.

Niki handed over a roll of gray duct tape. "I found this in a storage compartment."

Lazlo gave the cell phones to Niki. "Look at recent calls or saved contacts."

"Russian technician designed phones," said the older Russian, smiling. "Everything erases."

Janos switched to English. "Our friends are multilingual, at least English as well as Russian. There's a Hungarian phrase for what we need to do. *Felfuggeszt hagy.*"

"A similar English phrase is to hold one in abeyance," said Lazlo. "Better abeyance than death."

Mariya took one of the automatics from Janos and aimed it professionally, joining in the conversation, obviously discomforting the Russians. "We could put them in a safe deposit box if we found one large enough."

More tape was found and all four helped with the abeyance process, the Russians on their stomachs on the Class C's back bed facing forward with arms behind their backs. Knees bent, feet up, and not only taped together, but taped to their wrists. While they spoke with the two, Janos moved them around. "To keep blood circulating."

"Your English is good," said Mariya.

"Why have you been killing old men and relatives of old men?" asked Lazlo.

"You must have heard of the Civilian Conservation Corps," said Niki.

"How about Doctor Marta Voronko?" asked Mariya.

Janos pressed his automatic first below one chin, then the other. "And Sonia Nagy."

Finally, the older of the two said, "Nothing rings the bell."

"What about the name Demidchik?" asked Lazlo.

A slight reaction from the younger man.

"Or the Chernobyl murders?" asked Janos

Another reaction followed by the older man eyeing his partner.

"Or trafficking young women in Ukraine so you can sell them abroad?" asked Mariya.

"We were to keep an eye on you," said the older man. "The reason is unknown to us."

"I overheard you talking about money for Putin's coffers," said Janos.

"Of course," said the older man. "Isn't it always about money?"

"Certainly you've heard of the Chernobyl murderer who stuffed Chernobyl soil into victims' mouths."

"Of course we've heard of it."

"The investigation interferes with your trafficking networks."

"We don't know anything about that."

"So, what about this?" asked Lazlo. "What about money accumulated before the second war being used to kill old Civilian Conservation Corps men and relatives who dare investigate?"

Silence, then Lazlo nodded to Janos.

"I overheard you earlier," said Janos. "You know about the key I received from Eva Polenkaya. Your comrade Sergi wants the fortune. I'll call and say you plan to betray him."

The younger man's eyes widened. "You know Sergi?"

"Shut up!" said the older man in Russian.

As evening came, Janos drove the Class C followed by Niki's Caravan south to the campground near the state line and the Lucerne Valley Marina. They shared sandwiches with the Russians, feeding them bites and giving them water. Rather than all staying in one place, Niki and Mariya drove the Caravan to a motel over the state line in Manila to stay the night.

Lazlo and Janos would stay in the Class C with the Russians, perhaps learn more and decide what was next. Janos called the number on the rental agency agreement using one of the Russians' cell phones. He complained the SUV stopped running and the agency should send a tow. Afterwards the number he'd called was indeed erased from the cell's memory.

The marina run by Rose Buckles' niece was down the road from the campground. Next morning Niki and Mariya would be back and they'd decide who'd visit. After dark, Janos took a short walk with the phones designed by "Russian technician, to the marina parking lot, pulled the batteries at that location, then returned, spreading the phones and batteries across a field of scrub.

According to Pescatore's last message, a pair from Ukraine was in the area; the man an associate of Lazlo Horvath who'd contacted Niki Gianakos. The original mark had quadrupled. Guzzo's message back to Pescatore told of the two in a rental, east coast accents, tragic accident. Although on retainer, he also received body-count bonuses. As he sat in his motel room, he suspected this would increase. Pescatore insisted the assignment was nearly concluded and he could look forward to retirement. Even so, a money trail was appealing.

The Green River Best Western had restaurants on both sides. He'd backed the 350 pickup into a spot behind the motel in an unlighted area near a dumpster enclosure. He showered, changed to fresh cargo pants and hooded sweatshirt, walked across parking lots, and picked up his phone order from a steak house. While waiting for change, he gave the young woman behind the cash register the Guzzo smile. She did not smile back, did not even look at him. But when he walked out the door he glanced back and saw her watching.

The cool evening air, the quiet, the sound of his own footsteps. Things coming to a head required caution. Not far away, on the other side of the gorge, he'd left two hoods burnt to a crisp. Pescatore had connections built up through decades—US crime families, international Mafias, intelligence agencies.

Guzzo detoured behind the motel to the keyed rear entrance. Because of the bright lighting in close to the motel he could barely see the 350 near the dumpster enclosure. He checked to make certain he closed the passenger window, then recalled having done so after his arrival. In closer to the motel but still at the lot's perimeter, a white Lincoln Navigator was also backed in with its tailgate off the edge of the lot and onto the scrub. Not a handy spot from which to unload baggage. Wyoming plates, perhaps a motel employee. Yet it was a new Navigator. Except for trucks towing trailers with drilling equipment straddling the marked parking spots at the perimeter, other vehicles in this part of the lot were beaters and pickups—motel and restaurant employees. He recognized a rental agency sticker in the Navigator's windshield. He pulled out the small flashlight he always carried. Drink empties, fast food wrappers, and an empty binocular case. He doused the light and looked up quickly at the motel. A curtain on the second floor swung back into place.

Instead of going directly to his room on the first floor, Guzzo climbed the stairs and walked slowly down the hallway. The smell of grilled steak and garlic bread oozed from the bag he carried. As he walked past the room where the curtain had momentarily pulled aside, he stopped to listen. Nothing but televisions. He turned around and headed back to the stairs. At the bottom he looked out at the lot. No change. He climbed the stairs again and quietly opened the door to the second floor hallway. No one.

Back in his first floor room Guzzo spread his feast on the room desk and emptied pockets. He plugged in phones, checked one to make sure the motion detector he'd left near the 350 was activated, and turned on the television. The usual news channel crap—more on Anthony Weiner, complete with underpants bulge, hackers breaking into a Senate computer, and an old Boston mob boss arrested. If they'd waited, someone like him would have been assigned to hit the old fart and they'd save all the legal fees. Guzzo grabbed the motel channel lineup card, found TCM, and went there.

On screen a younger Martin Landau points a pistol at James Mason. The first bit of dialogue is from Mason with an astonished look, "Leonard?" Then comes the shot fired at Mason who, realizing it's a blank from Eve's pistol, slugs Landau. Guzzo pulled his chair closer to the desk and began eating.

Hitchcock would have enjoyed being here, zooming in on hints about the Navigator in the parking lot. Though he never told Vera, Guzzo relished these moments. A good steak, a decent motel room, a test of his second sight, and the puzzle. It was good to be the killer.

CHAPTER 26

Middle of the night, Russian discomfort complaints became gastrointestinal. The older man spoke of bladder and intestinal pain. The younger was blunt. "Soon we'll shit our pants."

Lazlo and Janos checked the duct tape supply, concluded they had plenty, and released one at a time. First they had the older Russian hop into the small bathroom. They dropped his pants, praised his colorful shorts, and sat him down. When the older Russian was back on the bed secured in backwards fetal position with fresh tape, they gave the younger Russian his turn. He was quicker, with steady streams and sighs of relief.

"Aren't you going to wipe my ass?" he asked in Russian.

"You'll have to live with skid marks," said Lazlo in English.

With the Russians secured, Lazlo motioned Janos to the front of the Class C where they sat in driver and passenger seats and leaned close. "I wonder if these two and your SBU contact are connected," whispered Lazlo. "Tell me again about yesterday's call."

"I assumed Smirnov was home drinking alone. Yet his conversation contained hesitations as if considering what another person might think. He's not acting alone. His agenda is outside his agency, perhaps involving the female contact in the US."

"When should we mention his name to the two back there?" whispered Lazlo.

"Wait until we can watch their faces. For now I'm going up to my bunk."

"And I'm going to my table made into a bed."

An hour later, amid snores within the confines of the Class C, Lazlo's cell phone rang its Kafkaesque pinball tone, the screen saying it was Jacobson.

"I have a request," said Jacobson. "We've intercepted overseas and New York messages. Unknown content, yet the messages are to cells in your area and the Chicago area. I'd like to keep in touch and have the two in the Lincoln Navigator watch your backs."

"Who's at our backs?"

"Russians and organized crime."

"Ukraine SBU?"

"Not sure, they're good at covering."

"About the Russians," whispered Lazlo. "They're in here with us snoring away."

Jacobson laughed. "You and Janos work fast. Remember, the two in the Navigator are there to watch. If you need them, be sure to call."

Kiev, mid-morning. Yuri Smirnov arrived late, wheeled to the elevator by the building guard. He closed his office door, wheeled himself behind his desk, and sat in the sun.

Last night's call from Janos Nagy had been on his supposedly secure cell phone. Nagy provided nothing and he'd wanted to call his US contact, but because of his drinking and the questionable cell, he'd waited. He turned from the window, opened his right hand desk drawer, and removed the SBU encrypted phone. He looked at his watch; US time would be middle of the night, or very early morning.

After several rings a sigh came from the phone.

He spoke Russian. "I'm sorry to have awakened you, darling. All parties are in the area of interest. Soon, one of us will be receiving information along with the key. Do you understand?"

A woman, tired from having been awakened, replied in Russian. "I understand."

Hearing her voice brought back fond memories of their lovemaking long ago when he was in better health.

Mariya and Niki arrived at camp before dawn with coffee and breakfast sandwiches in noisy paper wrappers. Janos turned on the lights. "I thought American motels had free breakfast."

"Too early," said Niki. "We picked up drive-through last night and microwaved it this morning."

The older Russian spoke from the back. "No baked goods?"

"Did they complain during the night?" asked Mariya.

Janos stood and spoke loudly. "Earlier when I called my friend Smirnov at the Ukrainian SBU the young one bellowed."

To this, the younger Russian looked confused, and Janos continued.

"Smirnov simply laughed. And of course the SBU has no record of them in any of the aliases we found in their possession."

As agreed, both Lazlo and Janos watched the Russians carefully, looking for reactions. They'd moved them about earlier. There were no reactions and Janos shook his head.

"Soon we'll leave for our meeting at the marina with Rose Buckles' niece." Lazlo paused, both he and Janos studying the Russians. Again, no reaction.

Janos said, "We'll eat first, then Russian roulette before the sun comes up."

The older Russian smiled, the younger looked worried.

No reaction to the names Yuri Smirnov or Rose Buckles. Yet reactions to the mention of Russian roulette. The Russians ate voraciously as if it were their last meal.

Guzzo stood at his motel room window, curtains open, lights out. His personal and equipment bags on the bed. The room faced west, the beginnings of sunrise shining on distant boulders. The 350, drilling equipment trucks, and the white Navigator layered in dew in the parking lot. He left his bags, put out the do not disturb sign, and headed down the hallway where he could smell the motel's free breakfast.

He paused in the lobby holding a morning newspaper studying others in the breakfast room. Drilling crew workers finishing up. Three elderly couples and a family with three children alternately grazed the breakfast bar. A little girl reminded Guzzo of his girls. He imagined them at the breakfast table with Vera, felt a twinge of homesickness.

A young man and woman arrived. Both dressed casually, the woman African American, the man Caucasian. Everyone in the breakfast room seemed comfortable with this except the elderly couples, who stared at CNN on the wall-mounted television more than before.

After the elderly couples finished and were gone, the young man glanced at Guzzo while waiting for the toaster. Guzzo made certain his long sleeve shirt covered his tattoo and put down the newspaper. He noticed the young man, wearing short sleeves, had a sunburned right arm.

After getting a cup of coffee, Guzzo stood perusing the fare. The African American woman was behind him at a table eating yogurt and a banana. The young man filled a cup with orange juice, placed it on the table, and went back to waiting for the toaster.

"Motel toasters are the slowest in the world," said Guzzo.

"You travel a lot?" asked the young man.

"A requirement of the service," said Guzzo, purposely smiling.

A hesitation before the young man smiled back. The toaster popped. "Finally."

"Next time try the waffle maker," said Guzzo. "It's faster."

Guzzo took bagel and coffee back to his room and stood eating at the window. When the man and woman walked to their Navigator, he hoisted his bags, hurried down the hall, and waited at the back exit until the Navigator was gone. The sun, flame-colored on the western hills, reminded him of the two toasted in the Dodge Charger on the other side of the gorge.

The Lucerne Valley Marina store was packed with fishermen, fisher-women, and racks of gear. As promised by Etta Pratt, Clancy Vargo's hair was very red and very long. Niki introduced herself with a brief mention of having questions about Rose Buckles. Clancy asked another woman behind the counter to cover for her. Lazlo, Janos, and Mariya, feigning interest in colorful fishing lures, followed when Niki motioned to them.

Clancy was slender and perhaps 50. Her red hair, when she turned, down to her waist in an intricate braid. They sat at a long table in a lunchroom/storeroom. After introductions, Niki filled Clancy in on basics—Niki's father having been at the Manila CCC camp in 1939, Doctor Marta Voronko's grandfather also having been there, the deaths of Niki's father, Doctor Marta's father and grandfather, Doctor Marta, and Sonia. Niki summarized

Lazlo's investigation into the deaths of George Minkus in Chicago, Buddy Minkus on his motorcycle in Colorado, and the fact Buddy's grandson, Cory Minkus, went missing after contact with Lazlo, his last known whereabouts Vernal, Utah.

A stocky woman with short hair interrupted saying the store was busy. When Clancy said this had to do with research into Rose Buckles' death, the stocky woman waved her hand, said she'd get someone from the dock to help, and told Clancy to take her time. After the visit from the stocky woman, whose eye contact indicated she might be the partner Etta Pratt mentioned, Clancy said, "Sue will handle the store. Let's talk."

"I admire your hair," said Mariya.

"Thanks," said Clancy. "I admire your accent."

"Etta Pratt said your parents were dead," said Lazlo. "I'm sorry."

"Heavy smokers and drinkers. The murder had its effect. Mom looked up to Rose."

"Did your mother speak of the Manila camp or the CCC boys?" asked Niki.

"The way Rose died was Mom's obsession," said Clancy. "Growing up I'd hear stories not only of what troublemakers CCC boys could be, but stories of Lincoln Highway workers, railroad workers, truck drivers, ranch hands, Indians off reservation, even ghosts and monsters."

"Do you mind if I say something?" asked Janos.

"I don't mind."

"You've been doing research concerning your aunt's death for some time. I wondered where you're at in your research regarding the nearby CCC camp."

"There was a Green River town camp," said Clancy. "Enrollees and staff there cleared because of a chess tournament with townsfolk. You're speaking of the Manila Camp. Correct?"

"Yes."

"It wasn't far from here, down the road south of Manila where the Uinta Mountains begin. The 1965 Sheep Creek flood washed all traces of the camp away. The only thing left of their work, besides the road to Vernal through the mountain, is the Ute Mountain Fire Lookout Tower. One thing I've been looking into lately is information that led me to a man in a nursing home in Vernal. He was a camp LEM—Local Experienced Man. He's in his nineties and as far as I know the only one left from around here. Sue and I spoke with him a few weeks back. He remembered Rose's murder, but there was something else he said that might help. He said there was a big ruckus at the camp a week or so after Rose was found. Didn't say what exactly, just some kind of ruckus nobody seemed to care about. By the way—Janos is it?"

"Yes."

"It's your accent and Mariya's accent. A couple days ago when I was off, Sue mentioned two men with accents here asking questions. They said they'd be back, but so far nothing."

After explaining the situation as best they could in a way that would not unnecessarily upset Clancy, she agreed to have her partner go out to the Class C to look in at the Russians. It took longer than expected. After peeking inside, Sue wasn't sure, saying one was younger and one was a bigger guy.

"Can you take the tape off their mouths?"

Janos held an automatic on them, telling them to stare at his trigger finger. One after the other, Lazlo removed the tape, had them speak, then replaced the tape. The Russians looked forward and to the side, but always at Janos' finger tight on the trigger of the automatic. Outside Sue apologized. "I'm sorry, I'd like to say yes. The accents are similar, but they're not the two who questioned me. They drove a black Suburban like the Secret Service."

In the parking lot, after getting details about the old man at the nursing home in Vernal, Janos and Lazlo told Clancy and Sue there might be more activity in the area because they weren't the only ones interested, especially if Sue was correct about another pair of men. They suggested Clancy and Sue call local authorities. Both agreed, saying no problem because the sheriff kept his boat at the marina. Also, they had a pistol and shotgun hidden behind the counter.

"Can I ask one more question?" said Niki.

"Sure," said Clancy.

"What's the derivation of your name?"

"My dad was Irish. It was Mom's idea because of her sister Rose. Clancy's Irish for redheaded warrior."

Sue hugged Clancy. "That's my girl."

"One other thing," said Clancy. "Rose's father was supposedly from somewhere in Eastern Europe. Family called him a redheaded Gypsy ghost because he disappeared before Rose was born. They said he played the violin."

After leaving the marina, with Janos and Mariya in the Class C following Niki and Lazlo in the Caravan, Lazlo couldn't help thinking of the redheaded violin-playing deserter he'd shot near the Hungarian and Romanian borders. No. What good was thinking 50 years in the past? Concentrate on the present.

He turned to Niki. "We should get rid of the Russians, yet keep them in abeyance."

"Leave them stranded in the mountains," said Niki. "Who'd give them a ride?"

"Excellent. And in a little while I'll call the Homeland Security pair in the Lincoln Navigator and send them on a goose chase to the marina."

"The crowd assembles while we go to Vernal," said Niki, handing Lazlo a slip of paper.

Lazlo read aloud. "Decken MaCade, Mountain View Care Center."

"I already put it in the GPS."

"The GPS is like my brain," said Lazlo.

"How?"

"It's as if I've been here before. A view from above, but in 1939. The gullies and mountains remind me of the Carpathians." Lazlo paused. "I can imagine it in winter. Victor and I—boys—sent to arrest a deserter. Victor shot and me shooting the violinist—the Red Gypsy. A family line of red-heads, the grandfather a redhead. Somehow red hair, specifically Clancy's, mixes in with the red walls of the canyon…I'm being foolish."

Niki glanced toward Lazlo. "Psychic connections are anything but foolish."

Rather than driving aimlessly searching for his mark in the Dodge Caravan, or waiting for word from Pescatore, Guzzo felt the Lincoln Navigator pair would eventually provide needed information. They were government agency, their interest in Niki Gianakos further evidence Pescatore's opinion of things coming to a head was true.

He followed without being observed. The Navigator pulled into a parking lot off the main street. He parked in a strip mall out of sight of the Navigator. He put on a watch cap and oversized weathered denim jacket he carried in the side compartment of his main bag. He shouldered his equipment bag, a well-worn backpack. In worn jacket and broken-in hiking boots, he could be a local ambling down the side of the road, or a homeless man.

As he walked through the strip mall lot, he noticed a black Chevy Suburban. A similar Suburban had tried following on his last trip to the area when he was driving the tow truck. Wyoming plates, darkly-tinted windows. No one inside. Brushing his hand at a front wheel well opening, he felt heat; the Suburban's engine recently turned off. He went over a rise behind strip mall dumpsters, pausing to look back using binoculars. No one in the

Suburban, but inside a laundromat two men who did not look like they were there to wash their underwear. One stood staring out the window. The other sat in a chair talking on a cell phone. Both wore dark shirts and slacks and had short haircuts. If there were more operatives, as Pescatore hinted, these two were better at keeping their distance than the crispy critters in the Charger, or the man and woman in the white Navigator.

Guzzo took a short cut through a park. The Lincoln Navigator was parked at the Green River Historical Society that backed up to open land with the interstate and the landmark Castle Rock in the distance. The setup was quick once he found a gully along the edge of the parking lot. Through binoculars he read the hours of operation. Because the Navigator was parked in the side lot, it seemed they were waiting for the place to open, which would be soon.

A car arrived, parked at the side, and a woman went around to the front and unlocked the door. After the pair from the Navigator went inside, Guzzo removed his long distance microphone from his bag and set it up in a growth of sagebrush, much to the dismay of a lizard that ran across loose stone in the gully. The visit to the historical society must have a connection to Niki Gianakos. Her father had been in the CCCs and she, like others, was most likely researching the Manila camp to the south. Guzzo aimed the directional microphone at the passenger compartment of the Navigator.

The two were in the building a long time. Another car pulled up, dropping off a very old woman who tottered in. He heard an occasional car drive past on a road behind him, but the guardrail blocked him. His plan, should he be approached, was to feign having spent the night in the gully. A police car drove past but obviously the officer did not see him, driving on to a Subway in the distance. The only creature aware of him was the lizard, making its way in fits and starts back to the sagebrush.

After nearly an hour, the woman and man came out of the building and got back into the Navigator. Guzzo was about to pack up so he could hurry along the gully back to the 350 when the windows on the Navigator powered down. Perfect, the couple began speaking.

"I feel sorry for that old woman," said the man, his sunburned arm out the window.

"The curator's panties were wedged," said the woman.

"Did you have the feeling the old woman didn't want to talk?"

"The curator's the only reason we learned anything, complaining about the Greek woman. At least we found out about the marina. Her saying the niece had a strange partnership was homophobic."

When the Navigator started, Guzzo put his microphone away and ran along the gully back to the strip mall. The black Suburban and the men who'd been in the laundromat were gone. Once he fired up the 350 it didn't take long to catch up. He kept his distance, using hills and switchbacks for cover. The Navigator crossed the bridge over the Green River and headed south toward mountains on the horizon. After Black's Fork there was a sign for Buckboard Marina, but the Navigator continued south. Eventually, after cat-and-mousing behind the Navigator for 50 miles on the treeless terrain, it turned east toward the gorge. A sign said "Lucerne Valley Marina and Campground."

The road angled southeast and downhill. It was curvier than the main highway, with lookouts and side trails popping up on both sides. Cars, pickups, and campers rushed past, the marina apparently popular. Suddenly, flashing lights on his tail. He pulled to the side with others. A State Police SUV sped ahead. The Navigator was also pulled to the side. He waited to get a few more cars between him and the Navigator, knowing the road eventually ended at the gorge.

A red Dodge Caravan came by going in the opposite direction. Guzzo tried to see the rear plate, but a motor home behind the van blocked his view. This wasn't the first red Caravan he'd seen on the way down from Green River. It would be a giveaway to U-turn on the narrow curvy road. He was about to pull out and keep going when another police SUV sped past, Dagget County Sheriff.

Guzzo's second sight began kicking in. Perhaps the police SUVs had to do with Niki Gianakos and her friend. He got the 350 back on the road, following two pickups pulling fishing boats. When he was within sight of the campground, reservoir, and marina, he stayed behind the last pickup. Ahead, he saw that the sheriff's SUV that had passed a short time earlier was pulled up beside the white Navigator in the marina parking lot. The woman and man from the Navigator stood outside, the sheriff apparently checking IDs while two state police officers looked on.

Guzzo's second sight went into high gear. The red Dodge Caravan that had passed followed by a motor home. If Niki Gianakos and her partner Lazlo Horvath knew they were being followed, calling the police to delay the tail is what an ex-cop would do.

He turned into the campground ahead of the marina, spitting gravel as he headed back onto the road. They'd be going south. Cops were back at the marina and he drove aggressively, moving slow vehicles aside. Finally, approaching the small town of Manila, he caught up and saw the Caravan turn onto Route 44 toward Vernal with the motor home close behind. Neither stopped in Manila and there was no Chevy Suburban. Second sight, and the close distance between the motor home and the Caravan, told Guzzo the vehicles were traveling together.

Halfway along the scenic byway through the mountains to Vernal, near an elevation sign at 9,500 feet, Niki pulled into a scenic overlook.

"Are they keeping up?" asked Lazlo.

"Janos is having to floor it on grades."

"That last sign said 8% downgrade and 10 switchbacks coming up. It'll kill the brakes."

"Here they come. Should we drive ahead and have them meet us there?"

"Hang on," said Lazlo, getting out. "I'll speak with them."

After the motor home parked, Lazlo went to the driver's door. The window was open and he heard the Russians in back complaining with various Russian curses about how Janos drove.

"I smell antifreeze and brake pads," said Lazlo.

"Like driving the Kremlin on wheels."

"I have an idea."

"We chain them to back bumper for ballast?"

"Good one, but I have another idea."

Guzzo saw the motor home struggling on steep upgrades. He'd been this way before; the downgrade to Vernal would be hard on brakes. He kept his distance, watched for others following, but saw only tourists or locals in a hurry. As he rounded an outside hairpin, the red Caravan and motor home were stopped at an overlook. He found an out-of-sight pull off large enough for the 350. Several vehicles sped past, transmissions downshifting like rats in cages. He took his binoculars, ran across the road, and climbed an outcropping of rocks.

After several minutes the Caravan moved on and Guzzo climbed down and ran back to the 350. He drove ahead, expecting to see both the Caravan and the motor home gone from the overlook. But when he rounded the curve, the motor home was still there.

He slammed on the brakes, pulled to the side, and backed the 350 out of sight. When the motor home moved forward he'd be able to see it. Perhaps the engine overheated. Perhaps they'd switched drivers, Niki Gianakos and Lazlo Horvath now in the motor home. But his second sight told him something else. All four in the Caravan and they'd abandoned the beast.

He started driving, but suddenly the motor home lurched onto the road. It gained speed on a long downgrade and he caught a glimpse of the Caravan far ahead. At the bottom of the downgrade with brake lights on all the way, the motor home's rear brakes were smoking. Obviously, whichever one of the four was driving had failed to shift into a lower gear. It must be the Ukrainians, thought Guzzo. One of the Ukrainians at the wheel, unfamiliar with oversized American vehicles. If it was the Ukrainians, rather than Niki Gianakos, the original mark, and her friend Lazlo Horvath, they were definitely in the way. At the speed they were going, Guzzo wondered if they'd rendezvous with the Caravan before nightfall. Pescatore's last messages kept running through his mind. The series of assignments coming to a head and the need to eliminate anyone in the way. Mountain driving, especially in a motor home, was difficult.

Being familiar with the road from having driven a large tow truck on it not long ago was helpful. Guzzo waited until the Caravan was out of sight. The drop-off was treacherous, the motor home unwieldy and vulnerable. No other vehicles in sight and Guzzo had a 350 with oversized tires and bull bars. When the moment arrived, when the physics lined up, he began passing the motor home and turned the 350 into its front end to change its direction.

He braked hard as the motor home's momentum carried it through the barrier and over the edge. A cloud of dust rose from below, turning distant pines gray. Even though no other vehicles were around, Guzzo imagined a frantic witness account—coming around the corner, seeing the motor home go over, how terrible it was.

After he parked and jumped out, the motor home was still crashing down the mountain, tearing itself to pieces. For a normal job he'd climb down and make certain they were dead. But the motor home was too far away and the red Caravan was still on the road, his mark either down there, or in the Caravan.

Shredding, tearing, and screws popping came from below. Guzzo could not see himself smiling but, as he ran back to the 350, knew he was—motor home construction in reverse.

CHAPTER 27

Typical Camp Manila celebration. Hooray, Barracks One powder monkeys finished blasting a mountain pass on the Vernal road. Camp superintendent congratulated Barracks One before a sullen look to Barracks Three. They'd clear the rubble. A bulldozer had gone through and they'd do the rest, hand-loading the trucks.

"Because it's a long drive you'll be on the Dodges an hour earlier."

The way he eyed them, crammed at the back table, everyone knew it was payback for the "accident" returning from the movie house. No more trips to Green River. Movies would be on the recreation hall's projector. There were a few groans, but none from Barracks Three.

It was a quiet night in Barracks Three, 38 men staring at ceiling knots and cracks. At lights out, Bela Voronko spoke up.

"Tomorrow on the mountain we'll be closer to God, who absolves us."

In the middle of the night one of the barge loaders from St. Louis wept. No one knew which except the two. Under normal circumstances there'd be a smart-ass remark, but these weren't normal circumstances.

Bela knew he wasn't the only one awake. He'd stuffed the envelope containing Rose Buckles' hair into his pillowcase. What if it were possible to speak with her? This hair once rooted in her head so close to his head. Would she approve of what they'd done? Or would she be angry? Especially with him because of his so-called "taking charge." He felt tears in his eyes, and knew, by the eerie hush of the barracks, other eyes were the same.

In a dark motel room in Rock Springs with the tan Buick parked outside, the lanky driver and his stocky partner also lay awake. They didn't shed tears or hold hair.

"It's crazy," said the stocky man.

"What they did, or what Big Sal wants us to do?"

"Both. Why can't he leave it?"

"His Uncle Rosario wants things like in the old days."

"Should dig his cronies out of their graves and have them do it. Ghosts chasing ghosts."

"What do you mean?"

"Those boys might as well be ghosts; they'll die in trenches and FDR's generals'll send telegrams."

"You worried they'll haunt us?"

"I don't like the boss using the word *needling*. How the hell do we needle them?"

"We give the officers and LEMs a hard time along with the Barracks Three boys."

"So, whoever's on the job with them tomorrow, that's who we needle?"

"Now you've got it."

"If Rosario had his way we'd plug a few and get the hell out. Our orders come from Big Sal, but Rosario talks to Al and the others. We do the needling, they plug a few and take off. Leaves us holding the bag."

"Big Sal won't let that happen. Rosario's practically dead and Big Sal's taking over."

"I hope so."

"You hope so. You're always saying you hope so. Get some sleep."

From the vulture's viewpoint there should be flesh. Yet, a flyover south to north at sunup revealed nothing except split boulders and dust settling. After sunup, movement drew the vulture's attention. Creatures aboard conveyances crawled into the rubble. All creatures eventually die. Therefore, soaring above the pass this day, and the next, was wise.

The worksite was a mess. After the two Dodge trucks cut engines and fumes faded, Barracks Three men picked up the faint acrid smell of spent gunpowder still in the mountain air. Decken MaCade, a new LEM sent from Salt Lake City after other LEMs quit, drove the lead truck. Smart aleck Barracks Two boys had razzed Decken, making fun of how he tied his tie just so, saying things they thought they knew about Joseph Smith, asking how many wives Decken had.

One of the St. Louis barge loaders drove the second truck, with the other riding shotgun. Bela, on the tail end of the second truck, was first to spot the tan Buick following in the distance. After the crew jumped off, the drivers restarted and turned around to back up to the mess. The Four Horsemen, Nick the Greek (War), Jimmy (Conquest), George (Famine), and Bela (Death) stood together watching the trucks negotiate the narrow gaps between boulders.

"You sure it was the same Buick?" asked Nick.

"I'm sure," said Bela.

"Wonder what they want," said George.

"They're here to kill us," said Jimmy, loud enough to be heard over truck engines.

Others standing nearby also heard and passed it around. Tensions were high, especially with staff hightailing it. Could be the same at all CCC camps. War putting everyone on a pinhead. A Barracks One powder monkey, in his spare time, painted pictures of naked women on pinheads. Everyone thought that was something, naked women on pinheads. But through the magnifying glass, they all looked like guys with tits.

After the trucks were backed in, Decken didn't give orders, but instead heaved the first large rock into the bed of his truck. The racket on floorboards got the attention of those staring at a vulture.

Work went on for a couple hours, filling the trucks, then several jumping on board to heave the rock and boulders off after the trucks drove north 100 yards to a steep downgrade where the rubble cascaded down like steel balls in a pinball machine tilted to the sky. At lunchtime, as the men sat on boulders chewing their bologna sandwiches and drinking cold lemonade, the two from the tan Buick showed up.

Both wore hats, jackets open and ties loosened. They parked in front of the two backed in trucks and walked up like district office bosses. Decken was the only one wearing a tie and khaki rather than denims and they went to him, eyeballing the others. One guy was tall with big shoulders, the other short and beefy. They talked with Decken as the others ate.

Afterwards the two went back to their Buick and spent a while turning it around on the narrow road. When they were gone Decken sat on a rock, looking like buzzards' lunch. He didn't move, not even wiping sweat from his brow. Bela walked up.

"Something wrong?"

"Those guys," said Decken, staring into the distance where dust from the Buick still hung. "I think I'll go back to Salt Lake."

"Why go back to Salt Lake?" asked Bela.

George Minkus joined them. "What did they want?"

Decken looked up to George and Bela. "They'll kill me."

"They said that?" asked Bela.

"Not exactly, but I got the message."

"What exactly did they say?" asked George.

"They said tonight me and the other LEMs and night guard better disappear or we can kiss our asses goodbye. That's when the short one opens his jacket and shows me his gun."

"He threatened to shoot you?"

"He showed me his gun. Ain't that enough?"

"That's enough," said Bela.

"What should we do?" asked Decken.

Bela considered this, looking at the other men.

"Tonight we'll discover whether we are men or boys."

Evening meal. No officers, no LEMs, only enrollees, the kitchen crew, and barracks leaders. The chaplain's assistant tried to say grace, but was late and mouths were full.

"You think Decken spoke with the superintendent?" asked Jimmy.

"Yeah, they deserted us," said Nick.

Bela scanned other tables. Everyone eating, not seeming to notice the absences of authority figures. "Perhaps we should wait before making judgments."

The evening dragged on. No classes. According to barracks leaders the instructors had a conference. As for officers, some kind of meeting in Green

River called by the district commander. If officers returned that night, they'd be back late. A few guys started a table tennis contest.

"Do you notice something?" Bela asked George.

"Besides desertion by the brass?"

"Yes, see how men watch the game, but are not following the ball?"

"You would notice that."

"Also, more men are smoking."

That night in Barracks Three men flipped through magazines or wrote letters. There was little talk, especially after Jimmy and one of the St. Louis boys moved chairs that were usually around the potbelly stove and leaned them against the doors at either end of the barracks. Last time they'd done that was when a bear was near camp.

After lights out they heard a vehicle outside. When they got up and looked out the windows, the faint outline of a Buick was visible in the dark. Inside the Buick a lit cigarette glowed. If someone tried to come in, the chairs leaning against the doors would simply tip over because the doors opened outward, but at least they'd know.

Bela heard bunkmates speaking softly in the darkness. He turned toward George. "I wonder if I'll ever get a chance to go back to my homeland."

"I thought this was your homeland," said George.

"Not where I was born," said Bela. "Where I grew up."

The passenger in the tan Buick glanced at the orange glow of the driver's cigarette. "Smoking heavy again? I don't blame you. If I had a cigar I'd light up."

They were parked near Barracks Three as planned. The only electric light came from the other side of the barracks at the latrine building. The driver glanced in the rearview mirror. "Didn't Al say the others were supposed to be back at the entrance road? I don't see a damn thing back there."

"Maybe they went with Al to get more ammo."

"Where'll they get ammo this time of night?"

"All I know is he said something about ammo. Keep your shirt on."

"Putting a scare into these boys is nuts. No matter what we do it won't be enough. Big Sal has his damn driver Lonzo call us and says put the fear of God into these boys. Al talks to Rosario and it's another story. What're we supposed to do? I didn't join this outfit to kill kids."

"Don't let Al hear you talk like that."

"How's a guy supposed to talk? Maybe we should get the hell out of here?"

"Then what?"

"Drive to Mexico, change our names. I was thinking of enlisting in the Army."

Silence for a while, then the driver heard a sound from his open window like the crackle of tires on stone. He studied the rearview mirror and noticed a momentary movement in the blackness behind them. "I think the others are back there at the entrance. Lights off but I heard tires. So, okay, let's say we go into the barracks, show our guns, and scare their skivvies off. You think it's gonna end there?"

"Only way Big Sal'll be satisfied is if we plug the kids responsible."

The driver put his cigarette out in the ashtray. "We'll end up with the Army after us."

"We arranged for them not to be here tonight?"

"But if they come back and find bodies—"

"All right, all right. We go in and scare the crap out of 'em. Al and the others will back us if there's trouble. But there ain't gonna be trouble from no goddamn kids!"

"You guarantee it?"

The passenger took out his revolver, held it up to the dim light coming over the roof of Barracks Three. "This guarantees it."

"All that guarantees is someone's gonna get it."

The passenger took his time putting away his revolver. "The way Al talks, and us being the ones that have to go in—"

"If we're being set up, I don't want any part of it."

"You and me both."

George Minkus once told Bela how, as a kid, he was able to creep up on anyone at night. He'd put on dark clothing head to toe, get his eyes used to the dark, control his breathing, and move slowly, feeling ahead like a bug with antennae. George snuck up on his parents and was introduced to sex. He snuck up on whoever was it in hide-and-seek. He'd always find a way, even when home was a streetlight pole with the lamp lit. He did this by patiently watching the other kid for a time, then using this knowledge to make his slow, insect-like moves.

Black socks for George's hands and feet came from Jimmy. Black pants and shirt came from Jethro. The knit watch cap was George's own.

After George crept back in through the little used narrow back door, out of sight of the Buick up the road, Bela and the others gathered in the center of the barracks at the potbelly stove. Bela and George sat with their backs against the cool stove while others lay or knelt on the floor, the 38 like puzzle pieces, all ears toward the whispering.

George became visible only when he pulled off his knit watch cap and the socks on his hands. "We're in trouble."

"What did they say?"

"They're supposed to scare us. They have guns and a guy named Al supposedly went for more ammo."

A shuffling in the puzzle around the stove. Bela knew others wanted to ask questions. "Everyone stay silent. It's best if only George and I speak."

"He's right," said George. "The less noise the better."

"Do they plan to shoot anyone?"

"I hate to say it, but they mentioned Big Sal, who I assume is Sal's father. Supposedly this Big Sal guy wants ringleaders shot."

Bela said, "That's me, if they need to shoot someone—"

George interrupted. "But after that, it seemed they'd be satisfied scaring the crap out of us. I had the crap scared out of me listening. Keeping control of my breathing was tough. The other thing…supposedly there are more hoods backing them up."

"The ones in the black Buick?"

"I didn't see it, but it could have been out on the road. These two are worried they might be patsies. Another thing, even though they arranged to have the officers gone tonight, they're afraid what the Army could do to them."

"That's on our side," said Bela. "But still, if they need to shoot one—"

"Forget it," said George. "We all agreed Sal got what he deserved. He planned another girl down the road. Isn't that right?"

Another movement in the puzzle, heads nodding.

"It's time for others to have their say," said Bela. "Beginning to my right, one by one, with no interruption, what should we do?"

CHAPTER 28

R ed Dodge Caravan speeding down the mountain. Dislodged rock on switchbacks crushed to gravel. Lazlo reached across the center console, placing his hand on Niki's thigh.

"I'm glad no one's in front of us," said Niki.

"Especially a motor home," said Lazlo. "It's 4:30. They're wheeling residents to dinner, we can speak with Decken afterward."

"If he hasn't fallen asleep," said Niki, glancing in the side mirror. "By the way, the motor home's out of sight. It'll take them a lot longer down mountain. What do you think they'll do when they get to Vernal?"

Lazlo turned toward the back. "What do you think they'll do? Janos? Mariya?"

With the stowaway seats down, Janos and Mariya lay on the floor. If someone followed only two would be visible. Janos and Mariya were wedged between luggage using Niki's sleeping bag for cushion.

Janos from behind the center console, his voice pulsating with each bump. "Although my plan to tie the Russians to the back bumper was creative, I admit yours was better."

Mariya beside Janos, her voice pulsating. "Niki, we deserve credit. We adjusted bindings and partially tore duct tape to make certain they'd eventually drive the beast."

"When they get to Vernal they'll have problems," said Lazlo. "Especially with their ID collections, cash, and phones gone."

Niki came up behind a Mazda convertible, the passenger taking photos. Niki repeatedly blasted the horn and the Mazda pulled off at the next overlook.

"Sorry I riled them," said Niki.

"Don't be," said Lazlo, feeling a buzz in his pocket. "We have cell coverage. It's Jacobson."

"Lazlo, we've got intercepts. Someone with a connection to the killings. No name or ID, but in particular, the one who killed Niki's father is after her. The pair in the Lincoln Navigator will watch your back. They think they've spotted a man in a black pickup. You still there?"

"Yes."

"Also the Russians—"

"We took care of them."

"I'll call again when I know more."

Vernal came up fast. When the GPS indicated a turn, Lazlo had Niki pass it and go around the block to see if anyone followed. The Mountain View Care Center was on the opposite side of the street. Niki turned into an alley.

Lazlo turned to the back. "Janos, Mariya, go inside and wait for us."

After Janos and Mariya crawled out the side door and disappeared behind a fence, Niki circled the building and squeezed into a parking spot next to another red Dodge Caravan. The back entrance was locked, forcing them to the front. Instead of using the sidewalk, they cut through a garden. Once inside, Lazlo scanned the road in both directions, no black pickup.

A two-bed room. The aide wheeling Decken in said the roommate would be a while. They had Decken to themselves. He was skinny, wearing flannel shirt and bib overalls. His face weathered, wisps of gray hair tangled like sagebrush over his hearing aides. He was on oxygen, nose tubes connected to the tank on the back of the wheelchair. Below the armrest a label with "Decken MaCade's damn chair" printed on it.

Decken smiled at Niki who sat on his bed beside his chair. "You know how old I am?"

"69?"

"I like her. I'll be 94 next month."

"Let's see," said Niki. "When you were an LEM at the Manila camp you were 21?"

"Kids in charge of kids."

"I realize it's been a while, Decken. Clancy at the Lucerne Marina mentioned a camp ruckus in 1939 after Rose Buckles' murder. Can you tell me about that?"

"You're not the first asking questions. I kept quiet until Clancy visited for about the tenth time. It's my age creeping up. Not that I've forgotten, just didn't feel the need to tell anyone."

Niki put her hand on Decken's arm. "My father Nick Gianakos was in camp in '39. He died recently. They called it an accident, but it wasn't."

A grin toward Niki's hand. "Barracks Three, I remember the name. The Four Horsemen in Barracks Three: your father Nick, Jimmy Phillips, George Minkus, and Bela Voronko. Can't recall what was for lunch, but 1939…Yeah, a ruckus. Powers that be snuffed it out. Worried where they'd end up in the service if they couldn't handle things. Poor leadership, loose lips sink ships, that kind of thing. War coming had everyone out for himself. Toss the camp ruckus on the back burner. Years ago I'd have said I wasn't sure if Barracks Three boys were involved. But times change and I'm old. Don't look sad. You think they had anything to do with Rose Buckles' murder? It's opposite."

"Opposite?" asked Niki.

"Justice," said Decken. "Other visitors over the years also had boys in Barracks Three. Wanted to know how things were at camp and what happened. Kept my trap shut. I was yellow. Don't shake your head. They come here to find out why their enrollee from Barracks Three died the way he died and I say I don't know a damn thing when I do know a damn thing!"

Niki waited.

Decken wheezed, steaming up his breathing tubes before continuing. "Some said enrollees saved red hair. Rose Buckles had red hair like her niece. Clancy got me to realize how yellow I've been. No more excuses. Sure, times were rough, and I was in the Navy in the Pacific. I'm a goddamn veteran, but that's nothing when I think how it went in '39 at the Manila camp.

"The camp's gone, especially after the Sheep Creek flood. But something's left behind. I tried to help them. Eventually someone'll come for me because I know about the hiding place."

Decken went silent for a moment. Niki rubbed his arm. "The hiding place?"

"Yeah, at the fire lookout tower."

He laughed and rubbed his eyes. "Let'em come."

He pulled his arm away, wheeled his chair backwards, and opened his nightstand drawer. He reached deep inside for a zippered black bag. When he pulled a revolver from the bag he got a reaction from all four. "Let'em come." After putting the revolver back into the bag and shoving it into the drawer, he had trouble breathing. During the effort to show his revolver he'd dislodged his oxygen tubes. Niki got the tubes back in and rubbed his shoulder.

"Thank you…thank you."

"No problem. My dad got upset when I asked about his time at camp."

She waited, and finally Decken began speaking again. "The Barracks Three boys had no choice. They defended themselves. Afterwards they stashed something. A note, the Four Horsemen said. A note hidden at the fire tower so someday the truth'll come out. They called it the Rose Buckles cache.

"It's not in the tower. They had to renovate that thing for wood rot. What they did is…When you passed through Green River did you see Castle Rock?"

"We did," said Niki.

"What the boys did, they made a replica of Castle Rock about 200 paces southeast of the tower. It's a pretty big. Took the whole barracks to move the rock to a spot on a firm ledge. They planted trees around it. So, there's this note, and maybe something else, underneath a Castle Rock replica at Ute Mountain Fire Tower. After the war, when I was feeling my oats one night, and being they called it a cache, I tried to look under it. But you'd need a front loader. I began worrying it was called the Rose Buckles cache and…"

Decken stared at Niki with tears in his eyes. "What makes me feel bad is, I promised I'd keep their secret. But by now, I figure they're all dead."

They left the Mountain View Care Center the way they'd come in. Niki and Lazlo through the garden, Mariya and Janos along the fence. Heading back north on 191 toward Ute Mountain with Mariya and Janos again lying on the back floor, all four wondered why there was no sign of the Class C with the Russians on board. As they began the climb into the mountains, Mariya spoke from the back.

"I thought I would have to show him the hair from Marta's jewelry box. I've carried it with me all the way from Kiev. The way he glanced at me when he told of the hair—"

Janos interrupted. "Since town there's been a black pickup truck. At first far back, now closer."

Niki drove faster, but slowed when they heard sirens. She pulled to the side for a State Police car followed by an ambulance.

"The pickup pulled over, but is behind again," said Janos. "It's large with double rear wheels. It passed others; now there are only two cars separating us."

"You have your pistol from the Russians ready?" asked Lazlo.

"Yes. Only a driver in the truck," said Janos. "A man. He tries to see ahead. He had a chance to pass but did not."

The Lincoln Navigator on the road to Vernal pulled in among flashing emergency vehicle lights. After confronting the local sheriff at the marina, Finley let Jennifer ask about the torn away guardrail while he watched for Niki Gianakos' red Caravan. Gaper slowdown southbound and northbound, an officer waving traffic to keep moving. A red Caravan went by going south, but didn't have the Michigan tag Jacobson provided.

"It's a long way down," said Jennifer when she returned. "You can barely make out the wreckage. A motor home torn to shreds. Heard them radio in. No seatbelts. Two men onboard sliced and diced by framework. New Jersey plate. They're checking with Jersey DMV because no IDs were found. This fits. I overheard the woman at the marina tell the sheriff about two guys in a motor home before he ran us off. Trouble is, Jacobson said the Ukrainians meeting up with Niki Gianakos and Lazlo Horvath are a man and woman, not two men. "

"What now?"

"Continue down to Vernal. We can't watch any backs here."

"Wait. There's the Caravan heading north, Michigan tag. And that pickup, the guy driving is the one from the motel."

Jennifer nosed the Navigator out, blocking southbound traffic. Eventually, with a perturbed look, the officer directing traffic let her into the northbound lane.

Lazlo held the Flaming Gorge map with Ute Mountain Fire Lookout Tower marked. When possible Niki overtook cars. Janos watched the pickup out the back window. Niki took Route 44 toward Manila and the fire tower, only one car between the pickup and the Caravan.

"We can't go to the fire tower with him behind us," said Niki.

Lazlo studied the map. "The turn is just ahead. Janos, see if he turns or hesitates. We need to know if he knows what Decken MaCade told us. It's called the Sheep Creek Geological Loop. There's the sign!"

"Wait!" shouted Janos. "The white Lincoln Navigator. It's behind the pickup."

"Now what?" asked Niki.

"We can't stop," said Lazlo.

Mariya sat up on the floor, looking out the side window. "It's strange. I see distant rock the color of the hair from Dr. Marta's jewelry box. Hair taken to Ukraine and now back here."

"The fire tower's on the scenic loop," said Niki. "Should we double back?"

Mariya held onto Niki's seatback. "The old man said the camp was on Sheep Creek. On the way down I saw a sign for campgrounds."

"There's the creek bridge," said Niki.

"We're around a bend," said Janos, kneeling up in back. "Invisible for the moment."

"There's a campground!" shouted Mariya.

Niki hit the brakes. "No pickup in my mirror. Hang on!"

"All clear!" shouted Janos. "Get away from the road!"

The Caravan leaned dangerously, its tires squealing.

"You did it!" shouted Janos. "The pickup and Navigator went past!"

"What now?" asked Mariya.

Lazlo looked to Niki, then back to Mariya and Janos. "The map shows the Uinta Fault. We've fallen into the Earth. It's near sunset. The man in the pickup knows more. The fire tower can wait. We should return to Decken MaCade."

When the road straightened, Guzzo knew he'd lost the Caravan. The white Navigator still on his tail.

Final assignment. Failure not an option. Eventually he'd find Niki Gianakos and Lazlo Horvath in their red Caravan. For now, he needed to deal with the pair in the white Navigator.

Motorcycles at an overlook on the left. He cut across and stopped, shut off the engine, got out, and heard the squeal of brakes as the Navigator pulled to the side in the distance, dust cloud emerging from the blind corner. He climbed a boulder and saw the Navigator waiting, parked in canyon shadow, the double lenses of binoculars glaring.

Guzzo walked back to four motorcyclists, Texas tags, riders watching the sunset. Two couples in their 60s cradling helmets.

"Beautiful sunset," said Guzzo.

"One of Our Lord's wonders," said a woman.

"Traveling light?"

"Left our gear at the Manila motel. Our truck and trailer's there. You don't think I'd ride that thing from Texas."

One of the men said, "Doug and I are riding down to Vernal tomorrow. You know any good places to overnight?"

"Best Western," said Guzzo, recalling he and Cory Minkus having a beer.

In minutes the sun was down and mountain shadows became one large shadow. The bikers mounted up, started their V-twin Harleys, and headed north back to Manila.

Guzzo inspected the drop-off. He needed to find the Caravan, but rid himself of the tail. The Caravan would stop in Manila. If he didn't find it there, he'd go to the marina. If not there, Green River.

He trotted along the overlook and found guardrail supports of old wood. North around the switchback where the Harleys disappeared, car headlights appeared. He counted off seconds to see how long it took the car to circle the cliffs and reach the overlook. He recalled having timed Marta Voronko's father's car in Ukraine. After the car passed, he climbed into the pickup, buckled his shoulder belt securely, and sped north to the next switchback. Once there he caught a glimpse of the Navigator's headlights. They'd already begun moving. He spun the pickup around, cut the headlights, and sped back, throttle to the floor.

After sunset it darkened quickly. Jennifer drove into the canyon opening. "We'd better not lose him."

Finley lowered the binoculars. "Not so fast or he'll spot us at the next overlook."

Jennifer: "At that accident, when you had signal, Jacobson say anything about this guy?"

Finley: "Texts through a Green River tower from phones in Chicago. He's on the job."

Jennifer: "A hit or follow?"

Finley: "Jacobson's not sure."

Jennifer glanced toward Finley. The glow of dash lights flickered in her eyes.

Finley smiled back, retrieving an image of Jennifer in her two-piece and wondering where they'd stay tonight and if there'd be a hot tub. He imagined elderly couples staring at the mixed race couple in the tub. He took a sip of iced tea and replaced his cup in the holder. Later.

The road needled between huge boulders ahead of the overlook where the motorcyclists had been. When Jennifer rounded the curve the full length of the overlook came into view. The pickup that shouldn't have been there was there, not facing away or toward them. Lights off, it came across the road from the right shoulder, perpendicular.

Nowhere to go. The pickup with its huge bumper T-boned the Navigator and shoved it sideways, wailing and leaning, smashing into and over the guardrail. Everything spilled out of cup holders and the center console. Jennifer screamed Finley's name and reached out to grasp his hand as the Navigator went end over end down the cliff face. Two brains did their best— quick fleeting thoughts of childhood, high school, college, academy graduation, gun range training, last night at the motel—trying to make sense of life.

Although the Navigator was heavy, he'd plowed into its side. The only damage to the pickup was the bull bar bent at the frame connections. He pulled alongside the torn guardrail, blocking it should anyone pass. Simply a guy admiring the red sky. Both headlights and taillights worked; no obvious electrical damage. He left the 350 running.

He retrieved night vision binoculars from his equipment bag, stooped down between the pickup and the sheared guardrail. The Navigator's lights were out. It was on its side, no fire. At first no movement, but then a man squeezed through a broken rear side window, lay across the door a moment, then slid off and limped backwards, stumbling to the ground.

Both in the Navigator needed to be dead, especially the young man who'd make the connection to this morning's chance meeting with the smiling gentleman at breakfast.

"Motel toasters are the slowest in the world."

"You travel a lot?"

"A requirement of the service."

Guzzo imagined himself smiling. *Bond, James Bond.*

The man sat up. Guzzo scanned the surrounding canyon walls, removed his automatic from his shoulder holster, along with its silencer. When the man stood and turned back toward the wreck, Guzzo let the binoculars hang on their strap, braced against the remaining guardrail, and fired a single shot to the lower kidney. When he studied the man lying on the ground with the night vision binoculars he saw enough blood to assure him the man would bleed out. Below the Navigator on the driver's side there was now enough blood to assure him the trapped woman would also bleed out.

After putting everything away he stood at the 350's open window. The temperature gauge read normal and he smelled nothing unusual as it idled. At first he looked north, wondering where he might come across the red Caravan. Years of assignments coming to an end, Pescatore speaking of closure. Back in Vernal the red Caravan had exited a nursing home parking lot.

Old men in nursing homes. Time to contact Pescatore. Vernal would have cell coverage. Guzzo got into the 350, belted up, and drove south instead of north. He wondered what it was like here in 1939. He knew the road he was on was blasted and cleared by CCC boys. Probably hotter than hell hauling rock in the sun. He imagined sitting in the shade of a boulder watching the slobs at work not knowing someday he'd come for them.

The Mountain View Care Facility's back lot was brightly lit.

"Visitors are gone," said Lazlo. "Only workers' cars."

"We should not park here," said Janos. "Although we have a head start coming back here, if the others turn back, they already know the van."

"Should I drop you?" asked Niki.

"We should stay together and each know where the van is," said Lazlo.

Niki pulled out of the lot and started down a side street back the way they'd come. "I know a place." She drove toward the bright lights of restaurants, then turned left. "A hospital sign, I saw it on the way in."

Previously Guzzo would be given the mark and there'd be time for planning. Those in charge becoming desperate. He'd need to be quick and brutal to set his family free and, if possible, cash in.

While he sat in a Vernal barbecue restaurant booth among patrons swilling beer and pounding down meat, Pescatore called, using the newest encrypted phone.

"Why are you calling?"

"Your text about the nursing home. This is the loose end. You're in the right place at the right time. Unfortunately, so are the Greek from Detroit and the Ukrainian from Chicago."

"How can I be certain they haven't already—"

"They were there earlier questioning resident Decken MaCade. Names of enrollees and staff from the 1939 Manila CCC roster didn't have his name because he wasn't there long enough. He was overlooked. You need to find out what MaCade knows."

"Then it's not simply a matter of silencing?"

"Only if you find the location of a so-called cache. Phone calls impersonating concerned relatives uncovered the nursing home rumor mill. An aide spoke with Decken MaCade's roommate who overheard MaCade speaking with a local woman. A hidden cache story. Something hidden by CCC boys in 1939."

"Why didn't I go for MaCade sooner instead of targeting relatives and researchers?"

"He just surfaced!" Guzzo heard frustration in Pescatore's voice.

"You've trusted me until now. Please be brief and honest. I'm the one in public."

Pescatore continued more calmly. "It's the location of information about what happened in 1939. Inquisitive Swiss banking officials are following a family money trail. A descendent, discovering the origin, wants to end it, but needs the information in the cache destroyed."

"So he—or she—is after funds stashed in Swiss banks?"

"Yes, funds having funded a vendetta. What matters is to put it to rest."

"If what CCC boys hid in 1939—"

"There's nothing for us there! We're being well paid to destroy what they left behind!"

Guzzo continued. "Do you know the term, *MacGuffin*?"

Pescatore did not answer.

"What if it's impossible to find and destroy this so-called cache?" asked Guzzo.

"You'll have to end it by getting rid of them all."

"All?"

"Here are the names. First the locals—Decken MaCade, the old man at the Mountain View Care Center, Sherman Leahy, his roommate, Clancy Vargo, who runs the Lucerne Valley Marina. She was overheard speaking with MaCade. Niki Gianakos from Detroit, Lazlo Horvath from Chicago, and the two recently from Ukraine, Janos Nagy and Mariya Nemeth."

Guzzo did not tell Pescatore that, of the four, he assumed at least one or two had died in the motor home "accident." He also didn't mention the two in the Dodge Charger or the two in the Lincoln Navigator. At this point he'd hold back some cards.

As Guzzo jotted down the information, the waitress came with her pad. She saw he was on the phone but did not leave until he covered his notepad and stared at her.

"Tell me one more thing. Should I get receipts from the victims?"

"Very funny. Best case scenario, get to the old men as soon as possible, get the location of the cache out of them, find and empty it, finish off the others, and bring the cache contents here."

"If I can't find the others?"

Pescatore shouted. "They're after the same thing you're after! You'll run into them!" Then, in a calmer voice. "As I said, Guzzo, it will be over soon."

Very soon, because the Mountain View Care Center was only a few blocks away.

Niki parked near the hospital emergency room portico. An ambulance beneath the portico, male EMT closing the back doors while female EMT got into the driver's seat. Janos and Mariya knelt in back looking at where they were. The ambulance drove out, the automatic sliding door of the entrance opening then closing as the ambulance passed.

"A good spot," said Mariya. "I hope we need it only for parking."

"There's always someone at the emergency room," said Niki. "We're down the street from the Mountain View Care Facility. Meet here if we get separated."

They followed signs through the hospital until they were at the front entrance. A young guard who'd been following stopped them.

"May I ask who you visited?"

"We were here to visit my father," said Niki.

"What's his name?"

"Nick Gianakos."

"Hang on a moment."

While the guard leaned over the desk giving the name to a receptionist, they left, went off the sidewalk outside the door, ran across a lawn, leaped over bushes, crossed the street, and paused, catching their breaths. Niki suggested they hold hands like couples on an evening stroll. Niki and Lazlo walked ahead, Janos and Mariya a few paces back.

"I have a feeling about this," said Mariya. "I remember speaking to Sonia before she and the Kiev Militia guard were murdered. This red hair I hid down in my shoe and things Doctor Marta told Sonia. A killer hired to erase what happened at the CCC camp. I have a key to a bank box in one shoe and the red hair in the other. What does it all mean?"

"The answer will be at the fire tower," said Janos.

"I hope, after tonight, we can go there."

"What will we do when we get to the nursing home?" asked Lazlo.

"Say we're taking Decken for a walk. Come on, we should walk faster."

Lazlo held her hand more tightly. "Perhaps it's time to call the police. They could put MaCade into protective custody."

"Would the police believe our story?"

"We'd end up in jail," said Janos.

"I'll call Jacobson," said Lazlo. "If we give him a description of the pickup and tell him about the Russians in the motor home—"

All four stopped abruptly. In the care facility parking lot, beneath bright lights where they'd decided not to park, was a battered black Ford 350 pickup with oversized tires, dual rear wheels, and a bull bar in front that was obviously bent backwards.

CHAPTER 29

Barracks Three, late night huddle around the potbelly.

Contact the night guard? No, according to Decken night guard and officers were told to disappear.

Sneak over to the motor pool and grab a truck? Crazy, since the night of the "accident" LEMs were told to remove truck keys.

Run away like chickenshits? Nobody wanted to risk being kicked out. How'd that look when applying for jobs or enlisting in the Army?

Hide out in the empty Barracks Five building? No, they'd helped board up that building and pulling nails makes racket.

Hide in the woods overnight and sneak back in the morning? Hell no, the hoods would probably get pissed enough to shoot someone next day at the job site.

The more they considered options, the angrier they became. Why should they hide? So what if paid-off officers and LEMs were frightened. They'd joined the three Cs boys, now they were men!

In the heat of discussion the 38 agreed to hold their ground. How about fixing the doors at both ends of the barracks? Tie rope to the handles, the other end up to the nearest rafter. Was there enough rope and would it hold?

Cut the lights. Nick said he'd fix it so the lights wouldn't go on. Stuff clothing beneath their blankets. In the dark it'd look like they were there but really weren't. Climb into the rafters and wait it out. No one would see them with lights out. But hoods would have flashlights. Damn it, maybe they'd have to drop down on them. Sure, there were only two in the tan Buick. But what about the other Buick?

They moved about the dark barracks, searching for broom handles, ball bats, stove irons—anything to defend themselves. They'd stay put. If a guy had to piss, he'd use the bucket near the door. There were a few things to use for weapons. What little rope they found wasn't enough to tie off the doors.

And so they climbed, helping one another up. Using the only barracks flashlight, Nick put on gloves and disconnected the hot wire at the first bulb in the rafter string and fixed it so he'd push down the wire to make the connection.

The driver lit up another cigarette, used the match to check his watch before blowing it out. He grabbed the Remington double barrel leaning against the dash. "It's three already. My pockets weigh 50 pounds with all the shells."

The passenger had his .38 in his lap and stuffed his jacket pockets with slugs. "For good measure I'm taking the Tommy gun."

"Seeing your Tommy and my shotgun should scare some crap out of 'em."

"We scare the crap out of 'em and if Al wants to plug someone, let him do it."

"What if Al rats us?"

"We go to Mexico or Canada."

"Canada's closer. When war starts and the Army's recruiting, we come back over."

The passenger reached into the back for the Thompson submachine gun. "I hope it don't come to that."

"Wait a minute. I see lights."

A camp truck drove along the barracks row, pulled between Barracks Three and the latrine, and the lights went out.

"Now what?" said the driver.

"Someone too lazy to walk to the can," said the passenger. "We wait until he leaves."

After the engine rumbling outside Barracks Three quit, the only sounds were whispers and the squeak of rafter timber. Bela and Nick shared a rafter, facing one another at the light socket. Flipping the light switch would do nothing unless Nick made the connection by pushing the hot wire down with his gloved hand.

The narrow back door, not the front, gave off a squeak. Bela could barely see a single man. The light switch was at the front door. The man whispered.

"It's Decken. Anybody awake?"

"What should I do?" whispered Nick.

"Turn them on," whispered Bela.

Decken shaded his eyes and looked up at the men in the rafters. "Holy hell."

"We're waiting," whispered Bela.

"You sure they're coming?"

The men nodded.

"Cut the light. I left a truck. It's loaded with picks and shovels. Trouble is, there's not much gas."

Nick lifted the wire, it sparked, and the lights went out.

"Good luck," whispered Decken. The door squeaked and he was gone.

"The truck's at the back door," whispered George. "Same door I snuck out."

The Buick's driver blew out another match and looked out the windshield. "It's 3:30—Hey look, it's Al with his Tommy and the others. Must've walked through the woods. If there's shooting, we're driving out of here."

There was no shooting. The lead man pulled the door open partway and squeezed through, followed by the other two. No lights went on. The only sounds were some thumps like a bunch of guys jumping around. Then it was silent.

"I guess they already scared crap out of 'em," said the driver.

"Let's go," said the passenger. "Scare more crap out of 'em and drive the hell out of this place for good."

Both got out with their guns and walked to the barracks. The driver said, "It's us, Al," as he pulled the door open.

When Nick sparked on the lights, two more came in, holding guns but dazed. The first three were on the floor, two holding their heads and moaning, one not moving.

Bela held the Tommy gun he'd grabbed pointed at the new arrivals. "I know how to use!" he shouted. "I watched Nazi boys!"

George Minkus held a .38. "My uncle's a Chicago cop!"

Jethro held a pump shotgun. "We use these in the hills!"

Barracks Three men were spread out, holding other pistols gathered along with picks and shovels. The new arrivals stared wide-eyed, short guy with a

Tommy, tall guy with a double barrel—the two who'd scared the crap out of Decken the day before. When quiet Paul Fontaine walked straight up to him with a cocked '38, shotgun was first to acknowledge the odds, lowering his double barrel. Tommy gun held out until Bela aimed down and shouted.

"Nazi boys shoot knees for fun!"

Bela, Nick, and George gathered guns and had the goons kneel with hands behind their heads. Four knelt. The two St. Louis boys sat beside the fifth. Both were in tears, a pick with blood on its tip on the floor.

"I didn't mean to kill him."

"How could you know in the dark? How could he know?"

Nick swung down from the rafters after permanently connecting the lights. He grabbed a stray shovel and glared at the hoods while speaking to the St. Louis barge boys. "We knew what might happen. We all did it."

"What'll we do now?" asked Jimmy, holding his shovel like a baseball bat.

"We ask what they'd do if they were in our position," said George.

Jimmy stepped closer. "Sal couldn't handle being out-punched. You took Henry for a ride. Where is he?"

"Must've had an accident," said one of the men, smiling.

The smile set things off, Barracks Three adrenaline exploding with overlapping shouts—drown them in the river, put them in their cars and shove them off a cliff, kill them on the spot, load them in the truck under a tarp and bury them next day on the road to Vernal.

Smiling goon said, "You lugs'll get yourselves to early graves."

Barracks Three men stared hard, at the same time re-gripping whatever they held—gun, shovel, or pickaxe.

Should they bust bones? Hold them 'til morning? Turn them over to the camp superintendent? No, they couldn't trust the superintendent. One suggestion was to empty their pockets, send a couple guys with any keys they find and look for the other car. Maybe take them to their cars before reveille, put them inside unarmed, and make sure they drive away.

"This is too good for them," said Bela.

"I don't suppose any of them will admit to killing Henry," said Jimmy.

Two of the goons immediately nodded toward the dead guy. "He did it," said one. The others nodded.

"Don't trust them," said Nick.

"I agree," said George.

"Be a shame if they ran away like wild horses and joined the Army," said Paul Fontaine.

"Be a shame if they came back to avenge their dead guy," said Jethro. "We'd be forced to kill'em. I ain't giving up this gun."

"How can we guarantee they don't come back?" asked Bela.

The goon the others called Al during the excitement was red-faced. "Make up your minds for Christ's sake!"

"All right," said Bela. "One of you go to truck and get shears we use for thick branches. We'll give each a reminder not to return by cutting off trigger fingers."

The goons seemed to shrink as if the barracks floorboards were giving way. Even Al, who'd sneered prior to this, looked worried.

"How will we know if they shoot with their right or left hand?" asked Nick. "Oh yeah, we cut off all the trigger fingers. Yeah."

"It's our only choice," said Bela. "All in agreement, raise your hand."

Because of planning done in the dark around the potbelly before the men arrived, and now knowing Henry had been murdered, the 38 Barracks Three men raised their hands, even the St. Louis barge boy still sitting on the floor beside the dead man.

The kneeling goons with their hands behind their heads looked back and forth to one another.

A man went out for the shears. They were long-handled with thick cross-cut blades. He put the shears on the floor in front of the kneeling men. Several began arguing about who'd do the cutting. The argument grew, men not arguing who'd have to do it, but who'd get to do it. Bela turned away from the goons and glanced toward Nick. All was going as planned.

Henry going AWOL after his successful grudge match with Sal was nuts. Then there was the staff's sad sack reaction to Sal's "accident." No matter how anyone acted when they went down into the gully to lift the GMC and drop it on Sal, no matter if some had reservations, they'd all agreed. Each of them keeping hair belonging to Rose Buckles—hair Sal brought into the barracks—was their blood oath. They'd become men doing what needed to be done.

Still, Bela knew it was he who'd talked the others into it. Nothing could convince him otherwise. He was as guilty for this as he was for escaping his homeland and leaving others behind. Not long after arriving in the US, he found out, by way of a letter from his mother, that the Nazis had taken his girlfriend, Nina Zolotarev.

Bela turned back to the goons kneeling on the floor, feeling anger boiling inside. He stared at each in turn. "Then it is agreed, we draw straws for each finger."

The man who'd gone out for the shears spoke up. "There's red sky to the east. Reveille's not far off. Let's get cutting."

CHAPTER 30

The ski mask was hot. No one at the reception counter. A 60s era camera and push button lock guarding the inside entry. Guzzo put one hand on the counter, vaulted, and duck walked behind the counter to a doorway. No one in a back office. Desk, filing cabinets, copy machine, piles of paperwork, and a facility map. He located the room, Decken MaCade and Sherman Leahy. A doorway out the back of the office open. Scent of dried urine. A fat female aide in blue slacks and flowery top walking the other way. Soon after she turned a corner, Guzzo found the room, took off the ski mask, and pushed open the unlatched door.

A curtain separated the beds. Sherman Leahy near the door, lights out, eyes closed. Beyond the curtain, CNN logo and split screens on bed two's wall-mounted television. Captioning on, sound off.

Decken's face was gray, wrinkled, spotted like a barnyard belly. Wisps of white hair waved in the building's HVAC circulation. His nose tube sweat reflected CNN strobe.

"Who the hell...?" he asked, reaching to both ears to turn up hearing aides.

"Don't you recognize your great nephew?"

"I got no nephews."

Guzzo pulled back his jacket sleeve, revealing his tattoo. "Remember my Desert Storm tattoo, Uncle Decken?"

Confused look. "Why you wearing rubber gloves?"

"You need to tell me something. It's important. My friends were here earlier and you told them. Now I need you to tell me where the CCC boys hid their cache so I can help. Get it? I'm here to help."

"If I don't tell?"

"They're my friends, too. If you can't tell your own nephew—"

Decken shook his head. "I ain't telling."

Guzzo moved in, shadowing the television glow. "I'll have to kill you."

A brief pause, a childlike voice. "Go ahead."

"And I'll have to kill old Sherman behind curtain number one."

Decken's eyes widened. The reek of sour breath, but no words. He coughed, sputtered, turned, pulled open a nightstand drawer, and fumbled with toothpaste tubes and spit cups before bringing out a .38.

Never allow a gun to be pointed more than a second. A second later Guzzo held the gun and Decken rubbed his wrist.

Guzzo aimed the .38 at bed one, tenting the curtain. "Well?"

"If I tell, you won't shoot him?"

"That's the idea."

"Look inside. One of the bullets is missing."

Guzzo retrieved a rolled up wad of paper from one of the six, unrolled it, and held it beneath the bedside lamp. "This the exact location?"

Decken nodded. Guzzo smiled. Decken smiled. Guzzo closed the .38's cylinder, studied the thickness of the pillows behind Decken's head, and noted Decken's hands firmly clasped on his chest in coffin pose. Guzzo turned off the bedside light.

On the muted television, CNN news had gone to an ask-your-doctor-about prescription medication commercial, required warnings scrolling wildly.

The pickup parked beneath bright overheads was dusty, its bent bull bar flecked with white paint. All four did a dance of indecision as they approached, keeping the pickup between them and the entrance.

"There's a wheelchair in the entry," said Lazlo. "I'm the shittiest looking. I'll get into it and become a resident."

Niki knew in her gut the pickup driver killed her father, and her brother. She imagined him throwing her father from the roof of their building. Her father feisty, once he made up his mind, like Decken MaCade with his .38 stashed in his nightstand drawer. And here was the pickup—Wait, passenger side window facing her not reflecting light.

Niki gave her Caravan keys to Janos. "Go! You're the fastest. Get the van."

Janos took them and started running back toward the hospital. Mariya ran with Janos.

Lazlo walked ahead with his pistol out. "I'll go in—"

Niki saw movement in the vestibule. She grabbed Lazlo's sleeve, pulled him back. "Lazlo, I must do this!"

She ran, the pickup shielding her from the care center entrance as the door swung open. She scrambled through the truck window, climbed over the console into the back, elbows and knees striking hard objects in the narrow space behind the front seats. Should have taken Lazlo's gun. Smell of cigarettes and stale beer. The pickup door opened.

Lazlo caught off guard, conjuring up a younger man able to run and leap into the pickup bed. But he was breathless, gripping his pistol, watching the pickup disappear into the darkness.

After climbing over the reception counter and going through an office, he knew where to look. Muted television, commercial for an exercise device. Something whining. The sulfurous scent of gunpowder. Lazlo turned on the overhead lights.

Both men dead, shot in the head. Decken sprawled on the floor between the beds. Blood from both spreading, the roommate's into his pillow, Decken's outward onto the floor and beneath the beds. A thick pillow beside Decken with two holes and powder marks. An older .38 special near Decken's right hand. Hearing aide on the floor whining its feedback. Crime scene first glance left the impression Decken used pillows to deaden the shot into his roommate, then himself. First investigator would look for Decken's fingerprints on the gun.

Lazlo ran, almost knocking over a woman in blue slacks and flowery blouse. "Hey, I thought I heard—Hey!"

"Call police!"

The van pulled up to the entrance as Lazlo ran out. He dove onto the back floor, its sliding door already open. The door powered shut as Janos sped off. A text came in on three phones, Janos, Mariya, and Lazlo reading the same message.

"Heading north. 191. Not seen in back."

As Janos sped through Vernal toward Route 191, Lazlo detailed the murder-suicide setup, gripping the seatback to keep from being thrown around. When the van stopped cornering he sat up. Behind them, a half-mile back, the flashing lights of a police car headed the other way toward the Mountain View Care Center. Ahead, mountains thrust skyward millions of years earlier spoke with the stars.

The map from the cylinder of the old man's revolver was in Guzzo's pocket. He'd memorized it. Manila at the top, Vernal at the bottom, Routes 191, 44, and the Sheep Creek Loop in detail, along with an entry road to the Ute Mountain Fire Lookout Tower. He'd seen Sheep Creek Loop signs earlier that day. The map had an X labeled, "Under Castle Rock boulder, 200 paces SE of tower."

The lights of Vernal faded. It cooled as he climbed into the mountains and he closed the passenger window. He took off the latex gloves and threw them into the back seat. He saw no one behind, but watched for headlights when switchbacks began. He'd be to the fire tower in less than an hour, but no need to risk being pulled over or hitting an animal.

Rocks and boulders in the headlights would have a lot to say if they could speak. One particular boulder to his left was rectangular like a bank vault. Perhaps 1939 funds were put in many banks. In the cache beneath the boulder he'd find the key, not what the CCC men had done to deserve death years later, but what they knew.

Pescatore said bring what he found to the fish market. The farther north he drove, the more Guzzo thought of the cache as the key to a fortune. The only place he and Pescatore met was the fish market. Where did Pescatore live? A high-rise downtown? Pescatore had accumulated power and money. If Guzzo simply supplied the contents of the cache…He'd make a decision when the time came. Certainly not a future in Orland Park cutting lawn, spreading Weed and Feed. He and his family deserved more.

Orange cones closed off the pullout where he'd pushed off the motor home. Somewhere in a Vernal morgue, bodies of the two in the motor home were probably shredded to bits. The pullout where he'd pushed off the white Navigator and shot the man who climbed out was not blocked, the torn-out section of guardrail out of sight. Obviously no one had reported this "accident."

After turning onto Route 44 toward the west edge of the gorge, Guzzo drove a long straight stretch and in the side mirror spotted headlights a mile back. Could be someone from a lodge or campground along the gorge. As the road snaked back and forth, the headlights disappeared and he searched ahead for Sheep Creek Loop. With the window closed, the smells in the pickup had changed, perspiration mixed with a sweet smell.

Over the years, Lazlo heard stories from men worried about wives, sweethearts, and daughters, out alone at night. He'd been Father Gypsy in the Kiev Militia, the burden of victims weighing heavily. For him lovers remained simply lovers. Yet now, after knowing Niki only days, he was being thrown about on the floor of her van. He's finally met her and she dives through a killer's open window! As he hung onto the seatback, Lazlo could smell her, the sweet scent of the woman he wished to spend his life with.

"Janos! You see them?"

"Occasionally a taillight!"

"But why—?"

Mariya reached between the front seats and held Lazlo's arm. "Deep breaths, Lazlo."

Lazlo grasped Mariya's hand. "Do you have the envelope Sonia gave you?"

"Of course, I've carried it in my shoe since we left Kiev."

When Mariya gave Lazlo the envelope with hair Doctor Marta's grandfather had saved he put it in his shirt pocket and clutched it to his breast. "Bela Voronko saved hair. George Minkus saved hair. Niki's father saved hair. Janos! Faster!"

The fire tower access road was an unpaved two-track climbing back and forth between pines. At the top it widened to a small parking area surrounded by new growth pines, cleared brush piles, and sharp-edged rock like rusted saw teeth. The tower, painted white, stood on the partially cleared plateau, a haunted cabin on stilts. The only lights below were miles north, the town of Manila. Guzzo checked his compass and drove off the smoothed parking area around the side of the tower, the 350 straddling rock like a boyhood toy tilting back and forth.

As promised by MaCade's map, the Castle Rock miniature stood out in the headlights, well off the parking area on a down slope protected by old growth pines, a few of which appeared to have burned in a recent fire. He did not get out to walk the 200 paces. Instead he drove up to the rock, its face ten by ten feet, but not so thick. It sat on a sagebrushed rubble bed. Someone had graffitied it with initials obliterated by time. The only character distinguishable was a plus symbol between two sets of initials. The plus was crooked, as in X marks the spot.

When the driver got out but left the door open, Niki stayed put on the floor. Her knees were sore, metal tools in a vinyl bag having gouged her. Inside lights had not come on. She inched up slightly and saw him with a flashlight inspecting the Castle Rock replica. She listened for sounds of another vehicle. Had Lazlo, Janos, and Mariya gotten her text? She was about to climb into the front seat but the man returned, boots clacking and shuffling on hard stone. When he got back in she felt the seatback shift and curled up, trying to make herself smaller. After he slammed the door the pickup lurched forward, seesawing over rock, then a jarring thump as the front end made contact with the Castle Rock replica.

The engine growled, tires spinning on rock. She searched the vinyl bag she'd knelt on. Jack, handle, and lug wrench. She pulled out the wrench, gripped its end to swing it. But suddenly the ceiling and backs of the seats were lit from behind and she caught a glimpse of the driver turning as she ducked back down. He seemed an ordinary looking man in his 40s. But this was the man who'd killed her father.

Lazlo knelt behind the center console as Janos neared the pickup, stones from spinning dual rear tires pummeling the van, cracking the windshield. Straddling large rocks, Janos accelerated closer, headlights on the driver who turned and smiled. When the man faced forward, Lazlo caught a glimpse of Niki's hand come up from the floor directly behind the driver's seat. She held something. Lazlo pulled out his gun. Ahead of the pickup the Castle Rock replica was tilted at an odd angle.

The pickup's backup lights lit, the impact throwing Lazlo forward onto the center console. Janos put the van in reverse but the pickup kept pushing. Rather than snaking between larger rocks as Janos had done driving in, the pickup pushed the van, its underpinnings sounding like a jackhammer at work. In the parking area, Janos turned the steering wheel and the van careened sideways.

"Keep the lights on him!" shouted Lazlo, reaching across to the sliding door handle.

The pickup circled to the driver's side of the van as Lazlo jumped out the passenger side rear door. After Janos powered the sliding door shut, Lazlo ran behind the nearest boulder, taking aim at the cloud of dust created by the van and pickup circling madly in the small parking area.

Guzzo saw two in the van. Before their arrival, the 350 had done its work, the Castle Rock replica tilted to one side. Charred pines kept the replica from tumbling down the mountain. The shine of metal in the shale hollow. He'd need to eliminate the two in the van. Assuming Niki Gianakos, the original mark, had not been in the motor home, she'd get it now.

The van was a toy for the raised 350 with its six wheels and bull bar. The chase raised ancient dust. Guzzo had the angle, the embankment steeper along the edge of the parking area, the van trying to turn back but too late. He plowed it onto the rocks, then onto a steep rock-strewn pathway between pines. He backed up and slammed the van's rear corner sending it over on its side and down the rocky slope. At first the van slid, but as the slope became steeper, it went into a roll, headlights whipping back and forth before finally going out.

Guzzo pulled up sideways and aimed his flashlight out the window down the slope. The van in a cloud of dust below, its roof smashed against a tree. Airbags had gone off, fabric like dried animal skin visible. Because there was no movement, he'd have time to retrieve what was hidden. He'd make certain the two in the van were dead and wipe out his tire marks before leaving. They'd be discovered in the morning, a tragic accident on Ute Mountain.

Just as Guzzo was about the put the transmission in reverse and go back to the Castle Rock replica, a hand grabbed his left arm and something smashed into his right shoulder.

There were two! One outside, one in the back seat! He reached to the passenger seat where he'd placed his pistol. It was gone!

A shot from behind into his right foot slammed down the accelerator, then slipped to the side. He pulled his second pistol from his shoulder holster, aimed at the man outside hanging onto his jacket. Whoever was in the back with his other pistol grasped his arm and his shot went through the windshield.

The grip on his left arm tightened after the shot. The 350 still in gear, rolling at idle. He crossed his left foot over his burning right foot and pressed the accelerator, the pickup dragging the man outside who wouldn't let go. When a blow to his head came from the behind, he dropped the pistol he held in his right hand, grabbed the pistol hitting him, and fired toward the back seat.

A woman behind screamed and the man outside growled as he accelerated the pickup. The legs of the fire tower loomed up quickly and he stood on the brake with his left foot. The man outside and the woman behind crashed forward, the woman wedged between the seats, the man outside still hanging on. Despite being dragged by the pickup the man outside had an arm around his neck!

Guzzo tucked the pistol between his legs, grabbed the shifter, put the 350 in reverse, accelerated, and slammed the brakes as he spun the steering wheel, body-slamming the man into the side of the 350, and at the same time slugging the woman wedged between the seats. When he was about to accelerate again, the 350 went dead. While being slugged, she'd somehow gotten to the keys, turning off the ignition.

Guzzo felt on the floor and the gun that had slid from between his legs. He got a grip on it, aimed out the window, and fired.

Niki's left arm aflame, a bullet had shattered bone. The driver's door open, the man gone. She crawled onto the driver's seat, scrambling with her good arm to get out. There'd been the crash, the van gone, Janos and Mariya gone. Somehow Lazlo had gotten out of the van and—

"Lazlo!"

Lazlo and the man on the ground in the dark. As she struggled to push herself out, there, on the floor, was a gun, the smell of gunpowder as she grasped it in her right hand and fell to the ground. She got to her knees, felt for the trigger, fired a shot into the air. The canyons echoed it back. The dark mass of Lazlo and the man struggled before her. If Lazlo could he'd have shouted something when she fired, but there was only the sound of gurgling gasps for air, Lazlo being choked to death in the darkness.

She moved in close but was kicked by a boot. The killer on top, strong and young. She had a pistol, but even if she aimed correctly, would the bullet go through the man and into Lazlo? It was too dark, the struggle an ancient creature kicking at shale, gasping its last gasp. Despite her useless burning left arm, she joined them.

Gripping the automatic tightly in her right hand and holding her finger carefully away from the hair trigger, she pushed her face between them, smelling, listening. Her neck twisted to one side as the killer became aware of her.

"You're next!"

On her back, her left arm flailing helplessly in a world of pain, she wedged her right hand with the pistol to the center of the killer's mass to fire into him. But he grabbed the pistol and flung it away into the darkness.

Mariya's legs torn at by sharp rock as she climbed, nearing the lookout tower plateau. Janos trapped in the van, legs crushed but alive. Janos insisting she take his pistol.

Over the last sharp-edged rock she saw them. A tall man holding a flashlight in one hand and a pistol in the other aiming down at Lazlo and Niki. Lazlo on his back, gasping for breath. Niki beside him, her jacket sleeve dark with blood. Mariya aimed the pistol she held, but they were too far away and if she missed...

The man waved Niki up. "I'll shoot him again!"

Mariya watched as Niki struggled to her feet. The man held his pistol and flashlight on Niki, limping behind her to the pickup. He reached in, started the engine, and had Niki walk ahead into the headlights. He went back to Lazlo and swung the pistol, hitting Lazlo in the head.

Niki screamed, "Lazlo!"

The man turned. "Shut up and move!"

Mariya crawled forward and stood. The truck's headlights lit up the Castle Rock replica, tilted awkwardly to the side. The man had Niki climb into a hollow at the base of the rock. He gave orders Mariya could not hear above the pickup's rumbling. Niki began handing things up. The man made a pile on the ground. A rifle with a cylindrical magazine caught in the beam of the flashlight. A Tommy gun like she'd seen in American gangster films!

Mariya moved in closer. She was barely able to walk to where Lazlo lay breathing heavily. It was too dark to see if Lazlo's eyes were open. She turned to get in close enough, but instead of the man standing at the edge of the hollow, only Niki was there, Niki reading from a yellowed sheet of paper she held up to the light from the pickup's headlights. Suddenly, the pistol Mariya grasped was snatched away and she was thrown to the ground.

Although in a world of pain, Lazlo held his breath and closed his eyes when the man shined the flashlight on him. The man had taken his pistol. He played dead, then turned to watch as the man led Mariya to the hollow lit by headlights. He blinked his eyes. The spinning eased but he could not get up. The headlights blinded Niki. She'd not seen Mariya until now. They spoke but the pickup's rumble was loud. Their body language, bending forward slightly, made Lazlo realize they wanted the man to assume both he and Janos were finished.

Niki handed over a sheet of yellowed paper. The man pocketed it and gave orders. Niki and Mariya were forced, despite their conditions, to carry several guns, including revolvers, shotguns, and two Tommy guns, from the cache beneath the Castle Rock replica to the pickup. The way the man had Niki and Mariya hold the guns by the barrels, there was no way they could turn them on him without being shot. They also carried what appeared to be ammunition boxes.

Mariya and the man both limped while Niki could not carry anything with her left hand. Niki shot in her arm and Mariya injured by the crash. Lazlo concentrated on the man's limp, looking for weakness. From the shine of blood at the top of the man's right boot it appeared he'd been shot in the foot.

After several loads were dumped into the pickup bed, the sounds of metal on metal made it obvious the man was searching the ammunition boxes. A minute went by before the three were back at the cache, the man ordering them into the pit, saying he needed them to look for something. Lazlo tried to sit but managed only to raise his head before pain overtook him. He watched carefully. Niki and Mariya's lives depending on detail.

Mariya glanced up, saw the man look back toward where Lazlo lay. She whispered something to Niki. When the man turned back, Lazlo heard him. "No talking, just find it!" Lazlo saw Mariya remove her shoe and put it back on.

The key! Mariya had been carrying the Brooklyn safe deposit box key in her shoe!

After more shared whispers, Lazlo knew Niki and Mariya would attempt escape. He needed to get to his hands and knees, perhaps get the man's attention. As he tried in vain to make his move it happened.

"Is this what you're looking for?" shouted Mariya.

Lazlo saw it all. The thrown key, the speed of the two getting out and around the boulder while the man ran after the key. By the time he retrieved it from the ground behind him, they were gone. The man turned, ran to the side, fired several shots into the darkness, took a step forward, and stopped. He had what he wanted squeezed tightly in his hand. He limped to the pickup, climbed in, and leaned sideways to use his left foot for accelerator and brake.

Lazlo readied himself as the pickup's backup lights lit and the rear wheels spun it backwards directly at him. With all his strength, thinking of Niki, he rolled sideways and felt flying stones as the truck roared past, then lurched forward to the parking lot exit.

The pickup's engine echoed in canyons as it made its way down the mountain. There were footsteps on gravel, Niki calling to him.

In the dark Niki came to him and pressed firmly on his shoulder wound. The rumble of the pickup faded.

"I'll hold it," he gasped, sitting up. "Please, both of you, see to Janos."

The female pilot and male EMT in the helicopter taking off from the Vernal hospital helipad saw emergency vehicles flashing like deranged fireflies converging on the Mountain View Care Facility. "We're out of here," said the pilot as she throttled up to gain altitude before heading to Ute Mountain.

At altitude heading north, they saw two emergency vehicles swarming toward the care facility break away and also head north, following Route 191 through the Ashley National Forest. Routes 191 and 44 were part of a scenic byway. Unfortunately all they could see from the helicopter was darkness and emergency lights trying to keep up. A few minutes later they saw flashing lights in the distance to the northwest.

"Did dispatch say who called?" asked the pilot.

"A cell phone in the fire tower," said the EMT. "A guy named Horvath climbed the tower and someone was awake in the Manila office to get the 911."

"The Manila sheriff got woke up," said the pilot.

"A dollar says she's got pajamas on under her uniform."

"You're on."

"Would she have had time for a bra? I mean, she's bigger than even you."

"Don't be a smart ass," said the pilot, turning on floodlights.

Canyon rock cast sharp shadows dancing against smoother boulders, shadows from blasting and busting up and clearing done in the 1930s.

CHAPTER 31

Before dawn, a hundred yards from the crossroad locals considered downtown Manila, a black 1939 Buick Four-Door Touring Sedan and a tan 1939 Buick Century Sport Coupe were backed in side-by-side on a cattle guard. A distant streetlight cast ghoulish shadows on the faces of four men inside each of the Buicks. The back seat men wore dark jackets and hats, their ties off, having become part of mummy-like bindings holding arms behind their backs—bits and pieces of rope, Scotch tape, and whatever the men in the front seats, who wore work uniforms and caps, could find in their barracks building. The Sport Coupe back seat was tight; the tall man and stocky man crammed together. The Touring Sedan back seat was roomier; the two back there leaning against the doors. Out of sight on the floor, the man the others claimed was responsible for Henry's disappearance didn't need tying up because he was dead.

Of the 38 Barracks Three men, six were chosen to drive the goons to Manila. The St. Louis barge boy, whose friend accidentally killed the guy on the floor, sat in the black Buick driver's seat, while Nick, the electrician, sat beside him holding a pistol on the two live wires in back. George, from Chicago, sat in the tan Buick driver's seat, while Bela, the Ukraine vampire, sat beside him holding a pistol on the two in back. A hundred yards up the road Jimmy the Big Apple and Jethro the Georgia baritone were in a phone booth beneath the streetlight. Back at camp Quiet Paul Fontaine had collected coins for the phone from the pockets of the hoods.

No fingers were lopped off by the crosscut sheers brandished by the Ukraine vampire. The hoods weren't worked over like a couple Boston toughs suggested. The hoods' spokesman named Al said they'd get theirs. This was answered by tales of Barracks Three men avenging others. George included Henry's geological stories, the ancient area rock not giving a damn about humans who were like ticks to be popped. Bela told the men Sal killed the girl and by doing so, killed himself. As planned, Barracks Three men were unanimous. Rather than cutting fingers, they put on an act, demonstrating how tough the CCC had made them and saying they'd killed others. Of course they knew bluster wasn't enough and would not release the men until after a couple important phone calls.

Jimmy and Jethro trotted back from the phone booth and opened the doors of both cars, making sure the hoods could hear.

"It was the cat's meow," said Jimmy, clapping Jethro on the back. "He sounded exactly like them."

Bela got out and stood with them between the open car doors. "So everyone can hear, who did he sound like?"

Jimmy pointed to the coupe's back seat. "Like the short guy in there." Then Jimmy turned and pointed to the sedan's back seat. "And like the loud one in there."

Bela put his hand on Jethro's shoulder. "Show them."

Jethro stood taller, like a guy ready to croon. Sounding exactly like the stocky guy in the tan Buick, he began. "He says, this is Lonzo. So I says, I got news from Manila. The Lonzo guy says, what news? And I says, the CCC guys got our guns and they killed one of us. Lonzo says, the boss ain't gonna be happy. And I says, too bad, 'cause we're taking off. The Lonzo guy asks where, and I says, some other family, maybe Luciano or Genovese or Costello."

"I read up on gangs in the newspapers," said Jimmy proudly.

Jethro continued. "Then I called the phone number we found on the other guy." He changed his voice to sound exactly like the loud guy named Al who squirmed in the sedan's back seat. "Someone sounding like a kid answers. Says his name's Felice. I tell him I'm calling from Manila and next thing I know an old man named Rosario answers. So I pretty much tell him the same thing I told the Lonzo character, only this time I add that us boys don't like the idea that Little Sal killed the girl. The Rosario guy doesn't talk, mostly listens. So I tell him maybe we'll run away to Italy like Luciano. The old guy's breathing heavy the whole time I'm talking. At the end he says, 'You guys are dead, all of you. Dead!'"

The four live ones in the back seats stared silently, the distant streetlight illuminating the whites of their eyes. When Al stopped squirming, Bela knew they had them.

After the call, Lonzo left the family apartment building to tell Cavallo his Uncle Rosario also received a call and there'd be an emergency meeting in the room above the garage. Last time they met there was when Cavallo's cousin was sent to prison. Lots of shouting. This meeting was similar, Lonzo and Felice told to wait outside. During the meeting Uncle Rosario did most of the shouting between bouts of coughing.

"I thought we had good men! All of them will be dead! My nephews disappoint me at every turn! First, your idiot cousin puts himself in prison! Then, your son kills himself!"

Cavallo pounded the table. "He didn't kill himself! Those boys killed him!"

Uncle Rosario coughed and spit. "Why? A girl! Your son, a fucking murderer!"

Cavallo imagined reaching across the table to strangle his uncle. He waited for the gasping to stop. "We'll kill those sniveling boys!"

"Is that what you want, Nephew? More men disarmed and shamed? It's a stain on the family!"

"I don't give a goddamn about stains! I care about avenging my son's death! The political bullshit was your idea! Family legacy! My son who'd already run a man down with the Packard—what a laugh!"

"I'm not laughing. I know about him killing a drunk. After running over him I heard he backed up and hit him again. He was supposed to receive discipline in the CCCs. He was supposed to be the future of the family."

Cavallo stared into his uncle's bloodshot eyes. "By climbing your fairy tale ladder? Heroin money in Switzerland? What good is it?"

Both paused, breathing heavily.

Finally Uncle Rosario spoke. "What about our men? One killed and the rest—"

Cavallo interrupted. "Don't forget them saying they might go to Genovese or Costello, or escape to Italy. You think other families know about the heroin?"

"Older ones might know," said Uncle Rosario.

Cavallo recalled the funeral, Francesca screaming as she leaped into the casket only to be dragged out. The beautiful casket with gold-plated handles.

Next morning the tan Buick headed north to Rock Springs, then east on Lincoln Highway.

"Still think we should go to Canada?" asked the passenger.

The driver shrugged. "Gas jockey back there said roads up to Jackson and Cody are rough. I'd hate to have to turn around."

"Yeah, these crossroads look like shit."

"Maybe Chicago and go north through Wisconsin."

"Why do you suppose the CCC boys left gas money in our wallets?"

"They want us to run."

"At least we didn't have to get rid of no body. You think Al will come this way after he dumps it?"

The driver lit a cigarette. "I don't give a damn anymore because they'll be gunning for us. If Al wants to go back to New York, let him. We'll drive to Chicago and head north."

"But without guns or ammo, what are we supposed to do?" said the passenger, hitting the dash with his fist.

"We figure out a way to make some dough. Take it easy on the car. It's all we got." The driver took a drag on his cigarette and blew smoke into the passenger's face. "We'll get where we're going when I say we're there. Then we'll sell the car and split up."

The passenger sunk lower in his seat, looking like a fat kid. "Split up?"

"I move faster on my own. If you don't like it—"

"All right, all right," said the passenger, looking out the windshield at the jagged teeth of the Rockies.

"I might join the Army," said the driver.

"Which one?"

The driver threw his cigarette out the window. "Don't get smart."

Earlier that morning, before sunrise, the six who'd made the trip to Manila and sent the hoods on their way returned to a barracks ready for inspection. With only an hour to spare before reveille, they shared the phone calls with the others, Jethro doing the voices again. Even after this, some were worried the hoods would return.

"They will not return," said Bela.

"He's right," said George. "There's nothing in it for'em."

Jimmy, the barracks leader who'd gotten back some of his steam said, "It's obvious officers and LEMs were paid off. We've hidden all the guns and ammo in the truck. You guys figure out a hiding spot?"

Everyone nodded, looking toward quiet Paul Fontaine.

Silent Joe Palooka from Chicago stepped forward. "Paul's got the spot and I wrote a note we can leave in it."

"Okay," said Jimmy. "Let's bunk for a few minutes."

Reveille, latrine rush, and breakfast went off as usual. Silence from other barracks men and staff about anything going on was strange. Decken got his truck filled with gas and requisitioned another. The men were worried they'd be split up with crews from other barracks, but that didn't happen. It was as if everyone, right up to the camp superintendent who joined them at mess, knew what went on during the night needed finishing off.

It was a bright crisp summer morning. Sure, it would be hot later that day, but in the morning it was wonderful. They even saw a few wild horses that had ventured into the canyon, perhaps running with a cattle herd.

On the way to the work site on the road to Vernal, Paul Fontaine, riding shotgun, had Decken detour onto the Sheep Creek Loop. The second truck followed. The Dodge and GMC engines moaned as they climbed to the fire tower with all the men aboard. They parked to the southeast side near the

Castle Rock replica Henry had been finishing when he disappeared. Only problem was, the replica was on its side and needed to be put upright.

Decken climbed the fire tower to have coffee, keep the ranger's attention, and fill him in on the plan to create a Castle Rock monument. The men started by shoveling a rock base in which the boulder would sit.

"You think they can stand that thing up?" asked the ranger.

"There's 38 of them and two trucks," said Decken.

"They better not wreck those trucks," said the ranger, looking down with his binoculars.

"Don't worry," said Decken. "Here, let me have a look."

Once the base, lined with sharp-edged rock from pebble size to man size, was complete, 38, minus the one who drove the Dodge, inched the boulder up using their strength combined with the pushing force of the Dodge. It's rear wheels spun a little with the initial push. During the tipping process, out of sight of the ranger and Decken, the men quickly emptied the contents of the Dodge into the cache before the boulder rolled gently into place.

Once the Castle Rock replica boulder was set up, the Dodge backed away, the driver got out, and the Barracks Three men took off their work hats and bowed to the ranger and Decken who'd moved out onto the balcony of the tower.

"It looks great," said the ranger.

"A tribute to the young man who discovered it," said Decken.

"It's on a flat, high and dry, not in the way or anything," said the ranger. "I'm going to tell the forest service to leave it be."

Decken took off his hat. "Tell them it's in honor of a CCC man who's gone."

The ranger took off his hat. "I'll make note in the fire tower log so no one disturbs it."

"The CCC thanks you," said Decken. "Maybe someday a President will come here and tour the place."

"Maybe so," said the ranger. Then he shouted, "Beautiful work, men!"

The 38 men put their floppy work hats back on and saluted.

The ranger and Decken saluted back.

At summer's end, radios brought news of Germany's invasion of Poland. European countries, one after another, declared war. The US remained neutral. During hospital visits to Uncle Rosario, who'd had a serious stroke and was obviously near death, Salvatore Cavallo Senior put up with his uncle's ranting and coughing, and also with Felice constantly at the bedside. When awake, the only thing his Uncle would say was, "There's too much talk of neutrality! Are we no longer men?"

Uncle Rosario hung on and eventually Cavallo invited his driver, Lonzo, to be with him. Conversing with Lonzo and Felice, while his uncle slept, gave Cavallo a new perspective on life and death. With their help a plan for the future of the Cavallo family emerged. Despite their mediocre positions in the organization, both Lonzo and Felice impressed Cavallo.

While his uncle remained physically but not mentally in the room, the three spoke of *Omerta*, the code of honor. After his uncle's stroke, Cavallo hadn't had a chance to speak in detail about the consequences of the CCC boys taking his son's life. With his uncle out of the picture, Cavallo, Lonzo, and Felice agreed the death of Little Sal, especially in the aftermath of Cavallo's men sent running with tails between their legs, would be impossible to keep under wraps. At least one runaway man or CCC boy or staff member would talk. It would spread across the east coast and around the world. The family name shamed. It would get back to Sicily and men would shake their heads at the cowardice of the Cavallos. During one hospital room conversation, with the hallway door closed, Cavallo asked Lonzo and Felice what they would do.

Lonzo spoke first, his voice as deep as Uncle Rosario's gutteral breathing. "If it were me, I'd need to take care of those boys. It'd be tough with war coming, but I wouldn't let it rest no matter how long it took."

Although Felice's voice was high-pitched like a boy, he spoke slowly and zealously. "It's not me on the spot, but I agree." Felice nodded toward Lonzo. "We've both given our word this is between us and will never leave this room."

"How will it look if I hire thugs to kill the CCC boys?" asked Cavallo.

Lonzo nodded toward Felice. Felice continued. "You don't hire thugs, at least not now. You put the funds in a trust."

"Lawyers?"

"Not that kind of trust," said Felice. "During my time with your uncle I learned about the warehouse of heroin dumped by the aspirin company. Both Lonzo and I are aware it was sold off in New York and other cities. Your uncle said it had to be done before its potency wore off. Somewhere back then—he didn't say the year—it was sold to organizations throughout the world disguised as being from the Orient."

Lonzo simply nodded agreement.

Cavallo glanced at his uncle breathing hard and open-mouthed. "You know everything. Can I trust you tomorrow and the day after and for years to come?"

They nodded.

Cavallo reached across the bed with both hands to where Lonzo and Felice sat in their chairs. They grasped hands above his uncle's legs, staring back and forth into one another's eyes.

"This is our ritual table," said Cavallo. "We three share the family's loyalty and honor. This is what I wanted for my son, and now you are my sons. We are different, yet we are the same. Do you agree to be members of the Cavallo family from this day forth?"

"I agree to be a member of the Cavallo family," said Felice.

"I agree to be a member of the Cavallo family," said Lonzo.

"Very well," said Cavallo. He let go of their hands. "Now, what should we do?"

"Let Felice speak," said Lonzo.

Felice sat forward. "Your uncle told me about the Jew."

"The Jew?"

"Yes, the last one you dealt with is neither Italian nor Sicilian. This makes his position in New York unique. With Jews being oppressed by Hitler, the moment is right for an alliance."

"What kind of alliance?"

"Jews arrive in New York to escape Nazis. Last year Berlin had its Kristallnacht. Jews need to hide whatever they can. With help from your Jewish comrade, and the fact your uncle has already used a Jewish bank to place his key, it's possible to keep funds hidden under Jewish names. No one cares about Jews, but their wealth is another story. Because the family funds are held in Swiss banks, it can be protected. War will come. Funds hidden under Jewish names is expected. After the war, the funds can be used to return honor to the Cavallo name."

Cavallo acknowledged Felice's statement by reaching out again to join hands with both men, the three nodding as Uncle Rosario came awake with a spasm of coughing that shook the bed as if a bomb had been dropped on the hospital.

CHAPTER 32

Two bullet holes, one in the windshield, the other in his right foot. Although vision through the cracked windshield began blurring, he slowed in Rock Springs, careful not to attract the attention of a night shift cop. His journey east began by cutting the headlights and nudging the 350 through the locked fence. It was dead quiet, no dogs as on warning signs. He broke into the office where he'd seen emergency medical kits.

The bullet had gone clean through, centered behind the second and third toe. A sink, clean shop towels, antiseptic, painkillers, and bandages made it possible to drive the rental Camry onto Interstate 80. His bandage job was thick, like a cast, and he found a wooden cane amongst the shop's junk. He left a wad of cash for the truck and busted gate, confident a chop shop wouldn't call the police. At sunup he crossed into Nebraska. At sunset, having stopped twice for gas, food, and toilet, he drove into Illinois. His foot throbbed for 1200 miles, keeping him awake. He lifted his right leg over the center console and alternately aim air-conditioned or heated air at his foot.

Halfway through Illinois he sent Vera a text. He'd be home soon and the girls should be in bed. The message signaled Vera he'd need help.

It seemed an ordinary weekday evening in his Orland Park neighborhood. Being close to midnight, many houses were dark, a few living rooms dancing with television flicker. He glimpsed an old black and white movie, a man and woman speaking to one another in a car, the filmed backdrop of a 1940s nighttime city scene in the car's oval rear window. Maybe a Hitchcock movie, the two discussing the *MacGuffin*.

A motion detector light on a neighbor's garage came on as he turned onto his street. He'd placed the garage door opener on the passenger seat, allowing him to drive the Camry directly in and close the overhead door behind him. Vera was ready, having moved her Suburban over and cleared the girls' bicycles and toys. The *MacGuffin*, gathered from the cache beneath the Castle Rock replica on Ute Mountain, was in the Camry's trunk, wrapped in the tarp taken from the 350 along with shop rags he'd used for blood and prints.

Guzzo stumbled to his knees stepping up from the attached garage into the house. Vera took over without speaking, motioning him to stay on the floor. She brought brandy, held him for several minutes, warming his hands beneath her robe, then helped him to the bedroom, past the closed door where the girls slept. Except for exclamations in Ukrainian as she cut open the cargo pants and unwrapped his foot, she didn't speak or question him until she'd rewashed the wound, soaked it, and carefully rewrapped it.

He lay back on pillows, taking an occasional sip of brandy as he watched Vera. She'd given him a couple Vicodins and this, combined with the brandy, calmed him. He'd completed his job, cleaning up the mess as best he could and getting back home. Vera deepened his sense of well-being by massaging his right leg and staring into his eyes from the foot of the bed. After she removed his shirt and washed bruises and scratches he'd ignored, she climbed into bed with him, holding him close, yet careful not to disturb his leg or foot. Although he continued dwelling on the assignment's outcome, especially Niki Gianakos and others left on the mountain, hoping anyone alive was unable to identify him, Vicodin and Vera holding him wiped the slate clean.

He awoke at 3 a.m. Vera stood at bedside holding a soup bowl. "You slept three hours. Perhaps now you can speak?"

"Another Vicodin."

"I've heated soup. Have some first. Please tell me we will soon be out of this business. The car you drove. I opened the trunk but did not disturb what's inside. What can I do?"

"Remove the Wyoming plate. If someone sees the car they'll assume it's a new purchase. Bring the bundle wrapped in the tarp in here. It'll be safe in our bedroom."

"What is it?"

"Believe it or not, a pile of guns and ammo from 1939."

"1939?"

"Hidden by men from a CCC camp. A note in the ammo box says a man in camp murdered a local girl and he'd murder again if they didn't act. Local justice. They killed him and made it look like an accident. Sound familiar?"

"Why didn't they turn him in?"

"The note says everyone was paid off. The murderer was a mob boss' son. Therefore my assignments. But now there's something for us."

Guzzo stared at Vera a moment, feeling his beard stubble prickle his cheeks as he smiled. "The family named Cavallo, with nothing better to do with their fortune, socked money away in Swiss accounts."

"How is there something for us?"

Guzzo reached down to the floor at the side of the bed, pulled his wallet from his cargo pants, removed the key, and held it up. "I've got this."

"A key?"

"Our future, Vera. The key to a possible fortune if we make the right moves."

Vera took the key, staring at it as if praising an icon. "Guzzo, is the ammunition box with the note describing all this also wrapped in the tarp?"

"Yes."

"*We are a strange Kiev couple.*" Near consciousness, the Ukrainian phrase, along with an English word, Sidekick, along with Kiev memories—syndicate strip clubs, a bomb exploding his office window, him down on the pavement outside the Chicago Blues Club, sent there by Yuri Smirnov of the Ukraine SBU. Something wrong. Smirnov asks questions yet provides few answers…

"Janos. Janos!" A familiar voice. His sidekick!

A blur of white and gray. "Mariya?"

A warm hand on his cheek. "Yes, I'm here."

"Where?"

"The hospital in Vernal?"

"Vernal?"

"Utah, Janos. Look at me. On the mountain, the van crashed, you were trapped, Niki and I came for you. The helicopter brought you. Detectives questioned us most of the night and into the morning."

Focus returning, the streets of Kiev receding. A hospital ceiling, hospital electronics on a stand, hospital sounds.

"Mariya."

"Janos, Niki's also here."

"Bandages…Mariya, your forehead…Niki, your arm. Lazlo?"

Mariya moved closer, her breath on his face. "We're fine, Janos. My scratches and bruises from the van wreck. Niki's gunshot wound taken care of. Lazlo's in another room. Despite being shot and nearly choked to death, he was able to drag himself up the stairs of the fire tower and call for help."

Sadness in Mariya's eyes, something missing. Janos recalled a vague conversation, male and female doctors hovering. A decision. He reached out with his right hand and touched Mariya's cheek, then plunged his hand beneath the blanket and discovered the void where his right leg should be. He yelled, not in English, not in Ukrainian or Hungarian. In another language reserved for moments of agony.

The bed turned over and over, a carnival ride gone wild. A foul taste, soup half digested. The nightstand clock showed 3:22. But why p.m. instead of a.m.? Guzzo sat up, launched himself toward the open doorway, held onto the doorframe to keep from falling. He steadied himself, watching as the open door to the girls' room slowly stopped coming up over him. He stumbled ahead. The girls' beds unmade, dresser drawers open. He called Vera's name but the house remained silent. Anger in his voice as if his voice knew something he did not.

The Camry in the garage. Vera's Suburban gone. No fresh scent of an engine recently started. The Wyoming plate still on the Camry. The kitchen showed no indication of lunch or dinner, only remaining soup in a pan. Amber Vicodin prescription container on the counter beside the stove, emptier than it had been. Next to the soup bowl a puddled soupspoon and two teaspoons with powdered remnants of crushed pills. Vertigo bouncing him off walls as he ran through the house. Message light blinking on the house phone. He pushed the play button.

A man's voice speaking Ukrainian. Words familiar were the Ukrainian pronunciations of Kiev and Zhulyany Airport along with an arrival time. He played the message again. The man mentioned Vera's name at the beginning and referred to himself as Yuri at the end.

Back in the bedroom Guzzo found the bundle of guns from 1939 and the ammo box, but the note left by the CCC men was missing. While dressing he heard a hum beneath the bed. He lifted the bed skirt and pulled out his cargo pants. He emptied the phones from the pockets and saw that the last phone he used to speak with Pescatore was lit. The message said, "Something wrong. Come to market ASAP. Someone close cannot be trusted."

Many hours earlier he'd spoken with Pescatore on this same phone from the restaurant in Vernal. He held his finger over the symbol that would place the call, but instead shouted to the ceiling.

"The key! Vera!"

The county detectives were gone, apparently back at their office comparing notes. They assigned two uniformed guards to sit outside two hospital rooms. Second shift nursing staff considered Janos' request strange; the doctors on duty did not. Janos wanted the leg saved. The doctors insisted they would have tried reattachment, but it was badly crushed and too much time had passed. To satisfy Janos, Niki called Jacobsen. Shortly thereafter, a call to the hospital director from higher authority did the job and Niki had no trouble convincing the staff to carefully wrap the leg and put it in a freezer for safekeeping.

Niki and Mariya spent the day alternating between Lazlo's room and Janos' room, doors closed to keep out hallway noise. Because of Mariya's forehead bandage and Niki's arm sling, they looked like street brawl leftovers. With the second bed in Janos' room empty they were finally able to convince staff to move Lazlo from his room so they could be together. Two recliners were wheeled in. Niki and Mariya took turns resting, but mostly used their phones trying to make sense of what had happened recently, and in 1939. After dinner brought in by staff, when it was obvious both Lazlo and Janos were asleep, Niki and Mariya spoke quietly.

"The glimpse you managed at the note in the ammunition box. Have you thought of anything else on it?" asked Mariya.

"It was so fast. A glimpse into the past."

Lazlo interrupted, speaking with eyes closed, his chin tucked into a padded collar. "If only I hadn't lost my gun. If only I'd turned him over and held him down. If only I'd gained the upper hand. He was strong. But not so strong the three of us would not have been able to hold him if I'd flipped him at the right moment. CCC men from 1939 could have dealt with him. Their spirits are here, in the mountains."

"You did everything you could," said Niki.

"I agree," said Mariya. "There's a trail of your blood up the fire tower stairway."

Lazlo again, "I'm sorry, Niki. You were recalling the note."

"An explanation with lots of signatures. I recall the words *murder* and *justice*. *Murder* in the first paragraph, along with a name, *Salvatore*. My guess is someone named Salvatore had, according to the signers, committed murder. It had to be Rose Buckles. Her niece and others in the area pretty much confirmed it."

Lazlo and Mariya remained silent. Janos snored gently. Niki continued.

"Something in the second paragraph, the word *justice* in the second paragraph surrounded by other words...I think *had to be done*, something like that. Also, the word *Hoods* stood out. The note had been in the box a long time. It was yellowed and stained green from old bullet shells. I did the best I could before he saw me. He checked the guns before moving them, but I was worried he'd think I'd loaded one and end up getting us all shot. The thing I remember most clearly was the bottom of the note. Scrawled signatures, pretty much impossible to read, but someone did print below the signatures, in all caps, *THE MEN FROM BARRACKS THREE.*"

Chicago's so-called rush hour, lasting hours, made Guzzo's drive to the fish market a nightmare. Women in other vehicles reminded him of Vera. Every back seat with children reminded him of the girls. Perhaps Vera was frightened. Yet there was the phone message. Was it a threat from her past? A man calling from Ukraine to intimidate her? But there was that name, Yuri. A man making a threat would remain anonymous. Crawling in traffic was like the flow of blood, his anger quickening his heartbeat. Although the Vicodin was starting to wear off, he was still dizzy. His foot throbbed and the Glock in his rear waistband pressed into his spine.

Nearing the fish market, an old man with a cane walking on the sidewalk reminded him of the so-called "accidents" he'd staged. All the elaborate plans created and executed successfully for this? Driving in traffic to either threaten Pescatore or ask for help from this man he now despised more than ever?

After getting out of the Camry, a large African-American man he'd seen about the place passed him wheeling a 50 gallon barrel. The man's coveralls were stained with fish blood and guts. Guzzo noticed in his peripheral vision the man glancing at him.

"From Wyoming?" asked the man.

"The car is," said Guzzo, continuing his limp up the ramp to the office with the help of the cane he'd brought with him from Rock Springs.

As usual it was noisy in the building. Another large African-American man he did not recognize dumped bucket after bucket of fish guts into the fish grinder. Pescatore was behind his stainless steel fish table wiping his filleting knife in his apron. Guzzo held himself up with his cane, removed his Glock from his rear waistband, and aimed at Pescatore.

"You've come equipped. Does this mean you're ready to work?"

"I'm here for answers."

Pescatore turned to a well-worn wooden side table. The filleting knife vibrated like a tuning fork after being stabbed into the wood. "You're supposed to provide answers, not me."

Guzzo stared into Pescatore's eyes, the whites pink and glistening like fish eyes. "Last time I was here you were concerned things were heating up. I'm back to tell you they have. Did you expect me back, Pescatore? Are you part of a larger plan?"

"I don't know what you're talking about."

"Vera's gone."

Pescatore paused a moment before answering, wiping his hands in his apron. "Gone? What can I do?"

"Talk."

"About what?"

Guzzo moved closer, aiming the Glock where Pescatore knew he would receive a painful gut wound if he did not answer satisfactorily. "You can either tell me how you're involved with Vera and a man named Yuri, or you can tell me how you'll help locate them. It's up to you."

Pescatore glanced over Guzzo's shoulder just as noise outside the office came inside. The door opened quickly, the two African-American men with handguns aimed his way. He turned to confront them but his cane slipped from beneath him when a blade sharper than any he could imagine sliced his throat. As he lost consciousness, the fish grinder in the next room vibrated the walls.

Voices, then something rattling. Janos opened his eyes, saw Mariya and Niki, but also Lazlo wheeling his IV and monitoring stand with one hand, his phone in his other hand.

"Did you get through to Kiev?" asked Janos.

"Yes, while you were asleep Chudin called back. They spotted Smirnov on a Zhulyany Airport security camera. A woman with two little girls pushed his wheelchair. A baggage claim camera spotted them again. On the way out with baggage, it appeared three men, one of whom was identified as working for Smirnov in the Ukraine SBU, followed. Unfortunately that was the end of the trail."

Janos lay back on his pillows. Although he knew his right leg was gone, he could feel it in his mind. "Lazlo?"

"Yes?"

"The key taken by the man on the mountain is now in Ukraine."

"How do you know?"

"Smirnov, the woman, the girls, and the three men following through the airport."

"Not very strong evidence," said Lazlo, glancing toward Niki and Mariya.

Janos looked to the three before answering. "If I can feel my leg, even though it's in the deep freeze, I can feel other things."

The two African-American men were busy behind the fish grinder, opening the trap door on a chute long enough to allow ground up material to fill a barrel before closing the chute and switching barrels. The business end of the grinder, a feeding trough shaped like a squared off tuba, was full, but sinking. During the holidays workers joked it jiggled like Santa's bowl full of jelly. Atop the mishmash of fish guts and bones lay an arm, bleeding red like Santa's suit. There was a tattoo on the unbloodied portion of the arm. Although most Desert Storm tattoos were made up of flags, eagles, and weapons, this one simply had the word *STORM* on the wrist with an arrow pointing to the hand.

As the workers made ready to dump more guts into the jiggling mass, one said, "That tattoo must have hurt like hell and took a while to heal."

"That's why I got mine on my upper arm," said the other man.

A wooden cane leaned against the vibrating machine.

Outside, a flatbed truck half loaded with barrels waited. When full the truck would head to the drying and pelletizing mill. Eventually the final product would be sold to animal feed companies across the Midwest.

CHAPTER 33

On a drizzly October morning in Washington, DC, Walter Jacobson from Homeland Security held a meeting at World Bank headquarters on H Street NW. World Bank, FBI, CIA, State Department, and Attorney General office officials were present. Switzerland, Ukraine, Russia, and Interpol each sent a representative. Lazlo, Niki, Janos, and Mariya were also there. Lazlo's arm still in a sling. Janos sat in his wheelchair.

Jacobson summarized events all the way from the aspirin company warehouse of heroin obtained by a Sicilian mob family in 1913, to the murder of Rose Buckles in 1939, to local justice initiated by men serving at the Manila, Utah, CCC camp, to subsequent questionable "accidents" of the men and family members, to recent murders in Utah, and finally the disappearance of an assassin and his family. Some at the meeting surmised the assassin mimicked the Chernobyl killer's work when murdering Dr. Marta Voronko. During this part of the meeting an argument ensued between the Ukrainian and Russian representatives.

"Although the man contracted to assassinate CCC men and relatives has not been found, my Ukraine comrades were able to track down his family. Ukraine SBU agent Yuri Smirnov flew them to Kiev. Smirnov was disloyal, working with Russian intelligence, Mafia, and perhaps other agencies following money trail. He recently obtained a lock box key from assassin's wife, killed her, trafficked two little girls, and in partnership with a Russian Jew posing as the owner of Swiss accounts, was able to get into them."

"How do you know this?" demanded the Russian.

"We tapped Smirnov's phone." The Ukrainian representative turned on a tape player.

Smirnov spoke in Russian to another man. Jacobson had an aide interpret.

"How can you possibly gain access to funds from before the Great War?"

"The Jewish woman. You should know. You assigned her."

"Yes, yes. Go on."

"After I take what is due for my services, as we agreed—Did we not agree?"

"Yes, go on."

"Afterwards, the funds can be used to improve the future of the Russian people. Isn't this, after all, what your leader requested?"

"Medvedev is my leader."

"But when Medvedev's term ends—"

"Stop. No need to say his name."

"No need to say his name because he himself recruited me."

"Yuri, you are worse than the Americans."

"Which ones? The Democrats or the Republicans?"

"They are all crazy. Someday our leader will be able to lead them by their noses."

When the Ukrainian representative stopped the recording, everyone in the conference room sat silent.

The Ukrainian and Russian had taken the meeting off course, even arguing about Ukraine's entrance into the Council of Europe in 1995, thus eliminating capital punishment. The Russian complained the Chernobyl killer would continue to live behind bars, unless of course someone provided a convenient way for him to commit suicide.

Jacobson promptly ended the meeting.

By afternoon drizzle in DC had ended and the sun was out. Niki and Lazlo walked hand in hand while Mariya pushed Janos in his wheelchair. They made their way north of World Bank Headquarters, through Edward R. Murrow Park and up 19th Street to a Greek café. Because it was well after lunch hour, they had no trouble finding a quiet booth. The booth was small, but they managed to squeeze in. Mariya and Janos, out of his wheelchair, on one side, Niki and Lazlo on the other side. As they got comfortable Niki heard a woman at a nearby table comment in Greek that the couples obviously enjoyed close contact.

Before leaving bank headquarters, Jacobson told Janos and Mariya he would make sure their visas were reclassified.

"Was Jacobson implying you'd be allowed to move to the US?" asked Niki, refilling their glasses from the bottle of Retsina.

Janos glanced to Mariya. "I believe he was inviting us. Eventually I'd like to return to see if I can discover the ones who killed Sonia."

"Why were the Russians and Ukrainians at the meeting?" asked Mariya.

"To stir the pot and get to the sludge at the bottom," said Lazlo.

"Can you imagine what 1930s mobsters would have thought if they'd known their legacy funds would eventually be used to fight human trafficking?" said Niki.

"Does Jacobson have the power to do this?" asked Janos.

"His idea of pairing up the World Bank and the World Court is a good sign," said Niki.

Mariya held Janos' hand. "I hope it comes true."

"Too bad we lost our home," said Janos.

"Your home?" said Niki.

"Our home on wheels. I miss it almost as much as I miss my leg."

Niki turned to Lazlo. "Since I no longer have the van you and I should consider a home on wheels."

Janos raised his wine glass. "To this I must conclude, bring on the Gypsies."

The others raised their glasses, "Bring on the Gypsies."

The waiter, with black hair slicked down in 1930s movie star style, arrived with the food, balancing four plates as if carrying priceless treasures.

All began eating except Lazlo. They paused when Niki said, "Lazlo, you've been quiet. Is something the matter?"

"I'm sorry, I was momentarily back in Green River. It had to do with Etta Pratt, the old woman in the Historical Society back room. She mentioned Rose Buckles' father being a Gypsy and a fortuneteller and playing the fiddle, but I didn't follow up. Instead, on a bookshelf—It's crazy to think of it now—I noticed several history books about the Hapsburgs. Did you know there were redheads in the Hapsburg line, especially in the Kingdom of Hungary?"

"You think Rose Buckles' father was from Carpatho-Ukraine?" asked Niki.

"Why all the Hapsburg books in Etta's back room?" said Lazlo.

"*Telepátia*," said Janos. "The Gypsy deserter you were forced to shoot?"

Lazlo leaned back and reached into his pocket. "Yes, the grandfather was a redhead, played the violin, and escaped to America. And even though investigators took most of the hair saved by Dr. Marta's grandfather for DNA analysis, I did manage to keep a few strands." He opened an envelope and placed the few strands of reddish brown hair stuck on new tape onto the table.

All four stared at the hair and thought a moment until Mariya said, "Assuming Janos and I return to the US soon, we might vacation together at Flaming Gorge and discover—I don't know—something more about Rose Buckles' father, and also about Jacobson's mention at the meeting of the six degrees of separation."

All four nodded and began eating slowly, obviously deep in thought.

Outside the restaurant a black Chevy Suburban with blacked out windows was parked across the street. Although it was October, the afternoon temperature had warmed and therefore telltale exhaust steam indicating the engine was running was not visible. Certainly, if there were one or more inside, it would have to be running to keep the air conditioning going because all the windows were closed.

With the street having dried in the sun, a puddle from the air conditioner condenser drain appeared below the Suburban. The air conditioning was running, the tubing from its condenser dripping onto the street. Any good investigator would see this.

CHAPTER 34

F all, 1939. Life at Camp Manila back to normal. Some claimed it was because of the changeover—new enrollees freshening the mood. Others, who'd been around all summer knew better. It wasn't simply the change of enrollees; it was the changes in command. Staff officers, including the superintendent, were weeded out following the "ruckus," as everyone called it. The weeding out went all the way up to the company commander in Wyoming.

Decken MaCade was one of the LEMs who stayed on and would winter over with new enrollees. They'd open up the Barracks Five building because it had two stoves instead of one. Part of Decken's role was to make sure the so-called "ruckus" that took place near the end of summer was downplayed. The new camp superintendent made it clear he'd be upset if he heard rumors concerning events that took place around camp that summer. For good measure he had the Barracks Three building boarded up.

Although the denim work uniforms remained the same, by the end of summer all the World War I olive drab surplus dress uniforms had been replaced by the new style tan dress uniforms. As Decken drove the canvas-covered Dodge truck with his load of men in their new uniforms to the Green River railroad station, he glanced in the side mirror at the GMC with its load following in his dust. Bela Voronko and Nick Gianakos rode shotgun beside Decken, men of few words since the "ruckus." Because it was cool out, the windows were closed.

"What will you do now?" asked Decken.

Bela answered first. "I think it would be best to enlist."

"Which branch?"

"Army Air Corps. I'd like to work on airplane engines."

"You think you'll ever go back to Europe?"

"That depends on war.

Decken continued. "How about you, Nick?"

"Back to Detroit. Even though we've got FDR's neutrality act for now, Ford and GM are making tanks and bombers. If war starts I'll join up. If not, my uncle has a restaurant."

Ahead, cattle were crossing the road, a cowboy on horseback trying to turn them around.

"Back at camp they were bringing cattle down from the Uintas Range for winter," said Nick. "I'm surprised to see strays this far north."

Decken slowed the truck until the half dozen cattle were clear, the gears grinding as he went for first without stopping. "You guys think we'll get into this war?"

Bela and Nick nodded and stared at one another. Then Bela said, "Unfortunately, the violence within some men can only be stopped with death."

Decken glanced to both of them as he shifted to second. "These days, any time death gets mentioned, I think of Rose Buckles." He shifted to third. "I'll never forget what happened to her. I never told you guys, but when I was in LEM orientation at the Green River camp, everyone there talked about seeing her walking down the street in one of her dresses. I saw her once in the café over there. She sure was pretty. One crazy thing I remember hearing is how she used to tell a story about Marco Polo discovering fishermen in Arabia drying fish and hammering them with rocks to feed their cattle. Some of the guys who fished in the river liked to repeat the story."

"A fine story," said Bela.

There was little room on the floor of the Dodge to the right of the gearshift. Both Nick and Bela had their feet propped on their duffels. Not much in the duffels, but there was something in each Decken knew of but dare not mention. Perhaps the locks of red hair Nick and Bela had packed inside were the reason both weren't very talkative as the Dodge drove down the main street, past the hardware store, Nan's Drug and Sundry, the IGA, and the Green River movie house toward the Green River station.

Although it had been released in the summer, *The Wizard of Oz* finally arrived in Green River. To increase attendance, the old man who ran the movie house allowed Tom to arrive early each afternoon and play the recording of "We're Off to see the Wizard" on his record player and amplifier system. Tom figured out how to get the record player to play the song over and over, allowing it to blast out on the speakers below the marquee all afternoon.

As he approached his movie house on foot with his newspaper in hand, the old man admired the marquee and smiled at the kids dancing in the November sun to *The Wizard of Oz* theme. Two trucks loaded with CCC men beneath their tarps drove past. The old man waved to them and the men closest to the backs of the trucks waved back through a wake of dust.

The old man could hear *The Wizard of Oz* theme in his office even with the door closed. Tom had made coffee and the old man sat at his desk with his cup and his *Green River Star*.

Nazis were closing Czech universities, murdering students, and sending hundreds to prison camps. FDR laid the cornerstone at the Jefferson

Memorial and Al Capone was released from Alcatraz. Below the fold was the usual small headline, "Mystery of Rose Buckles' Murder Continues." Soon, with all the war news, it would be on page two.

The old man took a sip of coffee and turned the page.

EPILOGUE—2018 GENEALOGY WEBSITE MESSAGE

Dear Ms. Clancy Vargo,

Please excuse my English. Family tree study and DNA presents to me your name. I see you live in USA state of Utah and therefore find somewhat difficult my belief. Somehow great-great grandfather is possible relation of your aunt with name Buckles. I live in Ukraine near once southern Hungary. If it is worthy of note, many in family tree have red hair. Any information will be greatly appreciated. Please have wonderful summertime.

ANNA HORVATH